Blue Sp[...]

Chrissie Glazebrook has worked [...]
and as a radio and television pr[...]
for the late Jackie magazine and has been published in a range of
magazines and newspapers, including a stint as Jenny Talia, a
spoof agony aunt. She ran away at seventeen to join a beatnik
colony in St Ives, Cornwall, returning to her Black Country home
after being busted for drugs.

In 1998 she gained an MA in Creative Writing and won the
Waterstone's Prize for Prose, and her first novel, *The Madolescents*,
was published in 2001 to great critical acclaim. She lives in
Newcastle upon Tyne.

Also by Chrissie Glazebrook

The Madolescents

Blue Spark Sisters

Chrissie Glazebrook

arrow books

Published by Arrow Books in 2003

1 3 5 7 9 10 8 6 4 2

Copyright © Chrissie Glazebrook 2003

Chrissie Glazebrook has asserted her right under the Copyright, Designs and
Patents Act, 1988 to be identified as the author of this work

Lines quoted from Anne Sexton on pp. 142, 243, 295, reprinted by permission of
Sterling Lord Literistic, Inc. Copyright Anne Sexton

First published in the United Kingdom in 2003 by William Heinemann

Arrow Books
Random House Group Limited
20 Vauxhall Bridge Road, London SW1V 2SA

Random House Australia (Pty) Limited
20 Alfred Street, Milsons Point, Sydney,
New South Wales 2061, Australia

Random House New Zealand Limited
18 Poland Road, Glenfield
Auckland 10, New Zealand

Random House (Pty) Limited
Endulini, 5a Jubilee Road, Parktown 2193, South Africa

Random House Group Limited Reg. No. 954009

www.randomhouse.co.uk

A CIP catalogue record for this book is available
from the British Library

Papers used by Random House
are natural, recyclable products made from wood grown in
sustainable forests. The manufacturing processes conform to
the environmental regulations of the country of origin

ISBN 0 09 941093 1

Typeset in Palatino by SX Composing DTP, Rayleigh, Essex
Printed and bound in Denmark by
Nørhaven Paperback A/S, Viborg

For Laura Hird

Acknowledgments

With infinite thanks to the wonderful Kate Elton; to the Random House team; to Jane Gregory, Broo Doherty and the staff at Gregory & Company, Authors' Agents; and to Lady Lisanne.

Love and black stuff to my friends in Ireland, in particular to Rose Doyle, Phyl Herbert, Rita Ann Higgins, Aidan Hynes and Enda Wyley.

Thanks also to New Writing North for a 'Time to Write' award which helped me to complete this book; and to Mike Campbell and North Tyneside Arts for providing writing space at the Buddle Arts Centre.

Destination: Haemorrhoid Oil

Toosh, toosh, toosh.

When I first spot the rabbit, it doesn't register as odd. It doesn't strike me as even a hundred decimal points of weird, not until later, when I'm on the aeroplane. This is how I know I'm on a mad tip.

Oh, triffic. Craziness is the last state I want to be in right now. Wits, gather round, lads, I need to keep you about me, to help me act like a functioning human. We'll soon be flying, lads, skimming amongst the clouds in a proper skygoing aircraft, bound for Dublin. The land of my fathers. My father, anyway. Don't want to lose you now, boys. Stick around.

See, I'm sitting on the top deck of the early-morning bus, gazing out of the grimy window. A zillion bees swarm in my stomach. My head's whizzing in that switched-off stratosphere on the far side of panic. Why? Because I'm running away from the place I laughingly called home. Because I'm hurtling into the unknown, heading for a new life. Big, big deal. And there's the rabbit, a black-and-white affair, shuffling, sniffing, twitching its nose. Aaahh, cute, is all I think.

The point is, the rabbit's on top of a bus shelter. On the roof. That's not something you see every day. Well, not ever. I'm seeing it all right, but my brain's spinning at 100 mph, too fast to file it under STRANGE.

Toosh, toosh, toosh.

What's my reaction? Do I whizz round in a double take à la Chandler out of *Friends*? Do I push the emergency button? Yell for the RSPCA?

Uh-uh. Jesus. I mean, how does a rabbit come to be on the top of a bus shelter anyway? Rabbits aren't mountaineers, like those hairy-arsed goats; they don't fall out of the sky, like frogs; and once they're up there, they can't abseil to the ground yelling 'hut-hut-hut', like the SAS. Anyways, nada, nix, big fat nothing, that's what I do, because it seems such an *un*strange occurrence.

This is how I know the madness is still on me.

Crazy or not, I'm sane enough to spot the CIA agents they've put on my tail.

Toosh, toosh, toosh.

The woman sitting opposite me on the Metro to the airport, she's the first one I clock. I've got her figured as a rookie spook on her first solo assignment. It's so obvious, the way she's pretending to read her *OK!* magazine when all the time she's secretly checking me out, peering inside my rucksack with her X-ray spex, trying to decode my body language, sucking thoughts out of my brain like sick through a sock. I pull the usual trick, making my mind go a total blank, picturing it as a computer screen. As soon as a thought flashes into my head, I press the Delete key. They're smart, the CIA, but Rowena M. Vincent is smarter. Face it, I've had to be, to dodge them all these years.

The woman gets off the Metro at the Regent Centre, giving the secret handover signal to another agent. I can't be arsed to skeg round the carriage to see who deliberately *isn't* looking at me. When you're used to being under surveillance, you don't need to see them. You just know. It's automatic, like breathing, or lying, or painting lippy on your mouth without using a mirror.

Toosh, toosh, toosh.

This'll be my first time flying. I was supposed to go to Paris once, with the school, only I came down with German measles, which was canny timing as it meant I could stay in bed for a week being waited on hand, foot and mouth instead of having to traipse round poxy museums surrounded by foreign people.

I'm flying, fleeing to Ireland. The Haemorrhoid Oil. Hell, I don't

2

even know if I need a passport but I brought it along in case. I left my so-called home in such an almighty rush, just a change of clothes and a few pairs of knickies stuffed inside my rucksack, plus money and a mobile phone.

Oh, and the photograph. A snapshot taken outside a Dublin bar on Bloomsday, two years ago. A picture of my dad. My long-lost dad, the legendary Lonnie Vincent. This is my quest, my mission, my goal: to trace my father, yea, even unto the ends of the earth. So, I'm on my way. Ireland, brace yourself.

'When's the next flight to Dublin?' My voice surprises me by sounding shaky.

The bird at the booking counter taps on a computer. Her face is peppered with freckles, on account of her eating too many ginger biscuits as a child, probably.

'Single or return?' she goes, without looking at me.

Toosh, toosh, toosh.

Sometimes you realize you've reached a crossroads, a waterbed or whatever, in your life. I don't hesitate, not even for a nanosecond. This is it, the point of, well – no return.

'Single,' I say.

Tap-tap. 'We have availability on the next flight, 9.55.'

'Cool,' I say. 9.55. I can't remember ever being out of bed this early on a non-worky morning.

She looks down her nose all sniffy when I hand over the cash, flicking through the notes like they're tainted. Which some of them might well be, as they came from my mum's vile boyfriend's pocket which I dipped before I left home, as a kind of parting shot.

'Check in at desk twelve,' she says, handing me the ticket to my new life so casual, as if it's a dry-cleaning receipt.

Toosh, toosh, toosh.

The bloke on desk twelve looks like he's got a head full of hangover. His eyes are red and flecked with sleep and he's sprawled out as if he's on the beach in Malaga. He frowns at me like I'm an

3

undesirable, someone seeking asylum, or more likely, escaped from one.

'Any baggage?' he mumbles.

'Say what?' I heard him the first time, but I'm giving him the benefit, a chance to be civil.

'Do you have any baggage?' He nods at my rucksack. 'Or will it be just the hand luggage?' Fortunately for him, he twitches his mouth in a bit smile so I decide to forgive him as he might have been out clubbing last night.

'No. No baggage,' I tell him. That much is true. I left it behind, all that emotional stuff I've been humping around for my sixteen earth-years. Dumped it with the garbage of my previous existence where it can rot to buggery for all I care.

Toosh, toosh, toosh.

'Window seat or aisle?' the bloke's saying. I'm about to go, *Window seat or I'll what?* but life's too short.

'Not a window,' I tell him. 'The other.'

He hands me a pass. 'Gate ten, boarding at 9.30. Enjoy your flight.' He yawns and collapses back into the slump position.

The airport's heaving with people in shell suits, jetting off to Alicante or Magaluf or wherever. Some of them, you can see they've spent the last month sizzling inside one of those sandwich-toaster sunbeds, getting a head start on a tan. How pointless is that?

I plonk myself down on a seat, next to a couple of old wifies dressed in identical jogging suits and canvas shoes, except one's in turquoise and the other's in candy pink. The biddies are tiny and stiff-looking, like figures made from icing sugar. They stare at me, then at each other, as if to say what's the world coming to. I don't see the point of pastel colours, me, especially when you're washed out and on the point of pegging it like they are. Not that I'm straight off the catwalk myself. I just threw on the first rags that came to hand, my yellow latex miniskirt from B'Zarr, a black body and lacy tights, plus my biker boots and leather jacket. It's a look I wear so often, it's

4

almost like a uniform. I cop one of the women giving me a sideways look so I glare back at her double hard until she turns away with a nervous cough and ferrets a tube of extra-strong mints out of her bag.

Toosh, toosh, toosh.

Another forty-five minutes to kill. My stomach starts growling like a cornered mongrel, so I take the escalator to the caff and join the queue for scran, behind a bunch of doddery people who take forever choosing between rubbery fried eggs and mushrooms shrivelled up like old men's willies. I bet they're away on a SAGA holiday: Send A Granny Abroad.

'If it isn't the young lady from the funeral parlour. How're ya?' I jump, startled, as a hand the size of a spade clamps itself over mine. My gaze heads north, past a massive chest and bull neck, taking in a square jaw splayed in a grin, slicked-back dark hair with silver wings, before coming to land on the crinkly eyes of, Omigawd, Hefty O'Hara!

'Er, good.' My voice creeps out in a kind of whimper. 'I'm good.'

'Didn't mean to scare you,' Hefty laughs, nearly choking me with the fumes from his aftershave. 'I'm just off for breakfast, will you join me?' He picks up a tray and slides it along the metal runners.

'Cheers,' I say. When Hefty O'Hara makes an offer, it'd be suicidal to refuse. According to my sources, Hefty is the hardest hard man of Newcastle's Wild West End. Smack baron, protection racketeer, capo di capi, if you believe all that stuff. A sudden pain shoots through my left kneecap, Freud's way of advising me to play along, obviously. I can't help wondering what the CIA must be making of this, assuming they're still after me. If that's the case, they're bound to have Hefty under surveillance as well as watching me, so they're getting a two-for-the-price-of-one deal.

Hefty orders a Jumbo Special with a pot of tea. For some reason my appetite's vanished so I say I'll just have a bourbon biscuit and hot chocolate drink. I go to pay for them but Hefty waves my hand away and settles up for the lot with a twenty, which he peels from a wad the size of a half-used bog roll. The notes are crisp and new, fresh from a bank job, at a guess. Hefty grabs the tray and strolls towards the Smoking section, me trailing behind him all bemused, like a docile cow thinking she's off to a field of daisies, then catching wind of a slaughterhouse up ahead.

Toosh, toosh, toosh.

Waving me to a seat, Hefty examines his Jumbo Special. The bacon's coming up for the third time in a sea of grease, the hash browns are as hard as house bricks, and the sausage is straight out of a dog's bum.

'Disgusting,' he says, as if he's read my mind. I manage a weak smile.

He loads his fork with cholesterol and munches in silence. I can feel his eyes on me but I concentrate on unwrapping the packet of bourbons. My fingers morph into bananas so I try to tear the cellophane with my teeth, but I'm canny nervous as owt with Hefty watching me and I can't get a grip. A flush burns my cheeks.

'You're making a right pig's ear of that.' Hefty takes the packet and slits open the wrapper with his knife, squeezing the biscuits out on to my plate. 'Here, eat up, Miss . . . what was your name?'

'Rowena,' I say, in a whimper.

'Rowena. There's a fine name.' Hefty takes a slurp of tea, sparks up a Silk Cut and picks a shred of bacon from between his teeth with a matchstick. 'And where'll you be flying off to?'

The biscuit crumbs taste like sawdust in my mouth. 'Dublin,' I reply. 'In Ireland.'

'Dublin, in Ireland!' roars Hefty. 'Well, there's a thing. And what takes you to Dublin, Rowena?'

Toosh, toosh, toosh.

A pukey feeling hovers in my throat. This man is one scary dude and I *so* don't want him around me, breathing my air, unnerving me, sucking away what tiny sliver of confidence I have left.

'I'm going to see my dad.' There, it's been said. I've made it real.

'And your dad lives in Ireland?'

My left knee starts jiggling like a lunatic beneath the table. My mouth twitches in a pathetic half-smile and an icy sweat breaks out on my forehead. 'Sorry,' I go. 'I think I'm going to be ill.'

With his neck-snapping hands, Hefty pastes a paper napkin to my mouth, grabs me by the armpit and steers me to the women's toilets. Jesus, the shame of it! He holds open the door and gives me a gentle shove. I just manage to make it to the nearest cubicle before a jet of hot spew shoots out of my mouth into the pan. Man, I sound like a rabid dog, barking and retching, until it feels as if my stomach's about to head up my throat and land with a plop in the blue-tinted water. It doesn't, of course, and after a bit the vomiting stops, leaving my innards raw but intact.

A poshgit woman wearing a blue pashmina and too much perfume glances at me through the mirror as I splash water round my chops.

'Morning sickness,' I confide, in a woman-to-woman tone. She twitches her mouth and scuttles out. It's written all over her: *Huh, another sponging teenage mum*, but I don't give a toss. All I'm concerned about is patching my make-up so the world won't know I've been throwing my lights up.

Toosh, toosh, toosh.

The Discman falls out of my bag, clattering on the floor. It's been buried under my scrunched-up clothes, the sound muffled, playing non-stop hard house. This is good news. It means the *toosh*ing was for real, not some schizo noise going on inside my head.

My face looks like ninety miles of bad road. Digging in my pocket I unearth some Sand Beige foundation but it sinks into my skin and disappears like the *Titanic*, hundreds of microspots surfacing like air bubbles. I wish I had some of that theatrical make-up that we used to slap on the bad cases when I worked as a funeral assistant. My scalp tightens at the thought. Stop it, Rowena. Get a grip. That was

7

in a previous existence. This is a brand new, box-fresh life. A wiped-clean slate, no previous offences to be taken into consideration, a totally blank rap sheet.

So why, God? What's with the Hefty factor? Why now? Just when things have a chance of coming good, why did you have to send a ghost from the past?

2

A Red Light for P!nk

Hefty O'Hara's waiting outside the door for me, puffing on a tab even though it's a no-smoking area. But no-one's about to argue, unless they fancy kipping with the kippers. If the rumours are true, he'd do your legs as soon as look at you.

'You OK now?' Hefty peers into my eyeballs. I nod, lowering my gaze to the silver crucifix glinting in his chest hair. 'We're boarding,' he says. 'Follow me. Here's your bag.'

He hands me the rucksack and I feel myself blushing. I wonder if he's been through it, rifled through my knickies, totted up the cash, flicked through the notebook where I've listed my funeral music in case of sudden death. I poke my hand inside the flap and fumble around for the photo of Dad. Still there.

Hefty's giant back leads the way to the departure lounge. He glances round occasionally to make sure I haven't absconded. No-one pays us any attention. He could be abducting me, forcing me into a life of whoredom or potato-picking or whatever, and no-one would lift a finger to save me.

'Put your bag there on the counter,' orders Hefty. 'For the X-ray.' I'm about to say, Jesus, I never knew we needed a medical, when I spot the conveyor belt. Hefty smiles a dangerous smile. Uh-oh. That'll be it, then. While I was revisiting last night's dinner in the lavatory, he'll have slipped a sawn-off shotgun into my rucksack. Drugs too, probably, every variety known to man, with a street value of zillions. I'm his wossname, patsy. So much for my new life. Life means life, in my case. I'll be banged up till my teeth rot and my bosoms hit my knees. The bag chugs along the rubber belt. I daren't breathe. Silver shapes float in front of my eyes. My armpits feel clammy.

But nothing happens. No red lights, no sniffer dogs, no wailing alarms, no CIA. Then I remember – I'm carrying my shoplifter's bag, the one I double-lined with metallic paper to deflect the microwaves and stuff. So what if Hefty *is* using me as a gunrunner? He could cram the rucksack with Kalashnikovs and Uzis, they still wouldn't show up on the scanner, more than likely. Saved by the Bacofoil!

'So, Rowena,' says Hefty, spreading out his muscly arms over the backs of two seats in the departure room. 'Have you been across the water before?'

'Eh?' I can feel my mouth stretching in an inane grin from the relief of not being arrested.

'Will this be your first time in Ireland?' he says.

'What? Oh, yeah.' My body's so floppy after being clenched with tension, I have to do a swift pelvic floor exercise to stop from wetting myself.

'It'll be a new experience then, travelling in a Fokker.'

I glance round to see if anyone's overheard Hefty's swearing. They're all staring vacantly ahead, eyes glazed, like contestants on *The Weakest Link*.

'Erm, I guess.'

'Not like your Boeings,' Hefty continues. 'Real boneshakers, these contraptions.'

'Right.' I slide down in the seat, glowing with embarrassment.

'And what's your da doing in Dublin?' Hefty continues with the third degree.

Just then a skinny lass in a Servisair uniform swishes up to a microphone and announces that the flight's boarding.

I feel suddenly nervous. My legs turn to sponge cakes. Hefty takes my elbow and heaves me up from the seat.

'Into the paddy wagon,' he says. 'Come along, Rowena, you'll be fine.'

We pile into a single-decker bus. There's not enough seats, so Hefty and I have to stand holding onto a metal pole, like gibbons in a zoo. As we tootle across the tarmac I peer through the window, trying to guess which plane is ours. They look enormous and a bit scary, like seagulls when you see them close up. The bus judders to a stop, right next to a wee toy aeroplane.

'Are you trying to squeeze the life out of that?' says Hefty, unwinding my fingers from the pole. 'Anyone would think it was a white-knuckle ride you're on.'

'Is this it?' I say. The little plane's different shades of green, with a shamrock painted on the tail. It's got propellers too. I thought they went out with the hand jive. On the front it says 'St Fidelma'.

'Concorde must be away getting its ashtrays emptied,' says Hefty. 'So we'll have to make do with this little fella.' As we climb up the steps, he makes the sign of the cross with his thumbnail.

My seat is 5C, near the front, next to an oldy bloke with nearly no hair. Hefty's supposed to be sitting further back but he leans across me and mumbles a few words to the gadge, who stands up, reaches for his jacket from the overhead bin and toddles off down the aisle. I splay my knees while Hefty shuffles past and parks his butt in the window seat next to me.

'What did you say to him?' I ask.

'I thought he might like to swap seats.' Hefty taps the side of his nose. 'Comes from having a long line of horse-traders in the family,' he explains. 'Anyway, you need looking after, Rowena, this being your virgin flight and all.'

Oh, brilliant. As if flying's not enough of a nightmare, I'm going to have my hand held by the Irish equivalent of Tony Soprano. Very comforting, I don't think! I poke around in my bag for the Discman and slap in a P!nk CD, so at least I won't have to make conversation about horses' heads and suchlike. I'm just about to plug in the earphones when a man's voice comes over the loudspeaker. He's speaking in foreign! I can't make out a word, it's complete gibberish. What if he's announcing there's a fire in the fuselage, or a terrorist bomb, and we're all going to perish!

'What's he saying?' My voice comes out a bit hysterical.

'He's welcoming us on board,' says Hefty. 'In Irish.'

I never knew they had a separate language in Ireland. How will I understand people once I get there? My toes bunch up tight inside the biker boots and I get this faint ear-buzz like I do before a panic attack. Then I realize I'm gripping Hefty's hand. Jesus!

'On behalf of the cabin crew, I'd like to welcome you aboard the Aer Lingus flight to Dublin,' says the voice. It's talking in English now. Whew, thank you, God. 'For safety reasons, we would ask you not to use mobile phones, CD players, or any other laser-operated equipment. You may, however, use laptop computers if you wish. We would remind you that this is a non-smoking flight.'

Sighing, I pack away the CD player. It's no-go the music, a red light for P!nk, then. Instead I decide to pretend to fall asleep or sink into a coma – anything so I won't have to talk to Hefty O'Hara, who seems to have cast himself in the role of my minder.

Truth is, I hardly know him. We sort of met when I worked at Crowther's, the funeral directors, in that former life I'm not going to talk about. When I say that we *met*, we more or less passed in the corridor, but Ray the driver/bearer spilled the beans on Hefty and his Irish relatives. According to Ray, the O'Haras are one of the three families in Newcastle that everyone's heard of but nobody crosses – well, not if they want to live. The others are the Gannons and the Stokers. They each have their own manor and run their own show. Drugs, loan-sharking, firearms, bank jobs, you name it. Suppliers of meatheads for the doors of clubs and pubs. Arsonists, perpetrators of insurance scams. Purveyors of summary justice, yea, even unto death. When archaeologists dig beneath the central motorway in a thousand years' time, they'll be amazed by what went into the concrete. According to Ray.

The O'Hara clan turned up at Crowther's to make arrangements for Danny's final journey. Hefty, a relative, still lived in the Old Country and flew over from Ireland to sort out – and pay for – the funeral. Ray said that Danny had been offed in a drive-by shooting. Tyneside was holding its breath, he said, bracing itself for a gangland war. Instant, violent retribution on an epic scale.

It never happened. Weird, that.

Ray reckoned there was speculation that Danny O'Hara's death was faked, that he needed to disappear for a while until the heat died down after some kind of grisly incident in the Ouseburn abattoir. Bollocks. Ray was present when Danny's body was brought in from the morgue. He saw the shamrock tattoo on his neck, the nose ring and trademark tongue stud, the hole ripped through his body, flaps of skin stitched together over what was left of his intestines. Fake that.

I met the O'Haras when they came to view the corpse, after it had been drained, embalmed, stitched up, glued, stuffed with wadding, and expertly remodelled to resemble a human being. Even then, just the toe tag bearing the name O'Hara scared the crap out of Ray, like he was dealing with Jesus H. fresh off the cross.

'See, that wasn't too bad now, Rowena, was it?' Hefty's voice brings me back to consciousness and I realize we're airborne. 'Will you have some gum?' He offers me a wrap of Wrigleys. 'For your ears?'

'No ta.' There's no way I'm sticking chuddy in my lugholes. I do a massive yawn. Something inside my head goes pop.

'So it's a holiday you're going on with your father?' asks Hefty. His hands are smooth and hairless, the nails buffed and shaped. Manicured hands. I wonder if the dried blood of his victims lies trapped beneath the fingernails, but he probably uses DNA remover.

'Yeah. No. Um, sort of,' I reply.

Hefty laughs, well, it's more a bellow.

'You'd best make your mind up, we'll be there before you know it. He'll be meeting you off the plane, then?'

I shrug. 'He doesn't know I'm coming. It's a surprise.' Ain't that the truth.

Just then the trolley dolly plonks a couple of containers on the dropdown trays in front of us. Inside there's a wee turdy bread roll, some butter and marmalade, and a chocolate chip muffin. I can't bear to look at it as my guts are still sore from puking up earlier.

'Your breakfast, flown right in from Cardboard Central,' says Hefty. 'Sure I'd have to be a desperate man to eat that.' He fumbles in his jacket pocket and produces a metal flask, then unscrews the top and takes a swig. 'Black Bush,' he explains, waving it under my nose. The sweet, sharp smell makes me wince and I have all on to stop from gagging. Throwing up over a mafioso wouldn't be the smartest stunt I've ever pulled and I don't fancy being fished out of the Irish Sea with my body riddled full of bulletholes.

'Thanks, only I don't drink,' I lie, my throat thick with nausea.

Hefty tucks the flask back in his pocket and shifts round in his seat to face me. 'And whereabouts in Dublin does he live, this father of yours?'

My face burns. I feel paralysed. Suddenly, hot tears spill out from nowhere and race each other down my cheeks.

'Hey, what's this in aid of?' Hefty hands me a proper hand-kerchief and reaches round my shoulders with his huge arm. 'Want to talk about it?'

So what do I do? I crack, don't I? Spill my life story, to a stranger, a gangster, of all people. Tell him how I've left home for good. How I'm running away to Ireland with nothing more than a two-year-old photo of Dad. How I haven't seen my father since I was a kid. How I don't even remember what he looks like, fuck's sake. I just know I'm desperate to find him.

When the crying dies down, Hefty pats my arm and says, 'What's he called, this dad of yours?'

'Lonnie,' I sniff. 'Lonnie Vincent.'

'Lonnie Vincent,' he repeats. 'And you've a photograph, you say?'

I nod. 'In my bag.' Hefty hands me the rucksack and I fiddle inside and pull out the photo. 'It's mad; I don't even know which one is him.'

14

Hefty holds the picture to the light and studies it. It's a photo of three men, dressed in T-shirts and jeans. They're holding pint glasses up to the camera, laughing. One of the men has a number two crop and an earring; the one in the middle is blondy with a tan; and the other has dark curly hair and a stubbly chin.

Hefty stares at the photo for ages. Then he turns it over and reads the writing on the back: *Toasting Joyce, Bloomsday, Cork Street, Dublin.* It's dated two years ago.

He looks at the faces again. 'And you don't know which one of these three rogues is your da?' I shake my head, no. 'How so?'

I chew my lip to stop from blubbing. 'It was years ago when he left home. I was only little. Mum got rid of all the photos of him. I just … I suppose I just forgot what he looked like.' My chin starts quivering. 'Then I found that picture in my nana's stuff. So I thought I'd run away to Dublin and find him.'

'Just like that,' says Hefty. 'It's a big place, Dublin. People can get lost there, whether they want to or not. Do you know anyone else in Ireland?'

I shake my head. 'I thought I'd go to this Cork Street place, try and find the bar, see if anyone recognizes him.'

'A bit of a long shot, that.' Hefty squeezes my hand. 'It's a good thing you ran into me, Rowena. A blessing, you might almost say. We're talking mean streets here; there's all sorts who'd take advantage of a young girl like yourself. I'll look out for you until you find your feet.'

'It'll be cool,' I assure him. 'I know a bit about Dublin. I saw *The Commitments* three times.'

Hefty punches my arm and roars. 'You're a real comic, Rowena. Saw *The Commitments*, that's a gem. Three times an' all. That settles it – you're definitely tagging along with me.'

Oh, triffic. As if life wasn't enough of a minefield, I've got a mobster for a minder!

3
Trublin Dublin

The bird in the emerald suit whizzes past, collecting the untouched breakfast trays. Shortly after, the man's voice comes over the speakers saying we'll soon be landing in Dublin. My knee starts jiggling again. I press down on it with my hand but it won't stop.

'Nothing to worry about, we'll be on the ground in a minute or two,' says Hefty, trying to reassure me, though I notice he's made the sign of a cross again with his thumbnail. The plane descends, making my stomach lurch and my ears go deaf.

Dublin. Dad. And Omigawd, Hefty O'Hara! What have I let myself in for?

While Hefty's waiting for his luggage to appear on the carousel, I weigh up my options. One: I could make a run for it, though with the eyes of Hefty and the CIA trained on me, any chance of escape would be slim – nay, skeletal. Two: I could play along with Hefty, let him help trace Dad for me, and then make a run for it. Three: I could throw myself on the mercy of the airport security people and tell them I'm suffering from amnesia, or I've been drugged, or abducted, and would they please put me on the next plane home.

Except I don't have a home any more. Not since I ran out on my mother who'll soon be getting married to her vile boyfriend. That door has been well slammed.

Even though I'm canny weak and ready to pass out, my brain's still unfuddled enough to realize that Hefty's my best – if that's the word – bet. Some scary thought, huh?

And I *am* getting frightened now. Because Vinnie O'Jones has clamped himself on to me like a conjoined twin, because I'm alone in a foreign country, because my stomach acid's on fire and my head's banging. But mainly because I don't know what I'm doing here, chasing a dad I can't remember, a dad who's probably forgotten I exist. How is he going to react when his long-lost daughter shows up out of the wide blue yonder? Will he remember me? Why hasn't he been in touch all these years? What if he hates me? What if he turns tail and walks away? What if he makes a statement on telly, denying me, poking the air with his finger to emphasize each point, like Mr Clinton? *I did not* – jab – *have family relations* – jab – *with that woman* – jab – *Miss Vincent*.

'Sharpen yourself up and climb in the cab.' Hefty's voice shakes me awake. The taxi driver packs Hefty's suitcase into the boot and we head off, me clutching the rucksack as though it's a lifebelt.

I gaze out of the taxi window trying to read the road signs but the words are in foreign, we could be in France or some other Third World country for all I know. I listen to the *whish whish* of the windscreen wipers. Rain, oh perfecto. The cab rumbles past rows of terraced houses, grey and grim. If this is Dublin, it's a class A dump. I rest my head against the window, close my eyes and twiddle my earlobe. It seems to trigger some sort of electronic deal in my brain. First I hear the faint buzzing of a dial tone, then I feel my fingers tapping out a number. 0800 BIG-G. The number rings out and clicks to connect.

'Hello,' drawls a sleepy voice.

'G-g-god, is that you?' I stutter.

'Speaking,' says the voice, stifling a yawn.

'It's Rowena here,' I begin. 'Rowena Vincent.'

'I *am* all-knowing,' says God, a trifle sarky-like. He must have been taking a nap and He's woken up a bit tetchy. 'Name your three wishes.'

Three wishes? I thought that was genie-in-the-lamp stuff, like in the Aladdin panto I saw at the Hippodrome.

'One,' prompts God. He sounds impatient. I can almost hear His fingers drumming.

Pulling myself together, I blabber, 'Can you make Hefty O'Hara not a true gangster, just an actor dressed up, like John Travolta in *Pulp Fiction*?'

'I said wishes, not miracles.' God sighs. 'Two.'

It isn't fair, putting me under pressure like this, but I suppose He's got a lot on His plate, what with earthquakes, genetically modified food, global terrorism and that.

'I'd like to find Dad real quickly. I want him to be glad to see me. And if it's not too much trouble, could you make him look like George Clooney only with a smaller chin? Or Brad Pitt, but not married, obviously.'

'Is that it?' sighs God. 'I've another call waiting.'

'Hang on, that was only two.'

'Out of time,' says God. He has no mercy.

'Er, cheers. Like, amen.'

Beep. God hangs up.

Beep.

'Just for a couple of nights,' says a voice. But it isn't God, it's Hefty O'Hara muttering into his mobile. I must have been dreaming. I knuckle my eyes. We've hit sunshine. The taxi's cruising down a long street milling with people, massive buildings, shops, a burger bar. Civilization!

'Be with you in ten,' Hefty's saying. He snaps the phone closed and stares out the window. The cab weaves and winds through the traffic. Drivers honk their horns like lunatics here, the noise could drive you mad, if you weren't already crazy. 'Ah, the Liffey,' says Hefty, sort of dreamily, and I'm thinking he must mean a pub or something.

'Where are we going?' A mild panic starts to set in.

Ignoring the 'thank you for not smoking' sticker, Hefty sparks up a tab and takes a deep drag. He probably thinks Silk Cut don't qualify as proper ciggies.

'To a hotel,' he replies, exhaling smoke through his nose, smiling. 'I'm taking you to a decent hotel, Rowena.'

My stomach clenches. Oh no, I've read about stuff like this, men picking up homeless girls, finding them a room and then selling them to saddos and sexual maniacs. Meet Hefty O'Hara, my pimp! No way, not in this friggin' life. If he thinks he's going to live off my immoral earnings he's way wrong. I'd rather take a bullet in the kneecaps than be a pervert's plaything.

'Don't look so worried,' says Hefty as the taxi judders to a stop. 'I know the management here and I've arranged for you to stay for a couple of nights, then we can think about tracking down that father of yours.'

He holds open the car door. My knees buckle beneath me. The rucksack slips off my shoulders on to the pavement. A tube of Twirl 'n' Curl mascara rolls out and disappears down a drain. As the cab reverses, I hear a crunch. The mobile phone, the last remaining link with my previous life, lies flattened in the gutter.

It's a sign.

4

The Cadogan Hotel

This is the first time I've been in a proper hotel. Mum took me to Whitley Bay once as an alleged 'treat' and booked us into a B&B on the seafront. The guest house had plastic butterflies stuck on the outside wall and a fake flamingo skewered into a flower bed. Apart from that, it was just a normal house, except it was run by a couple of queeny old blokes. Mum thought they were so elegant because they gave us napkins made out of proper tablecloth material, instead of paper serviettes, to wipe our chops. I tried to sleep with fingers in both ears in case they got up to disgusting homo stuff but Mum said they were probably well past that. I pointed out that one of them wore eyeliner but she replied so did Gloria Hunniford and she wasn't carrying on non-stop sexual shenanigans as far as Mum knew. She can be so unworldly.

Anyways, this is a real Dublin hotel, with plate-glass doors and wee trees like leafy green lollipops in tubs. THE CADOGAN HOTEL, says the sign on a brass plate. I clench my bum cheeks, aiming to look cool, although I probably look more like a constipated gibbon. A tingle spreads down my arms and my legs turn into lead weights. I'm paralysed, wondering what's in store for me on the other side of those doors. Maybe it's like *Stargate* and this is the portal to another reality. I'm totally spooked, feeling somehow that once I pass through the gateway my whole life will change in supercosmic ways. Seeing me hesitate, Hefty takes my elbow in his shovel-sized hand and steers me through the glass doors. Oh well, here goes nothing.

We're in a reception area. The carpet feels grassy and unreal beneath my feet. Behind the desk, a dark-haired woman in a green blouse tippy-taps on a computer. She looks up at Hefty and beams.

'Mr O'Hara, good to see you again.' She half-turns and raps on a door behind her. A head appears. A head with curly-cropped brown hair and long pointed sideburns. It's attached to a body dressed in a brown suit.

'H., how're ya.' The head's owner reaches across the desk and shakes hands with Hefty.

'Never better, Eamonn,' says Hefty. 'Never better.'

The brown-suited man glances at me. 'And this'll be the young lady who's to be our guest,' he says. I stare down at my feet. They look unfamiliar, as though I'm seeing them for the first time.

'Yes, this is Rowena,' says Hefty. They both stare at me like I'm a strange new specimen in a zoo. A flush burns into my neck. 'Rowena, meet Eamonn.' I shoot a quick look at him and nod.

'Well, sit yourselves down over there and I'll ring for some coffee,' says Eamonn. 'Is coffee all right for you, Rowena?'

I nod again, dumbly. What I'd love more than anything is a plate of chips and a couple of Solpadeines dissolved in Red Bull, but I need to suss out my situation. For example, who's paying for this? It's all very well for Hefty O'Hara to book me into a hotel but I didn't come to Ireland to squander my own money.

Hefty leads the way to a glass-topped table by the window and pulls out a pink velvety chair for me. It sighs as I sit down.

'What's with the frown?' asks Hefty, squeezing himself into the seat next to me.

What's with the frown! Here I am, alone in a foreign country, searching a strange city for a dad I can't remember, with only a two-year-old photo to go on. Then I'm picked up – abducted – by a gangster, packed into a taxi and transported to a hotel for who knows what nefarious purpose. And he wants to know *What's with the frown*?

'It's just . . .' I begin, as though it could be 'just' anything. Tears prickle behind my eyes. 'It's just . . .' Jesus, I'm so pathetic. Come on, Rowena. Get a grip. 'It's just that I don't know what to call you.'

Hefty roars. 'You're a dote, Rowena. Don't know what to call me, indeed. What would you like to call me?'

I shrug. 'Dunno. Mr O'Hara?' I venture.

'There's no need for formality,' smiles Hefty. 'We're friends, you and me, Rowena. Call me H., or Hefty, whatever you like. Let's not stand on ceremony.'

'OK,' I mutter. 'Hefty, then.' It nearly sticks in my throat. Me, Rowena M. Vincent, M as in Mobster's Moll, on first-name terms with a villain!

I'm staring at the pink-and-brown swirls on the carpet, wondering if someone deliberately designed it like that, and whether they got paid, or sacked. A pair of feet materializes, wearing DMs just like mine. For a second I think maybe I've split off from my body in an astral-projection-type thing and I'm standing next to myself. My eyes track upwards past the shoes to a pair of skinny legs, skinnier than mine, then to a tight black mini. Above that is a crisp white shirt. And crowning the whole thing is a mop of the gingerest hair I've ever seen in my life.

'Coffee?' The girl lays a tray on the table. Why is she asking me? She ought to know what's inside the silvery pot.

'Please,' I say, wanting to kick myself for sounding so submissive.

'Will you have some biscuits with that?' she says. 'Or are you sweet enough?'

I'm trying to decide whether she's being sarky and whether I should trip her up as she leaves, then Eamonn comes and says, 'Thank you, Texy, I'll see to it now.'

'Right y'are then,' she replies. Swivelling round to go, she winks at me. Despite myself, I flash a quick smile. The girl flounces off, drumming a rhythm on the tray with her fingers.

Eamonn rolls his eyes, in a you-can't-get-the-staff fashion. I study my nails. Jeez, I must have been chewing them without realizing, they're dead raggy round the edges. Bet I forgot to pack my manicure things.

'Sugar?' Eamonn offers me a bowl filled with paper sachets. 'Would you like sugar, Rowena?' he repeats.

'Cheers,' I reply. 'I mean, no, I don't use it.' What's wrong with me? I'm acting like a person with brain death. Maybe I've got new variant CJD from eating too many burgers. Maybe I'm knackered from jet lag. Or maybe I'm just scared witless.

'Wakey wakey, Rowena,' says Hefty. 'Drink your coffee, it'll give you a kick-start.'

As I lift the cup I notice my fingers are trembling and I have to hold it with both hands. The first slurp tastes so bitter I nearly spit it out. Call this coffee? It's totally vile, not like the milky Mellow Bird's I usually drink. As the caffeine hits the spot, the hot liquid sends a flush shooting up my neck and on to my face, and my forehead starts to tingle. I get a prickly sensation on my scalp and my finger ends go numb. My legs feel out of control and floppy, like a rag doll's. Oh brilliant, I'm going to flake out. Through a silvery mist, I see Hefty's arm reaching across the table to steady me. Everything's happening in slo-mo. Then my bum slides off the pinky velvet chair and I slump on to the swirly carpet, surrendering to unconsciousness.

5

The Unclear Family

Dad. My father, the legendary Lonnie Vincent. Why hast thou forsaken me? Where did you go?

The not knowing, that was the worst part. One day, the full nine yards: a dad, a mum, a nana and me. Next day, a gaping hole where Lonnie used to be. A void, a paternal absence, a state of dadlessness. Twenty-five per cent of our nuclear family blasted out of existence.

For nuclear, read *unclear*. The unclear family.

Mum refused to talk about it. I was too young to understand, that's what she told me. Nana Vincent backed her up.

What could have been so secret, so unspeakable, that they had to airbrush Dad out of the picture, rewrite history, revising and erasing as they went? Within a day, it seemed, everything disappeared: the photographs, Dad's clothes and shoes, the man-scented sticks and sprays from the bathroom, his books and vinyl record collection, even his guitar. That was the clincher, the sign that he wasn't coming back. When he played that guitar, he used to lose himself in another reality, strumming, plucking, riffing, his hardened fingertips riding the frets, creating harmony from discord, music from silence. Post-Dad, there was plenty of silence.

All that I have left is a two-year-old photo, a snapshot of three men outside a bar, laughing, raising their glasses to the camera. Dad sent the pic to Nana Vincent, his mother. On the back he'd written:

Toasting Joyce, Bloomsday, Cork Street, Dublin.

I'm guessing that Joyce was the woman who took the picture, a barmaid, possibly. But which of the three men was Dad? It had been years since I saw him. People change, sometimes for good, sometimes not. He'd been erased so completely from my life that I couldn't remember what he looked like, let alone imagine how he might look today.

The man on the left of the picture had a number two crop so it was hard to say what colour his hair would be. He wore an earring, nothing fancy, just a small ring, a sleeper, to stop the hole in his lobe from closing up. There was nothing distinctive about his features, nothing daddish, no giveaway lopsided smile like mine, nothing that made me keen to claim kinship with him.

The bloke in the middle had blondish hair, maybe chemically enhanced, cut in a style that was popular for a while with Second Division footballers. His face was a bit on the orange side, like he'd gone overboard on the fake tanning lotion or someone had given him sunbed gift vouchers for Christmas. There was a touch of upwardly mobile swagger about him, the aura of a Kappa-wearing charva boy made good. I think I'd have been disappointed if he'd turned out to be the one.

If I had to put money on it, if someone had pulled a gun on me, I'd have gone for the third guy. There was something of the gypsy in his dark curly hair, the three-day stubble, the flyboy grin. Maybe I inherited my psychic tendencies from Romany ancestors. I used to get whirly feelings in my head when me and Samantha Leach played in her dad's caravan, although Mum put it down to leaking fumes from the Calor gas canister rather than paranormal phenomena from ancient shades.

It's weird how my memories of Dad vanished pretty much overnight, along with his physical being and, allegedly, some cash and valuables from Nana Vincent's house. Mum said I'd been traumatized by his sudden disappearance, that nature was being kind by drawing a veil over the past, like amnesia was some sort of consolation prize for losing him.

As a father, Lonnie was pretty much self-contained. What did he do all day? How did he fill his time? I know that he went to university as a mature student, earned some kind of a degree, because his graduation photo stood on top of the TV, him in his robe and tasselled mortar board, smiling, but in a strained way, as though the hand of an invisible puppeteer was working him. What did his expression say?

Instead of being proud, Nana Vincent seemed almost embarrassed by his success, saying Dad was making a holy show of himself by mixing with educated people instead of getting on with a normal life. Scroungers, that was her opinion of students. Scroungers, layabouts and scruffy buggers who couldn't get proper jobs, couldn't hack it in the real world.

One time I tried to pin Dad down on what he did for a living. He told me he was a Social Enigma, which for some reason I thought meant he investigated people illegally claiming benefit. Or he'd say he was in demolition, working to break down stereotypes. Or in the Animal Liberation Front, rescuing people who'd got stuck in pigeonholes. Or he'd say he laid cats' eyes in the road so people could see the way ahead. Me, I took it all in, even though I suspected they were made-up jobs. When I was older, I learned to decipher the underlying message in his words.

He felt trapped. Paralysed. Held back by a family who found him too clever by half. He was sick, he once told me, of *living down* to other people's expectations. Lonnie Vincent was blessed with a brain. He had a lot to offer, but no-one wanted it.

I wonder if Dad ever did find himself, and more importantly, whether I'll ever find Dad.

6

Prince Diana's Necktar

My eyes blink open in the half-light. Patting around beneath me, I realize I'm lying on a bed, a single bed, with a woolly blanket draped over me. To my right is a small table with a lamp, and beyond that, another bed. The walls are made of butterscotch yoghurt, and the ceiling is covered in huge Ryvita crispbreads. Spaced here and there in the dimply tiles are little spotlights. I'm struggling to remember where I am, how I got here. There are no clues.

Elbowing myself up against the pillows, I take my bearings. In an alcove to my left, there's a door, and a sign that says FIRE EXIT. At least if there's a blaze I'll be able to escape. Opposite me is a long window with vertical blinds and a pair of heavy, half-drawn curtains. There's a dressing table with a swively mirror, a stool and a telly. Along the right wall is another door, slightly open, then a fitted wardrobe. Still no clues. It's all completely alien. I feel like Alice in Wonderland, after she followed the White Rabbit down the hole. Maybe I've had a deeply traumatic experience and I'm suffering from amnesia. Or I could have been involved in an RTA and lain in a coma for the last ten years. That would make me, what, twenty-six. Practically Jurassic. Jeez, I hope someone's been keeping up my cleanse, tone and nourish routine, otherwise my skin will have shrivelled like a walnut and I'll be spottier than a leper with acne.

It's no good, I'll have to investigate, check myself out in the mirror, see if I can find any clues to my present situation.

To test my limbly functions, I flex my feet and wiggle my toes. So far, so not paralysed. My fingers seem to curl and spread normally too, although the skin around my nails has been nibbled as though a small rodent's been at them. I run my hands through my hair. It feels stiff and bird's-nesty, which is a good sign as it means I'm most probably me after all. Now for the tricky bit: achieving verticality. Firstly I check round my throat to make sure I'm not wearing a neck brace as that would mean I had spinal injuries, or whiplash at least. All in order. Pinching my thigh to test for feeling, I manoeuvre myself into a sitting position and slide my legs to the floor. My feet touch carpet. It's so comforting to be in contact with the earth, to feel grounded. I move the soles of my feet around in little circles until they warm up from the friction. Bracing myself with my hands, I ease my bottom off the bed and slowly raise myself to a standing position. It takes a superhuman effort as I'm scared of falling and knocking myself into a coma, but I manage it. Only for a few seconds though, as my head comes over all sweaty and whirly and I flop back on the bed, exhausted.

The next thing I'm aware of is music. I let my brain settle and gradually I recognize it as 'Sing it Back' by Moloko. At first I think it's a new, crap mix as Roisin's voice is way out of tune, then I realize it's someone singing along to the track. Crinkling my eyes awake, I make out a greyish figure next to me. It seems to be floating, pixellated, like on telly when they fuzz out people's faces for anonymity. As my brain struggles to absorb it, the hazy vision sharpens focus and changes to black-and-white. Omigawd, I've turned colour blind! Rowena M. Vincent. M as in monochrome.

'Hey,' says a voice. 'So you do conscious as well, do you?'

It's the hair that pulls me back to reality. The thick unruly stuff, bright as a Sainsbury's carrot, on top of the black-and-white uniform. It's the waitress, the one who served the coffee, served it to me and – I recall with a sharp stomach-jolt – Hefty O'Hara. Oh, God.

'Where am I?' I moan in a vague, bewildered fashion, clutching my head to suggest serious memory loss. Then, just in case she's slow on the uptake, 'Who am I?'

The girl kicks off her Docs and flops on to the bed. 'Where, I can answer. You're in Room 204 at the Cadogan Hotel in the fair city of Dublin. As for who, if you don't know, I can't help you.'

A new track starts on the Moloko CD: 'Being is Bewildering'. For some reason it makes me want to cry.

'You look as if you could do with a drink. I could murder one meself,' says the girl. She brushes the hair away from her face and I find myself staring into the bluest eyes I've ever seen, the artificially *blue* blue of hotel swimming pools in Mediterranean holiday brochures. More a *too* blue than a true blue. She must be wearing coloured contact lenses. 'I'm Texy, by the way.'

'Texy?' I think, possibly aloud. 'Daft name, if you ask me.'

'I didn't,' she grins, 'ask you. Teresa, that's my given name, but it's just my family use it, and then only when I'm in the bad books. Which is most of the time,' she adds.

'I'm Rowena,' I say without thinking. Shit, bang goes the 'who am I?' scenario.

'OK then, Rowena,' she says. 'So howsabout that drink? What do you fancy? Mineral water? Tea? Coffee?'

'I dunno,' I mumble pathetically. 'Surprise me.'

'A clue would help,' she says, rolling her eyes.

'Something with a bit kick?' I venture. I'd guess she's maybe a couple of years older than me and legally able to drink, so one out of two ain't bad.

'Bang on! The minibar's a right rip-off so I'll go and raid the samples cupboard while they're busy with lunch,' she grins, swinging her skinny legs off the bed and slipping into her shoes. The door clicks shut behind her.

Time to take stock of my situation. First question, am I being kept a prisoner? Now that I'm sure my legs are functioning, I slide off the bed and pad to the door marked FIRE EXIT, the one that Texy disappeared through. Flicking back the Yale sneck, I open it, half expecting to see a solid metal wall with a massive ship's wheel thing that opens up to reveal a vault, like in bank jobs in the movies. To my amazement, the door opens easily on to a carpeted corridor with some stairs at the end. I peer both ways down the hallway, but it's dead quiet, no-one around, just more doors. The aroma of cooking meat wafts into my nostrils, making me drool. Jeez, it's been so long since my last meal, I could eat a scabby rat.

I close the door and go back into the room. On the surface it appears likely that I'm in a hotel rather than a prison. On the other hand, this place could be some sort of holding centre where trainee prostitutes are taught the tricks of the trade before being forced on to the streets or sent abroad to pleasure men who eat sheeps' eyeballs and wear tea towels on their heads. What if they make me learn belly-dancing? Or snake-charming? Or sell me to join the harem of some Eastern potentate, or as a concubine for a foreign despot and his fifty-three lookalikes? I'll just die if they make me ride a camel. I saw one close up at a zoo when I was little; a mangy thing half-covered in sofa-stuffing hair and baldy patches. Its name was Fang. The disgusting beast stamped its feet, hooves, whatever, then blew up its tongue to the size of a whale's bladder and hurled a half-litre gob of spit at me. Whoever designed camels should seek help.

My stomach starts growling. I'm so ravenous, my body must be eating its own muscle tissue. To take my mind off imminent starvation, I zap on the telly but it's just the boring midday news. Huh, no Teletext either, so I can't even check my horoscopes to see if I'm supposed to be having a good day. *Pisces: You will be abducted by a notorious criminal, flown abroad and enrolled in a school for teenage whores.* Nothing new there, then. I hit the red Standby button.

'I come bearing booty.' Texy stands framed in the doorway, two clinking carrier bags in her hands. Kicking the door closed behind her, she empties the contents on to the bed. 'Vodka, whisky, Tia Maria, Malibu, Bacardi, Mother's Ruin, take your pick.'

The bottles are mostly those wee sample ones you get on

aeroplanes, except for a huge one full of pee-coloured liquid. I check out the label: *Prince Diana's Necktar. Distilled in Sapporo.*

'What's this?' I ask, humping the monster on to my knees.

Texy glances up. 'Japanese Scotch, disgusting stuff,' she replies. 'A gift from a grateful punter.'

A grateful punter! So my theory was right. This is a house of ill repute – and Texy's on the game too!

She catches my startled expression. 'Not that kind of punter.' Lordy, she must be a mind-reader. 'A tourist,' she explains. 'Dublin's crawling with 'em. If they can't find a half-decent hotel, the poor buggers end up here.'

'Oops, sorry,' I stutter. 'I thought for a minute you were . . . you know, a hooker or something.'

'I'm flattered, not,' Texy grins. 'But you couldn't be more wrong, shweetheart. Now come on, choose your poison.' She tips out the second carrier on to the bed. It's full of cans, Bud, Special Brew, Guinness, and – there is a God! – Red Bull.

'What'll it be?' Texy plonks a plastic beaker in my hand. She rips open a can of Special Brew and takes a swallow.

'I'll go a Red Bull,' I reply.

'Not by itself, you won't,' she says. 'That's a flaying offence round here.' I watch as she pours two fingers of voddy into the beaker and tops it up with goldy fizz from the can. 'There, a VRB,' she announces. '*Sláinte.*'

'Cheers.' I take a sip. Eurgh, it's warm, like drinking urine, but I decide not to complain since she's been to all that trouble. Ferreting in my rucksack, I dig out a king-size box of Solpadeines, tear a strip in half and plink a couple of tablets into the drink where they fizz like good 'uns. 'Headache,' I explain.

Texy smothers a burp. 'You smoke?' she asks.

I nod. 'Sometimes. I haven't got though.'

'I'll roll you a fat one,' says Texy. 'That'll sort your head.' She fiddles under her shirt and produces a stash pouch from inside her bra. 'Stick some music on,' she says, gesturing with her elbow towards the bedside table. 'Under there.'

I kneel on the carpet to study the steely machine. It's a CD player and radio but my eyes won't focus properly and I can't decipher which knob is which. After twiddling this and that, a man's voice comes on the radio. He cracks a pathetic gag and laughs like a drain.

'Turn him off,' says Texy. 'Bloody Brendan O'Lunacy, he makes my flesh creep. Slap a CD on.'

There's no sign of any CDs but I remember Moloko was playing earlier so I stab a few buttons at random until I hear a faint laser-type *tzzzz* that means I've hit the right one. A few piano chords first, then the deepdown brass intro that leads into 'Pure Pleasure Seeker'. The VRB-Solpadeine concoction goes down a treat and I lie back on the bed, closing my eyes and feeling the voddy warm my innards. A lighter flicks and soon the sickly-sweet smell of cannabis drifts into my nostrils. The bed dips as Texy climbs aboard and offers the roach to my mouth. I inhale without opening my eyes and take the smoke deep into my lungs. Normally when smoking dope I get a coughing fit or an attack of hiccups, but this time it floats smoothly down inside me and sends my head gently spinning. Mmm, bliss.

'So,' I hear Texy say from a hundred miles away, 'what brings you to Dublin?'

My tongue feels huge and furry inside my mouth, like I've swallowed a stoat. 'Dad,' I reply. 'I've come to find my dad.'

'Ah.' Just one word, but the way she says it makes me feel she understands, knows the history, possesses all the wisdom in the world. Surrendering to the druggy buzzing in my head, I snuggle babylike beside Texy, feeling her body warmth radiate and soothe me, loving the bony knobbles of her coltish legs against mine. I rest my cheek against the comforting crispness of her shirt. Texy, my new friend, my guide in a strange and foreign world, my ally, my protector, my shield. Surely she was sent to me by angels.

7

BVM Pudding

Lord, I feel skanky. My T-shirt's damp and sticky around the bosoms and my neck is drenched in sweat. One side of my face is burning where I've been lying on it funny. I'm busting for a pee.

I'm disoriented, stretched out alone in a strange bed. Texy! For a moment I wonder whether she was a dream, until I spot the roaches in a saucer and an assortment of cans and empty miniature bottles on the carpet. Lordy, what time is it? Staring through the chink in the curtains it looks like early evening, dusk, gloaming, twilight, one of those funny-named things. Get yo' ass moving, woman.

Hauling myself up from the bed, I stagger to the door on the right and enter the bathroom, pressing a switch and turning on a fluorescent light. The white glare has me blinking like a pit pony and I shield my eyes, squinting through my fingers as I peer into the mirror. What a fright! I look closer. Something strange has appeared on my cheek, a blemish or perhaps a bite. Urgh, maybe I've been attacked by bedbugs. I examine it right up close in the mirror until gradually I make out what looks like writing etched into my cheek. It reminds me of that spooky lass Regan in *The Exorcist*, when the words 'Help me' materialize in angry weals. Triffic, I've been possessed. I stare and stare until my eyeballs feel ready to pop. There's a sort of smudgy bit, then a letter K, followed by a letter N and what looks like a misshapen T. What can it mean? As I watch, it begins to dissolve into my skin, somehow making it easier to read.

D . . . K . . . N . . . Y.

Oh Lordy, I must have dropped off to sleep with my face on my rucksack and the metal label embossed itself on my cheek like a

Dymo tape. I'm a real-life advert for Donna Karan New York. What a prize fool!

Perching sideways on the loo for a panoramic view of the bathroom, I release a damful of pee, followed by a beautiful soft and shapely poo, one of those smooth, never-ending ones where you lose half a stone at a sitting. After cleaning my nether bits I turn on the hot tap and empty a sachet of no-name bubble stuff into the bath. It smells of old ladies and furniture polish. The room fills with steam. I step into the water and slide down into the nauseatingly perfumed bubbles which have now taken on the odour of stagnant slimy liquid at the bottom of a vase of gone-off daffodils. Bleurgh!

Next to the taps is a wee tablet of soap, about half the size of a credit card. Fortunately it isn't perfumed, although it could stink of elephant dung for all I can tell above the disgusting pong of the bath lotion. It's crap soap too, popping all the foamy bubbles to buggery and not even attempting to form a lather. Huh, must be cheap foreign muck made from bog-trotters' entrails or something, not proper whale blubber like we have in England. I scrub and scrub but it's just redistributing the dirt, not cleaning it off. Maison well give up and try to exfoliate the dead skin with a brisk rub-down with a towel. Yanking out the plug, I step on to the mat and wrap myself in a fluffy white bath sheet, watching the water drain away to leave a ring of grey scum. I'm looking round for the Flash, then I remember I'm a guest in a real hotel. The servants can deal with my effluent, that's what they're paid for.

My belly's burning with hunger but I need to sort my face before setting out on a scran-seeking expedition. When did my skin last see cleanser? I dig in the rucksack and exhume my toilety stuff, dumped all anyhow in a Kwik Save carrier bag. Plonking my bott on the dressing-table stool, I steel myself to look in the mirror. Hmm, grimmish, but not over-the-toply gruesome, even with a DKNY logo on my cheek. Thunder rolls in my stomach. I decide to ignore it as I'd rather expire from starvation than leave the room without make-up. God bless whoever invented cosmetic cleansing wipes. They're like those wet tissues for sorting babies' bumcracks, only for faces instead of faeces. And they contain toner as well, leaving your skin soft enough to go without moisturizer if you're in a mad rush, which, trust me, I am. I smear a couple of wipes around my face, one in each hand to save time, avoiding my eyes as it would take forever to redo the liner and mascara and I truly can't be arsed. The tissues turn a foul digestive-biscuit colour from the residue of the Sand Beige Color-Stay which has been clagged on my face for x number of hours. My pores gasp and hyperventilate as the fresh air hits them but I show no mercy, dotting new blobs of foundation on my cheeks, chin, nose and forehead and blending it in at 100 mph. Sorry, skin, but you can't be seen stark bollock-naked in public. Then I smear some Red or Dedd lippy across my mouth, blot it with a tissue and apply a second coat. Now for the hair. I look like Siouxsie Sioux after a motorbike ride but there's no time to untangle the cotters so I backcomb it even stragglier and pin it up in a cone slide until it could pass as a punk-never-dies style statement. My fringe needs cutting but for now I drown it in spit, twist it into spiky bits and plaster it to my forehead. There, I'm human. Well, humanoid, close enough.

Clean knickies, push-up bra, black tights, slash-neck top, yellow latex miniskirt, biker boots, leather jacket. Check out the look. Not brilliant, but passable. Still, it's only Ireland, after all, and it's not as if I'm going out on the pull or anything.

I nearly jump out of my skin when the phone rings.

'Hi, it's Texy. Just called to see how you're feeling after your rest in the arms of Morpheus.'

'Uh, yeah, I'm radiant. Famished, though. I could murder something to eat.'

'Thought as much. How does a cheese toastie sound?'

My stomach grumbles in reply.

'I'm coming to get you.'

In no time flat Texy's rapping on the door. 'You needn't have

35

bothered dressing for dinner,' she says, looking me up and down. Her eyes shift to my face and focus on the embossed writing on my cheek. 'What the feck . . .?'

'Don't ask,' I say.

She shrugs in a good-natured way. 'Come on up to my palatial bedsit,' she grins. 'Munchies await.'

I follow her along the corridor, through a door at the end, and up some narrow, winding stairs that seem to go on for ever. The floor-covering, which starts off as bog-standard hotel carpet, becomes gradually scruffier and more threadbare as we ascend. To take my mind off the slight wheezing in my chest, I study the muscles in Texy's calves; they're like rubber balls moving up and down beneath the skin.

'How much further?' I pause, leaning against the wall to get my breath back. Mental note to pack in smoking before heart combusts and lungs turn to kippers.

'A few more steps, you wuss, then I'll give you a whiff of oxygen and a protein milkshake.'

'Just . . . need . . . siddown,' I gasp.

'We're here now. Eighth floor: camping equipment, rubber goods and leisurewear,' sings Texy. 'Staff quarters, or Gulag, if you like.' She fits a key into the lock of a purple-painted door. 'Anyone would think you'd scaled the north face of the Eiger with a camel strapped to your back, the fuss you're making.'

I attempt a laugh, with what remains of the air in my bursting lungs, then stagger through the doorway and collapse into a chair. One of my eyeballs feels loose, as though its membranes are slack. Maybe I've got altitude sickness from climbing to this room-in-the-sky, or a brainal malfunction. Rowena Loose Eye – that can be my aka name. I slump in the seat like a wrung-out dishcloth until gradually my heart stops pounding, my breathing returns to normal and the eyeball ceases to ricochet around my skull.

'Is this where you live, Texy?' I ask. She's bustling about in the tiny kitchenette, slicing cheese, buttering bread, slapping them inside a sandwich toaster, making me salivate.

'If this is what you call living,' she says. 'Personally, I'd just as soon be in a cave, living off berries and small mammals, wearing a hat woven from dried seagrass and nothing else, getting an all-over sun tan. Going native. Red or brown sauce?'

'Brown,' I reply. 'I suppose it's handy for work, though, no travelling, you just roll out of bed and you're here.'

Texy sends me a peculiar glance, as though I'm a halfwit. 'Being a waitress wasn't a long-term career choice, Rowena. I needed money and a roof over my head and this fitted the bill, but it's just a stopgap measure until I figure out what I want to do.' She hands me a plate. I rip into the cheese toastie like a savage, scratching the roof of my mouth and burning my tongue in a mad rush to stuff some sustenance inside me.

'You enjoying that?' Texy chews her food like a proper civilized human being, which makes me feel terrible for wolfing mine like a starving street dog. I resist the urge to lick the crumbs off the plate and concentrate instead on smothering a burp.

'Yeah, it really hit the spot. Thanks, Texy, I thought I was going to pass out from malnutrition.'

She wipes her mouth, takes the plates and stacks them in the sink.

'Fancy some dessert? I'll go and scout round the kitchen, see what leftovers are hanging around, if you like.'

I shrug, pretending not to care less, when actually my stomach still feels cramped with hunger pangs and I could scoff six giant helpings of treacle pudding, nee bovva.

'OK, but only if you're having some,' I sigh, in an attempt at half-heartedness.

'That's settled then,' she grins. 'Help yourself to coffee or tea if you fancy it. Back in two shakes of a lamb's tail.'

While Texy's away pudding-hunting, I make myself useful by washing the plates and tidying round the sink. Then I explore the flatlet, opening a door to reveal a tiny shower room with washbasin and lavvy. Everything here is so small, like furniture in a doll's house, making me wonder if the hotel hired a tribe of pygmies as staff, or ten-year-old children working illegally. From somewhere comes the sound of muted conversation; it's a man talking in a wheedling tone to a woman. Her voice is brusque, as if she's having none of it, although their words are indistinct. At first I wonder if it's a radio in a nearby room, but it's closer than that. It seems as though it's coming from the fabric of the wall. I press my ear against the tiles, trying to feel vibrations, but the voices seem more muffled, so I edge around the miniature room until it occurs to me: the noise is coming through the lavatory pan. Kneeling beside the toy-sized bog, lowering my head, the voices become quite clear.

You can't blame me for trying, Irma.

Don't you dare give me that old flannel. I'm sick of your lies. You can pack your bags and go back to live with her, I've had it up to here with your excuses.

'You're not regurgitating that cheese toastie, I hope.' Texy stands in the doorway, a grin bisecting her face. 'Or are you eavesdropping?'

A guilty blush burns my cheeks and my tongue ties into a reef knot.

Texy laughs. 'You're OK, you dote, we all listen in. It's the couple in the room below. Their yelling and screeching travels through the plumbing. They're cooks, see, they holler all the time. My theory goes that they were abandoned at birth and raised by a colony of Kilkenny cats. Aww, never mind,' she says, clocking my bemused expression. 'Now will you have a banana split?'

I nod. It's a relief to hear Texy's explanation, to know that the voices were real, that it's not some auditory hallucination, although it sure spooked me out to hear conversation floating up through the lavatory bowl.

While Texy creates a sweet confection of bananas and whatever, I nose around the room. There isn't much to see. The furniture is shabby and basic, chucky-out charity-shop stuff, light years away from the bay trees and glass doors, the springy carpets and velvety chairs in the public reception area a few floors below. The hi-fi looks as if it was made in biblical times, and it doesn't even have a CD player! There are no posters on the walls, no piles of shoes scattered around the floor, no heaps of minging undies; in fact, no sign of clothes at all. How can people outside the Third World live like this? It's too, too tidy and unbelievably primitive. The overall impression is of an impersonal and temporary-looking living space, the room of someone ready to ship out at a moment's notice. A stopgap measure, as Texy put it.

Naturally, I can't resist poking my nose in.

'Where do you keep your clothes, Texy?'

'They're in the drawers or hanging in the wardrobe, where do you think?' she replies, flapping her hand in the direction of a coffinlike box in the corner.

I slap my forehead. 'Duh! How stupid am I?' What I'm actually thinking is: clothes and wardrobe go *together*? In my experience clothes appear magically washed, dried and ironed on hangers hooked on the bedroom door, they get worn once or twice, then get transferred by unseen hands into the dirty-washing basket, and the cycle repeats endlessly. Wardrobes are for dumping impulse-buy stuff that you wouldn't be seen dead in, stashing shoplifted swag and plastic bags full of barely used make-up, pretty much a hidey-hole or a landfill site. Hanging clothes in a wardrobe? What an alien, yet novel, concept. It'll never catch on.

'Who's this?' I pick up a framed photo of a gadgy with little bitty silver hair done in a comb-over. He's sitting in a patio chair in a flower garden, gurning, flashing his gums at the camera. Someone's dressed him in a brown tank top, hand-knitted on big needles so the stitches are all droopy loopy. Attached to the top is a yellow badge in the shape of a letter B. This guy looks like a very old baby. I bet he's on drugs too.

'That's Bobbo, my granddaddy. Well, more my surrogate dad, as things turned out. I love him to pieces.' Texy licks her fingers and hands me a long glass dish. 'Here's your banana split, spoil yourself.'

Huh, soil myself, more like. It's a giant of a banana, the size of a cucumber, surrounded by ice cream and piped whipping cream, decorated with nuts and diced fruit and topped with a drizzle of wee-coloured gunge. I tuck in with gusto, but after a couple of mouthfuls I'm stuffed.

'Texy, this is pure scrumptious, honest. I don't want to seem ungrateful but . . .'

'But it's sickly, I know. I went a bit overboard on the maple syrup.' She points with her spoon at the sticky urine-type stuff. 'No need to force it down, it didn't cost a dime.'

'Cheers, Texy. Oh, man, I'm full to busting.' I pat my stomach and stir the remains of the pudding with the spoon, liquefying the ice cream, squashing the nuts and fruit, turning the rich, syrupy concoction into mush. We slob out on the chairs in an easy, companionable silence accompanied by the occasional gurgle of digestive juices. Chilling with Texy is ultra-cool, it feels like I've known her for yonks even though we only met today.

Texy's voice snaps me out of my reverie. 'What were you saying earlier about your dad? You said you'd come to Dublin to find him.' She licks a ciggy paper, smooths out a rollie and reaches for her lighter.

'Uh-huh.'

'So where does Mr O'Hara fit into this?'

'Hefty?' My stomach attempts a nervous roll, but it's too full to move. 'He reckons he wants to help me find Dad, but I'm still trying to figure out his angle, what's in it for him.' I'm tempted to tell her that he's planning to tout me as a sexual plaything for paying punters, lining his pockets with the proceeds of my body, pimping me out to unhygienic old men. Tempted, yes, but it seems better to lay the truth on her gradually, in dribs and drabs, in case she might be shocked or think that I really am some kind of a tart.

'I'm sure Mr O'Hara is just trying to help. He's got contacts,' says Texy. She's not wrong there. 'So you were saying about your father,' she prompts, adding, 'tell me to mind my own if you like. I'm such a nosy mare.'

'No, you're OK. I was wondering whether to mention it anyway, you being from Dublin.' Grabbing my rucksack, I pull out the photo of Dad and his mates and hand it to her. She turns it over and reads the inscription.

Toasting Joyce, Bloomsday, Cork Street, Dublin.

'Which one's your dad?' she says.

'I can't be sure, not exactly,' I reply. Texy shoots me a sharp glance, her eyebrows raised in a question. 'It's been years. He'll have changed for sure. Anyway, my mind kind of blanked him out.' It sounds crazy, even to me, but it's the truth. 'What about the pub?' I say, changing the subject to a safer one. 'Do you recognize it?'

'I know Cork Street.' She lights her tab and takes a pull, squinting through the smoke at the picture. 'In fact I know this bar,' she says. 'The Beggar's Belief, it's called.'

My stomach heads up to my throat and back again. 'You know it? Is it far from here?'

'Other end of the city,' she says, offering me the rollie, which I decline. 'It's in the Liberties, off the Coombe, up towards the Rialto end. Not exactly the bright lights of yuppiedom, but not exactly bandit country either. My granddad used to live around there, near the Guinness place. Tell you what, why don't we take a bus there? We could go to the Beggar's, show your dad's photo around, see if anyone recognizes him.'

Blood zooms round my body at supersonic speed. 'Really? You think . . .?' My front teeth feel itchy with nerves.

'Sure it's a long shot,' Texy concedes. 'But we've nothing to lose by trying – plus we can have a couple of drinks while we're at it, OK?'

'Suppose so.' Now that my fantasy about finding Dad is one step nearer to reality, I'm starting to brick it. A hundred 'what ifs' flood my brain, drowning rational thought. What if he left us to escape from me, his evil, twisty-minded daughter? What if I did something terrible that drove him away? What if and what if and all the what ifs to infinity.

Texy clicks her tongue. 'Could you try sounding a bit less keen?' My face crumples. 'We don't have to, Rowena. It seemed an obvious move, is all.'

'No, no, I really want to go there.' It sounds so false, so lame, me protesting, feigning enthusiasm.

'That's what we'll do, then.' Texy calls my bluff, pretending to take my words at face value. She grabs a bomber jacket from the wardrobe. 'No time like the present, eh?'

'I guess.'

Texy grins and shoves me towards the door. Her hand on the light switch, she turns and checks the room, then unplugs her mobile phone from the charger and stuffs it in her pocket.

'Holy Moly, will you look at that.' She points at the table, to the remains of my banana split. My eyes follow hers.

'What?' It's a swirly-whirly mess of fruit pulp and cream plus chocolate shavings.

Texy takes a step towards the table, swivels the glass dish round towards me. 'There,' she says, pointing to the leftovers. 'Can't you see? Those chocolate bits, they're the eyes. What's left of the cherry, that's the mouth. And the way the cream swirls round – if you put your head to one side and squint, it could be a veil. Look at it. It's like the face of the Blessed Virgin Mary.'

'Don't be daft,' I snort. 'Mush, that's all it is. Just sloppy, melty mush.'

8

The Secret Life of Dad

Who knows what Dad was doing in Ireland? He might have emigrated, or stowed away on a ferry, or run away to join a Riverdance troupe, or gone on a bender with Shane MacGowan and lost his memory. It could have been something as simple as a stag night; Dublin's a party hotspot and loads of people visit for a lost weekend of non-stop boozing.

But now I think about it, he did have a sort of connection with the Irish.

This day, right, I'd bunked off school and gone on a make-up robbing expedition in town. Well, I wanted some red mascara like Samantha Leach's even though it made her look as if she hadn't slept for a week. Also I needed a new top and ear studs to go with the mascara. After Boots, Top Shop and Republica, I sneaked the loot into Burger King so I could destroy the labels while treating myself to a giant Coke. Then, to my total horror, a woman on the next table started to breastfeed a baby. Can you believe the brass neck of her! She opened a bratflap in her bra, clamped the sprog's gob onto her nip where it sucked and slurped and made the most sickening noises. Apart from two lads who were sitting opposite and sniggering behind their hands, no-one took any notice, but to me it felt like a personal insult, as if she was doing it deliberately to wind me up when my nerves were already jangled from shoplifting.

Stuffing the robbed goods into my rucksack, I moved to a seat in the window, sipping the drink and watching the world go by until I'd calmed down. My face was burning with embarrassment from the disgusting wifey's behaviour so I rolled a couple of ice cubes on my forehead and neck to cool down.

That's when I saw Dad.

He was wandering up Northumberland Street, looking as if he was on another planet, weaving about, unsteady on his feet. Jesus, he's drunk in public! That was my first thought, but as I squinted through my fingers he seemed to correct himself and started to walk normally. Maybe he had a stone in his shoe, or a blister on his heel. Still I was concerned about him in case he'd developed sudden-onset MS, so I decided to trail him, keep an eye on his well-being. It was important to stay out of sight otherwise he'd give me a bollocking for sagging off school.

Once outside, I scanned the street with an increasing sense of panic. In the pedestrianized area, shoppers swirled and merged with each other like multicoloured clothes in a washing machine, but there was no sight of Dad. I ran down a couple of side streets, then wandered up and down the main drag peering into shop windows, checking out queues. Nothing. It's not like I was spying on him. Seeing him stumbling around had unnerved me and I wanted to be sure he wasn't ill.

Just as I was about to give up, I spotted him several doors away, coming out of a building. He walked a few steps then stood for a while, reading something, as far as I could make out from the back view. Edging along close to the shops, I pushed open the door he'd just left and glanced inside. It was a bank or a building society, one of those places with cashpoint machines in the lobby. From a safe distance, I kept him in sight and followed his progress up the street, dodging into doorways when he looked as though he might turn round. This was how it must feel to be a secret agent or a celebrity-stalker. Dangerous but exciting. Heart-stopping but impossible to resist.

My pulse raced when he paused outside a record shop called Hitz. I braked to a halt, lowered my head, pretended to check my pockets while still keeping him in vision. He stood there for ages but he didn't seem interested in the CDs and T-shirts and posters of chart positions. It appeared as if he was looking past the window display, at something or someone inside the shop. After a few minutes Dad moved away from the front and stood in the lane facing the side window. He took out a cigarette and lit it, cupping his hands and turning his back to shield it from the wind.

In the few seconds it took me to dart across the street and position myself in the doorway of Halfday's department store for a better view, someone else had joined him. A younger man, early twenties at a guess, wearing jeans and a hooded top, was standing in the alley right next to Dad. Without a word being exchanged, he sparked up a tab using the one in Dad's hand, then walked away. To a casual observer, they could have been strangers. But there was something in the gesture of lighting that cigarette, an almost practised effortlessness, that made me suspect they knew each other.

Dad was in no rush. He leaned against the wall in the lane and finished his cigarette. I watched him stub it out with the heel of his shoe. Then, zipping up his leather jacket, he set off up Northumberland Street once more. His stride was purposeful. He looked neither to right nor left. This man knew where he was headed.

More intrigued than ever, I followed him.

He was heading towards Haymarket Metro Station where I assumed he'd be catching a train to Four Lane Ends, towards home. Relieved, feeling a bit foolish for turning the afternoon's events into a melodrama, I was ready to call it a day, take a bus home, act like nothing unusual had happened. The incident in the lane had receded in importance, sunk into normal proportions. A guy in a hoody had asked Dad for a light. So what? End of story. I'd let my imagination run amok, turning an innocent, everyday happening into a conspiracy theory. Get a grip, girl.

But Dad didn't catch the Metro home, didn't even go into the station. He hung a left. I hung behind, skulking like a kicked mongrel, and watched him walk into a fun pub, a scary place with a list of specials, meaning cheap drinks, chalked on boards and music blaring from the windows.

45

Now what? If Dad was meeting his mates for a boozy session, I could be here until chucky-out time. Concealing myself behind a pillar, I considered the options, but not for long. Within two minutes he was back, accompanied by a man in a checked shirt. They stood close together and exchanged a few words, way too quiet for me to hear, then they smiled, shook hands.

'Nice one, Lonnie.' That's what I heard the bloke say before he went back into the pub. Dad turned up the collar of his jacket and set off again. He crossed over the road, strode along Percy Street and turned right in the direction of Gallowgate. I felt cold, hungry and wretched, plus I was itching to get to my room and experiment with the red mascara, but I decided to stick on his tail for a wee bit longer, just to make sure nothing weird was going on.

Slow down, Dad. He practically jogged up the road to the top of Gallowgate and my legs were pulled to buggery by the hill. That's when I saw him enter a building with a big sign in front. I waited in a nearby doorway for ages but there was no sight of him. In the end, with the breath steaming from my mouth in the freezing fog and feeling faint from hunger, I decided to cut my losses and head off home.

I never found out what was going on in the secret life of Dad. But even back then, he had a connection with the Emerald Isle. The sign on the front of the building had said Tyneside Irish Centre. Beneath the name, some crack about a forthcoming festival, pictures of fiddlers, a big splash about a showband, dancers, the best in Irish stand-up.

Yeah, right. A perfect line-up for my idea of Hades.

9

Taking the Liberties

Cork Street is way away from the touristy part of Dublin. I doubt it features on many picture postcards. The best I can say is that it's a long street, or it certainly feels long. Ugly, drab, depressing, are other words that come to mind. Texy says it's steeped in history but I reckon it should be steeped in soapy water and a strong solution of bleach. She also tells me the area is being regenerated, but demolition would be a better option.

Clutching my bag to my bosoms, I try to feel excited but the emotions are all jumbled up inside me. My new best friend, Texy, is showing me the hidden corners of her city, places a tour guide wouldn't know about, let alone set foot in. For this I should feel privileged. And I do, in a way. She's putting herself out to be matey, to help me to trace Dad, and it's kind of humbling to see how proud she is about this end of town, even though it's part tip, part building site where it's being dug up for some new rail system.

To be honest, the place is a real letdown. It had all been so different in my imagination, or perhaps something I saw in *OK!* magazine. Dad would be living in a loft apartment, high ceiling, wooden beams, polished pine floors, stainless steel kitchen, furnished in an achingly hip style, minimalist or whatever. He'd eat out in a French bistro with silver tables outside, like Starbucks only classier. Or he'd rustle up exotic snacks with food from the corner deli where they let him have goods on slate as he was their most discerning customer, a joy to serve. Cheese made from the milk of endangered goats, Mediterranean vegetables with unpronounceable names, bagels flown in from Jerusalem, his own special blend of coffee. He'd wear clothes fashioned for him by dusky maidens from somewhere abroad, who dreamt of his manly skin touching their fabrics into which they'd woven hot breathy kisses. My dad: loved, respected, *revered* by all. He'd be a wossname, entrepreneur, running a business empire – movie-making? Web design? Indie record label? – from his BoHo base in cosmopolitan Cork Street, as yet undiscovered by property developers, unsullied by tourism.

Huh, dream on.

'Here we are. The Beggar's Belief,' announces Texy, with a jokey flourish.

Bloody hell, what a dive.

You'd never guess the Beggar's Belief was a pub. There's no signboard, no name on the front, nothing to distinguish it from the wool shop or the butcher's on either side, both shuttered up with wire grilles. It's an ordinary building in a terrace of dingy shops, only with high-up windows so that passers-by can't see in.

'It's for locals,' Texy explains, pushing open the heavy, blue-painted door. 'Places like this, they don't encourage visitors. Or women, for that matter.'

No kidding. Inside, it's like a geriatric gay bar, packed with gadges lined up at a long wooden counter, others sitting round tables reading newspapers or playing dominoes, a couple of blokes down the far end throwing arrows at the dartboard. Texy weaves her way through the bodies and swirling baccy smoke up to the bar, leaving me marooned at the door. She says a few words to the barman, then beckons me over.

'Rowena, this is Cathal. Cathal, Rowena.'

A Ted, with a quiff and greased-back hair, nods.

'How old is she?' he grunts. He doesn't go big on pleasantries, obviously.

Texy says something I can't hear; obviously a lie about my age, as Cathal sighs and hands over the drinks. Texy passes me a double Baileys on ice, which slides down in one. 'Show him the photo, then.'

48

I fossick in the rucksack. 'It was two years ago, mind,' I point out. 'You might not have been here then.'

'We're a family business,' says Cathal. 'I was working here before I could see over the bar.' He takes the photo and turns it round in his hand, as though the people in it might be more recognizable viewed upside down. 'And what is it you're asking?'

I explain that one of the men is my long-lost father, that I need to trace him urgently as he's come into an inheritance from a distant aunt in Lima, Peru; that I can't remember which one he is since I contracted organic amnesia, but if his brain marrow turns out to be compatible with mine, there's a chance of a cure, which is another reason I need to track him down.

Cathal stares at me as though I'm an extraterrestrial, or a mentally disturbed person who's just escaped from an institution. He's a wee bit scary and I wouldn't be surprised if he's pressing some secret button beneath the counter to call the cops or the men in white coats to cart me off for under-age drinking.

'Quit babbling, Rowena.' Texy jabs me with her elbow, meaning *Shut it.* She edits my ramblings to a short, coherent sentence, asking Cathal if he recognizes any of the men in the photo.

'I might. Depends what it's worth.' He winks at Texy. She blushes. Me, I figure nowhere in the negotiations.

'You'll have my external gratitude, Cathal,' I gush. 'My undying thanks. Maybe even a cut of the inheritance. As commission, like.' But I maison well be invisible for all the notice he takes of me. He's gone all stiffypants over Texy, right, like she'd waste her time on a bar monkey with a so-last-century quiff. Still, at least he isn't after a threesome, which lets me off the hook. They lark on, chatting in low voices, flashing signals with their eyes.

'Stay put. I won't be long,' whispers Texy, scooting behind the bar and through a door marked PRIVATE. Cathal slithers after her like a sidewinder snake. Uh-oh.

I buy a packet of ciggies from the machine and a bottle of

Woodpecker from the no-mark behind the bar. Perching on a stool, I sip cider and chainsmoke, feeling sweaty and self-conscious. It's maybe twenty minutes later when the door opens and Texy reappears, her face flushed, hair mussed up like a ball of red candyfloss.

'C'mon, we're outta here,' she says. I slide my bum off the stool and follow her outside into Cork Street. We leg it down the road, then Texy pulls me into a doorway and puffs her cheeks, forcing air out of her lungs. 'Got a cigarette?'

I light two, passing one to her. She drags fiercely on it, then her body relaxes into a slump.

'What happened?' I say. 'You didn't have to offer him sexual favours, did you?'

'Hell, no,' she laughs. 'Just flirted a bit, put him on a vague promise. But look – I got a name out of him!' She fans a beer mat in front of my face.

'Let me see,' I say, snatching it out of her hand.

Scrawled in red biro are two words: MORAL ENRIGHT.

'He's winding you up, right? Moral Enright?' I splutter. 'What kind of a name is that?'

'A stage name,' says Texy. 'A stand-up comedian's name. He's the blond guy in the photo, the one with the fake tan. Worked the pubs and clubs, which is how Cathal knew him, I guess. He was well known on the college circuit; a bit of a cult, apparently, unless I misheard.'

She returns Dad's photo to me. It's starting to get creased and crinkly with so much handling. I take a good long look at the artist known as Moral Enright. How could he *not* be a comedian with that orange perma-tan, bleached hair and teeth, the showbiz smile? That's if Cathal hasn't made up the story to boost his chances with Texy. Assuming he's telling the truth, that would make Dad one of the men on either side of Moral; either the guy with a number two crop and an earring, or the one with dark curly hair and a stubbly chin. I search again for some clue, vaguely recognizable features, a family resemblance, but nothing stands out.

'I still can't tell which one is my dad,' I moan.

'Hang on, you haven't heard the best,' says Texy excitedly. 'The blond one, that's Moral Enright, OK? And this one here . . .' She points to the guy on the left with the earring and short crop. 'He was a barman who used to work at the Beggar's, name of Feargal somebody-or-other. He left under a cloud shortly after this picture was shot, ran off with the takings, according to Cathal.'

It's a while before the significance sinks in. 'So does that mean . . .?'

'It means, using a process of elimination, that your dad is the one on the right, the good-looking, curly-haired one with a two-day stubble. Handsome devil, innit?'

My heart leaps to my throat. I stare and stare at the photo until floaters appear in the corner of my vision. Dad. My dad. The long-lost, the legendary, the one and only Lonnie Vincent. His face is here in front of me, unmistakably Dad. How could I not have recognized him? It's so obvious now; he has the same lopsided smile that I inherited, and something about the shape of the eyes confirms that we share a gene pool.

'Sweet Jesus. Sweet, sweet Jesus.' Are these words the best I can say?

'Rowena, don't you see,' says Texy. 'Forget the barman, he's just a red herring. You have a picture of your dad, plus we've got a name, and not an everyday one at that. Moral Enright should be dead easy to pin down. He's bound to show up on a search engine on the Internet.'

'Yes, but . . .' I begin. 'But what if it's just a fan photo, like Moral was doing a gig up here and Dad happened to be in the audience? Moral won't have a clue, he won't remember Dad.'

'Stop being so negative,' says Texy. 'They could be best mates for all you know. Your dad could be, I dunno, Moral's roadie, or he might be a professional entertainer, do some kind of a turn himself. He could have appeared on the same bill under a stage name. He might even be famous! Rowena, this is so exciting.'

Exciting, but complicated also. It's hard enough to absorb that Dad was pictured with a stand-up comic, without Texy doing my head in, confusing me with outlandish possibilities. Long-lost Lonnie Vincent – reborn, renamed and even more remote. My brain feels like it's ready to burst with pressure. I need to lie down.

Back in Room 204 of the Cadogan Hotel, Texy decides that a celebratory raid on the minibar is called for as the samples cupboard will be locked up for the night. I down a couple of voddies but instead of loosening me up, they make me morose, cranking up the misery several notches. We lie on the bed and share a joint but it tastes so strong I'm afraid it'll make me sick.

'You kill me, Rowena. I don't get you at all,' says Texy in a pot-giggly voice. 'You're on the way to finding your father . . .'

'Don't say any more. Just don't,' I warn her. 'I'm in a scary situation, you wouldn't understand. Can you keep a secret, Texy?'

'Sure.'

'It's about Hefty.'

'Mr O'Hara? What about him?'

'You'll think I'm off my head, but it's serious, honestly, Tex.'

She waves the spliff at me, meaning *Get on with it*.

Taking a deep breath, I babble, 'I need to get out of Dublin pronto. Tomorrow. I'm going to leave first thing tomorrow. I want to find Dad, of course I do, but I need to get away from that gangster, Hefty O'Hara.'

'What are you talking about, gangster? You sure come out with some weird shit.'

'He *is*,' I insist. 'He's in the Mafia. The Murphia, whatever you call them here. He tricked me here to force me into prostitution, then sell me as a sex slave, or an erotic dancer.' There, I've said it.

Texy bursts out laughing. 'What the feck are you on about? Mr O'Hara's a proper decent chap, he's a businessman.'

'Yeah, the sleaze business, the pimp racket, the under-age sex market. He's a wossname – a *procurer* of young girls. I have to escape, otherwise he'll cart me off for plastic surgery to give me a new face, obliterate my identity, then no-one will be able to find me. I saw it in that movie, *LA Confidential.* He'll have me disappeared. The man's dangerous; I'm not shitting you, Texy.'

She rolls towards me on the bed, steadies me with her hands on my shoulders.

'Hey, what is this – Paranoia Central? Just relax, Rowena.' She sucks on the joint and passes it to me. 'It's almost as if you're afraid of finding your father. The minute we find a lead, you decide to do a disappearing act. And to pin the blame on Mr O'Hara being a *gangster* . . .' She shakes her head. 'It's too ridiculous for words.'

I hand her the spliff, turning my back towards her. We lie in silence for ages. Looks like nothing I say is going to convince her. I consider telling her all the stuff that Ray told me – Hefty's brother being killed in a drive-by shooting, the gang war that never happened, the bodies in concrete overcoats – but she's dead set on the story about Hefty being a businessman.

'Listen,' she says eventually, rubbing my shoulders, 'I'm going away on holiday tomorrow. Well, kind of a holiday. I'm off to visit Bobbo, my grandfather.'

Oh, triffic. Here I am, in danger of being humanly trafficked, and Texy, my only friend, is off on her jollies. I might as well chuck myself in the Liffey, now I've discovered it's a river and not, as I'd first thought, a pub. A deep sigh heaves itself up from my bowel.

After a few moments, Texy murmurs, 'You're welcome to join me if you like, it'll give you a breathing space.'

The bugles of the Fifth Cavalry echo inside my head. I snap into life. 'Could I? Could I really? Jeez, that'd be brilliant. Honest, Texy, they'll be dragging me out of that river if I don't get away now. I won't be any trouble, swear down.'

She hesitates, surprised by my sudden gushy outburst, but only for a moment.

'Sure, you're welcome. It'll be fun having you along, though Lord knows what you'll make of the place. Ballyloony isn't everyone's choice of holiday destination. Well, not *any*one's. Promise me one thing, though.'

'And it was all going so well,' I smile. 'I might have known there'd be a catch.'

Texy's forehead creases in thought lines. 'No catch, Rowena. Being polite, I suppose you'd call it. No biggy.'

'What then? What do I have to promise?'

'That you'll tell Mr O'Hara that you're checking out of the hotel.'

'*No way!*' I yell, a bit hysterically. 'He's the reason I need to do a runner so I sure ain't spilling the beans to him about my plans, and that's final.'

Texy's blue eyes drill into mine. 'Look, I know you think he's some sort of wiseguy but honestly, Rowena, you're way off beam. What do you have to go on? Rumour, gossip, folklore, hearsay? No. Has he ever done or said anything gangsterish to you?'

'Yeah, loads of stuff,' I reply. But naturally, the memory part of my brain refuses to co-operate when I try to dredge up an example.

'See, you can't think of a single thing.'

'Call it a gut feeling, an instinct, a psychic early warning system. I just *know*, OK? Hang on, when we were on the aeroplane he whispered something to this old bloke to make him move seats so Hefty could sit next to me. For all we know it might have been something about a horse's head, some kind of threat. Tell me that isn't dodgy.'

Texy rolls her eyes to heaven. 'What's dodgy about that? Mr O'Hara wanted to sit beside you because he was looking out for you. He was being kind, that's all. Nothing sinister about it. He's even asked for your hotel bill to go on his account. It's thanks to his generosity that you're here at all, not sleeping on the streets or dossing in some hostel.'

'Great,' I cry out. 'Does that mean he'll spring for the minibar as well?'

Sighing, she goes, 'All I'm saying is you should let him know you're moving out; it's the least you can do.'

Clearly Texy is either majorly deluded or worldly-ignorant but, against my better judgement, I decide to humour her, go along with her fantasy, pretend that Hefty is a genuine businessman.

'OK, then.' I blow out a dramatic sigh to show what a huge sacrifice I'm making on her behalf. 'I'll tell him in the morning.'

She plants a smackety kiss on my cheek. 'See, that wasn't too hard, was it?'

I smile. Naturally, I have no intention of telling Hefty O'Hara a thing. It's none of his business.

Come tomorrow I'll be outta here. On the open road to freedom, to Bally-bloody-loony. Rowena Vincent is on the lam again.

10

Running in the Family

Live fast, die young, stay handsome. It's the only way to go. That's what Dad said after our dog Georgie was murdered – yes, *murdered*, no bullshit. Some weird sadistic fucker was going round poisoning pets in Fozzy Hall where we used to live. Mum reckoned it was one of those pigeon fanciers off the allotments who'd turned dog killer because he'd already offed all the cats and he'd got the taste of blood.

Nancy Pancy Stephenson-Powell, the English bull terrier from number fifteen, was the first to fall into his murderous clutches. She loved a game of footie with the kids on the school field, leaping high in the air, barking her tits off, her chiselled features split in a mad grin. If she managed to catch the ball, game over. She'd scrag it to death, then scoot off and bury it in the soft earth near the rose bushes. Nancy Pancy was no oil painting until someone turned her into a still life. When her body was discovered behind the glasshouse, the school gardener became prime suspect. He was a shifty bugger, no doubt about that, his garden immaculate, a riot of colours, chocked with flowers and shrubs, fed with compost and well-rotted manure, probably all nicked from the school. A thief and a murderer. Plus his eyes were too close together like George Dubya's, which proved he was a bad 'un. So the local vigilantes, the SODs – Save Our Dogs – as Dad called them, put his windows through, ripped the plants out of his garden, threatened his kneecaps and advised him to find a different postcode. The bloke had a mental breakdown, sobbing in the street, all that stuff, and went to live with his daughter down south. Sorted. Nancy Pancy Stephenson-Powell, RIP.

Except that the doggy deaths continued. Mrs Miller's Yorkshire terrier, Dave Cotterell's whippet, the overweight basset hound from that poncy bungalow near the surgery. All victims of the infamous Fozzy Hall Pet Poisoner. No-one was ever charged with dogslaughter.

And then he murdered Georgie, aged six and a bit in human years, much-loved mongrel of the Family Vincent. Only son of Lonnie and Jean, darling brother of Rowena. Despatched to the celestial doghouse after a terrible death, fitting and foaming at the mouth, whining in agony, trapped in a shed with spiders scuttling across his spastic limbs, the stink of paraffin in his nostrils. And who discovered poor Georgie in his final throes? Why, me, of course. Me. I was fucking gutted. Hysterical, traumatized, probably, still bearing the emotional scars to this day.

Mum packed me off to Nana Vincent's house where I was stuffed with comfort food, chocolate Hobnobs and milky Mellow Bird's coffee, but there was no consoling me. I wanted to experience what Georgie had gone through, to punish myself for somehow causing his horrible demise. OK, I hadn't fed him the rat poison or whatever it was, but I was convinced I'd made the conditions right for him to be killed. Maybe I'd unknowingly committed a sin, told a lie, answered back, borrowed money from Mum's purse, something that disturbed the aura, swirling it up into a maelstrom of negative vibes, attracting madness, summoning evil as surely as if I'd sent a black-edged invitation card to the Devil himself.

Nana Vincent's job was to keep me away from the crime scene while Dad dug a grave in the garden as Georgie's final resting place. It was their way to prevent me from lapsing into one of my dark moods, brooding about Georgie's fate, plotting retribution, mutilating myself. Jeez, I'd forgotten about this weird stuff. Even way back in childhood I was self-harming, though in an amateurish, superficial way, nervous of hurting myself, squeamish about the sight of blood, not a natural-born cutter. This madness, then, it isn't a recent thing, it's more than normal teenage insanity. The craziness has been in me for years, since my age was a one-digit number. I'm shocked!

Stuff is starting to come back to me now, memories re-forming, making sense out of nonsense. Dad and his 'depressive episodes', as the doctor called them. His dark silences, times when his presence was so spectral it seemed more of an absence. Days – weeks, maybe – when he couldn't form words, couldn't summon up the spirit to move, when the black cloud hung heavy over him, oppressive, unrelenting, weighing him down to the centre of the earth. Now I can empathize, understand how he must have been feeling. I am my father's daughter. I carry his insanity genes, a mini-version of the man who withdrew into his own troubled mind and, later, disappeared into a new life, choosing the unfamiliar over the family.

Madness, it's all so clear, so obvious now, runs in the blood. And *running* runs in the blood. That's what we did, Dad and I both. We ran, vamoosed, had it away on our toes. When the going got tough we bogged off into the unknown, but surely better, life. Huh, that's what we thought.

Maybe we were just swapping one set of problems for another.

11

Ballyloony and the Parcel of Doom

At Texy's insistence I'm eating a proper breakfast, even though normally I can't swallow until eleven o'clock. She brings me a Full Irish, a giant plate of bacon, eggs, sausages, beans, tomatoes and fried bread. There are also slices of black and white pudding, glistening fatty things made of I dread to think what, which are not coming within miles of my stomach. Then, at the exact moment when I'm shovelling half a pig and the yolks of a dozen battery hens down my neck, Hefty O'Hara strolls into the dining room.

'Good morning, Rowena,' he says, sitting on the chair next to me and spreading a napkin across his lap. I almost choke unto death.

'Morning,' I grunt, through a gobful of farmyard animals. By the time I finish chewing this lot, it'll probably be afternoon.

Hefty's toffed up in a dove-grey suit and dark-blue shirt, pure Sopranos family-wedding-type gear. His dark hair, silver-streaked at the sides, reminds me of Paulie Walnuts. Texy hovers at his side, order pad at the ready. I nod at his get-up, shooting her a glance that means *now* tell me he's not a gangster.

He flashes me a deadly smile. 'And what are your plans for today?'

'Er, nothing much.' I'm caught on the back foot here, no time to prepare a response.

Texy jumps in. 'She's coming away with me for a few days, Mr O'Hara.' I could deck her for revealing our plans to him. 'We're going to Ballyloony to visit my grandfather.'

'Ballyloony?' Hefty's eyes switch from me to Texy and back again. His expression reveals next to nothing, but if I had to put a name to

59

the emotion that flits across his face, I'd call it surprise. 'Your grandfather's from Ballyloony?'

'Not *from* Ballyloony, not originally. He's in a care home there.'

'Would that be the place run by the Sisters of Blessed Relief?'

Texy raises surprised eyebrows. 'The very same, Mr O'Hara.'

Hefty turns a strange look on me. 'This is – how should I describe it? – a fortunate coincidence,' he says. 'I also have connections there; someone who lives in that home. A member of the family.'

See! I want to yell at Texy. A member of the family. *Now* tell me he's not a wiseguy. The Family. That's shorthand for the Mafia. Hefty stands condemned by his own words. But she's busy listening to his bare-assed lies, nodding, agreeing, a smile pasted on her lips, swallowing his story wholesale. How can she be so naïve?

'. . . so if you wouldn't mind, perhaps I could ask you girls to deliver a small parcel on my behalf. OK by you, Rowena?'

A sausage bunches up in my throat.

'A p-p-parcel?' I stammer.

'To my aunt,' explains Hefty. Behind his back, Texy wobbles her head like a nodding dog, indicating agreement. I'm beyond words.

'We'd be happy to do that, Mr O'Hara,' says Texy, the gullible fool.

'That's fine. Just scrambled eggs for me, then.' Hefty places his breakfast order, snaps the menu closed. 'And a pot of Earl Grey, please.'

My brain jumbles into a messy, raggedy knot of worry. Semtex, narcotics, unlaundered money, weapons of mass destruction. Who knows what evil lurks inside Hefty's parcel?

At three fifteen we board the bus to Ballyloony. Naturally, I refuse to carry the parcel of doom as there's no way I'm going to be blown to smithereens and leave only my dental records for the world to remember me. I heard somewhere about this woman who was so mashed up after a crash that she had to be identified by the serial number on her breast implants. I suppose it's too late to get a boob job now. Texy pooh-poohs my fears and stuffs the deadly package into her holdall where it sits swaddled amongst her clothes like a malevolent baby. She's had her nose round it like a sniffer dog but says it just smells of Jiffy bag. It doesn't tick or rattle. It's neither squidgy nor rock-hard. Texy thinks it might be a book, or a bag for toiletries, or maybe a video cassette. An ordinary, innocuous, every-day item, a genuine gift for an ageing aunt. Definitely nothing designed to bring down a government, destroy a high-rise building, poison a Pope, spark off a Holy War.

I wish I could be so sure.

'Let's dump it,' I urge. 'Please, Texy, chuck it out the window, just to be on the safe side. If the border guards catch me with something illegal they'll deport me, then I'll never be able to find Dad.'

Texy thumps me on the arm. 'What are you talking about? Border guards indeed! We're not even leaving County Dublin, you dope.'

'How was I to know? I never knew there was a county called Dublin. When you said Ballyloony, I thought it'd be hundreds of miles off, some Hicksville beyond the beyond of beyond.'

'You'd do better to ask than think, especially the way your brain's been wired, no offence.'

'It's just that my neural pathways stray off in the wrong direction sometimes.'

'Towards planets far, far away. Sure I won't argue with that.' Texy squeezes my shoulder. 'Hey, don't get upset, Rowena. I'll give you the craic on the Ballyloony set-up.'

Leaning against the headrest while trying not to disturb my hair isn't an easy manoeuvre, nor a comfortable affair. Even so, I manage to drift off into a terror-filled stupor and miss most of what she's saying. Some snippets incorporate themselves into a Tarantinoesque daydream about nuns, old gadges, and a frail silver-haired biddy with a semi-automatic rifle secreted inside her inconti-pads.

'You never heard a word of that, did you?' says Texy in a mock-accusing tone.

'I so did. I was resting my eyes to sharpen my ears,' I protest.

'If you say so. I'm not even going to mention the snoring,' laughs Texy. 'We're nearly there now anyway, so shake your sleepy head and get your stuff together.'

Knuckling my eyes, I peer through the window. We're in some kind of – well, I wouldn't call it a *town*, not even of the one-horse variety. But it seems to be a high street of sorts, lined with shops, a few people milling about, a cluster of parked cars, mostly old bangers, average age nine years, at a guess. The bus slows to a halt.

'Lady at the back,' calls the driver, peering into his rear-view mirror. 'Ballyloony?'

Texy bustles about, grabbing her holdall from the rack.

'I know, I know. Coming,' she replies, yanking me out of the seat, nearly dislocating my arm from its socket.

We clamber off the bus. It pulls away, leaving Texy and me standing next to our bags, marooned in the middle of some kind of market square. My joints are stiff. I'm bleary-eyed, befuddled and starting a headache. Triffic.

'Here we are. Ballyloony, centre of the cosmos,' says Texy.

'What now?' I ask, my voice dull and flat.

In front of us there's a row of shops, all painted the colour of digestive biscuits with some bricks picked out in black, like that's what passes for cool decor. Don't they get *Changing Rooms* over here? And check out those windows, man. Getro the Retro. They're full of rubbish out of the Old Testament, fluffy slippers, blouses and cardies in white and lemon and pink that even the ancientest old biddy wouldn't be seen dead in. Bicycle saddles, sacks of compost, keys cut while you wait, vinyl footstools, catering cans of no-name baked beans, wedding hats, novelty teapots. Ballyloony must be stuck in a time warp, around the late Fifties, at a guess. Maybe we've landed in a parallel universe, one that forbids cropped tops, that's never heard of Big Macs, where tongue studs are banned and wide-screen telly hasn't been invented. Pure Planet Drabbo.

'There's the hotel over there.' Texy jerks her head to the left. 'Give me a hand with the stuff.'

I trudge behind her like a pack mule, my back ready to cave in from humping the bags. Misery, thy name is Ballyloony. A pick-me-up, that's what I need. And a Red Bull to wash it down.

Texy heaves to outside a grim-looking building. It could sure use a lick of paint, and that's just for starters. I'm wondering if it's some old plague hospital left standing for historical reasons, or a mental institution from the dark days when they incarcerated fallen women, or what we'd now call single mothers.

'Here we are – our happy holiday home,' says Texy.

I gasp. 'This is *it*? We're staying in this dump? I thought you said it was a hotel?'

'And so it is, though not as the real world knows it.' Texy seems to find my amazement hilarious. 'What did you expect – a poncey chain hotel like the Cadogan, the place with less atmosphere than Mars? This isn't Dublin, Rowena, it's Ballyloony, countrified purgatory where the sinners are on remand.'

THE FLUES, says a sign above the door. It sounds like the name of an indie band, but it's more likely something to do with chimneys: smoky, sooty, lung-cancerous chimneys with generations of dead pigeons interred inside them. I bet chimneys are an outstanding architectural feature in these parts, along with prehistoric lavvies and Gothic septic tanks.

I trudge up the front steps – no such thing as disabled access here – and follow Texy through the door. Yes, I know it's a cesspit of a hotel, but at least they could make an effort at a reception area, some attempt at a welcome. A desk, perhaps, keys hanging from a board, pigeonholes, a bell, some old codger sweating over a crossword. None of that here. We're straight into a bar, a long room with flock paper on the walls, a wooden counter running the entire length of it.

Stools, huddles of tables and chairs, an aroma of stale beer, ciggies and beef gravy, and – God preserve us – Wheatus blaring out of the jukebox. Purgatory doesn't begin to describe it.

Texy kicks my shin. 'Will you stop looking as if you've wandered into a medieval torture chamber. The rooms are tucked away upstairs, they're nice, honest.'

My jaw drops. 'You've stayed here before?'

'Sure,' she says. 'I book in here whenever I visit Bobbo. It's cheap and . . .'

'Cheerless,' I butt in.

Texy does a facial expression which I recognize as crestfallen, making me feel guilty and horrible for being so mean.

'I'm joking,' I lie. 'It's a great place, it's got loads of character, a good vibe – at least, it probably will when it fills up. There's only one thing more depressing than being in an empty pub, and that's walking round a zoo when it's pissing with rain.'

'Whatever.' Texy shoots me a peculiar sideways glance. I've seen the look before on other people's faces. It means, roughly, that if they live to be a thousand years they'll still never work out where I'm coming from. Hmmph, suits me.

'Hello, how're ya.' A bloke with a mullet haircut appears at the other side of the bar.

Texy foot-nudges her bag along the floor. 'The name's Maguire. Texy Maguire.' I have to stop myself from snorting, as the way she says it sounds just like James Bond.

'Sure I remember you from last time you stayed. How could I forget a lovely face like yours,' says the bloke. Texy's cheeks turn pink. The guy disappears through a door, then returns with a desk diary.

'Let's see, what date would it be today?' He runs his finger down a page. 'Here we are, Miss Maguire today to the 20th, lovely room plus bed, breakfast and a fine old time thrown in at no extra cost.'

Texy explains about me, the uninvited, unbooked guest, the one in the corner losing her religion, or her will to live. Her voice sounds weird and a bit lispy, as if she's trying to act coy. The guy notices my existence for the first time. He says they'll fit me in no problem, it's a twin-bedded room anyway, and tells us how many euros he'll be duping us out of.

'Cheap at half the price,' he grins, as Texy fills out a registration form. 'The name's Matty, by the way, in case you'd forgotten. Anything you need, I'm your man.'

He leads us to the room. It's on the first floor, up some pale wooden stairs with ornate handrails, no lift. All the time Matty's chuntering on about how they'll be packed out in a couple of days, what with the Saint's Day and the bicentenary celebrations and that. I can't be arsed to listen as I'm suffering from anxious armpits and can't wait to climb into the shower to rinse the sweat off my body.

'Ta-daa.' Matty throws open the door like he's showing us into the Cistern Chapel or something. He demonstrates the light switches and kettle and toilet flush as though they're new inventions that we wouldn't be able to figure out on our own. 'Don't forget to sing out if there's *anything* you need, ladies.'

'Like what?' I say, as Texy closes the door behind him. 'A complete body massage, a lark's-tongue sandwich, a bedtime story? Puh-leeze.'

'He's not so bad,' smiles Texy. 'In fact, he's quite cute.'

'In the same way a pet polecat is cute.' I stick two fingers into my mouth in a pretend vomit gesture. 'That haircut – I mean, honestly!'

'Hair's fixable. Don't be so shallow, Rowena, it's what's inside that counts.'

I remove the hours-old chewing gum from my mouth, roll it into a ball and flick it at her in a matey gesture.

12

The Bison Teenery

To be fair, the room isn't half bad, considering how grim The Flues looks from outside. It's clean, no cobwebs, no mouse droppings near the skirting board, and the pillows aren't rock-hard. I can't be arsed to check for stains on the mattress. There's a tray with a tiny kettle plus coffee, tea and stuff and a couple of biscuits that remind me of the cork coasters we had at home, except they're wrapped in cellophane. Also there's a joined-on bathroom, meaning I don't have to scoot down a hallway half-dressed for a wash or a wazz. Lord knows why such basic facilities come as a surprise. What was I expecting – straw pallets to sleep on and an earth pit for a bog?

The shower is the only let-down. After fiddle-faddling on to find a reasonable temperature, i.e. somewhere between arctically cold and blisteringly hot, the water pressure refuses to function above a medium-strength drip. At home we had a power shower that pelted and stung the skin like bad-tempered hailstones. This must be the opposite, a weakness shower, the last dying drops of a baby stalactite exposed to the sun. It takes forever to lather and rinse my body and in the end I have to hope that my nether bits can fend for themselves.

After towelling myself dry, I slip into some jeans and a Nirvana T-shirt. It's creased to buggery from being scrunched up in my rucksack but who cares as long as it's clean.

'Fancy some tea?' I say, filling the kettle with water from the bathroom cold tap which I hope is fit to drink.

'Uh-huh, please,' says Texy absently. She's reading one of the leaflets from the bedside table. 'They're making a big deal of this bicentenary thing,' she remarks. 'Looks like they're expecting people from all over. Good job I booked the room well in advance.'

'What's a bison teenery?' A picture of a herd of stampeding shaggy-haired beasts forms in my mind as I struggle to unravel the electric flex and plug the kettle into an awkwardly placed socket.

'It's the two-hundredth anniversary of the saint's day on the 19th.'

'What month is this?' It sounds a reasonable question to me, but Texy finds it hilarious.

'Are you shitting me? You really don't know what month we're in? I wonder if you know what country you're in.'

'Don't be sarky, of course I do.' If you give me a minute to think about it. And if you don't ask me to point it out on a map. 'Come on, Texy, shitloads of stuff have happened to me recently, it's no wonder I'm confused about dates.'

'OK then, it's September.'

'Right,' I say, as the kettle boils and switches itself off.

Texy puts on a jokey gobsmacked expression. 'You actually believe me, don't you?'

'Uh-huh,' I mutter, pouring water over the tea bags.

'It's March, you eejit. *March!*'

'And when is this bison thing going on?'

'March,' says Texy. 'Nineteenth of March.'

Something clicks inside my brain. The date sounds kind of familiar, but I can't relate it to anything. I think and think, but the more I concentrate the hazier it becomes.

'That's when they celebrate St Vincenza di Verona, this Italian nun who was supposed to display the stigmata and perform miracles, if you believe all that stuff.'

'I don't know much about Catlicks.' My nose wrinkles as an embarrassing memory floats to the surface of my mind. 'Except this one day, right, I'd bunked off school to shoplift some make-up and it started to pour with rain so I dived inside a church to save getting soaked and ruining my hair. There was some kind of service going on. It was dead complicated, like a stage performance, all that chanting and swinging incense around and bells tinkling. The way people queued up for just a wee biscuit and a sip of wine, you'd think they were starving, like they couldn't wait to eat at home, or be arsed to find a Burger King. Then at the end people shook hands with each other, muttering words I couldn't make out, and the bloke who tried to grab hold of my hand looked like a dosser, or a kiddy-diddler. Well, I legged it out of the place dead sharp, didn't I? It was gross!'

Texy gives me a pitying look. 'But at least your hair wasn't hanging in rats' tails, so maybe religion isn't *all* bad.' She's taking the piss, but I refuse to let it rattle me.

We sip our tea in silence. Texy carries on reading about the saint and I check out a photocopied sheet of paper with details of the facilities at The Flues. It's so limited it could be written on the back of a postage stamp. Payphone in the lobby. Regret no room service. Breakfast served in the dining room between 8.30 and 9.30 a.m. Bar meals available lunchtimes and evenings. And that's it. No cheese-burgers or milkshakes on demand, no adult movie channel on the TV, no Internet access, no minibar in the room. How can they describe themselves as a hotel? I was right: it's just a pub, with a few letting bedrooms tacked on as an afterthought.

After we've feasted on cork-mat biscuits and tea, Texy curls up on the chair and sticks her nose into a book she found on the mantel-piece. *A Goat's Song*, it's called.

'Is it good, the book?' I ask.

'I'm just at the beginning.'

'What's it about?'

'I don't know yet.'

I peer over her shoulder. 'Some of those words look hard to read.'

'Hadn't noticed.' She turns over a page.

'I've never read a book in my life.'

Texy looks up at me. 'You're not serious? Of course you've read a book.'

'Nah. Not right to the end. It takes too long.'

'You kill me,' says Texy, turning back to the book, shutting me out.

I feel restless and fidgety.

'Where's this place where your granddad lives?' I ask, remembering the purpose of our jaunt.

'Not far from here. Less than a mile, but it's up a bugger of a hill.' Texy closes the book and parks it on the table. 'You won't believe the set-up they have at the convent, Rowena; it's mighty impressive, like a little working village in its own right.'

She explains that the community is run by the Sisters of Blessed Relief; that as well as the usual goddy nonsense, they organize commercial activities like a gift store where they sell candles and religious icons made in their own workshops. There's also a mini-factory where they make garments for sale to various religious orders, plus a bakery for altar bread and communion wafers that they sell to other churches.

'I thought that nuns just, I dunno, *prayed* a lot and did that navel-gazing stuff,' I remark.

'You're thinking of closed orders, contemplative nuns, where they never go out unless they need to go to hospital, or to see a dentist,' says Texy. 'There's plenty of places like that, but the Sisters of Blessed Relief are progressive. They're the biggest employers around here. Dozens of women from the town work there, in the laundry, the kitchens, the usual domestic jobs. And some work in the old people's home, of course.'

'What's that about, then? The care home? How come your granddad's in there, not in a Dublin one?'

'He's just lucky, I guess,' smiles Texy. 'It's something to do with an endowment from one of the benefactors, some clause saying that a number of places are prioritized for people who come from a particular part of Dublin. Hey, you know it! That area they call The Liberties. Thomas Street, the Coombe, Cork Street, all around there.

69

That's why some people refer to the care centre as the Home for Old Dubs – the *real* Dublin people. Bobbo was born within sniffing distance of the Guinness hop store, lived there all his life, brought me up there, too. Fortunate, really, as things turned out. He couldn't be in a better place.'

'So when are you going to see him?'

'Tomorrow, in the afternoon. Tell you what, I'll show you round some of the sights in the morning, if you like.'

'Yeah, triffic,' I say, my heart sinking to my boots at the prospect of being dragged round this gloomy necropolis. I'm already working out excuses to pull a sickie in the morning: legionnaires' disease, a touch of botulism, Ebola virus, narcolepsy.

'But tonight,' says Texy, 'we'll chow down in the bar and get a few drinks down our necks.'

'Yay, now you're talking!' I yell, punching the air.

Odd-Eye Joe

We speed-tart ourselves up. In my case, that means a swift going-over with eyeliner and mascara and only two coats of lippy, plus a fierce back-comb of the hair into a pyramid clip. I can't be bothered to change my clothes so it's jeans and the crumpled Nirvana T-shirt that reads, appropriately, NEVERMIND. My one concession to making an effort is strapping on my biker boots. Mental note to sprinkle talc on the inner soles before some innocent bystander gets gassed.

The bar's heaving with people on a poor man's night out. Vinegar and beer vie for top dog in the aroma department; pub grub must be doing a roaring trade this evening.

'I'll get the first round in,' says Texy, her blue-blue eyes glistening. 'What will you have?'

'Lager and blackcurrant.' I do a quick scan of the room for an empty table but there's none to be had unless we bunch up with a scruffy old bloke sitting on his own reading a newspaper. He probably smells bad, which is why he has a table to himself. Anyways, the last thing we need is to be trapped amongst the local knuckle-draggers so I lean against the jukebox trying to look cool and enigmatic, not that it's worth striking a pose in this company of deadlegs. From beneath my claggy black eyelashes I watch Texy as she orders the drinks. She's giggly and animated, the giveaway look of a bird on the pull. Matty's cracking jokes, laughing, his hair flopping in the sweaty atmosphere. She pays. He flicks the banknote and holds it up to the light, pretending to check if it's counterfeit. There's definitely a spark of something going on between the pair of them. Me, I'm forgotten, ignored, excluded, as per. The spectre at the feast, the hanger-on, the ugly mate.

'Could I nip in there?' A lad in ripped jeans and a leather jacket draws up to the jukebox. 'There's better music than this in hell.'

I shuffle out of the way and squeeze myself against a pillar, feeling like a cop on a stake-out, body flattened to a wall.

Jingling a mess of small change in his hand, the boy runs his eyes over the song titles. He's got brilliant choppy-cut hair, scrunched in a bedhead style, oozing straight-from-the-pillow sexuality. But his eyes. There's something not quite right about them. He glances at me, his gaze taking in the creased T-shirt.

'Anything you fancy on here? Nirvana, maybe? You're a fan of Kurt, I see.'

'No, not particularly,' I say, straightening the rumpled top as best I can without drawing attention to my bosoms.

'Just as well,' he grins. 'This bar smells of many things, but Teen Spirit ain't one of them.'

Despite myself, I smile, my mouth contorting in a lopsided rictus. *Very* attractive, in a Special Needs kind of way.

'I like C-c-catatonia,' I stutter, adding to my new mentally defective persona.

'I thought they split up years ago.'

'Uh, yeah. But I can still like them, can't I? It's not as if they're dead.'

'No, they've just gone into another room, one without a jukey. Take a look, there must be something you like amongst all this garbage.'

I shrug. 'Play what you want, I'm not bothered.' It dawns on me what's different about his eyes. They're odd-coloured. One is blue, the other brown. The wild, multi-heritage eyes of a street mongrel.

'OK, but don't blame me if it's your all-time foulest record.' He slips a coin in the slot, presses some buttons. A whirr, a click, then Bowie starts on 'All the Young Dudes'. Something clicks in my mind. Of course! David Bowie's eyes are different colours too. The boy stares at me, gauging my reaction. I stare at the nicotiney ceiling.

'You hate it, don't you?' he says. 'Now I'll have to set fire to my own hair to make amends.'

The stupid smile reappears on my mouth. 'I don't hate it and I don't love it. I'm . . . *undifferent* to it.' The word sounds wrong, but near enough.

'I'm Joe,' he says, offering his hand. I ignore it. 'And you'll be . . .?' *And I'll be damned if I'm going to be picked up by a complete stranger.*

'Rowena,' I say. 'From Newcastle, England.'

He takes a swig of his stout. 'What brings you to Ballyloony, Rowena?'

I swivel my neck round to check Texy's whereabouts. She's still flirting with Matty at the bar. Honestly, a person could die of thirst around here for all she cares.

'I've just, erm . . . I've just inherited a house – a castle, really – not far from here. It's a massive old pile, been in the family for, like, centuries. It's worth big bucks, only it needs a new roof before I can move in.' Lord knows where the words come from. It's as if a pathological liar has taken control of my tongue.

'Is that so?' Joe grins. 'Who'd have thought I'd be making the acquaintance of an heiress. And in the meantime, you'll be staying where?'

'Right here, in this gin palace.' I sneak another look at his mismatched eyes, then stare unashamedly. For some reason, a warm, melty feeling steals through my body and lands with a splosh in my stomach. Who'd have put money on a gorgeous specimen like Joe being in a backwater like this? OK, his eyes don't match, but that's cool-weird, not inbred-weird, and at least he doesn't have Billy-Bob gums and hillbilly peg teeth. It isn't just animal attraction, although I do find him fanciable. More than that, it's almost a glow of dawning recognition. The mushiness in my belly is the connection of one alien sussing out another in a hostile world. We belong to the same species.

Joe is an outsider. Just like me.

Straight out of nowhere, my conscience returns. Why oh why did I tell him I owned a castle? He's a local, which means he could find me out dead easy. I decide to come clean.

'Joe, that stuff I just said about the castle . . .'

'Let me guess. You made it up, right?'

I blush. 'How did you know?'

'I'm a mind-reader. Besides, we're a bit short on castles around here. Now if you'd said pigsty, *that* I'd have believed. So what's the real story – the truth, now.'

He pronounces it 'troot', which I find strangely appealing.

Just then Texy turns up with the drinks. I grab my lager and drain half of it in one go, golloping so fast it makes my eyes water.

'Sorry I've been ages,' she says. 'The bar was full of busy.'

'I noticed.'

'Matty's sent you an Aftershock to make up.' She offers me a shot glass. I knock back the blue stuff, then draw in breath at the sides of my tongue for the après-swally to kick in. 'Who's your friend?'

'I'm Joe, how're ya?'

She has the manners to shake his hand. 'How're ya, Joe. I'm Texy.'

'Can I get you girls another drink?'

She says yes, if that's no trouble, so he strolls off to buy a pint of Guinness for Texy and another lager and blackcurrant for me.

'Nice,' she says, her eyes studying his retreating back. 'I mean a real looker. He's got a deadly smile, and the cutest ass this side of Donegal.'

'He's OK, I suppose.' I'm trying to hide my secret attraction, though I see what she means about his derrière. It's tight and muscular and moves around sexily inside his Wranglers. 'Are we ever going to eat? This lager's gone straight to my head. Just a plate of chips would do me.'

'Sure. I'll order some once Joe gets back. Rowena, you don't mind if I stand at the bar and talk to Matty, do you? He's pure funny, makes me laugh my teeth off.'

'You fancy him, don't you?' It sounds almost like an accusation.

'Fancy him?' Texy twists her mouth in a bit grin, ruffles her hair. 'I dunno if I'd go that far. He's great craic, though, has me in stitches.'

'But the way his hair's cut, Tex,' I point out. 'And it's well overdue a shampoo.'

'Just my type,' she laughs. 'Male, hairy, full of grease.'

Joe returns with the drinks. 'Go and play,' I whisper to Texy. 'It's cool, honest.' She hotfoots it back to the bar.

'There's a table free over there if you'd rather sit down,' says Joe. I follow in a trancelike state, trying not to ogle his denim-encased tush as he manoeuvres through the drinkers. We plonk ourselves in a corner on an upholstered bench seat.

'Sláinte.' Joe clinks his glass against mine. He takes a mouthful of the black stuff, savouring the swallow in an almost orgasmic fashion. The creamy head leaves a trace on his upper lip and for an agonizing second I get an urge to lick it clean, to run my tongue along it. Jeez, what's wrong with me? My hormones are going postal! That's when I notice the scar on his face, running from the outer edge of his eyebrow past the cheekbone, nearly down to the side of his mouth. It doesn't have the look of a recent injury; it's silvery pink and blends in with his skin tone, but it's hardly unnoticeable. In fact it's fascinating and oddly sexy. I will myself not to stare but it feels as though my eyes are drawn to it like iron filings to a magnet. To distract myself I turn my head and focus on a middle-aged wifey with frosted hair. She's dripping with cheap bling and squeezed into a lurex top three sizes too small for her, displaying a creepy, crêpey cleavage. There, that'll kill any erotic thoughts that meander uninvited into my brain.

'Chips are finished, sold out.' Texy's back, and her voice makes me jump. 'There's no hot food left so I brought you this.' She slaps a sarnie on a paper plate in front of me. 'It's tuna mayo with sweetcorn on granary bread, OK?'

I stare at the plate as though it's a crashlanded UFO. 'I can't eat brown bread,' I hear my stupid voice complain. 'It's bad for my colon.' Immediately I regret referring to poo-related stuff in front of Joe. 'No, I mean tuna, I'm boycotting tuna because dolphins get tangled in the nets and die a horrible thrashing-about death.'

Texy rolls her eyes to heaven, exchanging glances with Joe.

'It's dolphin-friendly tuna,' she says, in mock exasperation. 'I checked.'

'But is it *tuna*-friendly tuna?' quizzes Joe. 'What's the difference? Tuna, dolphin, one or the other gets wasted.'

'I'll get you a packet of peanuts then,' offers Texy, deflecting the conversation. 'Or crisps, something to keep you going.'

'Here, I have some great nuts,' says Joe, unaware of the irony of his words. I daren't look at Texy or we'll both burst out laughing. He digs into his pocket and produces a paper bag. 'Cashews, pistachios, almonds. Earth's bounty, nothing added.'

'Cheers, Joe,' I say, aiming a wee smile at Texy, trying not to appear smug. She does that shoulder thing, turning her mouth down at the corners, meaning *Whatever*. 'See you later, Tex,' I say, effectively dismissing her.

'Sure,' she says, though she's the opposite of sure, wondering whether it's safe to leave me with a bloke who carries unadulterated nuts about his person. Her uncertainty doesn't, I notice, stop her shimmying back to the bar to continue her chatty with Matty.

This, as it goes, suits me fine.

Joe is easy to talk to, plus he's so good to look at. His face is fascinating because of its flaws. It's a face with a history. Although I know he's much cleverer than I am, I don't find it too daunting. Who else would I dare to talk to about real important stuff, religion for example? What's great about Joe is that I can admit I don't have a clue without feeling like a complete peabrain. This, for me, is new.

'Someone told me that religion is just a grown-up belief in an imaginary friend,' I say, amazed at remembering the fact.

'That's one way of looking at it,' says Joe. 'Or you might think of it as a cult that's been allowed to flourish.'

'What are atheists?' I say. 'Aren't they the ones who believe in nothing?'

'Atheists believe in anything,' says Joe.

'Oh,' I say. 'Right.' This is all getting too deep so I move the conversation to safer ground by telling him about the time I used to work as a trainee funeral assistant making dead people look nice for the rellies, tarting up the corpses for their final journey.

'To the afterlife, you mean?' asks Joe. '*That* final journey?'

'Nah. Up the crem to be toasted, or the boneyard to be buried six feet under. I can't see that it matters. When you're dead, you're dead. If I had to choose, I'd go for a Tibetan sky burial. They lay your body out on a hill, a mountain or something, hack it to pieces then wait for the vultures to pick your bones clean.'

Joe laughs to himself. 'And what if there are no vultures around?'

I shrug. 'Dunno. Buzzards then, I suppose, or condors, huge buggers with scrawny necks and beaks with hooks on the end for ripping flesh.'

'Of course. How stupid of me.' He slaps his wrist.

See what I mean? I can talk to Joe about real important things, like God and death and pop music, without feeling like a complete ignoramus. Time speeds up and without me realizing the lateness of the hour, suddenly it's chucky-out time at The Flues. He slings his jacket over his shoulder and we walk together to the door where Matty's waiting to lock up.

'I've had a great evening,' Joe says to me. 'Will we do it again some time?'

I nod, feeling strangely shy, not trusting myself to speak. Joe rubs my arm and leaves. Matty shoots the bolts and turns a key in the lock. I refuse his offer of a nightcap as my legs are jellified.

My arm feels warm and tingly in the spot where Joe touched it.

14

All the Old Dubs

Naturally, Texy and I miss out on breakfast. It beats me how people can lard out so early in the morning. It can't be good for their digestion, all that grease clogging their arteries before their heart's had a chance to wake up. Me, I couldn't care less about not eating until afternoon, I'm used to it. What grieves me is the fact that we're paying for bed *and* breakfast, but I don't expect the tightwads from The Flues will give us a refund. Crooks. The plus point of rising late is that there won't be enough time for Texy to show me round the sights of Ballyloony as she'd threatened. I'm in the mood for slobbing out all day, dozing, watching TV, gazing into space, maybe tackling the temperamental shower, maybe not.

Then it dawns on me that we have to visit Texy's grandfather in the Home for Old Dubs and immediately my head starts banging at the prospect, so I guzzle a couple of painkillers even though you're not supposed to take them on an empty stomach.

Secondly, I remember with a stomach-gripping shudder that we have to deliver the parcel of doom to Hefty O'Hara's dotty aunt. My blood turns icy cold as I wonder if this is my day to die. Maybe the sinister object in the package is programmed to explode when it comes into contact with a certain chemical, ammonia or something. Everyone knows what old people's homes smell of.

'Unggh.' Texy stirs in her pit, stretching and yawning like a lion. 'What's the time?'

'Half past time you were up,' I say, dangling a sweaty sock in front of her nose.

'Pooohh, get that thing away from me, it's worse than Gorgonzola,' she grumbles, but it does the trick and she hauls her body out of bed, pads to the bathroom. She performs her ablutions in a perfunctory wash 'n' go style.

Jeaned, booted and rucksacked up, Texy pronounces herself ready.

'Have you got the – the *thing*?' I ask. 'The P of D?'

'What? Oh, the parcel of doom?' she giggles. 'Sure, it's in here.' She pats her bag and I screw up my eyes anticipating an explosion, a second cosmic Big Bang. Texy Maguire, suicide bomber, endangerer of lives, gives not a shit. 'You're never going dressed like that?' She stares googly-eyed at my yellow latex skirt teamed with a black cropped top, diamond-patterned tights and biker boots, plus four earrings in one lobe and two in the other.

I feel put out. 'What's wrong with it?'

'For one, we're going to a care home at a convent. A *convent*, you get my drift. Like, hello! Nuns? Virgins? Brides of Christ?'

'Yeah.' I plant my feet and do the hands-on-hips thing. 'And?'

'They'll probably die of shock. I bet they've never seen a bare belly button in their lives. And you really should lose the ironmongery,' she says, staring at my earrings. 'Oh, forget it. But for two, we have to climb a pig of a hill and maybe a skirt the size of a hanky isn't the wisest gear.'

'Why ever not?' I'm astounded at her ignorance. 'It's better than pouring myself into skintight jeans. You'll end up with thrush or cystitis or that other thing, chlamydia. At least my skirt will let the air circulate.'

'Don't say I didn't warn you.'

I flick her a friendly V-sign. 'Stop acting like my mum.'

Joking and sniggering, we lock the door behind us and head down the stairs.

'Morning, Texy. How's the head?' Triffic. Just our luck to bump into Matty, heaving a crate of mixers, looking like death. I hope this isn't an omen.

'Head's good, Matty,' she says, and they both splutter with laughter at her witty double entendre.

'Edwina, how're ya?' he says to me.

'Rowena,' I correct him, doing my double-hard glare.

He slaps his forehead. 'Of course. *Rowena*, sorry.' He treats me to a lascivious once-over. 'You look stunning. Off somewhere nice?'

'Going to see my granddad,' Texy butts in. 'You know, up the convent.'

'He's in for a treat,' says Matty, goggling at my belly button. 'You'd better mind the Blue Spark Sisters an' all.'

'C'mon, Texy, let's hit the road,' I say, flashing an on/off smile to the mulleted mutant.

'Laters,' she says, blowing him a stupid kiss.

'Why did he call them the Blue Spark Sisters?' I ask, once we're clear of The Flues. 'That isn't their proper name, is it?'

Texy shoots me an old-fashioned look. 'It's just Matty being a mucky sod. I ain't saying, Rowena. You'll have to ask him about it.'

'Killjoy.' Now she's got me intrigued.

By the time we reach the Old Dubs' hangout, I'm dead, or as good as. That hill is a killer – a *serial* killer. My legs have seized up, my calf muscles are in knots, my feet are on fire, and my heart feels as if it's about to explode through my chest. Maybe they'll find a spare bed so I can lie down for a week and recover. Texy, on the other hand, is fresh as a newborn foal, except without the wobbly legs. Not a bead of perspiration glistens on her forehead, whereas I look as if I've been dunked in a barrel of sweat and hung out to dry.

The Sisters of Blessed Relief, Ballyloony. That's what it says on the sign. Nothing to do with Blue Sparks at all. Next to the nameplate is a map showing the layout of the place, just like in a retail park or a hospital. There's all sorts: a chapel, souvenir shop, grotto, retreat centre, craft workshops, rose garden, library and suchlike, plus a sizeable unidentified block which I guess is the private part where the Sisters eat, sleep, pray and generally chill. The old dudes in the rest home have their own map showing a circular building in the middle and several paths leading off. The little roads have names like St Philomena's Drive, St Vincenza's View, and St Peter's Close. St Peter's Close! That'll be the one where they put the gadgies who are ready to croak. Someone has a warped sense of humour.

At the bottom is a small sign advertising Vacancies, with a typed laminated card saying, 'Domestic Staff, part-time. Contact Sr Bonaventure, Administration Office.'

'Wow, this place is massive,' I say. 'Who'd have thought a poxy place like Ballyloony would have the world's biggest nunvent on its doorstep?'

'I told you, it's a working community, completely self-sufficient. There's lots going on here, though I wouldn't call it the biggest convent in the world. Biggest in the county, certainly. Well,' says Texy, 'you've rested long enough so we'll go and find Bobbo and deliver Mr O'Hara's gift to his aunt.'

'Can't I wait here while you do it?' I plead. 'My bones ache. I think I've caught multiple sclerosis.'

'You'll catch a smack on the head if you don't stop whingeing,' laughs Texy. 'On your feet, wuss.'

We enter the grounds and crunch our way along the gravel. By the time we reach the residential care home my feet are ready to give up the ghost. How come my biker boots have always been comfy until today, yet now they're pinching like two leather tourniquets? Texy pulls me along by the wrist as if I am a truculent toddler.

Inside the circular building it's like Door City. There's a reception-type desk surrounded by doors, doors and more doors. They're everywhere, some with dimpled glass panes near the top with signs saying Dietitian, Registrar, Physiotherapist, Gerontologist, Psychologist, as well as several marked Private which are possibly surreptitious smoking rooms for the staff. Then, down a corridor, I catch sight of one saying Chapel of Rest which reminds me of my previous career as Trainee Funeral Assistant and sends my stomach lurching. It all seems a wee bit on the spooky side to me, like maybe this is where they experiment on doolally old folks with no next of kin to pose awkward questions about their nearest and dearest. I'm almost expecting to see doors marked Cryogenics, behind which lurk freezers containing body parts suspended in icebergs, and giant microwaves to thaw them out come the revolution. Or an autopsy room where they remove non-diseased organs from dead codgers and transplant them into barely conscious ones to prolong their active lives. Or Eugenics, or Transformative Plastic Surgery, or Human Genomes . . .

Get a grip, Rowena. This is a care home run by the Sisters of Blessed Relief, not a real-life Dr Frankenstein's laboratory.

'Thank you, Sister Joseph,' Texy's saying to a wizened greyback who could sure use some rich emollient cream on her wrinkles. 'Come on, slowcoach,' she says, grabbing my hand. 'We're going to see Miss O'Hara first. They're ringing ahead to announce us. Security, you know.'

A young woman dressed in civvies meets us at a low-rise apartment block on St Philomena's Avenue. She leads us along a hallway smelling of vanilla air freshener and knocks on a door.

'Yes, come in,' says a voice, not the least bit quavery or doddery. Hefty's aunt has a ground-floor room overlooking a courtyard with a fish pond: goldfish, I think, or they might be koi carp or even piranhas, for all I know. She's sitting in a high-backed chair near the window, gazing out at the fountain. An image of Norman Bates's mother in *Psycho* flashes through my mind, then disappears as Miss O'Hara turns her head towards us, displaying her dentures in a broad smile.

An ancient music-hall act. An elderly showgirl. That's my first impression. Something theatrical, anyway. Her hair's thinning but long, gathered in a kind of ponytail held in a fake orchid scrunchy, the sort of accessory tweenies buy from Tammy shops. Although the roots are silvery, most of her hair is henna red, and her eyebrows are coloured in with brown pencil. The light from the window throws the bristles on her chin into relief. They look a bit stubbly, as though she has a shaving habit and hasn't bothered recently, giving her the appearance of a made-up momma walrus.

It's the eyes that spook me out. They're faded blue, milky, clouded over like an old dog's. Glaucoma, perhaps, or cataracts. I wonder if she's blind.

'Come in, won't you, over here where I can see you.' Not entirely blind, then.

Texy's fist in the small of my back propels me forward. She thrusts the Jiffy bag into my hand.

'Hello, Miss O'Hara. We've brought you a present from Hef . . . from your nephew, the one who lives in Newcastle, England.' I place the parcel of doom on the arm of her chair.

She chuckles. 'You can call him Hefty, bless your heart. He never would answer to Herald, his given name, Lord knows why. Now tell me how you know him.'

I explain that I'm from Newcastle too, how I bumped into Hefty at the airport, how he took me under his wing because I'd never flown in a plane and I knew no-one in Dublin. She picks at the package but makes little progress as her fingers are stiff.

'That sounds like Hefty. He was always protective of his sisters, wouldn't see anyone in trouble if he could help.' I try to attract Texy's attention, flashing my eyes at her to signify *Protective of their women relatives, see? That's Mafiosi for you*, but she avoids my gaze. I'm thinking the Corleone clan in one of the Godfather movies, where Michael wastes his brother but gives a home to his sister who's suffered domestic violence. I'm thinking Tony Soprano moving his mother Livia to the old people's home and stashing incriminating evidence. Why will Texy not see? It's right in front of her, as clear as a vinegared window.

Miss O'Hara gives up fiddling with the parcel, offers it to me. 'Would you mind, angel? My hands aren't all they were.'

I fumble with the sealed end of the bag. Trust Hefty to staple over the adhesive strip. My ticker thuds as the flap loosens. Is this it – the body-splatting big bang? But the worst that happens is a staple embeds itself in my thumb, drawing a microscopic spot of blood. I empty the contents of the bag on to the chair. It's a tape. An audio cassette. A proper bought one from a shop with a liner and all. I read the label out loud:

'*Circle of Friends* by Maeve Binchy.'

It's a talking book!

On a flowery gift card, he's written, 'To my dear Aunt Teazie, with love, H. xxxx'

'Oh, the darling boy, he remembered,' squeals Miss O'Hara delightedly. 'I borrowed the novel in large print from the library but I had to give up on it. Now I'll be able to listen to it all the way through. He's so kind and thoughtful, don't you agree?'

I'm stuck for an answer.

The time is eleven thirty.

Frignell! The words seem to come from nowhere. I nearly jump out of my skin.

The time is eleven thirty, repeats the computerized voice, louder.

'Who said that?' I look around the room, alarmed. 'Where's that voice coming from?'

'It's my clock,' says Miss O'Hara, reaching for a cube-shaped object. 'It tells me the time every half-hour. A great invention when your eyesight's gone. Good job I have my hearing. I hope it didn't startle you.'

'No, no, course not. But we'd better get going, Miss O'Hara,' I mutter, sucking the blood on my thumb pad. 'We're going to visit my friend's granddad in another building.'

'I didn't catch your name,' she says.

'It's Rowena,' I tell her. 'Rowena Vincent. And my friend Texy Maguire.'

'Thank you, Rowena Vincent. I won't forget your kindness.'

'It's cool, nee bovva at all,' I assure her.

As we're leaving I spot a framed photo hanging on the wall. It's a picture of Hefty, toshed up in smart togs, standing next to a beefy nun. Miss O'Hara is seated in front of them. They're wearing smiles to beat the band. What's that all about? We say goodbye, let ourselves out of the door and head for St Peter's Close and Bobbo Maguire.

'So no bomb in Mr O'Hara's parcel, then,' says Texy. The words 'I told you so' hang unspoken in the air. 'Just an audiobook for his aunt.'

'Sure, that's how it looks,' I admit grudgingly.

'What did you make of Miss O'Hara?' says Texy. 'Can you believe that hair? She looked like, I dunno . . .'

'A retired madame from a brothel, is my guess. Did you see her name on the card? Teazie! Teazie O'Hara. If that isn't something to do with the sex industry, I'm a blow-up doll. She maybe runs a string of girls for Hefty from the comfort of her own recliner. Who knows, she might have recruited some of the nuns for parts in porno movies.'

'Stop!' shrieks Texy, clamping her hands over her ears. 'Teazie is a nickname for Teresa, same as mine is. You are one sick specimen, Rowena. I can't believe you're slandering Miss O'Hara in the grounds of a religious establishment. You'll be punished if the Lord's listening in.'

'Yeah, right.' I do a sarcastic snort. 'Oh, hark, is that distant thunder?' I cup my ear in a theatrical fashion, then begin to shudder and convulse like someone having a seizure. 'Whoo, I'm sore afraid, Texy. What if God strikes me down with lightning, burns me to a frazzle?' Pointing skywards, I shriek, 'Tell me that isn't His face, there in that cloud. It is! He's coming to get me. Help me, please!' And I drop to my knees in a playful, prayerful pose, jabbering wildly as if I'm speaking in tongues, like a mad Pentecostalist.

Texy aims a kick at me. 'Get up, you eejit, before someone sees you. Uh-oh, too late.'

I follow her gaze. A couple of people visiting some oldsters watch, dithering, wondering whether to approach me with offers of help or drench me with a bucket of water. Do I care? I do not. Their expressions are priceless. But oh God, oh God, there, behind us on the path, are two wrinkly Sisters in full drag. The older one clumps along gripping a Zimmer frame. The other scuttles over to see what's going down. I'm still kneeling, scared to get up in case she knocks my block off for committing sacrilege, blasphemy or whatever.

'Child, are you ill?' she says. Her voice is kindly, in a mumsy way. Visitors gather round, rubbernecking, keeping at a safe distance from the incoherent madwoman.

I screw my eyes up tight and continue gibbering. Yadda yadda yadda.

Texy comes to the rescue. 'She, erm . . . She must have been hallucinating or something,' she says. 'She thought she saw God's face in that cloud.' Everyone stares skywards. 'The wind's taken it now, though.'

The ancient greyback crouches in front of me, her joints creaking, and places her hands firmly on my shoulders. I let the babbling tail off into silence and open my eyes to meet hers. We stay like that for a moment, staring at each other, then she hauls herself to a standing position and holds out a hand to help me up. I feel cheap and inappropriate with my belly button on show and the yellow latex skirt barely covering my bum cheeks, but she doesn't pass out with startlement.

'I'm all right now,' I say, dusting myself down and smiling. 'Thanks for coming to help, Sister. Can't think what came over me.' Her eyes are locked on to mine, making me feel uncomfortable. 'Well, gotta make tracks,' I bluster. 'We're going to visit someone in St Peter's Close. Toodle-oo.'

Texy and I leg it down the path. Once or twice I snatch a backward glance. The Sisters appear rooted to the spot, as still as statues, their eyes glued on me.

15

Meeting Bobbo

We hang around for ages at Bobbo's residence only to be told he's sitting in the garden, enjoying the fresh air. This is good news as there's a peculiar odour in the foyer that's making me feel nauseous, a cloying, cleachy smell that sticks to the roof of my mouth. It's a combination of wipe-clean chairs, Lucozade, institutional clothing and cut flowers just past their best. The universal smell of an old folks' home. I can feel it crushing my aura, depleting my serotonin, sucking the youth out of me.

My aura can't be entirely flattened, however, as I recognize Bobbo, with a powerful sense of déjà vu, before Texy spots him. He looks exactly as he did in Texy's photo, with his silvery hair combed over, his gums on display, wearing that grotesque home-made tank top over an assortment of shirts and jumpers, accessorized with the yellow badge in the shape of a letter B. I believe he's sitting in the same patio chair, too.

'Bobbo!' squeals Texy, running to him, embracing him in a fond squeeze. 'Bobbo, it's me, Texy. Teresa.'

'Sure I know who y'are. Don't feckin' patronize me,' he says, a mite grumpily. Glancing at his watch, he goes, 'You're late. Fifty minutes.'

The old fella seems to be in possession of his marbles.

Texy explains that we called on another resident first, then she unzips her mountaineer's rucksack and produces goodies, one by one.

'I brought you these, Bobbo. Face towels and that glycerine soap you said was nice.'

'Nitroglycerine, more like,' he says. 'Made me come out in a rash.'

'You can give it away to that nursing assistant you hate,' says

Texy, unruffled in the face of ingratitude. 'And here's the seed catalogues you asked for.'

'Fat lot of good they'll do me in here,' he says tetchily.

'You'll enjoy looking at pictures of the flowers, or you can cut them out and stick them on your pinboard. See on the cover – some of those pretty pink ones you planted in the garden at home.' I'd be surprised if he's allowed scissors. 'Socks. You can never have too many socks, Bobbo. And a puzzle to keep you occupied, stop you getting bored.'

She produces a wooden sphere, a 3D jigsaw. He'll never figure that out, not in his lifetime.

'Pah!' he spits. 'Did you bring the Black Bush?'

Texy hesitates. 'I've brought you a half-bottle, Bobbo, but we'll have to check with the staff first, in case it reacts with your medication.'

'Whiskey's all the medication I need. They dose me up with quiet pills, knock me out for their own convenience, lazy hoo-ers. As if I'd give any trouble.'

As if. Perish the thought.

'Anything else in that treasure chest of yours?'

'Vanilla fudge, chocolate marshmallows . . .'

'Daren't touch 'em these days. Can't chew 'em with these useless dentures.'

'Don't be awkward, Bobbo. You can suck them. I got you multivitamins as well, keep your strength up.'

'I get vitamins here, at least that's what they call them. They don't want me to have strength, they want me half-unconscious so I'm easy to manage.'

'Couple of vests as you said you were feeling the cold,' Texy continues. 'Steradent tablets to clean your false teeth, a pen, writing paper, envelopes and postage stamps – '

'And who would I be writing to?'

She looks directly at him. 'There's me, for a start. You used to write, Bobbo, and you still can, if you could be bothered.' Her eyes fill up. 'Sorry, Granddad, I don't mean to nag. It doesn't matter. Sometimes I think you forget about me between visits.'

His face softens, as though it's been magically ironed from the inside.

'Sure I'm always thinking about you, Teresa.' He leans forward and rests his forehead against hers, as they share a fond family moment.

I cough, one of those *Ahem* polite throat-clearing noises, to remind them that I still exist, even though they've chosen to ignore me.

'Bobbo, this is my very good friend, Rowena.' A blush steals up my cheek. Texy has acknowledged me as a friend, a very good one at that. It feels almost like a public declaration of love.

He looks me up and down in a not entirely approving way, like I'm a teenage hooker or a high-wire artiste on the run from a travelling circus.

'Pleased to meet you, Mr Maguire,' I say, offering him my hand in imitation of a human being with proper manners.

He bares his gums in a broad smile, takes my hand and pumps it. 'You look a lively young thing. Don't you be leading my granddaughter into bad ways.'

'I think he likes you,' hisses Texy into my ear. 'God knows why.'

The air's getting chilly. Bobbo's face has a bluish tinge and a dewdrop forms on the end of his nose, so we go inside to the residents' lounge for tea and biscuits. Texy pays for it by stuffing a €5 note into the donations box and I tell her it's daylight robbery and she should ask for change, but she shushes me up. Bobbo's mood begins to mellow, meaning either that he's forgiven Texy for being late or his quiet pills are kicking in. He rattles on amiably about the bicentenary coming up, saying what a load of fuss everyone's making just to celebrate a dead saint.

'Don't be such a killjoy, Bobbo. There'll be a lovely parade and you'll all get fancy food. It's a real special occasion.'

'They'll cosh us all with double medication on the day,' he says, 'to make sure we behave in front of the big knobs.' The image of dozens of semi-comatose old dudes being wheeled out for inspection tickles my twisted humour. I go into giggles behind my hand. 'It's a crying shame I haven't any decent clothes to wear. This thing isn't fit for moths.' He plucks at the tank top and grimaces in disgust.

'Leave it with me, Mr Maguire,' I hear myself say. 'I'll find a smart new outfit for you from the town.'

Texy digs me in the back with her elbow and flashes me a serious frown.

'What?' I whisper.

'Do you promise?' goes Bobbo, his face lighting up.

'I promise.'

And guess what, I don't even have my fingers crossed behind my back.

Texy says we ought to leave as it's time for Bobbo's afternoon nap and we shouldn't tire him out. She kisses his forehead, whispering that she'll visit him again tomorrow, but his eyelids are fluttering and he doesn't respond, so we sneak away.

'What did you think of my lovely grandfather?' she says, as we plod down the hill into Ballyloony town.

'He's pretty cool for an old gadgy,' I say. 'He's got attitude. I like that.'

'Sure he can be an ornery old critter at times but I love him to pieces. He brought me up from when I was ten, more or less. It can't have been easy for him, having a boisterous kid around. I owe him everything.'

'What happened to your mum and dad?'

She sighs. 'Long story. Let's just say they were so wrapped up in each other they had no time left for me.'

'Where are they now?'

'On the west coast,' she says. I'm thinking Los Angeles or San

Francisco, maybe Las Vegas, someplace swish and glitzy. 'Galway,' she continues. 'Living out the hippy lifestyle. Fair play to them, I don't bear a grudge. Some people aren't cut out to be parents. I've had to learn to accept that.'

A sudden outbreak of sweat dampens my hairline. My forehead tightens. Bile sours my throat. I halt, leaning for support against a garden gate. A ratlike dog yaps at me through the wrought iron.

'Rowena, what is it?' says Texy.

I wave her away. 'Just having a crazy moment. Time of the month coming up, hormones and stuff. I'm cool, honest.'

Truth is, my brain is pinging with Dad-thoughts.

Some people aren't cut out to be parents.

It sounds simple, but somehow against the laws of nature, nurture, whatever. I mean, if someone begets, as the Bible calls it, a child, knocks one out into the world, the least they could do is love and feed it, change its nappies on cue, supply it with pocket money for yay years, buy it up-to-date trainers and things. It just isn't on to decide they're not cut out to be parents. It's a total cop-out, unfair to the child, immature, a drain on Social Services, and leads to emotional scarring. That way lies a lifetime of madness.

'Should I knock on someone's door, get water for you?'

'Stop fussing,' I snap.

Texy backs off. 'All right, don't get arsey, I'm just trying to help.'

'Sorry.' I take a deep breath, do a couple of circle movements with my shoulders, then contort my mouth in a false smile. 'Truly, I'm sorry, Tex. Come on, we need to get back before the shops shut, hunt out some clothes for Bobbo to wear to the ball.'

'You weren't serious about buying him an outfit?'

'How could you doubt me, Texy Maguire? When I make a promise, I stick to it.' That's a dirty lie, but she doesn't know me well enough to realize.

We link arms and half-trot down the hill, leaving my panicky moment dissolving behind me.

91

My promise shall be delivered in spades. It's heartbreaking to see her granddaddy in all those shirts and that raggedy old tank top. He deserves better. Much better.

I've decided to treat Bobbo Maguire to a complete makeover.

16

Faking It

Texy decides to return to The Flues for a lie-down. This suits me fine as the last thing I need is someone looking over my shoulder when I'm shopping. Her taste in clothes can best be described as conservative and I have a hip, street style in mind for the new-look Bobbo.

To say the Ballyloony shopping experience is dire would be to underestimate the sheer shittiness of what's on offer retailwise. I meander through the In-Shop-type precinct trying to spot names I recognize: Top Shop, Schuh, Miss Selfridge, anything from the 21st century. Mission: Unaccomplished. The outlets have names like Plus Size Fashions by Máurin, Ciaran's Cookshop, and The Happy Nappy, Quality Babywear for Infants 0-4 years.

Ambling down a side street, I come to a shop selling sports gear, end-of-line stuff, plus that cheap, gaudy kit with never-heard-of labels. I browse through a rack of naffo trainers before wandering inside. An acne-scarred lad peers at me through half a ton of iron-mongery pierced in his ears, eyebrows, nose and bottom lip. Jeez, his face looks like it's been used for target practice, or he's growing it into an assault course for gerbils. As it turns out, he's canny helpful so I buy more items than I'd intended to, plus he gives me a bit discount, even though the clothes are cheap as chips to begin with. Handy, that, as I'm practically skint until I get to the hotel room where I've stashed my cash, loads of yo-yo banknotes, in a Tampax box. Once in the street, I turn the carrier bag inside out to hide the logo, so the world won't know I've been buying from a bargain basement and start sniggering behind my back.

I'm trudging back to The Flues when I spot what I think is one of those Army and Navy-type shops where they flog combat gear and hiking boots, plus cagoules, sleeping bags and ski masks for robbers. Achingly trendy, I think not. Actually, on a closer look, it's more of a sports equipment shop, snowboards and suchlike wanky wastes of time. I glance at the prices in the window. Bloody hell, the ski suits cost an arm and a leg that'll end up in plaster casts, and they're only shellsuits by another name. It beats me how they find customers around here; maybe it's a front for a money-laundering operation, or a fetishists' emporium.

The inside of the shop smells of something chemical, fake snow or antifreeze maybe, and as I troll through to the back bit, I nearly get knocked unconscious by a surfboard shaped like a fish. I could sue their ass for destroyment of brain cells. I'm looking round for staff but there's just one guy as far as I can see, flicking through a magazine and occasionally flexing his biceps to himself in the mirror. Sad-sad-sad. Ignoring him, I wander through the shop, looking for a type of garment that would keep Bobbo warm. Ah, here we are, outdoor wear, just what the doctor ordered for a hypothermia scenario. I riffle through the rack of coats until I find the perfect model – a Husky parka, filled with 2 lbs of duck down. Somewhere there's a baldy quacker waddling around, shivering its tits off. Still, who cares? I consider my moneylack situation and decide to pay a swift visit to my conscience. Fortunately, there's no-one home. I inspect the inside of the parka for security tags. Perfecto! It's not one of those electronic jobs, just one with a pellet of dye inside, a bugger to remove but a piece of piss to get out of the shop.

In the next section there's a display of wicked snowboarding hats. Wow, there's one called a Monsta Rasta which is a red, yellow and green beanie with loads of false dreads. Bobbo's gonna look well cool in that, plus his head won't drop off with frostbite. After mentally selecting it, I physically transfer it from the display to a huge pocket on the inside of the parka. To complete the look, I do the same with a pair of wraparound ski shades, nearly as huge as welding goggles only bright blue, with elastic to keep them from falling off. Bobbo, you's a hip dude, man.

OK, shopping list sorted. Now for the tricky bit. In sight of the biceps-obsessed assistant, I press a hand against my forehead and lean against a clothes rack. The clothes rack from which I've cunningly selected the right size of parka for Bobbo. The parka with a Monsta Rasta and ski goggles in the pockets. Trying to lower myself as painlessly as possible, I slide to the floor and land with a dull thud. I peek through the coats at the assistant, expecting him to bound across with a first-aid kit stuck to a wee surfboard, like on *Baywatch*. No response. He's probably checking his pecs or doing abdominal crunches. Poser.

'Uurrggh,' I groan. Nothing. Hasn't he heard of customer care? 'Eurgh. Eu-ur-rggh,' I go, in a more urgent tone. Zilch. I feel like punching his lights out, then we'll see how hard he is, but I settle for a wee pathetic plea. 'Er, 'scuse me, could you help me?'

I'm slumped on the carpet and the lad glances down at me as though I'm a care-in-the-community bag lady, rather than a high-spending customer with a big order.

'Need some help?' he offers, eventually deciding to shift his arse into gear. As he gets nearer, I almost gag from the pong of his aftershave, or scrotum de-sweater, whatever vile stink he's wearing.

'It's my . . . It's my heart,' I gasp in my best coronary-patient-clinging-onto-life voice. If that poncey perfume don't gas me to death first, I might add.

'Hang on.' He fishes in his ears and unplugs his personal stereo. Oh, triffic. 'Say again.'

I sigh. 'I think I'm having a myocardial infarction.'

He stares blankly at me.

'A heart attack,' I explain. Can it read my lips? Is it alive? Or is it on the New Deal or some such scheme for the jobly illiterate?

'Oh, shite,' he says. 'What do I have to do?'

'You could try keeping me warm,' I suggest, my hand fluttering towards the parka.

'Oh, right, yeah, sure,' he babbles, grabbing the coat and draping it over me. I wriggle my arms into the sleeves. 'Hang on, I'll get the manager, he's just outside having a smoke.' And this shop's supposed to be for healthy outdoor types! They want exposing on *Watchdog*.

'No, no,' I insist, recovering a bit too suddenly. 'I've got wossname, clausters, or aggro, that phobia where you can't stand people fussing round. It'll only exasturbate my condition. Get me a chair by the door, I have to have the fresh air.'

'I thought you had to keep warm.' He frowns, but he's way too simple to suspect.

'Look, mate, I've had a triple bypass, I know what's what. Just do it. Pronto,' I croak, trying for a bit death rattle. Jeez, it's a miracle my arteries *aren't* seizing up, what with all this quick thinking and hard brainwork.

He helps me up and I fake-stagger to the door, having a sly feel of his biceps on the way. Not bad. Pulling out a sort of bench covered in neoprene (which I *adore*), he sits me down and props the door open. Christ, better get the job over with, the weather's turned friggin' arctic out there.

'Are you all right now?' he says, beads of fear-sweat glistening on his forehead.

'My tablets,' I murmur. 'If I can just take my tablets, I'll be fine.' I fumble in the rucksack and find a couple of Solpadeines. 'Water,' I whisper. 'Just a wee dribble in a glass. Then I'll be on my way.'

That seems to do the trick. He can't wait to get me out of the shop before I start foaming at the mouth, so he can get back to waxing his shortboard or practising his squat-thrusts or squeezing his zits, whatever.

'Back in a tick,' he says, manoeuvring his thigh muscles at speed through the racks of overpriced goods.

Medical science would marvel at the miraculous recovery I make from my near-death experience. *Whoosh!* I'm out of that shop doorway faster than a greyhound from a trap.

My feet must sprout wings or something because I'm back at The Flues in no time flat, swathed in the parka and sweating to buggery, gulping for air and palpitating, my heart thumping at 200 bpm. *Ba-boom ba-boom ba-boom.*

Just then, at the most unflattering moment in my entire life, the bar door swings open. In strolls Joe. Drop-dead gorgeous, cute-ass Joe. He looks at the gibbering wreck that is me.

'Rowena, how're ya? Fancy meeting up later for a drink?'

'Mnngghh leurchh ggnn,' I reply.

'I'll take that as a yes,' he grins.

When I get back to the room, Texy's spark out on the bed which is good news, as I won't have to show her Bobbo's new clothes or explain why I'm wearing a parka bearing a security tag. I hide the carrier bag at the bottom of the wardrobe and bundle the parka beneath my bed, where it lies like a dead dog. Still freaked from my shoplifting activities and the unexpected meeting with Joe, I pop a tranquillizer, one of the pills I stole from Mum's emergency supply when I still lived at home, remembering too late that Valium and booze don't mix too well. Oh well, Joe invited me to meet him for a drink; it's not like the reddest hottest date of all time. I'll just have to watch my alcohol intake.

Truly I can't be arsed to fiddle on with the shower so I decide to risk a bath, even though I hate wallowing in my own effluent. The plumbing in The Flues is prehistoric. The pipes clatter and groan and the water trickles diarrhoea-brown for the first couple of minutes, then spits and spurts until it's clear. I hope it isn't connected to the sewers. Oh, bugger, there's no bubble stuff but there's a bottle of supermarket washing-up liquid on the shelf which will have to do. I squirt a few drops into the tub but it's that cheapo stuff so it doesn't foam much. The bath is enormous, big enough for a hippo, and by the time it's filled with enough water to cover my bits, it's practically cold again. I sluice myself at the speed of light then give myself a brisk rub-down with a towel but I'm shivering, the tiny bristles on my legs standing to attention.

Excitement. Anticipation. Jiggly belly. This is more than just hunger. I'm thrilled nervous about seeing Joe again, even though I've tranquillized myself, so hyped up I'm practically drooling. Behave, girl, get a grip.

17

Hell's Overspill

We arrive in the bar unfashionably early, slavering for chips. Worms are devouring my stomach. No food has passed these lips since I snacked on Joe's nuts last night and I'm in the mood for a blowout. I'm wearing my rockin' black denim ensemble and judging from the slack waistline on the skirt, my body appears to have shrunk. That'll be all the aerobic exercise I've done, schlepping up and down the hill to the nunvent and fleeing from the sports shop with the purloined parka.

Texy's wearing some of my make-up, even though she moaned about it being all Marilyn Manson stylee which I denied, as I grew out of my Goth phase at puberty. I can't truthfully say that black lipstick goes with her natural colouring. Perhaps if she dyed her hair deep purple or midnight blue it would look better, but even then she'd have to buy a complete new wardrobe to match. Tonight she's dressed in a short orange skirt which, admittedly, looks fab with her snake hips and really shows off her skinny black-clad legs in clumpy DMs. I look better, though.

The place is almost deserted. Matty's behind the bar reading the sports pages. His eyes come alive when he sees Texy and he stuffs the newspaper out of sight. She orders drinks plus chips and garlic bread for two, telling me to find a table and she'll bring them over. I've already spotted Joe sitting in 'our' corner, his nose buried in a magazine. As casually as I can, I saunter over.

'Hey,' I say.

He looks up, smiles. 'Hey,' he says, shuffling up to make space for me on the bench seat. 'What gives?'

It seems important to apologize for my demented state when we ran into each other earlier but when I start babbling he places his index finger on my mouth, shutting me up in his own sexy way.

'I never noticed anything different about you,' he says.

Huh, triffic. I was deranged, dressed in a shoplifted parka, sweating like a pig in a sauna, heart bursting out of my ribcage, and he considers that normal!

'So what have you been up to today?' he says. 'Did you make it up the hill to the convent?'

I screw up my face in a pained expression and Joe laughs, as though scaling a mountain and being crippled in the process is somehow amusing. Then I tell him how we delivered a package containing a secret tape to a gangster's aunt. My voice is shaky, reminding me that my nerves have been on hyper-jangle all day. I'm confused, too, about Hefty O'Hara, the deadly gangster (according to Ray) who goes to the trouble of finding a talking book for his aunt.

'You mustn't breathe a word,' I warn him. 'Otherwise I could get a bullet in the head.' I mime shooting myself behind the ear.

'We wouldn't want that,' he says, frowning and looking serious.

'This wiseguy, see, he's lining me up for a job in the sex industry, abroad somewhere, so it's best I pretend to go along with his plans, keep him sweet.'

'Sounds like a good ploy,' says Joe. 'It wouldn't do to arouse his suspicion. What's his name, then, this mobster?'

'I daren't say. He's so devious, he might have the place bugged. He's already duped Texy. She believes his old flannel about him being a businessman but that just shows how clever he is at fooling people. Oops, she's coming over now. Keep shtum.'

Joe nods gravely. At least he's taking me seriously, even if Texy's been hoodwinked.

'One lager and black, chips to follow,' she announces, slapping down my drink and perching on a chair next to me. 'Hiya, Joe. What's that you're reading?' He slides the magazine across the table.

'Just worky stuff, Texy,' he says. 'You'd be bored rigid.'

'What? What worky stuff?' I ask, nebbing over Texy's shoulder at the front cover. 'Computers? Is that what you do?'

'Sort of,' admits Joe. 'I work in the Internet café across the square. It was more a hobby really, but they pay me so I ain't complaining. Mostly it's serving cappuccino and latte and slices of carrot cake. That's Ballyloony for you; Silicon Valley it ain't.' He jerks his head towards the counter. 'The boy Matty over there, he pops in for a chinwag and a surf some days. Ah, here comes your meal.'

'Hallelujah! About time,' says Texy, as Matty delivers two plates of chips and a basket of garlic bread which she can darn well eat herself as I don't want my breath to stink like a sweaty sock.

'Mind if I join you?' says Matty. 'It's dead tonight, there's a pub quiz down the road, so Cilla can manage the bar on her own for a bit.'

'Feel free,' says Texy, winking at me and grinning like a ninny.

Brilliant. I'm starvulating, but now I'll have to watch my manners instead of cramming chips down my gullet at Mach 2. It's impossible to enjoy food when someone's watching, when you're trying not to eat like a savage and have to look out for grease running down your chin or ketchup forming a moustache round your gob. I manage to eat five whole chips and a burnt bit before I give up, wipe my mouth with a serviette, and announce that I'm stuffed.

'Waste not, want not,' says Matty, scoffing the lot in about two seconds, the gutsy guzzler. He pats his chest and burps. 'Let's put some music on, girl, liven this place up some.' Loading the plates, he struts off to the jukebox with Texy dancing attendance.

I'm still scooched up to Joe on the seat when he slides his arm across the back. He's probably only doing it to stretch his limbs but in my fantasy it feels like he's protecting me. When I shoot him a glance he stares straight into my eyes, making my stomach fizz and my heart perform a triple axel.

'You know what,' he says. 'You fascinate me.'

My cheeks burn. I wriggle on the slippy seat. No-one's accused me of fascinating them before.

'I want to know everything about you, hear your life story, find out what goes on inside your head.'

'Believe me, you don't,' I say, with feeling. 'It's gruesome, a complete horror flick. You do *not* want to know. Trust me on this.'

Joe smiles and squeezes my shoulder. 'I've never met anyone like you, unless it was in a past life. Where are you from? What distant world?'

'It sure as hell ain't Disney World,' I tell him. 'The dark side, that's where I come from. Hell's overspill, by way of Bedlam. I used to be mad once; my brain went haywire, totally out of control. But it's OK now because I had it treated by, you know, proper psycho medics.'

'You're trying to shock me,' he says. Little does he know. 'Why would anyone think you're crazy? You're just . . .' he pauses, searching for the right word, '*individual*, I suppose. You dance to a different drum. You're not afraid to be yourself. It's a rare gift.'

I slouch down on the seat, draw my knees up to my chest and clutch myself in a foetal position. Joe hodges up close and drapes an arm around me. A casual observer might imagine that I'm a basket case in deep crisis and Joe is my carer, but it feels strangely comforting, as though he's shielding me from all the bad stuff that the world can throw at me.

And I find myself confiding in him, although I'm selective about which details of my history to reveal. In one way, I've confessed the worst: that I was a teenage mental patient, a Madolescent. It isn't something I'm proud of, but I'm not ashamed of it either; it's more what you'd call a learning curve, a psychological sticking plaster, or a 'crisis intervention' as Dr Pooley described it, but not everyone understands that. Some people think I'm liable to run amok with a hatchet stabbing strangers in the street, when in reality my madness was a necessary phase, an obstacle I had to steer round, like the *Titanic* and the iceberg. Well, perhaps that's not the best metaphor but you know what I'm saying. You know what, I'm sane. My brain is ravelled again, more or less. Still, whether Joe believes me or not, it hasn't sent him running for the hills, which must be a promising sign.

Valium works its relaxing magic. Lager flows. I run off at the mouth, babbling on about How I Battled Depression, but in an entertaining, non-self-pitying fashion. At least that's the way it seems to me. And then suddenly, with the swiftness of a guillotine blade decapitating a Frenchman, I realize I've drunk way too much. I must lie down in a darkened room immediately. A rainbow floats before my eyes, splits into shards of coloured light, re-forms and drifts out of vision, over and over, ad nauseam. My stomach bobs around inside me like a cork in a barrel of brine. Inside my head, what's left of my brain shucks off its moorings, dancing a crazy salsa, bouncing off my skull.

'Gorra go bed,' I slur, attempting to stand. My legs buckle beneath me, the floor transforms into shifting sands, the walls close in like an iron maiden. I seem to recall being helped upstairs, half-dragged, half-carried, by – who? Joe, for one, and possibly Matty or Texy or a not-quite-so-drunk alcoholic plucked from a bar stool. I couldn't say even if my life depended on it, because that's when I black out.

When consciousness returns I'm lying on the bed in the room at The Flues, overcome by the whirly pits, feeling like death. The flickering gleam of a bedside lamp disturbs me. My eyes hurt. If I try to lift my head the walls dissolve, the floor wobbles and the ceiling spins. I resolve never again to mix Valium with booze on an empty stomach.

Eurgh, I feel really, really ill. Where is Texy? I need Texy. Not to nurse or curse or rehydrate me. Just to *be* here.

Try to avoid puking up. Lie perfectly still. Breathe evenly through mouth, in, out. Keep eyes closed. Empty mind of all thoughts. Sleep. Sleeeeep.

The sound of sniggering and shushing outside the door jerks me back to reality.

'Ah, Texy, wouldn't you let me come in, just for a minute.'

'Ssshhh, no, Rowena's fast asleep.' Huh, that's what she thinks.

'Honest, I'll be quiet, so I will. She'll never know anyone's there.'

'N-O. No.' Texy giggles. 'Matty, get yourself away, it's late.'

Matty! She's up to shenanigans with the mullet-haired barman! I hold my breath, straining my ears to catch their scuffling and fumbling outside the door. Then – oh, God! – I hear a low moan, a moan of sexual longing, coming from him. It's followed by a lengthy sigh, breathy with passion, from her. This is way too much for a sensitive human being to bear.

Gathering the duvet around me, I shuffle to the door and fling it open. They're entwined around each other, so close you couldn't insert a spliff paper between them.

'Could you *make* more noise if you tried?'

Startled, they disengage, like a couple of mating dogs drenched with a bucket of water. Texy tidies her hair and smooths her shirt.

'Rowena, did I wake you?'

'You'd have woken the dead with that bloody racket.'

'Aw, sorry. Away inside then, I'm just coming.'

'Yeah, sounds like it.'

Matty snorts. I want to punch his lights out. Texy flashes me a meaning look and shoos – *shoos!* – me back into the bedroom. Trailing the duvet behind me, I trip and bang my knee on the chest of drawers. Talk about a dignified retreat.

I'm burning up, furious that Texy showed no consideration for my delicate state, that she put her carnal desires before me, even after I'd practically expired from alcohol/Valium poisoning in front of her eyes. Furious that she's been sleazing with Matty while I, in my weakened, fragile condition, could have choked to death on my own vomit. Doesn't she know I'm out of my head with anxiety about finding Dad and losing Hefty, without having to worry about Matty taking advantage of her? Jeez, I'm practically flattened, banjoed, starfished by responsibilities.

Eventually the noise of their laughter dies down and their slurpy snogathon ends. Texy skulks into the room, her cheeks flushed like a baboon's bottom.

'Would you bring me a drink?' I say.

She pootles to the bathroom and I listen to her pee. 'Here,' she says, holding out a toothbrush tumbler containing tap water.

'Cheers,' I say, sipping the tepid liquid. 'So you've been playing sluts 'n' studmuffins with Matty, you tartlet? Sorry I went a bit schizoid back there, Tex. I feel bloodier than roadkill.'

'No harm done.' I spot her doing a secret smile to herself.

'Do you fancy him, honestly?'

'Don't sound so surprised. He's real good fun, plus he's got a lovely hard body. I've had my eye on Matty since I stayed here last year.' She does a big saucy wink and licks her lips. 'Who are you to talk, anyway? You and Joe seemed pretty wrapped up together, gazing into one another's eyes all evening.'

'That's different,' I protest. 'Me and Joe, it's a . . . a *spiritual* thing. He wasn't trying to get inside my pants.'

'Huh, like you'd fight him off if he was. I think not, Ms Vincent.'

'Go to sleep, I'm knackered.'

But her words set me wondering. Running through the options in my head, I try to work out my feelings for Joe. He's good-looking, his bed-head hair is completely fab, plus the duelling scar on his cheek makes him look dead romantic and mysterious. Even though I was sarky and horrid to him when we first met, it didn't bother him; he's so friendly and easy to get on with. I like him loads and yet, and yet . . .

The curse of Rowena is holding me back, warning me not to get too attached. Every time I allow someone to get close to me, every time I drop my guard, let them know I care – *poof!* – they vanish out of my life.

Dad, for example.

18

The Disappearing Dad

It didn't turn nasty. We're not talking *Fight Club* here. It wasn't even much of an argument. Ozzy Osbourne yells way louder and fouler than that over Poptarts or doggy-do. You might call it civilized, or mature, or any of those fancy words to disguise it, wrap it up in something that suggests it was logical, or made a kind of sense.

But it didn't. It made nonsense. A nonsense that would haunt us for the rest of our lives. OK, *me*, then.

I know why Dad left.

Sitting in the upstairs loo, flicking through Mum's *Take a Break* magazine, I could hear, if not the actual words, then certainly the tone of their conversation. It sounded serious. Dad wasn't asking if she'd like a carry-out, or if she'd taped *Inspector Morse*, or paid the electric bill. I ducked off the bog, unable to flush for fear of being discovered and outed, and positioned my ear against the door to try and catch their words.

'I don't want to be married any more, Jean,' said Dad. 'Not to you; not to anyone. I can't handle the responsibility.'

There was lots of to-ing and fro-ing. Accusations. Recriminations. Rebuttals. It wasn't pleasant. The most shocking aspect was that it was so ordinary. Ordinary in a marriage-breaking, family-wrecking, relationship-ending kind of way. Why couldn't he have made it sound more dramatic? He'd lost his heart to a rent boy, say. Or he'd decided to go for gender reassignment and become a nail technician? Why did it have to be such an everyday reason?

I felt embarrassed, ashamed, humiliated. Plus shocked and scared, naturally.

It isn't you, it's me. Dad didn't utter those words, but that's about the gist of it. When a man says that, according to Mum's *Marie Claire* magazine, he means the opposite: *It isn't me, it's you.* But that would be hurtful, and men don't like to be blamed, can't stand losing face, prefer to feel wronged than be total bastards, which is in fact what they are.

Is it any wonder that I tucked his killer words inside my head and shoved them to the back of my mind? That I chose to forget his pathetic reason for abandoning us – his wife, mother and child? Does it explain why I can't remember anything about him?

19

Stained and Skint

In the morning Texy's nowhere in sight. I figure she might be having breakfast until I check my Swatch and discover that it's afternoon. My belly feels swollen, distended, like the belly of a starving child from some unheard-of African region. On the plus side, at least I don't have flies buzzing about in my nostrils. Hey, stop it, Rowena. Thoughts like that invite bad karma.

After rinsing my bits in the bathroom, I swallow a couple of headache tablets and make a cup of tea with four sachets of sugar, as if my teeth aren't rotting quickly enough. That's when I discover Texy's note propped against the kettle.

Gone to visit Bobbo. See u later. Have fun. T. XxX

I'm abandoned, left to my own devices for the rest of the day. What oh what should I do? I'm flailing around in search of a purpose. This is so unlike me. I'm Rowena, the self-contained loner. Trouble is, it's begun to feel so normal, so easy, to hang with Texy and Joe that I almost miss them when they're not around. Uh-oh. Must beware of allowing other people to enter my comfort zone.

Dum-di-dum. I consider treating my face to a deep-cleansing routine in an attempt to nuke a line of spots studded across my forehead like an autopsy scar. Nah. Safer to let sleeping zits lie. Then, remembering the new clothes acquired for Bobbo, I decide to remove the security tag from the Husky parka.

Like I said, the tag is one of those with a pellet of dye attached, as opposed to the electronic ones that set off the alarms. The way it works is that if someone – a shoplifter, say – tries to remove the tag without using a special tool thingy, the pellet punctures and the dye shoots everywhere, over the robbed garment and on to the person's hands. Worst of all, it's that inedible stuff that won't scrub off even if you exfoliate a hundred times with scouring powder; you have to wait until the skin flakes off naturally.

The trick is to slide a plastic bag over the tag before attacking it with pliers, or scissors at a pinch. When the tag is wrenched off, the pellet breaks, and the liquid dye explodes into the bag, leaving garment and hands pristine and ink-free.

Ee-zee.

Well, that's the theory.

The reality is that I lose my grip as I'm fumbling with the tag, causing some of the dye to splash on to the scissors. In the panic, the handles dig into my palms, leaving two bright red blotches the size of 50p pieces slam dunk in the middle of my hands.

Ink-redible. Red-inkible.

Then, mental in mid-frenzy, I wipe a hand over my sweaty forehead, so now my stupid spots are stained a fetching shade of crimson too. That's taught me a lesson. I'm never, never going shoplifting again. Or at least I'll be sure not to rob any gear with dye pellets in the tags.

This is surely God's way of punishing me for robbing the clothes, or for dissing starving kids, or . . . Or just to punish me for being me.

At the precise moment when I'm hiding Bobbo's parka, a rap sounds at the door. My instant thought is that it's the police, that they've had me under surveillance and they've turned up to arrest me for shoplifting, catching me with the stolen goods, quite literally, red-handed.

'Who is it?' My voice is croaky with panic-stroke-guilt.

'Phone-a-Fuck. Your shag for the evening, who d'ya think? Open the door, you weirdo.' Texy sounds exasperated.

Kicking the Husky under the bed, I undo the lock to let her in.

'What's with the warpaint?' Texy stands framed in the doorway, goggling at my red-stained hands and forehead.

'I've been eating cherries,' I lie. 'No, bilberries, loganberries, or was it beetroot?'

'Make up your mind,' she laughs.

'Cake. I remember now. It was definitely cake, with red icing.'

'Eurgh, cochineal.' She screws up her face in disgust.

'Cochy-what?'

'That red food colouring, cochineal. Mexican insects ground into a paste, that's what it's made of. Horrible.'

'Yeah, right. Like they'd put dead bugs in a cake.' Now I know she's winding me up.

'Suit yourself,' shrugs Texy. 'Does that mean you're not hungry, since you've been force-feeding yourself with stodge?'

The thought alarms me. 'Nah, man, I'm famished, gagging for a fix of chips.'

'Chips again?' she says. 'I've never known anyone with such an unbalanced diet. Don't you ever eat vegetables?'

'Chips *are* vegetables,' I point out. 'Potatoes, that's what they're made with. Egg, chips and baked beans, they're my favourite. Hey, I guess that makes me a vegetarian.'

'Right, and it makes me the Pope's lovechild. Dope.' She throws a pillow at me.

So that's that sorted.

While we prepare ourselves for another evening in the bar and I figure out how to hide my shame and scarlet stains, Texy recounts her day with Bobbo. She reckons he was in a good mood, not a grumpy grumbler like yesterday.

'He asked when you were going to visit him again,' she says. 'He's definitely taken a shine to you.'

'Triffic,' I say, but not in a sarky way. Bobbo's a wicked dude and I can't wait to see him in his new outfit. As casually as possible, I say, 'I've bought something for him to wear so he doesn't freeze to death. He'd just better like it, that's all.'

Texy does a double take. 'You've *what*? Really, Rowena?'

110

'Don't sound so surprised,' I snap, offended. 'You didn't think I'd let him down, did you?'

'No, no,' she says, all of a fluster. 'Rowena, you can be such a total darling sometimes. Let's have a look.'

'You'll have to wait. We'll take it to him soon enough. I really can't be arsed to take it out of the bag right now. I'm spitting feathers here, man, gagging for a drink.'

'Come on then, it's my round.'

The bar is busy tonight, mostly with old penshies and a gang of scruffy blokes who look as if they've been exhumed from bogs. There's no sign of Joe. Even though we never arranged to meet I'm half-expecting him to walk in, and my stomach flips like a tossed pancake every time the door opens. The chips have a peculiar taint, like the fat needs changing or mice have crawled into the fryer and been frizzled to death. Also, it took forever to disguise my stains with concealer so people won't think it's virulent dermatitis or I'm morphing into a lobster. I'm wearing my black lace fingerless gloves and a scarf tied in a bandanna to cover the line of scarlet spots on my forehead. Complete waste of time.

I can feel a mood settling over me like a storm cloud.

Naturally, Texy wants us to prop up the counter so she can flirt with Matty, which makes me feel as comfortable as a nun in a lap-dancing bar. But the very worst thing is when I go for my purse to buy a round of doubles and I find out how little money I have left. The blood in my veins turns to ice. Someone must have robbed me!

My throat seizes up as I gulp air in panic, then try to compose myself and pretend nothing is wrong. Excusing myself, I float trancelike to the latrines and lock myself in a cubicle. A slick of sweat breaks out on my forehead as I count and recount the banknotes, trying to figure out mentally how many yo-yos I've got through since I left home. Gradually, sickeningly, it dawns on me. No-one's robbed me; I've spent it myself. I'd forgotten about paying for the flight and loads of other stuff like Bobbo's new clothes. It all adds up.

I'm practically bankrupt. A destitute abroad.

By ten thirty it's clear that Joe is a no-show. I'm sick to my stomach, so I say goodnight to Texy and laughing-boy and creep upstairs to the room. A glance in the mirror makes me wish I was dead. The spots on my forehead are glowing like red fairy lights. The stupid bandanna, fingerless gloves, wild hair and black-rimmed eyes make me look the double of that slutty Goth, Magenta, out of *The Rocky Horror Show*.

Jesus. My life is shittier than a bucketful of pus.

Not bothering to remove my make-up, I crawl into bed, so exhausted that the muscles in my leg twitch violently just when I'm about to fall asleep. When slumber eventually comes, I dream of Dad. The faceless Lonnie Vincent, dressed in a bandanna, motor-cycle leathers and carrying a winged helmet, lopes towards me in his biker boots.

'You are my beloved daughter,' he says fondly, 'in whom I am well pleased.'

'Cheers, Dad,' I mumble. 'When will I see you?'

'Soon. Keep the faith, Rowena.' He mounts a powerful Suzuki. 'Remember to keep the faith.' And he roars off into the distance, leaving me alone, yet in a crazily optimistic state of mind.

As dawn breaks in Ballyloony, the answer to my money problem is fixed in my brainbox. Of course, it's simple as a pimple, thanks to the cryptic clue from Dad. *Keep the faith*. It's an easy code to crack.

He's telling me to get a job at the nunvent.

Texy is still crashed out in her pit this morning so I decide not to disturb her. For the first time since we hit The Flues, I make it to breakfast. My stomach must be rotting away as it's been so long since it had a proper meal. A bowl of Frosties, two rashers, toast with blackcurrant jam and two cups of tea later, I'm set up for the day, if not the week. For a bit of extra confidence, I pop an upper and wash it down with some bitter fruit juice. Yuck. I'll just do the business at the nunvent, sort out a job, then at least I'll be able to stick some money in the kitty and hold my head high. Many things I may be, but sponger isn't one of them. As a fringe benefit, I'll be able to claim sanctuary at the nunvent in case Hefty O'Hara decides to grab me and export me into the international vice trade.

20

The Scared Heart

I'd forgotten about the hill to the nunvent where the Sisters of Blessed Relief hang out. Their gaff is at the top of a steep winding road, like K2 with grass verges. Lactic acid burns the backs of my legs from the exertion of schlepping up the never-ending incline. My calf muscles are bursting through the skin. I'll bet my hamstrings are fucked. Heart pounding, gasping for air, I steady myself against the wooden sign. My neck feels sticky with sweat. Sisters of Blessed Relief? Sisters of the Oxygen Mask would be a better deal.

I remember to check out the vacancies sign we saw the other day.

Domestic Staff, part-time. Contact Sr Bonaventure, Administration Office.

Once my breathing's under control, I trudge the last few yards up a path between loads of shrubs, bushes and stuff, and press a buzzer at the side of the door. A disembodied voice sounds through the squawk-box grille.

'Who is it?'

'It's Rowena. Rowena Vincent. I've come to see Sir, um, Bonny Denture.' That can't be right. Trust me to forget the name. I should have written it down.

'Do you mean Sister Bonaventure?' queries the voice.

'That'll be the one. Sister . . . What you just said.' Duh, she'll think I'm brain-damaged.

'Do you have an appointment?'

Jeez, what is this – a National Health Service convent? I could be seeking emergency spiritual treatment to save my mortal soul, or bringing them glad tidings of great joy, such as they've won the Lotto or something.

'No,' I mumble. 'I've come after a job.' This is when I notice the flickering red eye of a CCTV camera aimed at me. I run my hands through the tangled mess that is my hair. It must look like pony-chewed straw.

'Have you been in an accident?' asks the voice. 'Are you injured?'

Triffic. That's all I need, a triage nun, assessing how long I'll have to queue before someone deigns to see me. Why would she ask if I've been injured?

Then I remember about the stains on my hands and forehead. She must think it's blood.

There's some shuffling noises behind the door, followed by the sound of someone unsnicking a Yale lock. The door swings open to reveal a woman in unflattering spectacles and a bosom like a shelf. She's sporting a thick clump of fringe. The rest of her hair's hidden under a nun's headdress thing but I'll lay odds it's a pudding-basin job. She could be Ann Widdecombe's twin. Another woman, a gangly, stick-insect type with a faint moustache, appears behind her. They both reach out their hands, take me by the arms and usher me inside.

The hallway smells of furniture polish, that special anti-static type that stops the dust clinging. A line of chairs, their backs straight and stiff, stand to attention against the wall. It reminds me of the corridor outside our head teacher's office at school where me and my mates – the Fractious Element, as we were collectively known – were forced to sit awaiting punishment for misdemeanours. I must have perched there for, I dunno, weeks, if you add it all up. What a waste of my life. No wonder I always got crap grades.

A shaft of warm sunlight hits me out of nowhere, like a sudden glare from an arc light, making my scalp sweat, turning my head swimmy. I slump into one of the hard chairs, sending a shock up my spine and nearly dislocating my coccyx.

'I'm Sister Michael Mary,' says the Ann Widdecombe lookalike. Michael Mary? What kind of name is that? Is she going through some kind of identity crisis? Does God allow transgender nuns? 'Come with me and we'll get someone to look at you.'

I follow her like a sheep: a docile sheep with a newly docked tail. A fiery pain shoots through me where I banged my bum-bone on the chair. Maybe I'll contact one of those firms that sue people for hardly any reason, stick the nunvent for compensation; the Church could easily afford a few grand. Sister Michael Mary pauses next to a door with a cross painted on it. Perhaps it's the First Aid room. She motions me inside. It's some kind of office, dominated by a desk as big as a queen-size bed, with loads of pictures round the walls.

'Take a seat – Rowena, did you say?' She offers me a plastic chair with spindly legs.

'Yeah. Rowena. From Newcastle, England,' I add, though she's probably never heard of it, being locked up on this brick-built desert island with a bunch of old biddies and no telly, more than likely. It beats me how people exist without TV to keep them in touch with the world. It must be like living in a permanent *Big Brother* house, only without the hot tub and swearing, or the possibility of sex.

A smile crinkles her popply chin. 'Sister Bonaventure is on her way. Will I get you a drink while you wait?'

'Thanks,' I reply. 'I mean, no thanks.' Not if it's like that cat-piss they serve in Bobbo's visitors' lounge.

Sister Michael Mary exits the room, easing the door closed behind her. What an eejit. Fancy leaving a total stranger alone in this office. And *me*, of all total strangers. I could be rifling through the files, nicking pads of Post-it notes, sniffing the Pritt Stick, anything. I unlock my fingers which are Lego-slotted together with nerves. Aaagh! The red dye on my hands makes them look like something out of a slasher flick, as if a maniac's stabbed them in a frenzy of bloodlust. What a friggin' mess. Stuffing them inside my pockets, I find a wrap of chewing gum which must be at least two years old. The inside of my mouth is dry as the Sahara from the upper I swallowed earlier, so I decide to risk the gum, even though it's way past its sell-by and probably reduced to powder. Actually it's not all that vile as prehistoric chuddy goes, although it smells of halitosis rather than spearmint. Still, at least it's stimulating my saliva glands and preventing the formation of harmful bacteria that lead to plaque.

Check out those wild pictures on the walls, man. There's one of a woman in an off-white frock, her dimpled hands clasped in prayer, a golden halo crowning a nightmare hairdo. She's gazing upwards at some cavorting cherubs. OUR LADY OF BLESSED RELIEF, it says on the label. From the dreamy, spaced-out eyes she looks more like OUR LADY TRIPPING OUT ON HALLUCINOGENIC SUBSTANCES. Next to that there's one of Jesus – hey, even *I* know what Jesus looks like! – with shoulder-length hair that's way overdue a restyle. He's wearing Jesus sandals (of course) and one of those hippy-type kaftans; it's fallen open to reveal some sort of red-and-gold internal organ. THE SCARED HEART, it reads. Hey, Jesu lover of my soul, I'm right with you on that one. There was hardly ever a time when my ticker wasn't trembling with fear or dread, and that goes x100 for now.

The door opens. A woman glides – that's the only way to describe it – *glides* into the room. She's tall and elegant, like a model's granny, and her complexion's flawless even without make-up; pale, creamy skin with a yellowy tinge, like Hint of Barley emulsion paint, or mild jaundice. The nun's headgear covers her hair, leaving just an inch of chestnut roots exposed. This is a surprise; I expected all nuns to have grey hair, thought it was in the job description. She seats herself behind the desk, facing me.

'My name is Sister Bonaventure.' The voice is smooth, honey-gargled. 'And you're Rowena, I understand. From Newcastle.'

'Yeah. Erm, yes,' I correct myself. 'Newcastle, England.'

'How may we help you?' I sit there, hardly breathing, struck dumb, Beckham shooting non-stop penalties into my ribcage. Sister Bonaventure smiles, waits, and as there's no response, rephrases the question. 'Tell me what brought you here.'

'I, er . . . I was, you know, like, *sent*.' It's the truth, but it sounds like something a mentally unstable person would say.

'Sent.' Sister Bonaventure's eyes are hazel-coloured, with a strangely un-nunnish twinkle. Her eyebrows are shaped in a perfect arc. I wonder if she plucks them in secret. 'Could you elaborate?'

'*Sent*, you know. I don't know how else to put it. It came to me in a flash.' I'm about to tell her about my money worries, how I need to earn a few euros to pay my way so I can stay in Ireland and search for Dad, but it seems too long-winded and I truly can't be fussed. 'Well, not a flash, more a dream or a vision where my father appeared to me.'

Sister B. looks at me for ages, not speaking. Then, choosing her words carefully, she says, 'Tell me if I understand this correctly, Rowena. You're saying that our Father appeared to you in a dream and sent you to us.'

'Got it in one, Sister. Spot on, that is. My father, yes. He was definitely, like, guiding me, telling me to come here. No doubt at all.'

'Then you're welcome.' A beam spreads across her face. 'You're much more than welcome,' she says, rising from her seat, walking round to the side of the desk where I'm sitting. She offers her hand in greeting. Instinctively, I reach out to shake it, then remember the streaks of red dye on my palms. What will she think? They look like defence wounds on a victim of that psycho in *The Texas Chainsaw Massacre*. Snatching my hand away, I cram it in the pocket of my denim jacket.

'My hands are dirty,' I blather. 'I've been doing some weed.' Triffic, now it sounds as though I've been smoking marijuana. '*Weeding*. I mean weeding. In a garden.'

Sister Bonaventure leans against the desk. She's so tall she can rest her bum on top of it.

'Tell me, Rowena,' she says, almost in a whisper. 'Are you of the faith?'

The rational part of me ought to know that those are the words

118

coming out of her mouth, but the speed has made me so strung out they reach my brain garbled, scrambled, like an encrypted e-mail.

Are you off your face? This is what I actually hear.

'Oh, yes,' I reply, truthfully. 'Most definitely.'

'Then perhaps you've been sent to us for a reason,' she smiles.

'A reason? Oh, yeah, I nearly forgot.' I just stop myself slapping my forehead in a 'what am I like?' gesture. 'I was hoping there might be some work for me to do here.'

'Oh, there is much work to do,' says Sister Bonaventure, her voice warm and mysterious. 'Especially at such an opportune time. The Lord has indeed answered our prayers. You are more than ever welcome, Rowena.'

Salty blobs collect behind my eyes. I blink, trying to head off the tears at the pass, but it's too late. Here they come, rolling down my cheeks like rain down a gutter, my lips trembling, my body convulsing in great heaving sobs. That's all it takes, someone being nice to me. *You are more than ever welcome.* It's too much to handle, I feel overwhelmed by the whole niceness thing. Jeez, what am I like?

After an aeon and half a box of tissues, when I've recovered from the blarting jag, Sister Bonaventure says they'd be happy for me to start tomorrow. Just like that – no references, no vetting, no checking to see if I'm on the sex offenders' register. The arrangement suits me just fine. My past employment record isn't exactly blemish-free. Not if you count stuff like embezzlement and arson.

I nod. 'Thank you, Sister. Oh, thank you, thank you very much,' I gush, just stopping short of kissing the hem of her skirt. Pulling herself together, she tells me to present myself at eight a.m. and ask for Sister Michael Mary.

Yippee! I've landed myself a job, no probs. I'm in gainful employment!

*

119

Texy thinks I've gone mental.

'A job? You're on holiday,' she says. 'No-one works when they're on holiday.'

'It'll keep me off the streets,' I reason. 'And I'll be able to pop in and see Bobbo sometimes,' like that's a plus point. I haven't mentioned my money worries to her.

We have a couple of drinks in the bar on our own. It's Matty's night off and there's no sign of Joe. The booze goes straight to my head. When we return to our room I crawl into bed and – Gawd knows why – I say a silent prayer-type thing, not to God the Father on high, but to Dad, to thank him for tipping me off about that job at the nunvent.

Then the very strangest thing happens. Just as I'm drifting off to the land of Nod, a thought hits me with the force of a snooker ball in a sock. *Wham!* With full-colour clarity, I remember the Tampax box stuffed at the bottom of my rucksack. Uncertain whether it's a dream or a real memory, I sneak out of bed and crawl on hands and knees to the wardrobe, fumbling inside the bag until I find the box. My box of forgotten treasure. Breathless, almost dying with excitement, I thrust my hand inside and feel – oh, joy! – the bank-notes I'd stuffed there for safe keeping. Shitloads, hundreds, gazillions of euros, crisp and tightly folded.

How could they possibly have slipped my mind? I'm loaded – not boracic after all. This means, I realize with a thrill, that I don't need to take a job to survive. I'm financially independent. But if that's so, why did Dad come to me in a dream to point me so clearly towards the nunvent?

It's a sign. Yea, verily, it's a sign, but I'm way too knackered to figure out what it means.

21

Motorway Madness

Motorway Madness. The tabloid words screamed the news at millions of readers. People at breakfast tables munched, tutted and shook their heads while making a mental note to watch the full carnage on TV that evening. Metro passengers on their way to work scanned the headlines, intending to read the details at the office when they could be bothered to find their spectacles.

It took a while for the shocking reality to sink in.

Some of the people who'd been at the scene – firefighters, paramedics, police – stayed home the next day, piling on the post-traumatic stress by watching the drama being rerun again and again on the telly. Not a person in the country could have been unaware of it.

Me, I wasn't even born. I was nothing. Less than that, even. My egg hadn't hatched yet, let alone launched itself down Mum's Fallopian tube looking for action.

But Dad, he was there in the middle of it. It came down without warning, he said. One minute he was driving along the motorway, foot well down on the throttle, in a bit hurry, trying to make up some time. The next, like, whoa, where am I? Suddenly surrounded by thick fog, visibility down to zero, couldn't even see the brake lights of the car in front of him. He slowed down and didn't panic. Maybe he felt as though he'd passed into another dimension, or as though the world had ended abruptly and he was the last person alive. Alive but alone. He'd never experienced anything like this. The hard drive of his brain wasn't programmed for it. It was weird, frightening, alien.

He wound down the window. The weather outside was freezing, chilling his hands, numbing the bones in his fingers, stiffening his grip on the steering wheel. He heard the *vroom, vroom, vroom* of cars in the fast lane speeding past, hurtling into the unknown. Maniacs. Reckless, homicidal, suicidal.

Then he panicked. Braked to a stop, leaned over, grabbed his coat from the back seat, got out of the car, didn't even close the door properly. He had to get away from this nightmare. He ran, frantic and stumbling, across two lanes of motorway, not knowing – not caring – whether he'd be flattened by a truck, its driver focused on a full English breakfast at the next turn-off, or a lorry with livestock bound for the abattoir, or a florist's van delivering messages of love, apologies, sorry couldn't be arsed to get to the shops but happy birthday anyway. What he remembered was the silence, the dense, swirling silence. The silence punctuated by the muffled bangs of vehicles crashing into other vehicles.

Dad made it to the hard shoulder, scrambled up the embankment, feet slipping on the frosty earth, terrified of falling, rolling into the road, into the mayhem. He collapsed halfway up the mound, up the grassy knoll, sat there trying to control his breathing. His breath vaporized in the freezing temperature, droplets clung to the hairs in his nasal passages, his heart pounded in his chest.

He became aware of someone next to him. A man, oldish, with a tartan scarf tucked round his neck and breath smelling of mints. The man took Dad's hand, warmed it in his, and they flinched in unison at the constant thud of motor piling into motor. They never said a word to each other, not one word.

Then, through the sound-deadening fog, Dad heard another noise, a noise that clawed at his intestines, that made his eyeballs burn like molten lead. The terrible cries of people mangled in the carnage. Moans of agonizing pain, of unimaginable distress, final, desperate pleas for help.

And at last, thank God, the wailing sirens of the emergency services.

Motorway Madness. The expression entered the language, coined by tabloids, adopted by all.

Dad used his own language less and less. Nana Vincent told me that he retreated into long periods of silence, withdrew into his shell, stopped communicating with his family.

Did the events of that terrible day trigger off something in his dark side? Bring out the shadowy Dad who became a stranger to his wife, to his own mother, and, years down the line, to me, his daughter? Why am I even thinking about this?

22

Up the Nunvent

So here I am, suited and booted, for my first day as an employee at the convent of the Sisters of Blessed Relief. Well, more shoved and gloved, really. Texy had to resurrect my lifeless corpse with a couple of Solpadeines and shove me out the door, and I'm wearing tight-fitting latex gloves from a box of Violent Violet hair tint to cover up the crimson stains on my hands. At this ungodly hour the world is veiled in a drizzly mist. Maybe it's, I dunno, dew, or maybe my eyes are cloudy with sleep or early-morning glaucoma. Eight o'clock, that's the time I start work. Eight a.-friggin'-m., aka the crack of dawn. How pointless is that? It might be OK for the biddies in the House of the Rising Nun but it's deadly when you're hung over, which is probably why they don't go big on booze.

Sister Michael Mary answers the door. 'Good morning, Rowena,' she says, flapping me inside. 'We thank the Lord that you found your way to us,' she goes, almost in a whisper, as though it's some mysterious happening. 'He sent you just in time.' Feck knows what she's on about, but before I have time to question her, or even catch my breath, she's steering me through the shiny hallway and down a passage. 'I'll give you the guided tour,' she says. 'All part of our induction programme.'

She shows me into a long room with stone floors. It's dead cool, by which I mean chilly, as in refrigerated. Four wooden tables with sit-up-and-beg chairs line the room, poshgits' furniture, maybe from Ikea.

'This is the refectory,' she says.

I show her my expressionless expression.

'It's where we take our meals,' she explains. So I was right; they don't have a telly, otherwise they'd eat off trays on their laps. The panels on the walls match the table, half a forest in one room. I'd get clausters if I had to chow down in here; it must be like eating inside a wooden coffin.

'And here,' she continues, pushing open another door, 'is the kitchen where the food is prepared.' A gleaming cooker, the size of a small hatchback, takes up most of one wall. Then there's a fridge-freezer, an industrial microwave, two deep stainless steel sinks with shiny taps *and* a waste disposal, plus utensils for every purpose on earth hanging from a ceiling rack. It's gobsmacking, like something out of an advert in *Marie Claire*, no mountains of washing-up or overflowing ashtrays as in the kind of kitchen I'm used to.

'This is Rowena, who's been sent to help us,' says Sister Michael Mary to a woman scrubbing carrots at a long table. 'Rowena, this is Sister Cuthbert, our Delia Smith, as you might say.' They both chortle, as if it's the zillionth time they cracked the joke and they *still* find it funny. To be honest, Sister Cuthbert does have a hint of Delia, or maybe Delia looks like a nun with TV make-up.

'Welcome aboard,' says Sister Cuthbert, wiping her paws on her pinny. I notice the middle finger of one hand is missing. Maybe she chopped it off by accident. I hope she claimed for loads of compo. The amputated finger is totally the wrong one to lose for gesturing at someone to fuck off; still I don't expect they have much call for that kind of thing here.

Sister Michael Mary trots off along another corridor. Blinding sun beams down through skylights in the ceiling. I never knew the sun could shine so early in the morning; perhaps it's some Godly deal exclusively for religious establishments.

'These are the craft units, where we make goods for the gift shop. Prayer cards, statuettes, wall fonts, souvenirs.' She pushes open a door. Inside it looks like a warehouse. Metal shelves stretch along three walls, boxes are stacked up against the fourth. Long benches full of paraphernalia are set in a line down the room. On one, a row of greybacks paints statuettes of the Virgin Mary. It's a proper production line, only in slo-mo. The old girl at the end paints the robe blue; the next one colours the veil white, and so on down the line to the last one who dots in the features, eyes and suchlike. She probably has the best spectacles or the steadiest hands so they've given her the fiddly bits to decorate.

'This is Rowena, our newest convert,' says Sister Michael Mary. '*Sent* specially,' she adds in a whisper. The greybacks look up at me and gleam like a row of night lights. On the next table a couple of old wifies are sticking transfers on to plastic candle holders. These biddies are beyond ancient with doddery hands. The Parkinson Sisters.

'These hold candles for offering prayers to St Jude,' says Sister Michael Mary, as if it ought to mean something to me. 'The patron saint of lost causes. One of our top sellers, and we get a decent margin on them.' She picks one up and offers it to me. 'For you,' she smiles. 'As a welcome gift.'

'Right, ta,' I nod, stuffing the candle holder into my bag and toddling behind her out the door.

In the next room two younger women are setting out lines of rough pottery containers. My nostrils quiver from the whiff of paraffin.

'Moulds for the votive candles,' my tour guide informs me. I dunno what I'm supposed to say. Should I be impressed that they're sustaining the rural economy and employing the unemployable, or report them to the authorities for running a geriatric sweatshop making iconic tat for tourists? Just how kosher is this set-up?

Then we're out into the corridor again and Sister Michael Mary ushers me into yet another room. Machines hum. A steam iron hisses. 'This is the sewing shop,' she announces. 'We make garments for other religious orders, each to their own specification. Undergarments,' she adds in a whisper.

'Lingerie, you mean? Like in the factory in *Coronation Street*?' It's not exactly like Underworld, as the women here are actually working, not standing in huddles gossiping about the boss or plotting industrial action. But they look not unlike the lasses from the Street. For a while I can't nail it down, then it hits me. It's their eyes. They're staring at me with open curiosity; they don't have that glazed, vacant look of professional Christians.

Sister Michael Mary shoots me one of those patronizing smiles, as if I'm a retard. 'I don't think these garments would be classed as *lingerie*, exactly.'

She exhumes a pair of knickers from a basket, stout white cotton ones, not so much hi-tops as lo-bottoms, and way oversized, like Sumo wrestlers' nappies. I run the stiff, scratchy fabric between my fingers. Lordy, it must be like wearing Velcro next to the skin, or barbed wire.

'They're hard-wearing, made to cover every . . . Well, every *eventuality*,' says Sister Michael Mary. 'And these are the vests,' she says, displaying a woolly sleeveless monstrosity. I wrinkle my nose. The style police would soon hit their arrest quota here. 'Ah, come on, they might not be what you young people wear but they're very cosy,' she says. 'Besides, we don't have much call for hair shirts these days, nor sackcloth, with or without ashes.' I stare at her in a clueless fashion. 'Onward,' she says, shooing me out of the door.

I'm not sure if I can absorb any more, my brain's reached saturation point. It's not fair to bombard me on my first day, I might have to go off sick tomorrow with sensory overload. With all this fuss, anyone would think I was a business executive here to finalize a takeover, or the Queen slumming it on an official visit, instead of an underachieving bint from a council estate.

'And this is our computer suite.' Sister Michael Mary unlocks a door and leads the way into another room. The atmosphere is chilly despite the background hum of machines on standby. Maybe it's that air conditioning that comes on automatically as you enter the room, like in hotel bathrooms when the Xpelair switches on to waft away the smell of bodily emissions. The room's laid out in open-plan style, like something out of an office-furniture catalogue. There's a computer at each of the four workstations, and slidey hydraulic chairs that must be great for having races if the boss is out. The computer monitors are huge, about the size of patio doors, but that'll be because the nuns have old-age cataracts or aren't allowed out to the opticians.

'It's the latest technology, the Internet, e-mail so we can keep in touch with Sisters all over the world. We have our own website, produce a quarterly newsletter, and we even take orders over the Web for the goods we make here. It's all very hi-tech. We'd just upgraded but we've ground to a halt – crashed, you might say – as Mr Lander, our webmaster, has been called to a better place.' She crosses herself. 'Dingle, actually,' she adds, then tuts. 'Such a crime. Thousands of euros' worth of machines standing idle.'

I stifle a yawn. This whole deal is boring me rigid. 'So where do I fit in? What will I be doing?'

She takes my sleeve and pats it. 'We thought you could start on the domestic hygiene side of things. The Sisters look after their own quarters but we need to keep on top of the communal and public areas, dusting, vacuuming the stairs, keeping the wood polished, helping with the laundry. There's so much to do with the bicentenary coming up next week.'

Oh, so that's it. I'm nowt but a bottom-of-the-pile servant, a general fatscrotum. Still, it's not like I'm looking for a step up the career ladder, and the sooner I start the sooner I'll be earning money.

'Shall we set you to work then?'

I shrug. 'Suppose so.'

'Good. I'll introduce you to Enda, our housekeeper, who'll be supervising you. Just one more thing, Rowena, you're to enter and leave the building by the side door, the staff entrance, from now on, and always wear your uniform while you're inside the building.'

'Uniform?'

'Green-and-white checked overalls. Enda – and God – will provide.' Ha bleedin' ha. So already I've been relegated to the status of a peg wifey. *Very* welcoming.

23

Enda the Dragon

Enda the housekeeper fusses over me like a mother hen.

'Come in, come in, I'm not a dragon,' she goes, flapping her hands as if she's directing a driver into a tight parking space. 'Sit yourself down at the table, the kettle's just boiled. Will it be tea or coffee? I can't drink that strong stuff, it gives me the jitters, and you should see how it stains the cups, just think what it's doing to your insides. We've got the Nescafé there and the Mellow Bird's or the decaff if you're desperate or vegetarian.'

'Mellow Bird's please,' I reply, gulping back a mouthful of nostalgia. It's the coffee we used to drink at home, that place I've banned myself from thinking about. 'How do you make it?'

'Bless your heart, with milk, how else? I heat it up in me own little microwave in the kitchenette, three minutes per mug on full blast until the milk just begins to bubble, then blow on the top to stop it forming a skin, stir in a heaped spoonful of the lovely brown stuff and a couple of sachets of sugar.'

Jeez, I never asked for the recipe. What is it with this woman? She's fawning over me, running off at the chops, acting as if she hasn't had human contact in a while. Maybe she's a wee bit on the simple side and the greybacks keep her locked away in the basement where she's no danger to the public. Oh, triffic, my boss is a mental defective. Still, she makes a darn fine cup of coffee. The aroma wafts into my nostrils, the creamy head swirling on top of the light brown body just the way Nana Vincent used to make it. Pure, unadulterous bliss. The first sip shoots straight to my comfort spot, warmth spreading through my stomach, calming, relaxing, soothing. I can't remember when I last felt like this, excluding the odd Valium binge, of course.

'Help yourself to a Hobnob or three.' Enda slides a plate of biscuits across the table. 'Go on, don't stint yourself. Look at you, skinny ribs, I've seen more meat on a butcher's pencil.'

I'm about to protest in case I lard on a puppy-fat roll, but the cookies win out. Scraping the frothy bit of coffee and sucking it through a Hobnob has to rank up there with squeezing a ripe, juicy spot in the pleasure stakes, though the Hobnob has the edge in the taste department.

'So you've had the VIP treatment from the top brass, I understand. Tell me, strictly between the two of us, what do you make of Bonzo?' Enda stretches her sturdy legs and plonks her feet on a stool under the table. The casual yet practised way she does this suggests it's a familiar pose, a prelude to a good old gossipy chat.

'Bonzo?' I'm thinking, what is this – a chimpanzee sanctuary?

'Sister Bonaventure,' says Enda. 'Top Cat. Papal Pet of the Month. Miss Piety up there.' She nods her head towards the ceiling. Her hair's so thin the scalp shows through pink, with patches of shiny skin at the sides. Alopecia maybe, or female pattern baldness. Where the hair is intact, it's permed in one of those cauliflower styles, curled in florets. 'I'll bet she gave you the third degree.'

Although I'm warming to Enda after that canny coffee, experience has taught me to be wary of strangers. She could be on the payroll of the CIA or, worse still, the Mob, as represented on earth by Hefty O'Hara, my nemesis. Jeez, I'll have to lay off the drugs; they're making my paranoia flare up. I decide to play it dumb.

'She did, but I pleaded the Fifth,' I reply, making my voice little-girly and innocent. 'What's the verdict on her, then?'

'I'm not one to gossip.' This means the opposite of what it says.

'It isn't gossip,' I assure her. 'It's inside info, important for a newcomer.'

Enda sniffs. 'Overpromoted. Too much too soon. Connections, see.' She taps the side of her nose with a finger. 'It's not *what* you know, that's all I'll say on the subject. As for that Eminem, she's no better than she ought to be, either. I could tell you tales, Rowena . . .'

Eminem, I rapidly work out, is Enda's code name for Sister Michael Mary. M and M, see, two Ms. Sounds like Enda's got the dirt on everyone here and I reckon it wouldn't take much to prise it out of her. She's gagging for a good old bitching session.

'Pardon me for asking, Rowena, but why are you wearing those mucky rubber gloves?' she says. 'Are you trying to stop biting your nails or is it some kind of daft English fashion?'

'Growing my nails,' I reply, then realize that she might demand to see how chewed they are. 'No, I mean the gloves are from Top Shop, they're what Madonna wore on tour. Latex,' I say, immediately regretting it as she'll suspect I'm a rubber fetishist. 'I mean both. Nails and Madonna, like.'

'Make up your mind.' Enda inhales the coffee aroma and dunks a cookie. 'I think you're hiding something under there. What is it – dermatitis? Eczema? Psoriasis? Show Enda, I'll not tell on yeh.'

'Promise?' I heave a sigh. It's obvious she's not one to give up.

She crosses her bosoms. 'Promise.'

Peeling off the glove on my left hand, I expose the crimson stain. To my relief, it seems to be fading round the edges, leaving just a bright red oval in the middle of my palm.

Enda stares. 'When did that appear?'

'The night before last.'

'And you've the same on the other one?'

I nod, taking off the second glove and holding out my hand for inspection.

'God love you,' she whispers. She parts my fringe and scrutinizes my forehead. That's personal-space invasion, that is. The spots feel livid. They probably got infected from the dye, turned septic and now I'm suffering from toxic shock syndrome. I could be dead within hours!

'Don't touch them, Enda, they're still sore,' I warn. 'And they might be catching.'

132

'I doubt that.' Enda leans forward in her chair. 'I've heard the rumours about you being *sent*. This proves that you're special, Rowena. Chosen. You mustn't fear the marks. They're a sign, a blessing,' she says. 'Have they appeared before?'

'Once,' I admit. It was after a disastrous shoplifting expedition in Westgate Road when I robbed a dead expensive biker jacket with a quilted purple satin lining. The dye stained my hands bright blue that time, although I don't mention the fact to Enda. 'It fades after a few days. It's just a . . . an *allegory*,' I assure her, hoping she'll believe I'm suffering an adverse reaction to shellfish or something.

'It's a miracle, is what it is,' says Enda, crossing herself again.

The stains seem to impress her, for some reason. This is cooler than cool. She says I'm to be excused cleaning duties which means I can loll around like Lady Muck for the rest of the day. Problem is that it's boring as fuck as there's no telly or magazines to keep me occupied. Enda says she'll have to do the rounds to show willing, make sure her staff aren't malingering. She makes me promise not to leave her 'quarters', as she calls the storeroom and kitchenette, until she returns for her break, advising me to sit in quiet contemplation and not to scoff all the biscuits.

After she's scurried out armed with spray and dusters, I spend a bit of time rummaging through the supplies cupboard. There's nothing worth nicking, and the solvents give just the merest hint of a buzz even though I sniff until my nostrils implode and my septum nearly disintegrates.

To kill time I practise my burp-speak technique, an exceptional talent which has been neglected recently, involving sucking air into my throat and belching out a word. I used to be able to belch *hipp-o-pot-a-mus* no problem but the best I can manage now is *ba-da-bing* which is pathetic. If only I had some Red Bull to guzzle, or Pepsi Max at a pinch, to lubricate my larynx and swizzle up my stomach gases, but there's bott-all to drink here. Face it, milky Mellow Bird's isn't exactly top choice for stimulating belches. Oh, Jesus King of the

Jews, I'm bored-bored-bored to buggery. So bored, in fact, that I wash, dry and side the coffee mugs and clear the biscuit crumbs off the table, even wiping it down with a damp J-cloth, *and* rinsing it out. For me, this is almost unknown territory. I'm not a Teenage Housewife, baby.

After all that stultifying, brain-sapping activity, I must have dozed off, because the next thing I'm aware of is a chorus of whispers, hissing and shushing, in echoey stereo. My eyes blink awake. Omigawd, they've got me surrounded! Which 'they' isn't immediately clear; it could be the CIA, the O'Mafia, or the cops about to arrest me on that shoplifting rap.

'Ssshhh, don't spook her.' It's Enda's voice. I swivel my eyeballs to left and right. The 'they' surrounding me is a bunch of women, eight, nine of them, an army of domestics dressed in regulation uniform of green-and-white checked nylon.

'What the—?' I gasp, just preventing myself from uttering a profanity.

'You've no call to be alarmed, Rowena,' Enda assures me, flapping her hands to shoo my audience away. 'Stand back there, give the girl some air.' The women shuffle in reverse. They're all gawping at me as if I'm some strange specimen in a zoo. Just what is going on here? Maybe it's what they do to new starters, a ritual, an initiation ceremony, and there's tar and feathers to follow.

My eyes flicker round the room, scanning the women one by one. They're no beauties, and you can take *that* to the bank. I've heard of the Rose of Tralee, but these are more like rejects from the Bogwort of Ballyloony. I run my fingers through my feggy hair, aware that it must look like a manky old mop. The women stare at my hand.

'Will someone tell me what's going on here?'

The wall-eyed girl at the front jumps at the sound of my voice. The name-badge on her overall says PAULA. I can feel my blood starting to rise, my hands bunching up into fists. Maybe they're a lynch mob out to crucify heathens, or the domestic hygiene wing of the IRA armed with petrol bombs or AK47s beneath their overalls.

'They've come to witness a miracle, Rowena,' says Enda. 'Show them. Show them the stigmata.'

'Eh?' I glare at her, gobsmacked. 'The stig-*what*?'

'Jesus, Mary and Joseph, would you look at that!' Paula the wall-eyed cleaner points a finger at the table. 'There – the face of Our Lord!'

My gaze follows her finger. There's nothing to see except the old J-cloth I wiped up with. The dozy bint slumps to the floor in a faint, or more likely an epi.

'Stop!' I yell, holding out my hands in front of me. 'Stop all this.' I'm thinking they're all in on a massive wind-up, maybe some sort of performance art with me as a stooge, or I'm being filmed for a telly practical joke and a bunch of people will jump out of hidey-holes, squealing their tits off and yelling, 'Gotcha!' This seems even more likely when the women all sink to their housemaids' knees, crossing themselves and mumbling in unison. I want to punch their friggin' lights out, honest. 'Enda,' I plead. 'Make them stop.'

But Enda's down there on the cork-tiled floor, hands clasped, eyes pointing heavenwards. She makes the sign of the cross, creaks to an upright position and speaks to the women.

'Show's over. We've all seen enough to know what's what. There's work to be done.' One by one the cleaners file towards the door, each bobbing a kind of curtsey as they walk past me, including Paula who's surfaced from unconsciousness and goggles at me as if I'm a ghost.

Well, thank fuck that's the initiation ceremony out of the way.

I want to ask Enda about the cloth, but all the kerfuffle has worn Enda out. 'I need to rest my eyes for a while,' she says, stretching out her loggy legs. 'To recharge my spiritual batteries.' Yeah, right, baldy old sloth. Within seconds she's snoring away in the chair, her mouth hanging open like a deceased person's. I study her teeth.

There's no order to them. They look as though they've been hurled into her gob from a distance, like darts at a dartboard, landing wherever they will at impossible angles.

While she takes a nap, I grab the local paper in a vain effort to find a scrap of news. Nothing, apart from a short piece about some fiddler's forthcoming CD and the theft of some horse drugs from a vet's office. Even the horoscopes are boring, no windfalls, house moves or new love interest in sight.

An hour or so later she rouses from her after-lunch snooze, yawns, stretches and scratches her pinky scalp.

'I must have nodded off there, I'm disoriented. What's that you're reading?'

'Stars,' I say.

'Read Capricorn out for me,' she says. Huh, I might have guessed she'd be a goat.

'A new acquaintance will walk into your life. It says to treat me, her, I mean him, whatever, with utmost respect and generosity. Oh, and beware of a foreigner who will play fast and loose with your affections.' I add the last bit to make it sound exotic. Enda could do with some excitement in her life.

'Hmm,' she muses. 'It's rubbish again. What sign are you?'

'Pisces,' I reply.

'Go on then, let's hear what's in store for you. Hang on, Pisces, you say? We're in that part of the zodiac now. What date?'

'March nineteenth,' I say. It depresses me to think that I probably won't get any presents this year.

'The nineteenth of March?' she repeats. 'Holy Mary Mother of God, that's the date of . . .' She crosses herself and gazes at the ceiling.

'Oh, yeah, that bison thing,' I say. 'I knew the date meant something, but I couldn't remember what. My mind must have gone out of sync when I came to Ireland.'

Enda looks as if she's about to faint. 'That bison thing,' she says.

136

'Jesus Mary and Joseph, God forgive me. The nineteenth, that's our blessed saint's day. And it's your birthday too?'

'No big deal. I'm not expecting a present from you, Enda. Not an expensive one, anyway.'

She snatches the newspaper and wafts it in front of her face. 'I need a brew,' she says. I heave a massive sigh, but it's no good, the sarcasm's lost on her. 'Make it strong and put three sugars in mine, I need it for the shock.'

'What shock?' I ask. 'Been having a nightmare – *day*mare – or something?' My voice is supposed to sound full of genuine concern, but it comes out like a statement at an industrial tribunal: *I discovered the accused asleep, nay comatose, on the job, m'Lud.*

Enda's unfazed. 'Why, the shock of waking up and finding there's still an hour of work to struggle through,' she says, deadpan, as if she had any intention of lifting a finger. 'I'd like to meet the feckin' eejit who said a life of toil was good for the soul.' I can't tell if she's serious or not but I'm thinking that's rich, I've never met such a lazy-arsed cow, apart from myself, which goes without saying.

'Here's your tea. Sorry, Enda, but I overfilled the pot, water's spilt all over. Where's that J-cloth?'

She throws up her hands. 'J-cloth, she calls it! You're speaking of a holy relic,' she protests. 'It must be kept as evidence. I put it away for safety in that box, the one with the picture of St Francis on his ass. Hand it to me.'

I follow the direction of her pointing finger to the top shelf where a biscuit tin rests on a stack of sheets. On the lid is a painting of some old gadge sitting astride a donkey with sticky-out ribs and a pot belly, a classic case of worms. The donkey's way too small for him. That's cruelty, that is, the bloke's feet are nearly touching the ground and the poor beast looks as if it's on its way to the knacker's yard. And Enda reckons the man's a saint! Placing the biscuit tin on the table, I pour a cup of strong, sweet tea for my so-called boss. She eases the lid off the sacred container to reveal the sad, soggy J-cloth, a pink and white stripey affair, like an outsized angel fish in its final death throes. Then she makes the sign of the cross with her fingers.

'Why was Paula going on about the face of Our Lord?' I ask. 'Is she a bit . . .?' I circle my index finger next to my temple to indicate 'remedial' as I'm not sure if they do political correctness in Ireland, or if it's OK to be offensive.

'Look for yourself, Rowena. Surely you can see the likeness?' Enda turns the open tin towards me. All I see is a manky old rag crawling with germs, one that should have been binned or buried yonks ago.

I twist my head and view the J-cloth from different angles. 'It don't look like diddly squat,' I say. Am I the only person who can't see it? 'It's stupid, like that time the Virgin Mary's face appeared in my banana split.'

Enda jerks upright in her seat, suddenly alert. 'This has happened before? Tell me, girl, this is important.'

'Just the once, in my friend's room. I swished up my pudding and Texy reckoned she could see a face in the leftovers. It's mad, there was nothing there, honest, Enda. Just ice cream, Dream Topping, bits of chocolate and a cherry, that's all.'

'He works in mysterious ways.' Enda blows on her tea to cool it, takes a slurp and screws up her face, like the drink's poisoned or something. 'Dishcloths, ice cream, they're all the same to Him, instruments to get His message across. You, my girl, have come here for a reason, otherwise why would you turn up for our blessed saint's anniversary? Your very own birthday? Eh? Eh?' She nods rapidly to underline the point. 'Any garibaldis in the cupboard?'

This is pure time-wasting bollocks. I didn't come all this way to serve tea and biscuits like some kind of kitchen monkey. Focus, focus. Don't let the superstitious old bat's religious notions get in the way.

'Enda, I'm not making fun of you or your beliefs, but you've got it all wrong. I came to Ireland to find my father . . .'

The daft bat looks up at the ceiling and crosses herself again. I wish she'd pack it in.

'. . . and it was pure coincidence that I ended up here.'

'No such thing as coincidence,' she declares, like she's stating a scientific fact.

'I thought I was running out of money; I needed to earn some quickly so I applied here for a job. That's the top and bottom of it.'

Enda relaxes in her chair, resting her feet on the stool. It's a wonder her circulation doesn't stop from lack of exercise.

'You could have got a job anywhere. The cake shop, the dry cleaner's, McDonald's – they're always on the lookout. You were guided here by the Lord, I'll never believe different. You've found your father, Rowena, or rather he's found you.'

It's pointless talking to her. She's made up her mind that I've been sent to the nunvent on some kind of mission and nothing I say will convince her otherwise.

Then a really, really strange thing happens.

'Our Father, who art in Dublin, Lonnie be thy name.'

These are the words that I hear coming out of my mouth. Complete gibberish. What's wrong with me? It must be because I'm surrounded by goddies, greybacks, all these religious crackpots in the nunvent. Fortunately, Enda's too busy munching biscuits to notice.

'They've gone soft,' she complains, referring to the garibaldis, but it doesn't stop her scoffing the lot. She wipes the crumbs off her chin. This is beyond drudgery, but to humour Enda and keep her on track I rinse the cups in the sink, shake the water off them and replace them on the shelf.

'Can we go home now?'

There's a dragging ache in my belly that suggests the onset of a monthly condition. Triffic.

'Away, then. The Lord won't mind if I nick off a bit early with you.' Enda grabs her coat and runs up the stairs like an athlete. She can't half motor for an old 'un.

'Bobbo was asking after you again today,' says Texy. 'I thought you might have popped your head in at lunchtime to say hello to him.'

'Been plenty busy,' I lie. 'Enda the housekeeper – my line manager – she's a total slave-driver. I've been on the go non-stop, do this, fetch that, and she's going to train me how to supervise the other girls so I'll be working in a managerial capacity, kind of.'

'What's the point? You'll be out of there in a couple of weeks.'

'But they don't know that. It's quite flattering that they think I'm boss material.' I can't bring myself to tell her that my day consisted of brewing coffee, serving biscuits, washing up and fending off religious maniacs.

'Enough about work already. It's Friday, let-yourself-go night, and you've got a date. In fact, we both have a date.' I raise my eyebrows in a question. 'Joe and Matty, they'll both be in the bar this evening, so paint a smile on that twisted face and prepare to get lamming drunk.'

My stomach tightens and a part of me turns melty at the thought of seeing Joe again.

I'm beginning to see why Texy is hung up on Matty. Not that I could ever fancy him, mind, not in *this* lifetime. He's too obvious, too in your face, plus he has a mucky, though infectious, laugh. Me, I prefer subtlety in a bloke rather than someone whose eyes latch on to the nearest pair of breasts like a teat-seeking missile. There's also the business of Matty's unfortunate hairdo. Whoever cut it should be retrained or forced to mow lawns for a living, just to keep up with the latest styles. But like Texy says, hair is fixable; it's what's inside that counts, and Matty has a generous nature.

Joe, now, he's a completely different kettle of flesh. I mean *fish*.

There's a sense of restraint about him, a feeling that he keeps a part of himself in reserve. He's not the type to spill his guts until he's good and ready, until he knows and trusts someone. He'd be a brilliant torture victim. Not even wild whores could drag information out of Joe, not even if they clamped electrodes on his nipples or trimmed his toenails with a chainsaw. I admire that in a man.

Ironically, his holding back is precisely the quality that makes me want to do the opposite, to tell all, throw caution to the winds, yodel from the mountain tops about my train-wreck of a life. That must be the reason why I blurted out my history of crazydom, life as it is lived in the World of Maddage. It would have scared off a lesser person than Joe.

It also explains how I come to be telling him right this minute about my Dadsearch, my quest for a man whose existence doesn't even amount to a memory, or at least not a reliable one.

'I guess Dad got some things wrong just like anyone else, but to me he was a hero. It sounds weird, Joe, but I don't want anything to spoil my image of him, which is why there's a part of me that's frightened to find him.' These are the personal, private words coming out of my mouth, confiding my innermost thoughts to someone I never knew existed until a couple of days ago.

Joe turns to face me on the seat, his mismatched eyes melting into mine.

'It doesn't sound weird at all. Just a normal human reaction,' he says. Then, completely out of the blue, he goes, 'Do you like poetry?'

My face flushes with embarrassment. Actually I can't stand it but admitting that would shut down the conversation.

'Erm, some of it's OK,' I reply, praying that he won't ask me to quote my favourite. *There was a young girl from Beirut* . . . Uh-oh, better steer clear of that one. 'Why are you asking me?'

'What you said about your dad reminded me of something the American poet, Anne Sexton, wrote.'

'Oh,' I say, raising my eyebrows and trying to look intelligent.

Joe smiles. He isn't fooled by my phoney facial expression.

'Go on then,' I encourage him. 'Tell us, if you can remember.'

'She said, "It doesn't matter who my father was; it matters who I remember he was." They're such wise words.' He looks down at his knees, as if he wishes he hadn't said it.

'Joe, that's brilliant,' I gush. 'So it doesn't matter if my dad was like, say, Hannibal Lecter, as long as I remember the times he was kind to me, like when he bought me a PlayStation for Christmas?'

'Sort of along those lines,' says Joe. See, I'm not a complete ignoramus!

Next thing, I'm telling Joe all the business about Dad being photographed with Moral Enright and how Texy suggested we might dig something up on him off the Internet.

'Yup, that could work,' says Joe. 'Why don't you drop by the café in the morning and we'll give it a go? What have you got to lose?'

I'm stumped for an answer.

'Sure,' I reply eventually. 'I'd love to, Joe.'

What *have* I got to lose?

Amazingly, even though I'm not drunk, there's a hangover starting to kick off in my head.

'Fetch us a drink, man,' I say to Texy when we reach our room. 'I gotta take some painkillers. My skull feels as though it's in a vice.'

Texy is a wee bit mashed, judging from the way she pulls off her bra via the sleeves of her shirt and twirls it above her head like a stripper. I scrabble in my bag for some headache tablets and feel something strange inside. Pulling it out, I discover it's the candle holder that Eminem pressed on me as a gift.

As a joke, Texy fills a toothmug with wine so that when I dissolve the Solpadeines the fizz spills over the rim and dribbles down the sides.

'My cup runneth over,' I giggle, wiping my chin on a pillow. Then
– and I know it's a daft idea – I say, half-laughing, half-serious,
'Have you ever said a prayer, Texy?'

She snorts. 'Too bloody many. Prayed my little heart out when I
was a kid. Dashed them off for the sick, the sad, the starving, you
name it.'

'Does it work or does it piss God off?'

She raises her eyebrows at me. 'Who knows? I guess it's like
sending out a bunch of begging letters or playing the Lotto. Now
and again one comes good but you shouldn't get your hopes up.
You can't bank on them being answered, though some people seem
to think they can. Why do you ask?' She hunches up her shoulders,
as though she's dreading my answer.

'Just wondering. It must have tipped me over the edge, hanging
around with those goddy people up the nunvent. One of the nuns
gave me a present with all the words on. Texy, could we give it a go?
Would you help me say it?'

She makes a spluttering noise. 'What?'

'A prayer,' I repeat. 'To St Jude. Look.' I dangle the candle holder
in front of her.

'Are you crazy?'

'I thought you believed in that stuff. You're a Catlick, aren't you?'

'Lapsed,' she says. 'I don't know what I believe, if anything. I
sometimes think the church is there just to keep people in line by
brainwashing them, like the Moonies only with stricter rules and
more cred, and minus the communal weddings. Sorry, God,' she
adds, crossing herself.

'But saying a prayer, it can't do any harm,' I reason. 'It's not like
dabbling with a Ouija board, unleashing demons, bringing down
the forces of evil. It's more sending a wish out into the ether, only to
a named person: St Jude. Go on, Tex, let's do it.'

'You're mental,' she says.

'Well spotted.'

She relents, laughing. 'Oh, all right then, Miss Strange. But don't get mad if I have a fit of the giggles.'

The candle holder has three sides made of see-through stuff. On two of them there's a picture of a Robert De Niro lookeelikee – maybe it *is* him when he wasn't so raddled – clutching some kind of plate with Jesus's face painted on it. It reminds me of those overpriced, limited-edition commemorative plaques that you see in magazine adverts, marking the last-but-one living snow leopard, or a zillion years of Peter Rabbit, whatever. On the third panel is painted the words of the Prayer to St Jude.

Saint Jude, glorious Apostle, faithful servant and friend of Jesus, I read, *the name of the traitor has caused you to be forgotten by many, but the true Church invokes you universally as the Patron of things despaired of.*

Oh, God. Some of the words are long and unfamiliar and I'm not sure how to pronounce them so I open and close my lips in silence, beh-beh-beh-ing like a goldfish.

Pray for me, who am so miserable; pray for me, that finally I may receive the consolations and the succour of Heaven in all my necessities, tribulations and sufferings.

Bloody hell, talk about moany stuff. St Jude must be clinically depressed if this is what he listens to all the time.

Particularly (here make your request) and that I may bless God with the Elect throughout Eternity. Amen. St Jude, Apostle, martyr and relative of our Lord Jesus Christ, of Mary and of Joseph, intercede for us.

It's gobbledegook. The words are long and hard to pronounce, plus I was raised a heathen. Still, the thought's sincere so St Jude will have to make allowances for it all being a bit DIY.

'Can't find a candle so we'll have to use this.' Texy plonks an object on the table. It's a kiddie's night light from the bedside cabinet, battery-operated, one that emits a dim pink glow so that bairns won't be totally spooked if they wake up unexpectedly. Also it's in the shape of a toadstool house with an open front door and paintings of elves and pixies cavorting around inside. Inappropriate, but it's better than nowt.

'Kneel, you have to kneel,' I instruct Texy after she's switched off the main light.

'Puh-leeze,' she says with a cod-exasperated sigh, but she sinks to her knees.

'Ready?' I don't want her dashing off for a wazz in the middle of the proceedings.

'Yeah, yeah, yeah, I'm ready,' she says, clasping her hands and screwing her eyes up tight in a parody of prayer.

'No laughing, right?' I can see she thinks it's some big joke but I need to concentrate, stay on track. 'Right?' I repeat.

'Right,' she says, mock-serious.

I lace my fingers together and stare into the glowing toadstool, trying to drum up inspiration for some suitable prayer words.

'Dear St Jude,' I intone. 'It's Rowena here, asking for your help, what with you being the Satron Paint – I mean *Patron Saint* – of Lost Causes and that. We, that's Rowena Vincent and Texy Maguire, find ourselves wading in deep, deep guano.'

Texy stifles a splutter. Ignoring her, I continue.

'First off, Bobbo Maguire, that's Texy's granddaddy, he's a cause lost inside his own head. He lives up the care home for knackered old men. If you could look in on him now and again to make sure he's eating enough and not being a pest, we'd really appreciate it.'

'Is that it?' whispers Texy, fidgeting.

'I ain't started yet,' I reply.

Repositioning my knees, I address myself again to St Jude.

'Secondly, another family-type request. See, the reason I came to Ireland – God might have mentioned this to you – is because I'm trying to find my own dad. His name's Lonnie Vincent and I haven't seen him since I was thirteen. It's iffy, this one, because I don't even know if he's in this country, but I'm going to look him up on the Internet and I wondered if you could put a trace on him through

145

your own sources, Interpol and stuff. I'd be externally grateful if you could do this for me, St Jude.'

'Hurry it up, my knees have gone to sleep,' hisses Texy.

'Shut it, I'm nearly done,' I tell her.

'And finally, St Jude, if this doesn't sound too selfish, would you bless me and make the zits on my forehead go away. Cheers. Yours, er, faithfully, like, Rowena.'

Texy sucks her teeth. 'I don't believe you just said that stuff about your spots.'

'Why not? I thought I maison well ask while I had the guy online. Nowt to lose, have I? Come on, put the kiddywinkies' night light out and let's hit the sack.'

A grin big enough to cover three counties spreads across Texy's face.

'You kill me,' she says.

24

The Mouse Drop-in

Dragging myself into the land of wakefulness, I remember with a start that it's Saturday, and I'm meeting Joe this morning. Gorgeous, wise, cute-assed Joe. For the first time I'll see him on his home ground, the Internet café. The Mouse Drop-in. Is that some kind of joke about rodent poo? Out of bed, girl. A bunch of stuff to do.

Shower and moisturize body. Shampoo and condition hair. Cleanse, tone and nourish skin. The whole caboodle. After all the scrubbing and creaming, the mirror reveals a pinkish, glistening, half-formed thing, like a foetus or an axolotl. This is the naked, unrecognizable, stripped-down-to-basics Rowena, barely made, rarely displayed.

Minus make-up, my face looks as if it belongs to a stranger. Unringed by liner, unclagged by mascara, uncoloured by shadow or pencil, the eyes appear wide-set and almost almond-shaped. Brushing back the damp hair, the giant brow reminds me why I always wear a fringe. A five-a-side football team could play on the vast expanse between hairline and eyebrows. *Hi, forehead*, I mouth silently, smoothing the ingrained frown lines with my fingertips. Then it comes to me in a flash: I look like an extraterrestrial. A grey. An alien creature fresh from a Roswell autopsy table.

The public Rowena emerges as I apply the cosmetic mask, building up layers of skin with concealer and foundation, humanizing and shaping the eyes with shades of Purple Rain and Sooty Black, staining the lips Blueberry Pie, until my features resemble a trio of bruises set in alabaster.

Brilliant. Exactly the look I was aiming for.

Hair is more of a problem as it's shiny and slippy from

shampooing. I don't get this thing about swishy, tossy hair; it's a nightmare. Of course it should be clean so it doesn't get a build-up of dickies or ticks, but then it takes three days of backcombing and industrial-strength hairspray to make it manageable. Shampoo is bad for hair anyway as it robs it of natural oils and whatever. Once I read about this woman who never washed her hair at all, even though it was so long she could nearly sit on it, and she reckoned it cleaned itself somehow; I forget the science bit. The longest I went without washing my hair was twenty-two days, until Mum threatened to call the social services and have me taken into care, just when it was getting over that lank phase. Anyways, I attack it with sculpting mousse and firm-hold gel, backbrushing it until I look like a shit-scared cartoon moggy, then scrunch it up into a skull clip and spray until my scalp squeals, then spray some more until the follicles die and the hairs get rigor mortis.

There remains the problem of what to wear for a visit to Joe and the Internet café. Just what is the dress code? Geeky vest, shorts and knackered but vee expensive trainers like the baby boys who work for Microsoft? Maybe I could hire a Lara Croft outfit from a fancy dress shop to show I'm entering into the spirit of things? Hell, I dunno. In the end I plump for my jeans and a torn black cotton and lace designer top that I ripped off from TK Maxx, accessorized with leather jacket and boots for a kind of neo-Goth-bikerchick look. Why oh why did I never get round to having my belly button pierced? I'm such a wuss.

It's past two o'clock when I leave The Flues so already I'm majorly late for my morning coffee assignation with Joe. The Internet café isn't easy to spot. I walk past it twice thinking it's a launderette before I figure it out.

Beep-barp. A two-tone buzzer sounds as I open the door and again as it closes, a harsh, ear-grating noise that would drive me mad as a bus. Inside there's a window seat and three small tables with chairs. Further along are two benches, each with three computers and operators' chairs. On the right is a food counter displaying cake slices, wrapped half-baguettes and sandwiches, plus crisps and chocolate bars. A half-full jug of filter coffee stews on a heated stand. There is no sign of customers. At the far end is a door bearing a PRIVATE sign.

Where is Joe?

I wander down the aisle with the computers and perch on a chair. The screensaver shows the words *The Mouse Drop-in*. A picture of a cup of coffee slides in from screen left. A layer of froth appears, growing bigger and higher until it explodes *splat!* and the bits reform into the words *@last!* Mildly amusing the first time, but after five minutes it's starting to do my head in.

Where is Joe?

It's crazy, anyone could walk in and smash up the computers with a baseball bat or help themselves to a free coffee or rob money out of the till. No, Rowena, don't even think about it! This computer kit is expensive, they must have security cameras or surveillance equipment or – *gulp!* – more likely a webcam. I glance around casually, trying not to appear furtive, scanning the walls and ceiling for a hidden camera lens, straining my ears for a whirr or click. It's strange how your instinctive actions begin to feel unfamiliar under the glare of an invisible electronic eye. Breathing, for example. In, out. In, out. Simple, until you fear that your every gesture, each tiny word in the vocabulary of your body language, literally every breath you take, is being captured on camera, monitored, scrutinized, evaluated. Get a grip, woman. Repeat this mantra: *I am not paranoid. I am not . . .*

'Rowena, how're ya?'

I jump in startlement as Joe appears through the PRIVATE door.

'Hey, Joe. I was just . . .' Why do I feel guilty when I've done nothing wrong? Force of habit, probably. Years of practice. 'Just wondering where you'd got to. Sorry I'm late.'

'No problem, you're here now. Fancy a coffee or a bite to eat before we trawl the search engines for that dad of yours?'

My underarms feel clammy at the thought. I say I'll have a Sprite and some plain crisps. Joe cracks open a can of Fanta for himself and I watch his Adam's apple bob up and down as he swallows it.

He sits down at a computer. 'Pull up a chair and we'll go surfing,' he says. 'Do you know how to use the Web?'

I shake my head no. Once or twice I've used it but it's better to pretend I'm an absolute beginner in case I do something really dumb. Why oh why did I choose to eat a packet of crisps? It's impossible to munch them without making a racket or getting them stuck round my mouth so I pop them in daintily, one at a time, and suck them until they're salt-free and soggy.

'This is one of the best search engines,' he says, clicking the mouse. 'Remind me what your dad's name is.'

'Lonnie Vincent,' I say. My voice comes out a bit croaky due to the damp crisps sticking to the roof of my mouth.

Joe types the name in a box. Words fill the screen. 'Bingo!'

I nearly choke. 'What – you've found him?'

He runs his eye across the page. 'I've found *a* Lonnie Vincent. Bass player with the Bulletboys, a heavy metal band from LA. Could that be the one, do you think?'

My eyes water with nerves. 'Is there a photo of him?'

The mouse scampers across the mat. Joe clicks, then a picture scrolls down the screen. It's a tall, skinny bloke with blond hair halfway down his back. He's sporting leather trousers and a bare torso with well-defined six-pack. My dad, bleached, ripped and leathered up. The legendary Lonnie Vincent, King of Thrash!

Joe reads some more. 'Hang on, that won't be him. The Bulletboys were going strong in the Eighties, before you were born.'

'Oh.' That's all I can muster. Just, 'Oh.' My brain can't decide whether to be gutted or relieved. On to Plan B. 'Would you try Moral Enright?'

The search engine home page flickers on the screen. 'How do you spell Moral?'

'Like *im*moral, I think. As in *im*moral earnings.'

Joe grins to himself, types in the name. He scratches his head at the result. 'Nada. Nix. I'll use another search engine. Nope, no joy. Let me try different spellings.' I watch as he types *Morel, Morrel, Morell, Morrell, Moral N. Wright*, blah di blah, without success.

'He's a stand-up comedian, big on the college circuit,' I point out, recalling what the barman Cathal told Texy.

'That ought to help.' Joe's mad-pianist fingers race across the keyboard and the mouse clicks like castanets. 'Eureka!' he yells. 'Looks like we've nailed yer man.'

I stand up, peering at the screen over his shoulder. Joe's gorgeous choppy hair smells of exotic fruit, possibly watermelon.

Karma Comedian – **Moral** Adair

The wag of Waterford, **Moral** Adair, tells about life on the road, the pressures of celebrity and his spell in 'showbiz rehab'. The night Moral Adair cracked up in spectacular fashion ... formerly of comedy duo Adair and **Enright** ...
www.komix.com/madair.htm – 14k – <u>Cached</u> – <u>Similar pages</u>

'Gotcha,' says Joe. 'Now we're on to something, Rowena. His name wasn't Moral Enright after all. It was Moral Adair. His stage partner was called Enright, so it's an easy mistake. Here, I'll run off the web page for you to read.' One click of the mouse, then a sheet of paper shooshes out of the printer.

Karma Comedian

Moral Adair on losing control

The wag of Waterford, Moral Adair, tells about life on the road, the pressures of celebrity and his spell in 'showbiz rehab'.

The night Moral Adair cracked up in spectacular fashion in front of a rowdy student audience is not one he cares to remember. Or is ever likely to forget.

'I'd had the shakes all day. It didn't bother me, it was only Cork, who gives a toss? In any case, I'd never go on stage alone.' He mimics downing a glass of Bushmills, his favourite tipple. 'Standing in the wings, waiting to be announced, I was sweating like a roasting boar. Stage fright. First time I'd ever had the jitters, I always was a cocky bastard.'

When the MC called his name, Adair's legs buckled. He managed to stumble on to the stage. 'To be honest, I thought I was having a heart attack or a stroke. It wouldn't have surprised anyone – I'd been living the rock 'n' roll lifestyle bigtime for years. The reincarnation of Elvis, my manager used to joke, but without the corset. Or the talent. So here's me staggering around like a stunned bullock, and the crowd just laughed their todgers off – maybe out of relief that I'd got some new material at last.'

That gig was a turning point for Adair, formerly of comedy duo Adair and Enright. 'I lost it – lost everything – including control of my bladder. My career vanished down the drain right in front of me.'

And so it goes on, the sad self-pitying tale of a washed-up comic, brought down by booze and narcotics; a litany of lame jokes, like the one about how he fell from Grace, with a punchline you could see coming a mile off. And his spell in 'showbiz rehab'? A retreat in a monastery where he rediscovered his faith and vowed to pack in hoovering coke up his hooter. 'Life is about give and take,' ran one of his more profound statements. He reckoned he'd been take-take-taking and it was now time to give something back to the people who'd supported him and the friends and family he'd let down. Yeah, right.

'What a loser,' I say, almost embarrassed to think that Dad had stood next to him for a photo. 'I wonder what happened to him.'

'Hang on, I've found some more stuff. Funny how it helps to have the right name.' Joe points and clicks. The printer churns out paper. 'Look, there's a picture of him here, in some online newsletter.'

Under the heading 'Moral Inspiration' is a jpeg of our not-so-funnyman accepting a framed certificate from some wifey in a tent dress. She's gazing adoringly at him as if he's the Second Coming. Moral Adair, slimmer, darker of hair, less obviously tanned, smiles his unmistakable smile directly to the camera, his glittering teeth displayed to perfection. The smile begins and ends at his mouth. It doesn't come within twinkling distance of his eyes, which have a dull, corpse-like quality and an expression that translates as *Get me outta here*. I read the caption:

FORMER COMEDIAN MORAL ADAIR IS NAMED INSPIRATIONAL ROLE MODEL BY FCD PATRON, MRS D. HORAN.

The piece appears in the newsletter of Freedom from Chemical Dependence. FCD, short for FuCkeD. It's dated four months ago.

'Mr Moral Adair attends the Junkie Oscars,' smirks Joe. 'Top dog in the drugs rehab world – what an accolade.'

'The woman looks pretty spacey,' I comment. 'Maybe she's a reformed druggy too, plus she fancies the pants off Moral, anyone can see that.'

'You're such a sceptic,' smiles Joe. 'What it means is that it shouldn't be too hard to contact Mr Immoral Adair. We could track him down through the FCD, say we're reporters doing a motivational, kick-the-habit article or something.'

Pins and needles prick my scalp at the realization that I'm another step nearer to finding Dad. My eyes meet Joe's mismatched ones. I have an urge to hug him, but I resist.

Beep-barp. Enter two scruffy lads with lank, badly cut hair. They strut towards the counter doing that stupid Manchester roll walk. Oasis fans, eurgh. Joe taps their names into his computer and shows them which ones to log on to. I bet they're browsing sites about vampires or recreational drugs, when they'd be better off checking out cures for chronic acne.

'Fancy another drink?' Joe offers me a can but I shake my head and say I'll just have tap water. My nerves are getting to me and I'm scared that fizzy pop will bring on an attack of burps. The two lads snort and snigger like wee piggies as they click between sites. Half an hour passes. I can feel my dander rising.

Joe picks up on my darkening mood. 'Time, lads,' he says, checking his watch.

'Aww,' moans the spottier one. 'It's only five o'clock. You're not supposed to close until six.'

'I've had a sudden death in the family,' says Joe, straight-faced. 'Got to shut up shop early, get to the wake. Sorry, boys.'

They mutter and grumble between themselves, but pay up in a good-natured way before shoulder-shrugging their way out. Joe locks and bolts the door behind them.

Gathering the printoffs, I say, 'I'd better get going then.'

'Why, have you got something on?' Joe cocks his head at an angle, emphasizing his cuteness.

I feel awkward. 'No, but ... you have stuff to do. The family bereavement.'

He chucks me under the chin, laughing. 'You didn't believe that? I just said it to get rid of the two short planks so I could lock up.'

'What? Joe, you rotten thing. You shouldn't lie about death in the family, it opens the door to bad luck.'

He shrugs. 'Like I'd notice a bit more misfortune. I was going to invite you to my place for a cup of tea, if that doesn't sound lame.'

A hot glow spreads up my neck and on to my cheeks. Triffic. Now he'll think I've come down with scarlet fever.

'It sounds as cheesy as a Dairylea triangle, but I'll let you off this once. Let's go,' I say, edging towards the front door.

'Not that way,' says Joe. 'I live above the shop, it lowers the insurance premium. Watch out for the step.'

He shows me through the door marked PRIVATE and locks it behind him, then takes me by the hand up an uncarpeted flight of stairs. Showers of stars sparkle and fizz inside me.

'Welcome to my humble penthouse,' he says, unlocking another door and flattening himself against the wall to let me through.

I feel intoxicated by the sight, the sound, merely the idea of him, and when I squeeze past his lush body through the narrow doorway, I'm approaching meltdown.

Mind yourself, girl. Get a grip.

25

Ninja the Cringer

Joe's room is a mishmash of guess-the-decade styles and colours. There's a two-seater sofa in maroon with cream-coloured stripes, a leather recliner, a couple of beanbags, and one of those naff mosaic-topped tables. I think it's called Shabby Chic, meaning charity shop chuckouts, rubbish that's unsold at the end of car boot sales, Seventies time-warp stuff. Shite, in other words. The whole lot should be in a museum, or a skip. In contrast, there's a hi-fi system with massive zillion-decibel speakers that perforate eardrums at a hundred paces, plus a wide-screen TV with a video and DVD player.

My tongue knots itself in a double sheepshank. I'm inside Joe's abode, the place where he sleeps, washes himself, eats, chills, breathes the very same air that's in my lungs now.

'I love your flat, Joe, it's so ... *different*,' I say, in a passable imitation of a moron.

'No need for diplomacy, you're among friends,' smiles Joe. 'Find a CD while I put the kettle on.'

'Can I use the –?' See, I'm so wound up I can't form a sentence, can't decide whether to say loo, toilet, bog, lavvy.

Joe points. 'Through there, hang a right, second door on the left. Mind the gap.' As soon as the words are out of his mouth, I've forgotten them. Fumbling my way along the gloomy hall, I find the second door. I wave my hand around in the dim nothingness and touch a piece of cord with a plastic ball at the end. I tug it and lo! We have lift-off, we have a light-on situation, the genuine bright stuff issuing from a globe on the ceiling. Glancing at my feet, I realize I'm about to step in a hole where a row of floorboards has been removed. The gap that Joe warned me to mind. It's a nest of vipers down there, cables snaking through the void, looking dangerously electric. Skirting around it, I close the door behind me, pull my knickies to my knees and sit down on the loo, aiming my tinkle down the side of the pan so as not to be overheard.

A movement in the corner of my vision makes me clench my pelvic floor muscles, shutting off the trickle. Something stirs in the bathtub. At first it looks like a heap of clothes dumped there for washing. As my eyes refocus in the light, I realize it's a living, breathing entity. A crumpled, curled-up shambles of a thing, a creature covered in coarse ginger hair, like a giant rat that's crawled in off the streets.

It's a dog. An animal unlike any I've ever seen, including ones made in special effects studios for horror films. A plug-ugly Muppet of a dog, a skulking beast rejected from Sesame Street, the kind of dog that would make Rolf Harris recoil in revulsion if it turned up on *Animal Hospital*. The hound shoots me a wary glance, cowering, trembling, trying to disappear down the plughole. Oh, triffic. A dog with self-esteem issues. When I flush the bog, the beast's body shakes violently, as if there's a pounding jackhammer up his bum.

'It's OK, I won't hurt you,' I say in a friendly but firm dog-whispering tone. I offer him my hand to sniff but he turns away, trying to make himself invisible by ignoring me and hiding his head behind the taps. 'Screw you, then,' I tell him, as it's clearly a waste of time trying to gain the confidence of a clinically depressed canine.

Joe, gorgeous cute-ass Joe, is lounging on a beanbag. I fight the urge to launch myself over there and cuddle him unto death. Fortunately he doesn't seem to notice the hormones flashing off me like a hyperactive sparkler.

'Fancy some toast, Rowena? I'm making some for meself.'

'Thanks, I could murder some,' I say, following him through to the kitchen, trying to stop my eyes lasering into his bum.

Joe pushes a light switch. A fluorescent tube buzzes then

crackles into action, flickering enough to set off a seizure. He pops a couple of bread slices into the toaster. 'Rare, medium or charcoal?' he says.

'Medium.' I tear my gaze away from his butt muscles and study the kitchen. It's on the poky side but big enough for a Formica-topped table and two chairs with spindly legs. There's a tiny cooker, sparkling clean, meaning it's hardly ever used, plus a basic microwave oven, an ancient twin-tub washing machine, and a fridge sprayed red, plastered to buggery with magnets.

'You never told me you had a dog,' I say.

'So you met Ninja?' Joe laughs. 'He usually hides in the washing basket when visitors come, you're honoured.'

'What is he – you know, what make of dog?'

'He's a lurcher, technically speaking. Greyhound/Alsatian cross. But he's too timid to lurch, so I suppose you'd call him a cringer. Ninja, the Ginger Cringer. Frightened of his own shadow, just a heap of jangling nerves covered in skin and rat-fur. He's the first and last of the breed. I might as well have bought a kitten to take out rabbiting with me, for all the use he is. Jam?'

'Just butter, ta. So does he live in the bathroom?'

'Mostly. He sleeps on my bed sometimes but he crawls underneath if a breeze gets up.' Joe turns the kettle on, slides two plates of toast on to the table and sits down, stretching his legs out sideways. 'As dogs go, Ninja is doggone useless. Not a bad guard dog though, just that he warns me by trembling instead of barking.'

We munch our toast. The water boils, the kettle switches off. Joe appears not to hear, or chooses to ignore it, and the subject of tea is never mentioned again.

'Can I take a look around?' I say.

Joe nods. He leads me down the hall, pushes open a door opposite the loo and flicks on a light. It's a tiny boxroom; a vision in orange. Walls, ceiling, bed cover, everything in different tones from pale apricot to to deep burnished copper. Even the floorboards are stained a fetching shade of amber. The effect is of being crushed by a giant sunflower.

'Spare room,' he announces. 'Or guest bedroom, if you like.'

'Wow,' I say. 'This is cool, Joe. Was it your idea?'

He shifts his weight from foot to foot, almost as though he's embarrassed to be outed as an interior decorator. 'I guess,' he admits. 'Bloke in the DIY shop next door had some stock left over from a promotion so I used it up. It wouldn't be everyone's taste.'

'What's your bedroom like?' There, the words are out. I've no shame, me.

Joe stares at his feet. 'A bit of a kip at the moment. It needs some working on when I get the time.'

'Aaahh.' I make it sound like a disappointed sigh.

'You can see it if you like,' Joe says, 'as long as you understand it's nowhere near finished.'

'Sure, sure,' I say, nodding my head and frowning to show my grasp of the situation.

Joe's room is at the end of the corridor, through an archway decorated, if that's the word, with fake gargoyles on each side. Their bulldoggy faces remind me of something out of that movie *The Omen*. Spooky, Gothic, butt-ugly. The door is black, heavy-looking, dotted with metal studs, like the entrance to a torture chamber, or Frank N. Stein's castle. I'm half expecting Riff Raff, the scraggy-haired butler, to limp round the corner and jiggle his misshapen body in the Time Warp.

But what lies beyond the reinforced door? Lordy, what if Joe's into the S & M scene? Maybe he's luring me into a home-made death row where the flayed bodies of virgins hang on meat hooks from the ceiling, some still clinging to life, limbs twitching in agonizing pain, blood dripping from raw, gaping wounds, lashed by bullwhips, tortured by cattle prods, their few remaining brain cells swollen with regret. Regret that they'd said yes to Joe's invitation to come up for tea . . .

Jeez, what's got into me?

'You ready for this? You look as if you're in a trance.' Joe's voice sparks me into normality.

'Lead on,' I say, trying to sound light-hearted.

He turns a key in the lock and pushes the door. It opens silently, without a hint of a creak, shattering my expectations. Instinctively I duck my head and screw up my eyes to protect me against the mad fluttering and dive-bombing of a horde of bats. Again, nothing.

Joe stabs a button on a remote control. The room's shadowy interior glimmers into life, as a sunrise effect spreads along the walls, then the ceiling, alternating rainbow colours glowing, dimming, glowing again. On the opposite wall, sinuous shapes in pinks and purples brush against each other, colliding and separating, then grouping with others before dissolving into different shapes, a chaotic but beautiful ballet played out on a giant plasma screen. Ambient music reverberates inside my head, tones of undiscovered instruments synthesized in a gloriously sensual cocoon of sound. At first barely audible, the music gradually builds, simultaneously soothing and uplifting, until it surges to a throbbing climax that makes my brain vibrate inside my skull.

'Well? You like?' Joe studies my face, gauging a reaction.

I feel liquefied, blissed out by the hypnotic waves of vision and sounds undulating through my body, inside and out.

'It's . . . It's amazing, Joe, like landing in a fantasy world, galloping bareback on unicorns. Like being transported into space, seeing the planets close up, spinning on the rings of Saturn, riding on the moons of Jupiter.'

'Hey, that's enough,' laughs Joe. 'Let's not get carried away here.'

'But it's such a magical feeling, like being lifted on clouds, floating into the stratosphere, all that otherworldly stuff. I've never experienced anything like it, Joe, and I've done all kinds of drugs.'

'I don't want to prick your fantasy bubble, but it's just my personal chill-out zone, knocked together with MDF, perspex and fancy wiring. There's a way to go before it's finished but, yeah, it's coming along.'

He zaps the remote, dimming the lights and sounds, then ushers me out, closing and locking the door behind him. We return to the main room.

Dusk is closing in, the half-light transforming the mismatched furniture into weird shapes in my mind. The sofa reminds me of a stocky man wearing an overcoat, maybe part of a military uniform. He's been in an accident with a vehicle. The lighter stripes on his back are tyre marks. The impact of the crash flung him across the road, smashed legbones, tibia, fibula, inflicted minor damage to vertebrae. Head injuries are involved. He's confused, feeling nothing. Endorphins, his natural painkillers, rush through his body, temporarily numbing him. Army training, drummed into him until it became instinct, asserts itself. *Atten-shun!* This is why he struggles to get to his feet, why his back is hunched in semi-collapse. He is, in a word, fucked. Just like the sofa.

Joe flips through a stack of CDs, selects one and slaps it in the player. It's a woman with a raspy voice singing something bluesy. Maybe I should ask who she is but showing myself up as an ignoramus would be too embarrassing. I look around the room. It's like a library, books everywhere: on shelves, on the window sill, in tottering piles on the floor. Me, I've never read a book all the way through, mainly because it takes too long and life's too short. But since Joe's a fan I'm willing to feign interest, so I pick one up from the top of the nearest heap. It's dusty and I can hardly make out the title in the semi-darkness.

'Hmm.' That's my stab at sounding intelligent. 'Fifty Crates in the Garden. Is it a good story?'

'Fifty what?' Joe glances at the book, then grins. 'Not fifty crates, it's Socrates. *Socrates in the Garden.* Poetry,' he explains.

My face flares. I feel so humiliated, I could chew off my own knuckles.

'It's as dim as a bat cave in here,' says Joe. 'No wonder you couldn't see to read it.' He switches on a lamp. A reddish glow warms the room. Joe pats the second beanbag. 'Why don't you come and sit here.'

Co-ordination deserts me. In the three steps it takes to park myself next to Joe, I stub my toe on the fireplace, kick over a pile of books, lose my balance and still manage to land bumfirst on the beanbag. 'S-s-sorry,' I stammer.

'You took the scenic route, so what?' Joe makes light of my clumsiness. He truly doesn't seem to care that I'm as ladylike as a marauding elephant in a tea room. Clumpyclogs, Dad used to call me that all the time. Perhaps if he'd called me Twinkletoes I'd have turned out daintier on my feet. A heavy sigh escapes from my mouth, surprising me.

'Penny for them,' says Joe.

Another involuntary sigh. 'I was thinking about something my dad used to say. Do you think, if someone tells you a thing often enough, it comes true?'

'Such as?' says Joe.

'Doesn't matter. Ignore me, I'm talking garbage.' A hazy recollection comes to mind of some hippy-drippy TV show about how positive affirmations, if repeated endlessly, can turn you into a different and better person. Anyway, I'm not sure I'm ready to be drawn into a conversation about Dad, not until I've worked out my feelings. They're still in a jumble after finding that stuff on the Internet.

As if he's a mind-reader, Joe says, 'I'll e-mail the FCD tomorrow, ask if they can give me a contact for Moral Adair.'

I stiffen.

'Or I could do it tonight, if you'd rather,' he adds helpfully.

'*No!* No, tomorrow's soon enough. My brain feels jiggly from information overload. I need to unwind, give it a rest. Too many new thoughts make it unravel. Oh, God, does that make me sound completely insane?' I stop, wondering if I've said too much.

'In what sense?' says Joe. 'You're one of the sanest people I know.'

'You should get out more,' I smirk, but inside I get a chest-swelling feeling that means I'm flattered and pleased. Rowena M. Vincent, sane? Sure, why not? It's a novel idea, one that takes some getting used to, but compared to the old me, I'm quite ravelled in the brain department, most of the time anyway.

'What makes you think you're crazy?'

'Nothing much, I was just testing. Told you I've been through some bad times but maybe it's an age thing, hormones on the rampage, just a phase we have to go through when we're young. Then we get old, our bodies fall to bits, and we die and get eaten by worms. Life, eh?' I tut.

Joe flashes me a deadly smile. 'I used to think I was so wild, a rebel,' he says, 'but I was just a daft kid. Had me first tattoo when I was fourteen, a holy mess it was an' all. I was out of me head on cider, me mate Brendan was ripped to the tits on speed. Lord knows why I let him loose on my body, but he was training to be a butcher and I trusted him, more fool me. It's a wonder I didn't die from septicaemia.'

'What was it, the tattoo? A name, or a heart, something like that?' I'm trying hard not to squirm, imagining myself let loose on his body.

'I wish,' says Joe. He rolls up the sleeve of his T-shirt and shows me what looks like a drawing of a messy ball of string. 'Brendan said leave it to him, he'd surprise me, and he wasn't kidding. It was a – don't laugh, Rowena – it was a bull's head, with a ring through its nose, snorting fire out of its nostrils. The naffest thing you ever saw, but what can you expect from a butcher?'

I ease up his sleeve and study the tattoo again. 'You'd never know what it's supposed to be. It looks like a mistake, as if someone went wrong and tried to scribble it out.'

Joe chortles. 'That's more or less what happened. I had corrective surgery, in a manner of speaking. Blind Bob, the real tattoo artist, tried to cover it up with a Celtic knot, *et voilà*.' He lifts his elbow and inspects the thing himself. 'It turned out more fucked up than ever.'

'Why is the tattooist called Blind Bob?'

'How long have you got?' I wiggle my bum on the beanbag to indicate all the time in the world. 'It isn't that Bob's blind, exactly. OK, he won't wear glasses because he likes to look hard. But he's more *dyslexic*.'

I try not to snigger. 'Just word-blind, then.'

'A few years back this biker asked Bob for a tattoo on his chest. A soaring eagle clutching a Harley-Davidson logo. If you just glanced it looked the business, you could practically hear the wings beating. But when he did the writing, Bob missed out the L and there it was, large as life. HAREY DAVIDSON.' Joe shakes his head. 'Tsk. Bad, bad mistake. The biker went back with his mates, they scalped old Bob, chopped his hair off at the feckin' roots.'

I paste my hand over my mouth. 'They never! So what happened then? Did they tie him to a bike by his feet and drag him out of town?'

Joe grins. 'Nah, nothing heavy. They warned him if he ever did another tattoo they'd chop his fingers off, so Bob sold his needles on the Internet, went into body piercing. No need to worry about spelling, see.'

I turn this over in my mind. Sounds logical enough. 'Are you . . .' I hear myself saying. 'You're not pierced, Joe?'

He shoots me a killer smile. 'Apart from the ears, you mean? No. But I'll let you in on a secret.' I budge up closer for confidentiality. 'Matty from The Flues, he's got a Prince Albert.'

'What's a Prince Albert?'

'It's what you might call an *erotic* piercing. In his little fella, y'know what I'm saying?'

'Oh, right,' I nod, as though I have a clue. 'Joe, could I ask you something real personal?'

'Sure you can ask,' says Joe. 'Doesn't mean I have to answer though.'

I stare into his blue and brown eyes, trying not to let my gaze wander to the scar. 'I don't want to offend you,' I begin.

Joe deals me another killer smile. 'Don't bottle it now. You're going to ask how I came by this thing, right?' He runs a finger down his face.

'No!' I protest. 'No way, certainly not, never in a million years. Well, actually, I was, yes. But I changed my mind, honest.'

Joe laughs. 'No big deal, Rowena. It's a duelling scar.'

'Oh.' I'm none the wiser. He cottons on to this and explains about duels without using long words or making me feel like a complete airhead. 'So,' I say, trying to sum up, 'you had a private quarrel with someone and sorted it out with deadly weapons?'

Joe fidgets. 'Not exactly, unless that's how you'd class a belt buckle.'

'But you were fighting for your honour, like?'

'It wasn't a duel in the literal, the historical sense, Rowena.' He sighs. 'Look, I don't mind giving you a blow-by-blow account but it doesn't seem right, with you trying to find your dad and all.'

'How do you mean, Joe? Where does Dad fit into this?'

He tugs a handful of hair. 'Because my dad was the one who scarred me, and honour had nothing to do with it. It was alcohol, that's what turned him into a raging brute.'

I clap my hand over my mouth in horror. 'Jesus, Joe, I should never have asked. I'm so, so sorry.'

'No need to apologize. You see where I'm coming from, though. I know you didn't go through the stuff that my family did, and I'm pleased for you. But my father was a waste of space, a vicious, drunken bully, and my one regret is that we didn't get away from him sooner. I was fifteen before I found out that God's last name wasn't Dammit, or that the word Mother didn't have to come before

F—, you know what I mean.' Suddenly he cracks into a broad smile. 'Here endeth the first lesson. Knock, knock.'

'Who's there?'

'Stopwatch.'

'Stopwatch who?'

'Stopwatch you're doing and give me a kiss.'

Just as I close my eyes and prepare to pucker up, he plants a matey smacker on my mouth. I feel short-changed and a tad foolish. The point is that we're both warmed up now, the awkward family-confession moment in the past. How could we ever have been stuck for words? He gases on and on, cracking jokes and telling me all kinds of stuff. Despite the kiddy kiss, I sense a growing closeness between us. The thought of it sets off a tingle in my undies until my body buzzes with excitement and my head feels about to float off into space.

Life is perfecto. At last, at last, I feel a weird sensation of – what? Happiness. True. Bizarre as it seems, I'm actually, truly *happy*.

Naturally, I have to hide this state of affairs from Joe.

He squeezes my shoulder in an intimate gesture, leans across and reaches an old biscuit tin from beneath a bookcase. Inside is a joint-rolling kit which is good news as my brain could use some narcotic relaxant.

'Your turn to choose the music,' he says, moistening two skins and sticking them together. I riffle through the CDs but as I recognize hardly any of them there's no option but to pick one at random. I slip it in the machine and press Play, holding my breath. It would be just my luck to choose Motorhead or something, with Lemmy screeching 'Ace of Spades' at a zillion decibels. But fortune must be smiling on me as it turns out to be Eva Cassidy's *Songbird* which my mum had at home. Not my style, but at least it's familiar and I don't need to show ignorance by asking who the artist is. Still, it's a wee bit of a surprise that Joe has it among his collection.

He's sitting on the sofa now, patting the seat beside him. The couch has stopped resembling a man in a car crash so I sit down and draw my knees up to my chest. Joe takes a pull on the spliff and offers it to me. I take it from him like a pukka dopehead, remembering not to wrinkle my nose at the smell as that's the sign of an amateur. First a wee suck to get my mouth used to the taste, then I take a good long draw, inhaling deeply until my chest feels hot and fit to burst and there's just the tiniest wisp of smoke to exhale. Jeez, it's strong stuff. The inside of my head gets the woozy tingles as if I've counted back from ten to six after a general anaesthetic.

Stay awake. Fight the urge to doze. This is what I have to say to myself on the rare occasions when I smoke dope. Don't drift off. Stay conscious. Ride the wave. Enjoy the buzz. The buzz-z-z-z . . .

Z-z-z-z-z . . .

26

Dog's Dinner

Joe *flick* a shimmering rainbow *flick* haunting music *flick* the sweet smell of dope *flick* Joe Joe Joe *flick* inserting his key into the lock *flick* sliding into bed with me *flick* his tongue *flick flick flick*

What the . . .?

I'm in bed. In *a* bed. Hell, I must have done my falling-asleep trick again. Some gracious guest, me. Struggling to focus my mind and get my bearings, I realize that it's Joe's spare bed. And I'm not alone. Jerking into consciousness, I draw my legs towards my chest, curl my toes and explore beneath the duvet with my feet. The stranger in the bed is a living, breathing thing, an entity of the non-Joe variety. I lift up the cover. There's Ninja, in a foetal ball, his muzzle nestling in my crotchly area. Ninja the Cringer, curled up in an attitude of supreme couldn't-care-lessness. If that don't beat all. Jeez, I hope it was some dream-type business I was having back there and Ninja wasn't actually, you know, doing tongue stuff. Still, who cares, he's not about to sell his lick 'n' tell story to the papers. *Ninja the Minja in Doggy-style Romp. He's Simply the Beast, says Rowena, 16.*

Mmm, it's so cosy having Ninja in bed. I run my feet along his body, loving the sensation of my toes against his ribs, the coarse texture of his coat almost punk in its standy-up roughness, the solid feel of him. Maybe he is a head case, a dog with special needs, but he's hard and bristly and mean-looking on the outside and that's what counts. My toes rub against an area of his back where his coat is thin and worn like a threadbare rug. Ninja has a baldy patch. His back leg twitches, then he stirs, stretches out full-length, does a jaw-cracking yawn and settles down again. It's amazing that he doesn't suffocate with his head buried under the bedclothes. I just hope he doesn't freak when he realizes where he is, which is, I'm assuming, Joe's spare room. I don't have a clue how I came to be here but my brain's too tired to worry. Warm, contented, swathed in sunflower colours, I drift off into sweet oblivion.

In the morning Ninja has vanished, leaving a small tuft of hair halfway down the bed as a souvenir and as evidence that I hadn't imagined it. I tiptoe to the loo and he's there, in the bath, his private comfort zone. He shoots me a glance, furtive like, but at least he isn't quaking with fear and he doesn't try to squeeze behind the taps which is a sign of progress. Best of all, when I offer him my hand, he sniffs it, then finds the courage to lick it, only the once but it's a start. It shows we have the makings of more than a one-night stand. He even lets me scratch the soft bit behind his ear.

'Good dog, Ninja. Big, brave, clever dog.' I figure that's all the bonding he can handle in one session. The muscles twitch in his tail, not so much a wag as a tic, but a move in the right direction.

After I've washed, dressed and coloured in a face I pad along to the kitchen. I'm gagging for a cup of tea. To my surprise, as it never occurred to me that he would be out of bed this early, Joe is sitting at the table, cleaning under his fingernails with a toothpick.

'Top of the morning to you,' I say, hoping he'll appreciate my attempt at Irish culture.

'There's some tea made,' he says, pointing to a brown granny-type pot. I pour half a mug for me and a refill for Joe. 'Hope you don't mind me putting you to bed. Completely zonked last night, you were. Sleep all right?'

'Fine, especially since I had company in the night.' I blow on my tea and take a sip, trying not to gulp too hard when I swallow.

Joe stops picking his nails and stares at me. 'Company? And how would that be?'

'The lovely Ninja, he crawled into the bed and we snuggled up together.'

169

'You're not serious,' says Joe. 'That dog would eat its own tail rather than go near a stranger. You must have dreamt it, Rowena.'

'I never,' I protest. 'I found some of his hair in the bed this morning, plus he licked my hand in the bathroom just now. We've got a whatsit going, a rapper.'

'A *rapport*?' says Joe, trying to keep a straight face.

'Yeah, whatever,' I go, blushing. 'Did you know he's got a baldy bit on his back? What if it's distemper, or canine scurvy or something? You should get it checked out at the vet's.'

'See those cork tiles?' says Joe. I look down and nod. 'I laid those meself but the mutt decided to have a nap on the floor before the adhesive was dry. When he got up he left half his coat behind, stuck solid. You can still see some of the hairs next to the cooker, I haven't got round to shaving the floor yet. There's not much call for fur tiles around here.'

'No wonder he lives in the bathroom,' I say. 'It's a DIY assault course out here. Jeepers, Joe, look at the time. I must get back to the hotel or Texy will think I've been abducted by aliens.'

Joe grins. 'Texy probably has other things on her mind. Matty, for one. Why don't you give her a ring, let her know where you are. It's Sunday, laze around and do nuttin' day.'

'If you're sure I won't be outstaying my welcome.' My voice goes all shy and my shoulders curl in a sickeningly coy manner.

'There's nothing I'd rather do than spend time with you.' Joe's eyes lock on to me, sending my spine quivering. When he passes me the phone, an electric current shoots from his hand to mine, like when you stand on a cheap carpet and switch on a household appliance, unless that's down to dodgy wiring.

I dial Texy's mobile. She sounds relieved to hear from me, but I can't tell whether it's because she's been concerned for my safety or if it's the other thing that she's just reminded me about. It had flown right out of my brainbox. I'd completely forgotten that we'd arranged to go and see Bobbo this afternoon. I'd already suggested to Texy that it would be a good time to deliver his new outfit too. Bloody buggery bollocky hell.

Explaining the situation to Joe, I'm almost in tears. Which would I rather do? Chill out all day with a gorgeous hunk who makes my body tingle, or drag myself up a 1-in-10 hill to make meaningless conversation with a grumpy old gadge? It's a tough call, right? Then Joe suddenly remembers he needs to update the anti-virus software for the computers, plus the disk needs defragmenting which takes forever and I'd be bored silly and it would be mean to let Texy down and stuff like that. It all sounds too convenient and I guess is his way of letting me off the hook, letting me know he won't be at a loose end, which is real sweet and confirms what a brilliant, thoughtful person he is. Not that I doubted it for a millisecond.

He gives me a business card with the Mouse Drop-in phone number and says to give him a bell when I have some free time. I slip it inside my pocket, fingering it as though it's made of precious metal or butterfly wings.

27

Texy Spells it Out

'You're a dark horse,' teases Texy. 'I wish you'd let me know you were staying with Joe last night, then Matty could have kept me company.'

'It isn't what you think,' I protest. 'We didn't *do* anything. Just had a cosy night in, then I had a spliff, didn't I, and came over all dopey-dozy? Joe put me in the spare bed and the dog must have crawled in with me.'

'A likely tale,' she says, aiming a jokey left hook at my chin.

'It's true,' I insist. 'We're just friends, Joe and me. Would you have, you know, gone for it with Matty? Done the business, like?'

She does a saucy wink. 'Is the Pope a Catholic?'

'I don't even know what the Pope looks like, let alone whether he's a Catholic,' I say truthfully.

Texy stares at me for ages. 'You kill me,' she says.

We haul Bobbo's new clothes up the hill to the nunvent, dividing the load between us. Texy carries the stuff in the sports-shop bag which isn't so heavy, and I manhandle the Husky parka. The easiest method seems to be for me to wear it, but by the time we've left base camp and climbed a few million steps the sweat is pouring off me in bucketloads. This isn't helped by Texy winding me up about being unfit, like I need reminding.

'Fucksake, give it here, you moaning Minnie,' she nags, pulling the jacket off me and shoving her arms into the sleeves.

'If you insist.' Maybe I should feel a teensy bit guilty about letting her cart all the clobber but what the hell, the gifts are for her granddad. I've nothing to reproach myself with.

'This must have cost a packet,' she remarks, testing the quality of the parka. That's without even noticing the high-class label.

'Bobbo's worth it,' I reply, trying not to sound too martyrish. 'He won't peg out from hypothermia, for sure.'

'More likely he'll melt to death,' says Texy, with a slight out-of-breath puff in her voice which makes me smile for some reason.

When we reach St Peter's Close in the Home for Old Dubs, Texy and I are in a similar state of knackeredness. I could murder a Red Bull but I suppose it's out of the question. A nursing assistant tells us that Bobbo is sitting in the garden. It comes as a shock to find him slumped in a wheelchair, bound tightly in a blanket, looking like an old Baby Jesus in a swaddling cloth. His skin is deathly pale but the tip of his nose is red, with a dewdrop about to break ranks. Whew, what a relief. I'd hate to think I'd gone to all that trouble to kit him out and he'd croaked on me.

Texy fusses around him, rubbing his arms to get the circulation going. I poke her and nod to draw her attention to the parka which she must have forgotten she's wearing.

'Bobbo, look at your lovely new coat.' She manoeuvres it on to his shoulders, grabs his armpits and lifts his body, tucking the parka in beneath his bottom. He gazes up at her. His eyes are glazed and vacant. 'Didn't Rowena promise she'd get you new clothes? Eh?' The old man stares into the distance and sniffs. His nose is so runny I can hardly bear to look until Texy mops it with a tissue.

'This is one of his not-so-good days,' she whispers. 'Don't be offended if he forgets to thank you for the clothes.' She pulls the hood up over his head. Bobbo resembles a frail Eskimo, an under-the-weather Inuit. Colour gradually returns to his cheeks, the blueish tinge giving way to a hint of pink.

'It's getting chilly,' I moan. 'Can't we go inside?'

Texy releases the brake on the wheelchair and trundles the old man towards the building. His eyes are downcast, seemingly blind to his surroundings. He hasn't uttered a single word. I wonder if the nurse has gone overboard on the quiet pills. By the time we reach the day room he's nodded off. Texy tells me to keep an eye on him while she has a word with the staff so I have to stand there like an eejit, checking occasionally to make sure he's still alive.

After aeons she returns with a woman wearing nun's drag, introducing her as Sister Monica. When she crouches to check on Bobbo, I realize from the creaky knees that it's the Sister who helped me up the other day. The day when I was making fun of God, claiming to see His face in a cloud. The day I babbled nonsense, pretending to speak in tongues. Lordy, I hope she doesn't recognize me.

She fannies on with Bobbo, talking to him as if he's a child, praising his new parka. He stirs from his slumber and lets her have the full force of his bad temper.

'Don't feckin' patronize me, woman!'

Texy breathes in sharply and claps a hand over her mouth in horror.

'Now, now, Mr Maguire, sure I'm only trying to help.' Sister Monica seems unfazed by his outburst. 'There's no need for that kind of language.' She rubs his gnarled old hands. In an aside to Texy, she goes, 'We'll get him to bed, let him have a proper rest, and he'll be his own sweet self again when he wakes up.'

As she hoists herself to a standing position, Sister Monica notices my presence for the first time. A fleeting expression in her eyes tells me she recognizes me as the gibbering fool from the other day.

What do I do? I bob a curtsey, don't I? How mental is that? The woman's a nurse in a nunvent and I'm acting as if she's the Queen or something. Texy butts in to cover my awkwardness.

'This is Rowena Vincent, Sister. She works here at the convent.'

'Is that so?' smiles the sister. 'And what is your job, Rowena Vincent?'

My mouth loses touch with my brain. 'I'm a . . . I do . . . I work in, erm, *Cleanliness*.'

'Sure and isn't it next to Godliness?' Sister Monica does a tinkly laugh. 'You'll be in the housekeeping department, I take it, in the main block?'

I nod. She gives me a penetrating, though not unkind, look.

'I'm certain that we'll run into one other again.'

Incoherent, befuddled, confused. Why do I feel so stupid in the company of Sister Monica?

'Unngghh,' I grunt, in the manner of someone who was raised by wild animals in a jungle.

Bobbo, looking as though he could sleep until Armageddon, lies tucked up in bed, the Husky parka adorning the back of his chair. His other new clothes – the ones I paid hard cash for – are in his wardrobe, still in the shop bag, unseen by Texy or Sister Monica. Boy, are they in for a surprise when Bobbo models them in public.

Texy and I hold hands as we skip like downhill racers back to Ballyloony. She suggests calling at the tea room for a snack since it's too early for a bar meal. It's a poky wee spot, way too many tables crammed into a small space, breaking every fire regulation in the book, that's if they've heard of books in Hicksville, or fire regs. You'd think it was the arrival of the Queen of Sheba, the way people turn and stare at us, raw curiosity burning in their eyes. They've no shame, any of them. Squeezing through the furniture, we make it to a table in the corner. I feel faint, so utterly butterly famished I could scoff a dishful of dead rat stew.

'I'll go cheese on toast,' says Texy, pushing the menu towards me. 'What about you?' She runs her fingers through her carroty mop. A woman shuffles up to the table. At first glance it looks as though she's wearing a brown-coloured stud in her nose, then I realize it's a wart. Triffic, the waitress is a witch. Why is this no surprise?

'What can I get you girls?' she asks, brandishing a notepad.

Texy squeezes past her, loo-bound. 'Order mine, I'm busting,' she says to me.

'Cheese on toast for two,' I say. Someone has to take control, maison well be me. 'And a pot of tea. Oh, and a Red Bull.'

The witch raises one plucked-to-buggery eyebrow. 'A Red Bull?' she says with a schoolgirly laugh which is a disappointment as I was expecting a cackle. 'The nearest red bull is in Kearney's top field, and a rampant old beast he is.'

I glare at her. 'No, I mean – ' She returns my look with a blank one. Jeez, what's the point? They've obviously never heard of drinks that give you wings. 'Just get us a can of Lilt.'

'Will you have your tea now?' She flicks a damp rag over the table. 'Or when you get it?'

'Whenever.' I wave her away. She's doing my head in. Texy returns and seats herself at the table. I draw squiggles with my finger on the steamed-up window. After a few minutes the waitress comes back with eating irons wrapped in paper napkins, accompanied by two plates of unsavoury scran.

This must surely be the foulest cheese in the universe, yellow rubbery stuff with the texture, smell and taste of incontinence knickers, but I'm so gagging for food I manage to chew it into submission. The waitress doles out the tea things and plonks a glass of watery orange and a drinking straw in front of me.

'What's this?' I say. 'A can of Lilt, I asked for.'

She stretches her mouth in a haggish smile, revealing discoloured teeth. 'We don't have the Lilt, so I brought you some cor-jel. It's full of vitamins.' She looks pointedly at the spots on my forehead which are starting to itch like buggery.

'Thanks, that'll be just fine,' chimes in Texy, as she can see from my expression that I'm in a dangerous mood. 'Don't cause a scene,' she hisses.

The waitress trolls back to the counter. 'What's friggin' cor-jel anyway?' I ask.

'Moonshine distilled from the tears of angels by leprechauns,' replies Texy, straight-faced.

'You're kidding me, right?' She smirks. 'You're such a tease, Texy Maguire. I knew you were lying; there's no such things as lepric corns and anyway, this cor-jel stuff is just orange squash.'

'There's no fooling you,' says Texy. 'Come on, we're outta here. I'm not eating this muck.' We steer through the furniture and Texy pays at the till. On the way out, the waitress flashes her brown teeth at me in a witch grin. I flick her the finger, but secretly beneath my jacket in case she puts a curse on me.

Outside the tea room, I gulp fresh air into my steam-clogged lungs. The rush of oxygen sends me dizzy, spinny-headed, for a few moments. Tiny sparks ping and fizzle in my brain.

'I need to sit down, Tex. My head's whirling.'

'OK, let's go sit in the park, play on the kiddie swings,' says Texy. She heads across the road towards some iron gates. My aching feet lumber behind her on autopilot. I feel as clumsy, uncoordinated, out of synch, as a yeti in stiletto heels. We perch on a vandalized bench with missing slats. 'Come on then, spill,' urges Texy. 'I want to know everything that went on between you and Joe last night, no detail spared.'

I describe the flat, the second-hand furniture alongside state-of-the-art TV and hi-fi; the spooky door leading to Joe's room and the amazing light and sound system inside; the sunflower-inspired bedroom where I spent the night; and jittery Ninja who lives in the bathroom.

'And . . .?' says Texy. 'What about you and Joe? Don't leave out the juicy bits.'

'There's nothing to tell. We just talked about, I dunno, stuff.' I'd like to ask her about Joe's friendly kiss. For all I know, this could be the way they do stuff in Ireland. Maybe couples aren't allowed to snog until they're engaged to be married. In the end I bin the idea because it would be spilling too many beans before I've sussed out my feelings for Joe, or his for me. 'Hang on, though.' I slap my forehead. 'We did find a lead.'

'A dog lead?'

'No, you lummox. A Moral lead.' I explain about Moral Adair, the born-again comedian, alkie cum junkie in recovery, model of inspiration for Freedom from Chemical Dependence. 'Joe's going to e-mail the FCD, find out how to contact him.'

'Sounds like you're catching up on the legendary Lonnie. How does that make you feel?'

The question stops me dead in my tracks, like a mugger in an alley. How does it make me feel? Shit-scared, if you want the truth. Meeting Dad is my last shot at happiness, at a future, at a life. If I don't find him, or if our relationship doesn't work out, I'm done for. Finito. There is no fallback situation, no Plan B. All my eggs are contained in the Dad basket.

'How do you think I feel? Excited, of course. What a question!' My voice lets me down by coming out quavery. Texy isn't fooled.

'Rowena, no-one's forcing you to go through with this,' she says soothingly.

'I've come way too far to turn back now.' Tears gather behind my eyes. 'Anyway,' I say, struggling to control the tremor in my voice, 'why would I want to? Once I find Dad everything will be . . .'

The words hunky and dory stick in my craw and the tears come rolling out, racing down my cheeks, smearing my make-up, splashing off my chin. Texy budges up on the seat and hugs me; that's when I totally lose it. Great heaving, suffocating sobs rise in my chest, my body begins to shudder uncontrollably, a string of spittle hangs out of my mouth. *Very* attractive.

'Let it out,' she says, like I could stop if I tried. She hands me a tissue and I dab my eyes carefully so as not to ruin my make-up, then blow my nose like a tuba. Helping me up, she links her arm into mine and says we should go back to our room in The Flues so I can get some peace and privacy. That's when I notice two lads leaning against a tree, smoking. It's the unibrowed Oasis freaks from the Mouse Drop-in, leering at me from beneath their greasy fringes.

'Just ignore them,' says Texy, noticing my fingers bunching up into fists.

My brain is exhausted, overwhelmed by feelings too weird to comprehend. Nothing is simple. Certainties have grown into king-size doubts. What seemed a straightforward plan when I headed for Ireland now feels crazy, unworkable, the product of an unhinged mind. Finding Dad was supposed to be the answer to everything. But what was the question?

'You're bound to be confused,' Texy says, her voice grown-up and counsellor-like. 'It's such a big deal, coming to a strange country, knowing no-one, searching for your father – a stranger. Jeez, it takes some guts, Rowena, I have to hand it to you.'

We're in our room at The Flues, sharing a bar of dark chocolate. Texy is propped up against the headboard, I'm curled up on the bed, my head in her lap. She strokes my hair, untangling the knots, a strangely soothing experience. Maybe it's a form of hypnotism, like tickling a trout or upending a rabbit. Whatever the trigger, my pulse stops racing, the uneven heart rhythm returns to normal and I can breathe without hyperventilating.

'It wasn't like I had a choice,' I explain, munching a square of choccie. 'My life was fucked up big style, nothing on the horizon but bad, bad karma. I had to get away from Newcastle. Finding Dad seemed the obvious answer, the only solution.'

She leans down and kisses my hand. 'There's always a choice, only sometimes the clouds in your mind are too dense to see through.'

'What are you saying?'

She sighs. 'That the happy family myth is just that – an idealized image, a feelgood movie, a fairy tale. Take my mother and father. We'd never have got along together, not without one of us blowing the others up. They'd have become resentful and I'd have felt cheated because they didn't fit my idea of the perfect parents. The

179

best thing was to call it a day, make positive changes, so they went off to hug trees and grow lentils, while I moved in with Bobbo, which turned out best for all of us. I don't feel an ounce of bitterness towards them. Just because they're my parents doesn't mean hanging myself with the umbilical cord. We want different things, it's a fact of life. You have to move on, deal with it, not cling to some fantasy notion of "family". Hey, listen to me, the walking cliché. I should get a job on daytime television.'

We snuggle up together. Texy's wise words shine a light through my brainfog, allowing me to view things more clearly. A choice. I have a choice. Perhaps I don't have to pin all my hopes on making a new life with Dad. Jeez, he might have another family now, a young wife, a couple of sprogs, free-range hens, a pet weasel. He must have had his reasons for leaving Mum and me.

Something clicks in my mind. A vague memory of Nana Vincent saying that Dad – her son – needed space to find himself; and Mum responding sarkily, along the lines of 'He should try looking up his own arse.' Despite myself, I giggle out loud.

'What's tickling you?' says Texy.

I relate the story to her. 'I don't know if I remember it, or imagined it, or dreamt or overheard it. But you have to admit, it's funny.' We both start sniggering, then laughing full-on, until eventually we're rolling around the bed clutching our stomachs, helpless, roaring insanely, streaming tears. By the time it subsides, my cheeks and diaphragm are sore, my whole body aches from the sudden outburst of hilarity.

Then, and this is so weird, like an alien voicebox has been implanted in my body, I find my mouth forming these words:

'Texy, I feel so happy. It's been such a lovely day – no, the whole weekend's been spot on. You and Joe, you make me feel shiny inside. You're brilliant, both of you. Real, proper friends. It's almost as if I've discovered for the first time what life should be like.' Or at least, for the first time in ages.

Who would have thought I'd be uttering – and meaning – these words? Miserable, moody, sullen Rowena. Happy, *moi*? You betcha. Not before time, either. How long does happiness last? I'll be seventeen soon. Don't I deserve something good in my life instead of heartache, depression and constant angst? Sure I do, because – like in the hair product commercial – I'm worth it. We finish off the chocolate.

The electronic chirrup of Texy's mobile interrupts the blissful moment.

'Hello.' Texy mugs a daft face as she answers the phone. 'Yes, hold on, she's right here.' Offering me the handset, she whispers, 'It's Mr O'Hara for you.' I make frantic signals with my arms but it's too late, she's already told him I'm here.

'Rowena Vincent speaking, how may I help?' My voice goes up and down with nerves, breaking like a pubescent choirboy's. Texy stifles a chortle behind her hand.

Hefty introduces himself, says he hopes I'm enjoying Ballyloony and thanks me for delivering the gift to his aunt. He wants me to give her another message, like I'm his personal slave or something.

'She's expecting me to visit her tomorrow but I have to be away on urgent business. Would you apologize and tell her I'll be there for the saint's day celebrations on Thursday?'

'OK,' I say, lolling my tongue and pulling a cross-eyed face down the phone.

'It won't be too much trouble, I hope. It's a devil of a hill to climb to get to the home.'

'No problem. I'm working at the nunvent so I have to trudge up there anyway.'

A pause. 'You have a job at the convent? What a resourceful young woman you are, Rowena.'

The tone of his voice makes my gills turn green. 'Right, gotta go, bye,' I blurt, pressing the button to end the call.

'What's wrong?' says Texy.

'How did he get your mobile number?' I'm burning up with rage. 'See, the Mafia must have an insider, a plant, in the phone company.'

'I gave him my number before we left Dublin, you dope. What's got into you? How come you've turned into Miss Angry all of a sudden?'

'Me and my runaway gob!' I holler. 'I could pull out my own teeth with a claw hammer for spilling my private business to Hefty O'Hara. I could fillet myself for telling him about my job at the nunvent. He'll be using me as a go-between, a crookie's runner, to deliver messages to his aunt. I bet they're secret warnings coded in Mobspeak.' In truth, I'm mad at Texy for forcing me to speak to Hefty and even madder at myself for forgetting that he's a clear and present danger, something that seems impossible to drill into her.

Texy frowns and aims a playful thump at my arm. 'Rowena, will you just get over this mad idea that Mr O'Hara is some kind of gangster. It was funny at first, but the joke's wearing a bit thin now. He's a bona fide businessman, end of story.'

'That's just your opinion,' I snort.

28

The Devil's Griddle

By the time I reach St Philomena's Avenue it's past eight in the morning. It took forever to haul myself up the hill as there's a dragging ache in my stomach which can mean only one thing: my mollies are getting closer.

I'm hoping Miss O'Hara will still be in bed so I can leave Hefty's message with an underling, but no such luck. There's a dogleg queue of old biddies with sticks and walking frames, hobbling into the dining room for breakfast. In amongst the decrepit crew, Miss O'Hara stands tall, straight-backed, henna-ed hair screwed back in the orchid scrunchie. I wave to catch her attention before remembering that she's visually impaired so I stand in front of her, touch her cardigan and make my presence known.

'It's Rowena Vincent, Miss O'Hara. I came the other day, remember?'

'Of course. Hello Rowena, you're up and about early.' She smells chemical, as though she's been prematurely embalmed.

'Late, actually,' I correct her. 'I work here now, over in the Cleanliness department, we're supposed to start at eight, but I promised Hefty I'd call in to see you. He phoned yesterday; he asked me to pass a message on to you.' And I had to come as I value my kneecaps, is the thought that's whizzing through my head.

Her milky eyes look into mine. It's spooky, not knowing how much she can see. 'I hope he isn't going to let me down, not for the saint's day.'

I set her mind at rest, telling her that he'll be arriving on Thursday as he's away on business until then. Probably meeting a consignment of asylum-seeking virgins to add to his string of hookers. I'm just thinking that, not saying it out loud. At least, I hope so.

Miss O'Hara thanks me and asks if I'd like to sit with her at breakfast, but the thought of eating with a bunch of clapped-out old girls, all that dribbling and denture-clacking, makes me feel ill, so I mumble something about getting the sack if I don't get to work immediately and she says goodbye and thanks me again. Why do old people always act so grateful? It strikes me as a form of emotional blackmail.

On the way out I notice Sister Monica. She's deep in conversation with another nun, two penguins having a conflab over the price of fish. To my surprise, it turns out to be Eminem, Sister Michael Mary, the one who gave me the guided tour on my first day. They look up and stop nattering for a second, smiling in my direction. I smile back and give them a cheery wave, relieved in a way that I've been spotted in the old ladies' home as it gives me an excuse for being late for my dust-control duties. I'll say I was donating my time free of charge in the cause of charity, bringing succour, spreading joy and stuff to coffin-dodgers. The Sisters wrinkle their faces in reply and watch me leave the building. I'm sure they're gassing on about me, though what they can find to say is anyone's guess.

The gardens appear to have had a seeing-to. Rows of bedding plants have been stuck in the ground even though a cold snap could kill them off overnight. Waste of friggin' money; still, details like that won't bother the Church, they rake in loads every day from gullible believers who struggle to put a meal on their own tables.

I pass an old bloke digging round a clump of saplings, giving them air, tidying up the place. He's bent double.

'Morning,' I call out.

'And a fine one at that,' he replies, standing up straight, rubbing his back and leaning on his spade. He removes his cap and scratches his head, turning his face towards me. Sprouting from it is a bushy white beard, so thick and luxuriant he must have fed it with fertilizer. He looks like a garden gnome, or a hairy old leprechaun, or something else I can't quite put a name to. For a moment I almost recognize him, and then the thought-fragment flies out of my mind. Talk about the attention span of a gnat. I wish. All this religious malarkey is rubbing off, eating away at my senses.

It's gone half past eight by the time I reach the side door of the main building, the trade entrance to the nunvent. It would have been impossible to sneak in anyway, as I find myself in a crowd of buzzing skivvies and a scene of chaotic activity.

'What's occurring?' I ask wall-eyed Paula. She's unravelling a heap of bunting, passing a string of pennants along a line of overalled girls. At the far end is a ladder where a woman built like a navvy is hammering the decorations to the wall.

'It's to make things look nice for the visitors,' says Paula. 'For the saint's day on Thursday. Enda should have explained to you about the preparations.'

'She never mentioned it,' I say, although she might have done, if only I'd been arsed to listen.

'You'd better hurry up and get changed,' says Paula, her face creased with worry, 'before the Sisters spot you.' I follow the direction of her good eye to see Sister Cuthbert, the kitchen nun with a missing finger, barking orders like a sergeant major.

'Left. More to the left. No, that's too far. Back a bit. Straighten it up there.'

Bloody hell, what a shambles. I could have done without this in my present state of premenstrual bellyache. Pushing past the skivs in the doorway, I make my way to the Cleanliness department. After all the hubbub outside, Enda's hangout is like an oasis of calm.

'Sorry I'm a bit late, Enda, I had to take a message to one of the residents in the old folks' home. Plus I've been awake half the night *and* my head's come up in bumps.' I don't bother to mention the cramp in my gut or we'd be here all day discussing assorted ailments.

'A bumpy head? Let Enda feel it.' She plonks me on a chair and stands behind me, inspecting the raised lumps, muttering to herself. 'Do they itch? Are they painful?'

Actually, it's happened before, after I'd eaten aubergine. Some sort of food intolerance, but it doesn't hurt and the bumps disappear after a few hours.

'This is a new one,' Enda admits. 'I'll have to look it up in the book, but it's all part of the, er, the *syndrome*, no doubt about that, no doubt at all,' she concludes in a snap diagnosis. 'I suggest you nibble a Jaffa cake with your eyes closed – best bump-soother in the world. And if you're making a coffee, I'll join you. There's nothing sadder than drinking alone.'

Heaving a massive sigh, I fill a couple of mugs with milk and stick them in the microwave. Enda stretches her legs under the table and spreads out a newspaper.

'You'd best wear a clean uniform today,' she says, waving her hand towards a pile of green and white check overalls. 'There'll be dignitaries wandering in and out, poking their noses in. There's a rumour the bishop's due sometime. Hmph, that's all we need.'

I toil away making the coffee, silently cursing my lot in life.

'Lord, will you look at this,' exclaims Enda. 'Kearney's bull escaped and had his way with a herd of cows in the bottom field.' She peers at the newspaper, pointing out an article with a picture of a massive bastard of a beast adorned with a rosette. This is what passes for front-page news in this Dead Men's Gulch of a town. Enda whistles and reads some more. 'Sure it's a bad day to be a cow. They found some more with the flesh sliced off their flanks while they were standing in the field.'

'That'll be aliens,' I inform her. 'I read about it in a magazine. Extraterrestrials. They take samples of Earth beings to clone for who knows what gruesome experiments on their own planets.'

She huffs. 'It'll be gypsies, more like, or Romanian refugees, cutting free steaks for themselves.'

'But it doesn't hurt the cows. They get better,' I assure her. 'The wounds heal over and they're good as new in no time.'

'Until the bandidos get peckish again. Look sharp, Rowena, get that uniform on.'

I groan, rummaging through the pile of overalls until I find one that least resembles a tent.

'Why all this fuss?' I ask, slipping the disgusting uniform over my togs and pulling the belt real tight so I don't look like a sack of spuds. 'What's the big deal about the saint's day?'

'It's the bicentenary, remember,' says Enda. 'Two hundred years since St Vincenza was martyred. You'd best keep a low profile on Thursday.' She nods at the ceiling. 'That lot upstairs, they won't want us menials mixing with the high-ups or the praying public.'

The morning drags by, a succession of assorted hot drinks, biscuits and Enda feeling the non-existent bumps on my head which she swears are shrinking thanks to the magic of Jaffa cakes. Marooned in our underground bunker, we witness none of the ceremonial preparations, the pulling of weeds and polishing of poorboxes, the ritual scrubbing of the grotto to clean off limescale and graffiti.

My belly is rumbling and groaning bigtime, and the pinging of my ovaries confirms that the curse is upon me. It's almost a relief when Enda nicks off for a gossip with her bingo partner in the laundry, leaving me to suffer alone. I hold the Cleanliness fort, killing time by making up answers to the crossword in the local paper. 1 across: GONADS. 2 down: OCCULT. And so on. It's one of those supposedly easy puzzles, none of the words longer than six letters, but the clues make no sense so I just fill in words at random. I manage to fit in a QUIM which pleases me no end for some reason. It's such an underrated, underused word, plus it looks great written down.

It's no good, I'll have to pop some Solpadeines to ease the gutbusting agony tearing away at my insides. I can hardly bear to wait for the tablets to dissolve. A groan like a cow in labour roars out of me, giving a nanosecond's respite before the pangs return with double knobs and bells on. This is a killer premenstrual pain, much worse, more all-consuming, than being possessed by the devil.

Enda returns from the laundry, gossiped out. She stares at me from the doorway, an expression of concern flushing her face.

'Whatever is the matter with you, girl?'

Apart from the excruciating belly cramps, I've experienced a lightning mindflash. A revelation, one might say. I've just remembered who the old gardener reminded me of. I almost pass out with shock at the realization.

'Enda, I bumped into someone in the grounds this morning.' It sounds so demented, I'm wondering whether to tell her. If she's in an arsey mood she could grass me up to the Sisters and they'd have me sectioned as a mental case.

'And?' she says. 'Who was it?'

'You won't tell them, will you?' I roll my eyes towards the ceiling. 'Promise me, Enda.'

'I promise,' she says, crossing her hands over her saggy bosoms.

'It was . . . It was a man. A scruffy bugger, dressed in mucky old clothes, he was. Pretending to be a gardener.'

She drops the concerned expression. 'Then that's probably what he was. We have some of the local volunteers in giving the place a going-over, making it look nice for the whatsit.'

'The bison teenery,' I offer.

'That's the one.'

'But he wasn't a gardener, Enda. He was loitering under false pretences.'

'He didn't put his hands on you?'

I shake my head. 'No, nothing like that, but I recognized him, Enda. He looked just the same as in the pictures I've seen of him.'

'He's a celebrity?' says Enda. 'Someone off the television?'

188

'Yes and no,' I say, meaning yes, he's famous and no, he's not on the telly.

She sighs. 'Just tell me, Rowena. I can't be doing with guessing games.'

I draw a deep breath.

'It was . . . It was *God*. It was, Enda, swear down. It was God the Father, the man who lives up in the clouds. By his beard shall ye know him.' Yikes, I'm spouting biblical gibberish again. But this time, it's really real. I've seen Him, the Big Man, the guy upstairs, resting against a spade, pretending to be a gardener.

Enda steadies herself against the table with one hand, clutching her rosary with the other, kissing the crucifix bit.

'Lord God Almighty,' she says. 'First the girl exhibits the holy head-bumps, then God materializes before her in the garden.'

'Aarghh!' I let out a groan as premenstrual agony sears through my insides. The devil grips my gut and twists, wringing my stomach lining like a dishcloth. I gulp for air. The Evil One allows me a pain-free moment lasting half a second. Then, showing not a milligram of mercy, thrusts a red-hot poker into my ovaries, cauterizing my Fallopian tubes, instantly scrambling any eggs that might be trying to escape my burning belly. Too weak to support my body, I sink to my knees.

'For the love of God, Rowena, tell me what's wrong.'

Flipping my stomach like a barbecued burger, the devil tosses it on to the griddle of hell, forcing fiery heat through my internal organs, searing my intestines, burning them like a string of supermarket bangers, making them spit and sizzle, strangulated hernias emerging like pig fat through sausage skin.

'I'm calling a nurse, so I am.'

'No!' I scream. My insides have now disintegrated into charcoal, the excruciating pain floating away like flakes of ash on a summer breeze. 'No, it's all over now.'

Enda flusters round me, helping me to a standing position. I feel dazed, spinny-headed, pins and needles sparking on my brow. She leads me from the store cupboard into the kitchenette, guides me to a chair, sits me down, then places a cup of tap water in front of me. A complete role reversal, as it's usually me pandering to her every whim. I decide to milk the situation.

'Is there any coffee going? And Hobnobs, chocolate ones preferably, to bring my blood sugar up, balance my electrolytes and stuff.' Enda pats me on the shoulder and scuttles off. I listen to the clattering of cups, the crackle of biscuit wrapping, the patter of biscuits being tipped out and arranged on a plate. The satisfying, comforting, pleasurable sounds of someone waiting on me hand and foot.

After I've dunked, slurped and burped, Enda quizzes me about my dramatic collapse.

'I had this agonizing pain in my side, here,' I say, indicating my waistband. 'Unbearable, it was, just like someone was ripping me open with a pitchfork.'

'Ooph,' utters Enda in sympathy.

'As if a vacuum-cleaner attachment with jagged teeth was digging into my body and sucking my insides out.' I'm trying to make the story more colourful and interesting for her.

'Ooph,' repeats Enda, using her catch-all word for pain. 'Or as if,' she goes, egging me on. 'As if someone was driving, say, a sharpened nail into the side of your body?'

I nod. 'Possibly. Totally gut-wrenching, excruciating, it was. Felt like I was being, I dunno . . .'

'Crucified?' she offers, her eyes boring into mine. 'Not that I'm putting words into your mouth.'

'I suppose that's one way to describe it.' Actually, I was going to say disembowelled, but I couldn't remember the word in time. Still, crucified seems to satisfy Enda. She crosses herself.

'Do you still have the marks on your hands? And on your forehead?'

Oh, not that again. I tug my fringe to cover the line of spots. They're not quite so livid today but someone messing with them isn't going to help them heal. Bunching my hands into fists, I hide the faint staining on my palms from Enda's sharp gaze.

'They're fading, Enda, just like I said they would. In a couple of days there'll be nothing to see.'

'Then perhaps we should take photos before they disappear altogether,' says Enda firmly. 'Evidence, see. We'll need evidence.'

Evidence? What is she on about? Omigawd, maybe she's in cahoots with the cops! Enda's a grass! She's collecting evidence of the dye stains from the security tag so the gardaí can charge me with robbing the parka. I should have known never to trust god-botherers, they don't have a clue how we people in the real world have to struggle. If I hadn't nicked the coat, Bobbo would have pegged it from hypothermia, then Texy might have been jailed for elder abuse. That's it! That's my defence, my mitigating circum-stances. I was stealing – no, borrowing – a coat to save an old gadge from freezing to death. They're bound to fall for that one. The story of the Good Samaritan is in the Bible, which means it's gospel so they can't touch me for it.

'Maybe I should bring a camera to work tomorrow, take a few snaps,' continues Enda. The stupid woman doesn't realize I've rumbled her game. 'If the marks fade we'll have no proof, not until they reappear.' It wouldn't surprise me if she suggests touching them up with a dab of lipstick to fabricate evidence, stitch me up like a proverbial kipper.

'No, no photos,' I insist. My best ploy is to scare the daft bint with a religious argument. 'Cameras are the tool of Satan. Didn't you know, Enda, every time you take a picture of someone it steals a bit of their soul for the Devil. He's on some sort of commission deal with Kodak, I reckon. There's hardly a soul left intact in the world, Old Nick keeps chip, chip, chipping away, taking a slice of mortal spirit with every snap. He's got spies in all the Boots stores, all the

Supasnaps shops, all the places they develop photos, making sure he doesn't miss anyone. That's why there's no supermodels in heaven; they've no souls because they've been photographed so many gazillions of times. Straight to hell on a handcart, the skinny bints. Where do you think Princess Diana is? On a fluffy white cloud plucking a harp? No way. Just think of all the paparazzi following her around, clicking away, nicking bits of her soul. Sweating like a fat lass in the eternal bonfire, that's where she'll be. So that's why I don't do photos.'

It sounds plausible, even to me, and I made it up off the top of my head.

'You're a funny onion, so you are.' Enda leans back in her chair, grinning. 'I never heard such coppernosity in me life. Would you look at Padre Pio, there's hundreds of pictures of him and he bore his wounds for fifty years, bleeding constantly and smelling of roses. It's the Vatican, see. Full of bureaucrats, paper-shufflers, number-crunchers, like her upstairs, that Sister Bonzo. They needed hard evidence before they'd so much as utter the word "canonization", let alone consider it as a possibility. Nobody doubts Padre Pio now he's a saint, bless his soul.'

I haven't a clue what the dizzy wife's rambling on about, but nobody's firing me out of a cannon, that's a dead cert.

Enda stares at me for a moment, then gives in. 'All right, fair play to you; if you're so set against it, then no photographs. But there's already rumours going around about the, y'know –' she rolls her eyes and nods her chin in the direction of my hands, 'about the stigmata. And your crown of thorns.' She points to the spots on my forehead. 'Now you've experienced the pain of the wound in your side too. And the Lord God appeared to you in the gardens, not to mention those bumps on your head which must mean something. It all adds up to one thing, Rowena. You've been picked out, chosen. There's no denying it.'

Rumours? Stigmata? Crown of thorns? Lord knows what the silly old mare is rattling on about. I bet she's going through the meno-pause and her brain's spongified through hormone deficiency. Although, if you ignore the religious claptrap, it does seem that some weird shit has been going on around me: the dreams of Dad that led me to the nunvent and reunited me with my 'lost' money, the coincidence about my birthday being on the saint's day, stumbling across God among the bedding plants . . .

There couldn't possibly be anything in it.

Could there?

She hasn't done a tap of work this morning and now she leaves me alone again while she pootles off for more gossip. A whistle-blowing type would report her to the Sisters.

The day passes at a hundredth of real time. After stacking cleaning materials in neat piles for the dustbuster girls, presenting dockets and chitties for Enda to sign in her spidery writing, ensuring a clear audit trail, I'm completely knackered, mentally and physic-ally. My brain's numb from performing menial tasks, and there's a mutiny going on in my stomach. What I really, really want to do is crash out on the squashy bed at The Flues and remain unconscious for twenty-four hours.

Fat chance.

When Enda returns from her latest wanderings, she's accompanied by a nervousness of skivvies, twittering and wittering like a shed-load of pre-Christmas turkeys. My first thought is that they've called a union meeting to demand more flattering uniforms or environ-mentally friendly dishcloths, but if that's the case, why are they all gawping at me?

Enda pulls out one of the chairs. 'Sit down, Rowena. We have some news. Tell her, Paula.' She pushes the wall-eyed lass forward to face me. 'Go on, girl, don't stand there staring like an eejit.'

Paula clears her throat. 'I overheard the Sisters talking about you. I wasn't listening at the door, honest; I was polishing the fingerplate.'

'Get on with it,' snaps Enda. 'No-one's accusing you of eavesdropping.'

'They were in Sister Bonaventure's office, a few of them. Eminem, Cuthbert, Sister Monica, I didn't recognize all their voices. They were talking about you, Rowena, discussing you, like.' She lowers her gaze and backs away, as if I'm royalty or something and she'll be beheaded if she makes eye contact.

Enda pushes Paula to one side, impatient with the girl's slowness.

'It seems the rumours I mentioned have reached the ears of the Sisters. What's more, they're taking them very seriously.' Enda puffs out her chest, assuming the role of top dog.

'I haven't a clue what you're talking about,' I protest. 'Rumours? If someone's been spreading lies and tittle-tattle, just tell me. Name names. I'll sort them out.'

The skivs whisper and fidget in discomfort at my show of aggression. If I yelled *Boo!* they'd wet their knickies. Enda seats herself next to me at the table.

'Calm down, girl, while I explain what's going on.' The others gather round and listen in awed silence, gazing at me to gauge my reaction.

This, according to Enda, is the case for the prosecution.

1. I showed up at the nunvent quite out of the blue, claiming that I'd been directed there by my father, who came to me in a dream. My arrival coincided with the lead-up to the saint's day bicentenary, the most important celebration ever held by the Sisters.

2. Although I tried to conceal them, it was immediately evident that I bore the stigmata, the wounds of Christ, on my palms, and the marks of a crown of thorns on my forehead. Later, I exhibited severe pain in my side, the site of another of Christ's wounds.

3. The face of Our Lord materialized in a J-cloth that I'd been

handling. Added to that, a likeness of the Virgin Mary was said to have appeared earlier in a half-eaten banana split.

4. Sister Monica witnessed me speaking in tongues after I'd seen a vision of God in a cloud.

The room is silent while everyone absorbs the details. Enda looks smug, as if to say, *There, I told you so.* Eventually I find my voice.

'Oh, come on, it's bollocks,' I spit. 'Complete rubbish. Total pants, religious mumbo-jumbo, that's all. A chain of misunderstandings, coincidences.'

Enda sniffs. 'No such thing as coincidence, I've told you before.'

'But it makes no sense. What are they getting at? I ain't no saint, and that's the copper-bottomed truth.' To be truthful, I've noticed the strange looks people have been giving me but I assumed my lipstick was smudged or my skirt was caught up in my knickies.

'The point is,' says Enda, 'that they – all right then, *we* – believe there's something in it, that your turning up here is significant in some way. Not only that, but they've put the bishop in the picture. Isn't that right, Paula?'

'I wasn't earwigging.' Paula rushes to defend herself. 'Sister Bonaventure was talking loudly down the phone because the bishop's hearing is poor.'

'So it doesn't matter how strongly you protest, the Sisters believe what they want to believe. Don't you quote me, it's only hearsay.' Enda backtracks, realizing anger could turn me into a loose cannon. She checks her watch. 'That's enough now, girls. Time to head home. That means you too, Rowena, and don't lie awake worrying all night. I'm your line manager, I'll protect your rights.'

Why do her words not fill me with confidence?

What a crazymad day this has turned out to be. Things don't improve when I get back to The Flues and find a note from Texy.

Rowena,

Off to the pictures with M. No need to wait up (fingers X-ed!).

Oh, triffic. Just when I need her to offload the weird doings of the day, she decides to go for a shagathon with Matty. Typical.

To ease my bellyache I take a long soak in the bathtub, stinking the water with Texy's aromatherapy bubble stuff which I find in her toilet bag and wrapping myself in her fluffy towel. Warm, scrubbed and tingly, I turn on the TV and endure a game show where this woman shrieks like a banshee because she's won a washing machine. She's so hysterical with excitement it makes me wonder how she's managed until now: taken her laundry to the river and bashed it on the rocks, perhaps. Her yelling sets my teeth on edge so I switch off the telly, resisting the urge to hoy it out the window and trash the room to buggery like a coked-up rock star.

Desperate for something to occupy me, I end up reading a touristy leaflet about the saint, which is boring as hell but kills a couple of minutes.

St Vincenza di Verona
d. 1803 Feast day: 19 March

Vincenza was the daughter of a merchantman, a native of Verona, Italy. From a young age she was blessed with wonderful visions and the gift of knowing the future. Realizing that Vincenza was very holy, people came to ask for prayers and advice. As a reward for her great love, Jesus gave her the privilege of suffering His own wounds in her hands and side. The humble Vincenza tried to hide them.

At the age of 28, she founded a new religious order of women called the Sisters of Blessed Relief. Their particular work for Jesus would be to tend the old and sick of mind. Vincenza lived only five years after her congregation began. During a heretic uprising, she was stoned and both her eyes were struck out. Vincenza's death was painful but mercifully, she did not linger. However, she helped her sisters from heaven because the community continued to grow and open new convents and is today spread throughout the world, in cherished memory of this brave martyr.

Beatified in 1950, she was canonized in 1975 by Pope Paul VI (1963–1978).

Bloody hell, and I complain about *my* miserable life! At least I haven't had my eyes gouged out by maniacs or been pelted unto death with rocks. Still, neither had she, at my age. Vincenza sounds like a spunky lass, nothing wussy about her, unlike me, her cowardly namesake, who's too scared to meet her own father.

I read on about the celebrations for the two hundredth anniversary of her death. There'll be a parade with an icon of the saint, a bonfire, multicoloured paper lanterns, streamers and banners and for this one day only, children are allowed to ask for coins in the streets. That is so not on, it just encourages aggressive begging; there ought to be a law against it.

Still, at least Vincenza is not just remembered but *celebrated* on her birthday, martyrdom day, whatever it's called. No-one's the least bit arsed about mine, and I'm still alive!

29

Waiting for Daddo

'Of course I'll be there,' Dad assured me. 'I promise.' How many times had I heard this lie? Did he mean it, believe it, as he uttered the words, or were his fingers crossed behind his back?

Nodding wordlessly, I plucked his collar for comfort. My mind was filled with a mixture of hope and dread, wanting to believe that he'd turn up for the play, his eyes glistening with pride; but envisioning the one empty seat in a full house.

OK, it wasn't a major part. Pease-blossom, a stupid fairy in *A Midsummer Night's Dream*, along with Gemma Probert's Mustard-seed, Claire Malcolm's Cobweb and Samantha Leach's Moth. Privately, we named ourselves Piss-blossom, Bastard-seed, Gobweb and Mott. Four girls less sylphlike would have been hard to find. I think Miss Pegg cast us out of spite, to humiliate us because the wizened old crone disapproved of our Gothic tendencies. She made us drag up in gauze shifts dyed in shades of pink, and flit around the stage wearing flesh-coloured popsocks, trying not to thud and thump like a herdlet of teenage elephants. It was mortifying and a total waste of time, all the friggin' rehearsals, all the sitting around like cheese at ninepence, listening to Titania stumble over her lines while Puck forced out comedy farts and the Rude Mechanicals, popped up and pilled out, pretended they were in a porn movie, *A Pigbummer's Wet Dream*, or something.

Our first performance was in the afternoon, in front of the entire school. Degradation Central. You couldn't even glorify it by calling it a dress rehearsal as Claire spilt a bottle of Lucozade all over her costume and had to go on stage in something called a petticoat, borrowed from a teaching assistant. Lumpen. That was Pegg-leg's

198

verdict on our performance. Lumpen, wooden, and stilted. I pictured a pair of stilts made from lumps of wood and thought that maybe we weren't too bad. How hard can this acting lark be? We needed to work on our lines, said Pegg, even though each line consisted mainly of one word, two at most. I had to say, 'Ready,' 'Hail, mortal,' and 'Pease-blossom,' which goes to show what a crap writer Shakespeare was, and why you never see him on the telly.

So there we were, the sullen foursome, frowning, chewing gum, trying to look hard while simultaneously cringing from frock-shock. I tried to spot Dad in the audience but the lights dazzled me, making it impossible to see past the first couple of rows of seats. It went off OK, no thanks to Miss Pegg urging us on from the wings, making her eyes go big and pulling up the sides of her mouth to remind us to smile. Sod that for a game of soldiers. All I wanted was to get the thing over with, lose the pink rags they'd dressed me up in, then go home with Mum, Dad and Nana Vincent, maybe stopping at the chippy on the way. We had to take a couple of curtain calls, blinded by the flash of cameras, hunted by the viewfinders of whirring videocams. This was how soapstars must feel being hounded by the paparazzi.

The parents were milling round outside the hall, some taking surreptitious drags on ciggies hidden in curled-up hands. I hoped Dad would have the will power to wait until he hit the fresh air, not show me up as po' white trash by sparking up indoors like those sad baccy addicts.

Dad. Will power. The words don't belong in the same breath.

Surprise, surprise, he never showed.

Mum and Nana mumbled lame excuses, nothing that made any sense. Couldn't be avoided . . . he's very sorry . . . he'll make it up to you. And something urgent must have cropped up. In other words, neither of them had a clue, because he hadn't been in touch.

It wasn't the first time he'd stood me up, and it wouldn't be the last. I should have known better than to be dazzled by the glimmer of hope. Maybe he'd meant it when he said he wouldn't let me down, but once he uttered those terrible words – I promise – well, that was the kiss of death.

I put a brave face on it, pasted a smile on my mouth, but my heart was solid as lead in my chest. I set about building a new layer to thicken the barrier between me and the world: the invisible carapace protecting me from other people and the brain pain they inflicted. Every day, in every way, I'm growing harder. This was my mantra, and these my rules:

Look after Numero Uno.
Keep your thoughts to yourself.
Never ever let anyone see you cry. Act double hard at all times.
Trust no-one. They all let you down in the end.
Don't think about the past. It only fucks you up. Ditto the future.

I used to have this recurrent nightmare where my teeth worked loose and fell out. It was so real, so vivid, that it always came as a surprise to find they were still there in the morning. Years later, I read in a magazine that it was a classic insecurity dream.

The night of Dad's no-show at the concert, I pulled out one of my own teeth.

I chose the one that seemed easiest to jiggle. After a spectacular performance in front of Mum and Nana where I acted like I wasn't bothered by Dad's unexplained absence, I took myself off to bed with a mug of microwaved milk. In reality I was upset beyond comprehension, so distressed that I thought the milk tasted like the sputum of a dozen old men and hurled it out of the window on to what we laughingly termed the lawn.

Wild, mad, demented. I was all of these. Holding my breath until floaters appeared before my eyes, I scanned the bedroom for things to destroy. A wrecking spree was called for. First I disembowelled a toy panda with a nail file, yanking out its foam-rubber intestines and impaling the skin of its empty body on a wire coat hanger. Not so cuddly now, eh? Then I ripped out the mane of a My Little Pony by its roots and slashed its belly with the nail file in a frenzied attack before hanging it by the neck with its reins until it was dead. Hung, drawn, quartered and flayed alive. Not so hot to trot now, are we, My Little Phoney?

But still I was exploding with fury and bent on destruction.

Ransacking the jewellery box that Dad gave me for Christmas, I tore beads from their strings, bashed the ballerina until her neck cracked and her stupid head fell off, then kicked the shit out of the innards. Hah! No more tinkly music, no more Blue bloody Danube, no more presents to use as blackmail. I'm not for sale. You can't use me, toss me aside like a stinky old trainer and then expect me to come running because you buy me a cheap gift.

I spit on you, Lonnie Vincent!

Trashing the room wasn't enough for me. Vandalism didn't make a scratch on the surface of my rage. Surrounded by the wreckage of my life, still I searched for something to smash, something to hurt, to deflect the pain inside me.

That's when I decided to pull out a tooth from my own head. That's how mad I was.

I felt around inside my mouth for one I could get a good grip on. It was, as I later discovered, a first molar. Taking it between thumb and forefinger, I wriggled it, gently at first, to lull it into believing I meant it no harm, presented no danger. Perhaps it mistook the rhythmic rocking motion for a caress, because I felt a tiny movement, a gradual but slight loosening of the tooth inside its housing. For a while I paused, testing for pain, but there was none. And so began the assault – there is no better word – on the innocent, unsuspecting tooth. I would not rest until it was extracted, from my throbbing gum untimely ripp'd. Until I could twirl it between my fingers, hold it up to my eyes and examine it. Until I could tongue the bloody cavity it had once occupied. Until, most importantly, I could savour the pain of its absence.

What was I thinking! Was I mentally deranged?

I was eight years old.

Skivoid duties pass off uneventfully at work, even though my nerves are on edge in case there's more talk of propelling me into the spotlight on the saint's day. I'm trying to avoid bumping into the Sisters in case the sight of me sets them off on some crazy tip. Also I'm steering clear of the skivvies as far as I can because I'm in no mood for their kneeling gigs or near-hysteria.

Enda actually deigns to do a bit polishing in readiness for the bishop's visit although I don't suppose she'll run out of elbow grease, lazy cow. She says I should keep a low profile today which is fine by me. She sets me on organizing the storeroom which means climbing up a set of wobbly steps, taking down piles of towels and cloths, shaking them out, folding them up again, and putting them back in the same place. What a friggin' waste of cosmic energy. I feel a right sweaty Betty too, probably because of my premenstrual cycle, and keep squirting myself with spray perfume in case I start to get whiffy. Naturally, Enda finds a religious explanation.

Twitching her nostrils about my person, she says there's a strong scent of dried roses in the air. I'm about to correct her, tell her it's Ocean Breeze which is about as far from roses as you could imagine, but then she comes out with a load of schtick about the odour of sanctity, whatever that means. She's convinced that it's further proof, not that any is needed, of my specialness, my chosenness, my giftedness. Jeez, is there no let-up?

Fortunately my belly isn't unbearably achey today but the muscles in my arms feel as though they've seized up from all the unaccustomed activity. By the end of the shift they're stiffer than a corpse's and the biceps are almost protruding from my arms, as if I've been pumping iron all day in a gym.

Trudging down the hill to the town, I'm wondering whether to call at The Flues to beautify myself or whether I should go straight to the Internet café to see Joe and catch up on the Dadsearch. I plump for the latter. My heart thuds with excitement as the door to the Mouse Drop-in swings open with that maddening *beep-barp*. The place is busy, full of wanky student types on the computers, others slobbing out with drinks at the tables waiting for a space to come free.

Joe spots me arrive and saunters up looking like sex on legs, his tousled hair suggestive of just-got-upness even though he's been working most of the day. I just manage to stop myself going 'Phwoar'. He strokes one finger against my cheek, sending a zillion volts shooting through me.

'Glad you came by. I've found out more stuff on Moral Adair.' The sound of his voice thrills me, even if the news makes my heart plummet to my boots. 'I don't know how long these layabouts will be hanging around. Another half-hour at least. You look tired. Do you want to go upstairs, put your feet up, and I'll be there as soon as I can?'

A blush of confusion spreads up my neck. 'If you're sure you don't mind.'

'I'm sure I don't want you to leave, which amounts to the same thing.' He steers me through the door marked PRIVATE, hands me the keys to the upstairs flat and plants a fleeting kiss on the bridge of my nose, discovering a whole new erogenous zone.

My body glows with longing. I'm aching to hold him, encircle him in my arms, brush my mouth against his. Why oh why am I holding back, keeping him at arm's length? Because I'm terrified of getting it wrong, of imagining that Joe might be attracted to me when he's only being kind, feeling sorry for me because my dad fecked off and left me. Is that what he thinks of me? That I'm some charity case?

Little Orphan Roey, dragged in from the gutter, forced to scrub floors in a nunvent, a poor friendless, fatherless child? He's such an enigma it's impossible to tell.

'OK then,' I sigh, as if I need to consider it. 'A power nap should sort me out. I just need to . . .' My mind's racing. I just need to *what*? Scrape the fur off my tongue, brush my teeth until they squeak, spray the scent of ocean breeze into my armpits. Check gusset, change out of lacy black thong into scuzzy specials, voluminous knickers for *that* time of the month. Oh Lordy, feet! Mustn't forget about them. I read in a survey that smelly feet are the number one turn-off in a relationship. Hang on, why am I obsessing? Joe and I have no relationship, apart from a matey one. He could almost be my brother, in which case sue me for incestuous thoughts. Also my feet don't get sweaty, not since I recycled my trainers by dumping them in the bottle bank outside Safeways. Hey, stop wasting time, Rowena man, get yo' ass up there.

It feels strange being alone in Joe's flat, even though he's within calling distance. I perform the most cursory ablutions, change into my comfort knickers and acknowledge the bath-dwelling Ninja in a reassuring tone. Overcome with tiredness, I decide to lie down on the spare bed in case the furniture shapes in the gloomy living room spook me out. Crash. This is my knackered body collapsing on the sunflowery bed after closing the door so that Ninja can't crawl in with me.

I'm just starting to relax when Ninja's nose appears in the chink at the bottom of the door, sniff-sniff-snuffling like a truffle hound. Then he starts scratching the carpet, going wild, as if he's digging up a tasty bone.

'Stop it, Ninja,' I hiss. This sets him off whimpering, then whining, then barking like a proper guard dog. 'Fuck's sake, Ninja,' I say, as firmly as I can without yelling. I can see from his shadow that he thinks this is some kind of game. He's wagging his tail and launching his front legs at the door, scrabbling with his paws, woofing with excitement. Oh, triffic. So now I'm responsible for this vandal of a dog unravelling the carpet, scuffing the paintwork to buggery, turning Joe's comfort zone into a hobo's flop. Kneeling down, I position my face against the gap under the door and click my tongue to get Ninja's attention. He pauses for a moment to work out what's what, then comes out with a deep throaty snarl as if I'm an intruder armed with a machete about to hack his master to pieces.

'It's me, Ninja,' I whisper. 'Rowena, your friend. You slept in my bed, remember? I'm trying to take a nap so please shut the fuck up, there's a good boy.'

'Don't be teaching him bad language.' The door inches open and there's Joe, resplendent in a Jamiroquai T-shirt and a pair of tracky bottoms. Have I died and gone to heaven? 'Sorry, Rowena,' says Joe. 'Was the mutt playing up?'

I haul myself to a standing position with what scrap of dignity I can muster, considering I've just been caught lying on the floor cussing a dog.

'Has everyone gone downstairs? Have you closed the shop?'

'Yeah, I called time early again. Look, why don't you take a nap in my room. I might join you; I usually relax for a bit after work, if that's OK with you.'

He takes my hand, sending lightning down my spine, across my shoulders, an electric storm ending up, fizzing and sparking, in the knicker region.

I feel as though my legs are floating into Joe's room on their own, as though they belong to a parallel me slightly removed from the normal mind/body configuration. Fortunately Joe doesn't seem to notice, or is too polite to remark on it. He pats the bed, inviting me to park my butt, only Ninja gets there first so I'm left perching on the edge with both feet resting on the floor. The dog grins, sticks out his tongue and whips the tip of his tail on the duvet like this is some manic territorial game where he dares me to claim a piece of his bedspace.

'Behave, you bad hound, where's your manners,' says Joe, pushing Ninja on to the floor. 'Go lie on your own bed.' Ninja slinks across the room and flops on to a beanbag, sighing and rearranging his features into a pissed-off expression. I slide my bum further on board, while Joe zaps the remote to dim the lights so they still change colour but in a more muted, less obvious way. Another zap and some music comes on, pipes and squeezebox kind of stuff, but slow and strangely sad, a woman's voice drifting from speaker to speaker, pure yet hazy like a haunting dream. Not my usual taste, I prefer a thumping bassline reverberating in my head, throbbing in my belly, but I'm open to new sensations.

Joe eases his gorgeous butt on to the bed and spreads out next to me. This is such a weird and unsettling feeling, like being in a foreign country without a map or a mobile. Nothing new there, then. He shifts position, raising himself up on one elbow, cupping his chin with a hand, gazing directly, wordlessly, at my face.

My belly tingles. My cheeks burn with confusion.

'What?' I say at last. 'Why are you staring at me?'

Joe shuffles up closer. 'Can't I admire the scenery?' He reaches out a hand and strokes my cheek. My heart races. I hold my breath to stop myself from moaning. All kinds of crazy stuff is going on in the downstairs department. To break the tension I fake a yawn, a huge, lockjaw type that cries out for an anti-tetanus jab.

'Aurr-u-ugh, I'm pure bushed, Joe.' It's the truth. I'm knocked out, flattened by a wave of exhaustion. Plus my eyes are watering, my mascara's claggy and I'm worried in case he's noticed the spots on my forehead. Here I am, in intimate bodily contact with the lushest boy on the planet and what happens? I mutate into a warthog with sleeping sickness. Typical.

'Relax,' says Joe, his voice warm and smiley. 'Close your eyes, let your body float.' He folds the duvet over me, lowers the music volume until it's barely audible and leaves the room, clicking his fingers for Ninja to follow him. Overcome with a weariness that makes my skin creep, I drift, drift away, a beautiful, weightless surrender into the arms of the slumber god.

Later, when I surface into consciousness, the first thing I'm aware of is the noise of lip-smacking, the wet, satisfied sound of one who's just enjoyed a juicy steak, perhaps, and wants to savour the taste for as long as possible. A teeth-sucking, mouth-licking, spittle-making sound. It's issuing from the corner of the room, from Ninja to be precise, sprawled out on his beanbag. Whatever he had for dinner, it must have been the doggy equivalent of a cordon bleu blowout. On closer inspection, he's still eating it, grabbing it between his pointy teeth, ripping the flesh in a canine feeding frenzy. I watch in fascination as he tears it apart, mixes it with saliva, chews and finally swallows. It takes a while before it dawns on me exactly what is tickling his taste buds.

My thong! The black lacy number that I whipped off earlier before changing into a pair of comfort knickers. The beast must have been rootling in my bag. The dog is eating my pants!

'Ninja! Leave!' I yell, scrambling off the bed and crawling across the floor to the beanbag. 'Bad, bad dog,' I say, trying to retrieve the chewed bits of cloth from his mouth. He turns his head away and carries on ripping, jaws clenched round a scrap of the material grasped between his paws. 'Drop it now, Ninja, this isn't a game. Give it to me.' He narrows his eyes and growls, curling his top lip in an Elvis impression as a warning that he isn't playing a game either.

'I'd leave him to get on with it before he has your fingers off.' Sweet Jesu, it's Joe, and he's witnessing the violation of my thongular undies. I could expire from embarrassment! 'I dunno what he grabbed, I hope it wasn't anything expensive.'

'No. Oh, no, no, no, no,' I gabble. 'Nothing like that.' Somehow I manage to stop myself admitting it was a dead cheapo item nicked from a market stall.

'Enjoy your power nap?' says Joe, offering his hand to help me up from the floor.

'What? How long have I been asleep?'

'Fifteen, maybe twenty minutes.'

'You're kidding me. Is that all?' I feel alert, refreshed, alive, words that almost never apply to me. Slobbed out, sluggish, dead on my feet, much more my stylee. So the night is still young, Joe is still friends with me and I'm still up for it, whatever 'it' is. Who cares if my underwear is dissolving in the dog's stomach acid? I'm wide awake and ready for anything, except sexual intercourse, possibly. Or poetry.

'You want some music on?' Joe flips through a stack of CDs dead fast, like a card sharp shuffling a deck.

I nod. 'Can we have something normal on, not that weird stuff you were playing before? It sends me to sleep, no offence like.'

'Is that right?' Joe laughs, selecting a disc and slapping it in. 'We'll go for Anastacia, nobody sleeps when she's on.' I check the label. It's her first album, *Not That Kind*, and I'd forgotten what an amazingly raunchy voice she has, how it makes you want to get down and dirty. Instinctively I wiggle my shoulders, half-close my eyes and pout, losing myself in the music. When the second track starts I'm well gone, singing 'I'm Outta Love' at full belt, waving my arms, shaking my booty.

'Would you mind if I kiss you,' says Joe into my ear.

Would I *mind*? Although my instinct is to back away, he wraps one arm around me, tilts my face with his hand and touches his mouth to mine gently, moistly, so tenderly that it leaves me giddy and breathless. My head spins, my legs tremble, my stomach turns to jelly. I want to hold him tight against me, feel his body pressing into my intimate crannies, writhe hornily next to him, shamelessly offer him my wanton self to use any way he wants to.

Naturally, I don't, even though I'm at the second-raunchiest stage of my menstrual cycle. Confused and flustered, I back off, let the embrace dissolve into nothingness, act flippant. What is it with me? Like he's going to reject me after that soft, sexy kiss?

31

Holyunstoned

Just as I begin to relax, Joe springs a surprise by offering to update me on Moral Adair. My heart sinks to my socks. Why – when I should be jumping for joy? Face it, the only reason I'm here – in Ireland, at the Internet café – is to find out more about Dad, so why do I feel so uncomfortable? Dad is screwing things up for me again. I resent the way he's hijacked our potential lovemaking situation, turning Joe's thoughts of passion to a sense of duty, making Joe feel that he's overstepped the mark, crossed the dividing line between friendship and intimacy, that he has to keep our relationship on agreed rails. Or perhaps I'm scared that we'll unearth something to ruin my image of the fantasy father, discover that he's far from the perfect parent of my dreams. Maybe he's a criminal, doing time in prison for gunrunning, turkey-rustling or pig-smuggling. Even worse, what if he's a down-and-out, a drunken bum sleeping in hedgerows, yelling at people in the street, swilling cheap cider and begging for roll-ups? I'd die of shame.

Taking a deep breath and steeling myself for a disappointment, I say, 'Let me have it.'

Joe explains that a woman at the FCD replied to his message, sending him an e-mail address for Moral, although she couldn't say if it was still current. Madair@holyunstoned.com; just the ticket for a born-again recovering junkie.

'We'll need to compose a message about your dad,' says Joe. 'Something that won't put Moral on his guard, something that doesn't reveal too much about yourself. I've set you up with a Shotmail account so you can stay as anonymous as you like. You could be writing from anywhere in the world for all he knows.'

We go downstairs to the café. Joe logs on to a computer, launches the web browser and types in an address. A page appears, nothing fancy, just purple writing on a white background.

www.holyunstoned.com
THE OFFICIAL WEBSITE OF MORAL ADAIR
::: COMING SOON :::
"WAS LOST BUT NOW AM FOUND"

I frown. 'What's that supposed to mean?'

'It's a holding page,' says Joe. 'He hasn't got the website up and running yet. I checked the address he used when he registered the domain name but it was done through a nominee, which means we can't contact Moral by snail mail. He might not have given his real address anyway. We can still reach him by e-mail though, assuming he checks his inbox.'

I set to work writing a message by hand but have to scribble it out and start again several times until the words sound right. Meanwhile, Joe scans in the photo of Dad with Moral and the absconding barman so that we can send it as an attachment with the e-mail. This is to establish my credentials and also to nudge Moral's memory, if it hasn't already been eaten away by drug and alcohol abuse. Joe approves my sixth draft, which reads as follows, including a few minor amendments suggested by him.

Dear Mr Moral Adair,

I'm writing to you in the hope that you'll be able to help me in my quest to trace my ~~boilogical~~ biological father, Lawrence Vincent, better known as Lonnie Vincent, ~~formally~~ formerly of Newcastle upon Tyne, England~~, UK~~.

I am his ~~dauhter~~ daughter Rowena M. Vincent. My Nana (Lonnie's mother) gave me the ~~attatched~~ attached picture of you with Lonnie (right) and a barman (left) outside a bar called the

Beggar's Belief in Cork Street, Dublin. The photo was taken two years ago on Bloomsday. Someone has written on the back 'Toasting Joyce', ~~but I have no idea who Joyce is as she doesn't appear. Maybe she was holding the camera.~~

Do you ~~rember~~ ^{remember} having this photo taken? Did you know Lonnie Vincent? If so, could you tell me how to get in touch with him? It is very ~~impotant~~ ^{important} for me to contact him as he will learn something to his ~~avantedge~~ ^{advantage}, and that is the god's honest truth.

I hope you are keeping well ~~and mannaging to stay of the chemicals you depended on~~ and that you will find time to reply as it is v. urgent.

Thank you Mr Adair or Moral if its OK to call you that.

~~Sinscerley~~ ^{Sincerely},

Rowena M. Vincent

Joe reads it through again and says it's probably as good as it's going to get. Then he shows me how to send it using my very own personal e-mail address. It's a surprise to find he's set me up as madolescent@shotmail.com but he says he couldn't resist using the word as he'd never heard of it until I mentioned it the other night. He types in the message, attaches the picture, addresses it to Madair@holyunstoned.com and presses the send button. I feel dead nervous imagining it whizzing through cyberspace, wherever that is, and finding its way like a tiny computerized pigeon to Moral's inbox. Stupidly, I blow a kiss at the screen to wish it good luck, crossing my fingers behind my back to double it.

'Now all we have to do is wait,' says Joe.

'If only it were that simple,' I mumble, sighing.

'Or I could tell you about Joyce, if you want to hear.'

'Joyce?' The word almost chokes me. 'What do you know about her? Tell me, Joe, even if it's bad news. I can handle it, honest.'

He warns me not to be disappointed if Joyce is not the kind of person I've imagined. Then he tells me.

Could anyone be more stupid than me! It turns out that it isn't a woman after all, but a famous Irish bloke called James Joyce who wrote books and stuff. When I challenge Joe to prove it, he tells me this geet long story about how Bloomsday is named after a character called Leopold Bloom in *Ulysses*. He says that Bloomsday, which turns out to be on 16th June, was the day that Joyce the writer and a woman called Nora Barnacle first went walking in a place called Ringsend and it's, like, a big deal all around the world.

I'm stunned and speechless! In my worst imaginings, I thought Joyce was Dad's girlfriend and that maybe they were married and – horror! – she'd given birth to a kid or two, my half-siblings, snotty, smelly-bummed infants. Lonnie Vincent and his new clear family.

But at least Joe's knocked that theory out of the water.

32

King Arthur and the Nights of the Unstable

Back at The Flues, Texy is just emerging from the bathroom. I'm dying to hear about her night of lust. She looks as if she's done a couple of rounds with Mad Mike Tyson. Her face is puffed to buggery, dark bags like sacks of coal under her eyes.

'What happened to you?' I say, helping myself to a ciggie from her packet. 'Someone land you a sucker punch?'

'Didn't get any sleep last night,' she says, mumbling, too drained of energy to operate her mouth. 'I feel like the walking dead – at least I would, if I could walk properly. My legs are wobbly and unstable.' She twitches her swollen lips in a hint of a grin. Her date must have turned out hotter than hot.

'You're unstable, full stop. I take it you got shagged senseless, then?'

'Rowena!' she yells, sounding shocked at the very suggestion, before returning to a girly-secret tone of voice. 'You could say that. I feel bruised all over, especially, y'know, inside the sugar walls.' She tugs on her Marlboro. 'He's a well-made lad, is Matty.'

'Spare me the details,' I say, grimacing. Then, as curiosity wins out, 'Oh, go on, then, you maison well tell us.'

She budges up next to me, whispers confidentially in my ear. 'Put it this way: imagine blowing a didgeridoo . . .'

'You're kidding!' I thump her on the shoulder, pretending to be stunned. 'Really?'

'I was nearly, like, cleft in twain,' she giggles. 'Rent asunder.'

'And what about his King Arthur?' I say, trying not to appear overeager.

'King Arthur?' Texy frowns and wrinkles her nose. 'Me no understand.'

'Down there,' I say, nodding my head and making my eyes go big. 'His body-piercing. The ring on his thing.'

'King Arthur?' Texy lets out an explosive laugh. 'You mean his Prince Albert, you eejit. How did you know about that? Has Joe been blabbing about Matty's privates?'

'He might have mentioned it in passing,' I reply. 'So what about it, then, did it hurt? I bet it chafed a bit?'

Texy rolls her eyes and puts her finger on her chin in mock-concentration. 'Chafe? It's supposed to give extra stimulation, so no complaints on that score. It didn't exactly *hurt*, not until after we'd been going at it for three or four hours, then I started to feel battered about a bit.'

'Repent, thou whore of Ballyloony,' I say in a dramatic voice, pointing an accusing finger at her, booming like an Old Testament prophet. 'Lest thou be internally lacerated and rendered barren by the wrath of God.'

'Rowena, stop it, don't make me laugh,' she says, clutching her middle. 'My ribs feel like they've been through a crusher.'

'You're a filthy dirty mare, Texy Maguire,' I say, giggling. 'And as punishment for your sexual misdemeanours you shall buy the drinks all evening.'

'It's a deal.' She grinds her ciggy into the ashtray and plants me a kiss on the cheek. 'Not a word to anyone, yeah?'

'My lips are sealed. Unlike yours, you brazen harlot.'

It's like twat soup in the bar of The Flues, totally heaving with all kinds of people I don't want to mix with.

'OK, where to?' I say as we hover in the vestibule. 'Do you fancy a pizza for a change, I'm starving hungry?'

'Sure.' Texy and I link arms, bending our heads against a force nine gale, and stagger down the street. The wind rips at my carefully sculpted hair until it feels like candyfloss about to fly off its stick.

'Let's get out of this friggin' hurricane before we take off into the stratosphere,' I say. 'That might be a pizza place over there, next to the bus shelter.'

Texy braves a glance. 'It's only a chipper,' she says, 'but it'll do me.'

Some of the local youths are hanging out in the rackety shelter, hunched up in the wind, noses red, knuckles grazing the ground. This must be their version of a big night out.

'Got a smoke?' says one, daring to beg from me.

'Suck my gusset,' I snap back, shoving past him into the chip shop. His mates burst out laughing, taunting him, so my night isn't a total waste of time. Obviously these mouth-breathers aren't used to the sophisticated repartee of townies like me. Texy and I order a tray of chips each with loads of salt and vinny. They're disgusting, overcooked and limp, and hot for all of two seconds until the typhoon hits them, when they turn sour and greasy.

'I can't eat these deep-fried sluggy things,' I grumble, screwing up the tray and depositing it in a handy flower bed. 'We maison well go back to The Flues and drink ourselves mortal. At least we'll be within staggering distance of bed.'

'Suits me,' says Texy, booting her tray of chips into the air like a football. We cling to each other and fight the tornado along the street to the pub, bolting straight into the ladies' bog to see what we can salvage of our ruined hairdos and streaky mascara.

The bar is crowded, the usual row of serious drinkers propping up the counter, groups of peasants on the banquettes, men in Jurassic suits, women with blue eyeshadow and bleached-to-buggery hair. A few younger people slouch near the jukebox and around the pool table. Matty is nowhere in sight. Cilla the barmaid explains that he's in a meeting with the brewery rep and could be some time.

'Fancy some Red Bull with your vodka?' says Texy, forging a path to the counter. I nod. Jeez, this place is grim, it gives me the creeps. Nearly everyone is fifty years old and even the younger blokes are dressed in the types of hoodies and trainers that are *so* five years ago. I lean against the jukey trying to look enigmatic but I'm so uptight a wee tic starts twitching underneath my eye. Triffic. Now everyone will think I'm a hooker winking at prospective clients.

'Drinks,' announces Texy, plonking a glass in my hand. She takes a long swig of hers, eyes me up and down. 'What's up? Look at the face on you, it's like a pound of smacked tripe.'

I shrug.

Texy laughs. I'm mired in the slough of despond and all she can do is laugh! 'Ah, drink up, Rowena, things always look better when you're blootered.'

'You're not funny,' I snap. 'In fact you sound like that mad old housekeeper in *Father Ted*. She was Irish too. I rest my case.'

'Get outta here,' grins Texy, digging her elbow into my ribs. She raises her glass. 'Come on, after three. One, two . . .' We knock down the drinks but I feel so choked and confused, mine nearly comes back up my throat. I'm on the point of calling it a night, heading upstairs to bury myself in the duvet, when Texy says, 'Look, there's Joe just walked in.'

My brain snaps awake, like a computer springing to life after being in standby mode. A hot tingle spreads through my belly. Joe, Mr Gorgeous Tush-of-the-Century. I follow with my eyes, mesmerized, as he lopes up to the counter, jeans clinging to his muscle-toned bum, a wet dream in denim. Cilla pulls him a pint and he takes a sip. Wiping his mouth, Joe turns round and flashes the sexiest smile, lifting his glass in a greeting. Seeing him, remembering his kiss, makes me fizzy-knickered but also confused. Confused, awkward and unco-ordinated.

'How're ya,' he mimes.

'How're ya, Joe,' calls Texy.

Me, I'm struck dumb and paralysed, apart from the twitch below my eye. Duh, retarded or what?

'Let's go stand at the bar and talk to him,' says Texy. I'm rooted to the spot, unable to put one foot in front of the other for fear I'll lumber like Frankenstein's monster, or someone trying out prosthetic limbs for the first time.

'You go,' I manage. 'I'll stay here and put some music on.'

'And what's Joe going to make of that? He'll think you're not interested. I don't get you one bit, Rowena.' Texy mimes tearing her hair. 'You chuck your chances down the drain.'

Unlike some, who dredge theirs up from the sewer, is what I'm thinking. What's wrong with me tonight? It feels as if I'm sur-rounded by a negative force field, being zap-zap-zapped with death-ray vibes. Why this doomed-out feeling, this sense of fore-boding? It's Joe, or rather it's our hot-and-cold relationship. I'm mad into him but confused also, because I don't know where we stand or where we're heading. Get a grip, missus.

I let out a deep sigh and say, 'OK then, only you'll have to do the talking; I'm not in the mood. My brain's on a downer for some reason.'

'Not a problem, kid,' Texy assures me. 'We can't be sunny all the time. Your name's Rowena, remember, not Pollyanna.' How she can be so lovely in the face of my bolshie-mindedness beats me.

It's fine, though. My dark mood fades as soon as Joe bestows one of his smiles and odd-eyed special, just-for-you looks on me. Shivering fits, this boy is pure ultra-gorgeous de gorgeous. He makes me smoulder. How could I ever have thought of pushing him away?

'I thought the cat was supposed to have your tongue,' says Texy while Joe visits the latrine. 'But I can't get a word in edgeways between you two. When you're not nattering you're making cows' eyes at each other.' She pretends to stick two fingers down her throat. 'Look, I'm not playing gooseberry all night. I'm away to find

Matty, drag him away from the brewery guy, maybe play a tune on the didgeridoo with any luck.'

'You tart!' I spit, but not venomously. Joe returns and Texy slips away in search of some take-me-big-boy entertainment.

Joe spots a free table near the window so we park ourselves on the seat and I push my leg next to his slyly but casually, and revel in the warmth of it beside mine.

How we get around to discussing the merits of pro-biotic yoghurt I can't remember, but it proves we can talk on just about any subject. Joe says he isn't *Oh Fay* with those wee plastic bottles of drinky yoghurt. This surprises me as I thought he was up on health foods, nuts and stuff, but at least it gives me a chance to educate him on the benefits.

'It keeps your stomach in working order,' I inform him, 'by balancing the fauna in your gut.'

'The fauna, really?' he says, smiling. 'And the flora too, I'm guessing?'

'Flora's a kind of low-fat spread,' I point out with some authority, as Nana Vincent used to scrape it on her toast. It didn't stop her having a stroke, though.

I explain about Botox, the stuff people get injected into their foreheads to freeze the muscles to stop them getting wrinkles.

'It costs a bomb in beauty salons, but I read up about it in *Take a Break* magazine and it should be easy enough to do it from home.'

'How would that work exactly?' Joe asks.

'Simple,' I tell him. 'You open a tin of tuna or dressed crab, leave it in a warm place for a few days until it forms this stuff called botulin, then get hold of a hypodermic syringe from, say, a druggy or an insulin-dependent diabetic, and just inject it into the forehead. *Voilà*! Piece of piss.'

'You're amazing,' he says, and I feel a blush spreading out from my hair follicles, thrilled skinny that I've impressed him with my scientific knowledge.

Texy's hair is cockled up in shagger's tufts when she reappears hand in hand with Matty. I go to point it out but manage to stop myself by imagining how embarrassed *I'd* feel if someone did it to me. Not that I've indulged in sexual congress. No such luck. I'm beginning to wonder whether Joe has a problem in that department as he's never come on to me apart from the odd kiss. Maybe he's in the gayers, I dunno, but I'd sure like to find out.

Texy and Matty sit down at our table. It's obvious they've just done it; the air is crackling with pheromones and I think I can smell sex on them, even over the stink of booze and fags. They down their drinks in no time flat, then Texy says she's come to tell me that she'll be staying with Matty in his room tonight, leaving me free to do whatever.

After they leave, with Matty practically pole-vaulting his way out, I turn to look at Joe, trying to guess his reaction to the news that I'm unexpectedly available. He squeezes my hand, which is a promising sign, then whispers into my ear. Not so promising.

'I'll be getting off home; busy day tomorrow with the oldsters. You'll be OK on your own so?'

Choked, feeling humiliated and rejected, I nod. 'Yup, I could do with an early night too. Loads to do.' What a lie. Maybe I'll slap on a face mask, pluck my eyebrows, prune my toenails, some of that girly stuff, if I can be arsed. I can't help feeling cheated and mildly depressed, wondering if this is Joe's way of binning me off, dropping me.

I walk him to the door of The Flues, shuffling like some geriatric in oversized slippers.

'G'night then,' I mutter, unable to meet his gaze.

'Don't I get a kiss?' he says. This perks me up no end, but I decide to play it cool.

'If you like,' I reply, fighting the urge to pucker up and stand on tiptoe, which is a good thing as he reaches down and offers me the merest brush of his lips on my cheek. Is this it – the kiss-off? The final embrace? The sign that means *You're history*?

'Call in tomorrow after work, if you're not doing anything,' Joe says.

'I'll have to check the diary,' I reply over my shoulder, a mite offhandedly, slouching towards the stairs. Jeez, what is it with me and my self-destruct button? Why do I do this to myself?

33

Facing the God Squad

For once in her life, Enda gets her lazy arse to work on time. Trust me to be late, only half an hour, but still. She emits a puff of air, meaning that she's relieved to see me, but she's also wearing a strange expression, sort of pinched around the mouth like a camel's anus. I'm guessing it spells some kind of trouble.

'Rowena, put your uniform on and get upstairs double quick.' She rolls her eyes and jerks her thumb heavenwards. 'You've been summoned to an audience with the papal cow.'

'Eh?' My face screws up in a question.

'Sister Bonzo,' says Enda. 'She sent Eminem scuttling down here looking for you first thing. Go on then, instead of standing there looking dazed.' She forces my arms into an overall, lines up the Velcro strips and shoves me through the door. 'And if it's bother you're in, make sure you don't drag me into it.'

Paula passes me on the stairs, her eyes Bambi-wide, although staring in different directions.

'What the frig is going on, Paula?' I snap. 'Do you know why Bonzo's sent for me?'

She flattens her back against the wall, keeping out of my reach. 'I know n-n-nothing,' she says in a trembly voice, meaning the news has already travelled round the below-stairs grapevine. I'm considering shaking it out of her, grabbing her by the hair and slamming her head against the wall until she confesses, but that would make me even more late.

'Hey, no worries, chuck,' I say in a semi-kindly way. Her shoulders relax from their ear-level position and she scurries off to gossip to her workmates about her close encounter with the mad-woman from the Cleanliness department.

Even though I'm not particularly rushing, by the time I reach Sister Bonaventure's office I'm panting like an out-of-condition greyhound. Mental note to cut down the fag intake. I tap on the door, smoothing down the vile overall and checking for holes in my tights.

'Come,' purrs Bonzo in her honeyed voice. It occurs to me that she'd give great phone sex if she hadn't already signed up as a bride of Christ.

I enter the room, closing the door behind me, and stand there like a ninny while she finishes reading a letter or two. This is dis-gracious. My time is valuable. I could be, I dunno, microwaving a milky coffee to kick-start Enda with a jolt of caffeine or rearranging the biscuits in alphabetical order. After an age Sister Bonzo puts the correspondence aside, slides her glasses down her nose and does a royal wave of the hand which I interpret to mean I should park my butt on the chair opposite her.

'Ah, Rowena.' She removes the specs, folds them on the desk and exhales a lengthy sigh. 'Rowena, Rowena. Do you know why you're here?'

She stares at me wordlessly. At least she might clue me in on whether it's some kind of philosophical question.

'You got me on that one, Sister,' I shrug.

Her face is expressionless although I sense cogs chugging in her brain, as though she's struggling to come to a decision.

'I'll come to the point,' she says eventually. 'You'll be aware that we celebrate our saint's day on Thursday . . .'

'My birthday,' I butt in.

She ignores the interruption.

'. . . and that this year marks the two hundredth anniversary of her martyrdom?'

I nod. Jeez, my tights are snaggy around the knees, my second favourite pair too.

Bonzo takes me on a verbal tour of St Vincenza's life and achievements, creaming on about her being the foundress of the order of Sisters of Blessed Relief, how she bore the stigmata and suchlike, but skating over the details of her grisly death, the stoning and eye-gouging, which is the part that interests me most.

'So you understand the importance of the bicentenary to us, Rowena?'

'Er, I guess so.'

'It's vital that everything goes smoothly, that we're all – what's the expression? – singing from the same hymn sheet.'

'Vital, yeah.' I don't understand why they can't print extra hymn sheets instead of everyone craning their necks to sing from the same one.

She passes me a leaflet about Vincenza, and another one about wills, bequests and stuff, begging people to leave their moolah to the nunvent instead of to their families. I bet that'll go down like a knackered lift with the bereaved relatives, especially if they've been counting on the dead person's dosh to pay for a holiday or a new car. She advises me to glance through the pamphlets at my convenience though I don't believe in taking reading matter into the bogatory as there's all kinds of poo germs floating about. Sister B. mentions that pilgrims will be congregating from all over Ireland, plus others from Europe including some big cheeses from the Catlick world.

Yeah, yeah, I'm thinking. And . . .? What has any of this got to do with me? My stomach is dead grumbly from biscuit deprivation and menstrual jiggles. I truly can't be arsed to listen to the whole speech; it's like a boring history lesson, or being brainwashed into joining some bizarre cult. I will not cease from mental fight. Words aimed at my grey matter melt away like butter drizzling down boiled sheep's brain. Resist, resist. Do not succumb to Bonzo's hypnotic voice. Do not let her penetrate your thoughts.

'So how do you feel about that, Rowena?' Sister Bonaventure

thinks I've been entranced, but she couldn't be more wrong. My ears have been shut, deaf to her blandishments, the whole time.

'Er, cool,' I say, humouring her. 'I'm totally cool with it, Sister.' Lord knows what she's been rabbiting on about. As I close her door behind me, I hear a ping as she picks up the phone to make a call.

A welcoming committee awaits me when I return to Enda's quarters. The skivvies are buzzing with excitement, bombarding me with questions.

What did Bonzo say to you?

'Some old pants about the saint's day, how important it is to roll the visitors for cash, con them into sticking the nunvent in their Last Will and Testament. Sounds well dodgy to me, like a religious scam. Oh, and they're going to make everybody share the same hymn sheet, tight buggers.'

Are you going to do it?

'Do what? Read the leaflets, you mean? I doubt it very much. She told me to look through them at my convenience. How unhygienic is that? They're printed on glossy paper an' all, not even fit for emergency bum paper. It makes you wonder how the Sisters live, dunnit?'

Do they want you to wear a costume?

'She never mentioned anything about it being fancy dress, not that I remember. Mind, I stopped listening, switched off partway through. If it's a daft dressy-up gig I think I'll go as Lara Croft, or P!nk, it ought to be easy enough to knock up a costume.'

Will you be doing any lines?

'No way. I don't do coke in case it overstimulates my heart and makes me drop dead. Imagine the shame of being found in a toilet cubicle with a rolled-up twenty-quid note, powder up your snitch and your knickies showing. Anyway, I can't get excited about any drug that has to be snorted off a cistern. Eurgghh!'

None of their stupid questions makes a jot of sense so I wave them away and go to score some caffeine. It's a weird set-up, though. Why do I have a feeling that they know more about this malarkey than I do? They're flitting and fussing around me as if I'm the second coming or something. Aww, I'll wheedle it out of them soon enough.

Now I ain't saying the girls at the nunvent start giving me the superstar treatment, but there's a definite change in their attitude towards me. They're nicer, more respectful, as though I've contracted some exotic, non-contagious disease and need to be pampered. This suits me fine as it means I have practically nothing to do in the way of proper work, not even being Enda's personal domestic slave. Scaredy-cat Paula has cast herself in that role, popping in and out of the Cleanliness department several times to cater for our coffee and tea requirements, as well as introducing new lines of biscuits for our delectation. First it was chocolate-covered marshmallows with a crumbly base, then ginger Hobnobs. When I happened to remark that I preferred the chocolate ones, Paula was crushed and skittered to the shop in her lunch break to buy a packet. I'm considering going rockstar, having a rider written into my contract specifying a barrel of Smarties with all the yellow ones taken out, or a crate of Evian water and some organic cranberry juice as a mixer.

Enda laps up the attention, basking in my reflected glory. Next thing she'll be coming to work wearing shades, swinging her sarnies in a Gucci carrier bag. I can't say I understand this turn of events, this worshipping-me-like-a-saint business, but I'm not one to complain. OK, the skivvies chose to believe that business about the stigmata, the face in the J-cloth, but it isn't as if I deliberately set out to trick them.

Today has turned into one long coffee/tea/chocolate break, sipping, slurping, nibbling, munching, trying to stave off boredom. The downside is having to bear Enda's non-stop wittering: the history of her foot complaints, endless recipes for boiled ham shanks, corny homespun homilies, such as 'Eaten cake is soon forgotten.' That's certainly true in Enda's case. It beats me how she still has any teeth left in her head after the sugary snacks she shovels down her neck.

Our all-day brunch menu includes angel cake and iced fondant fancies, donated by Mary Belker from the bakery, plus Belgian chocolate beverage in a carton reeking of baccy after making the journey to work in Grainne the seamstress's handbag. Yuk, it's lumpy too, and tastes of salt, not destined to be a major seller in the instanto drinko line. It wouldn't surprise me if gold, frankincense and myrrh put in an appearance before long.

Six of us scooch up round the table while Enda recounts in minute detail every bloody programme she watched on telly last night. I'm on the point of losing the will to live when Joelle from the laundry charges in through the door, her eyes as poppy as ping-pong balls.

'The bishop's here!' she announces, almost hysterically. The news is met by a communal intake of breath from the huddled masses. 'He's gone straight into a meeting with the Reverend Mother, Sister Bonzo, Monica and the rest. Cuthbert's just taken them some tea. Sure wouldn't I like to be a fly on their wall?'

All eyes turn to me.

'What?' I say. '*What*?' This is starting to do my head in; it's like everyone's in on some big secret except yours truly.

Enda beams at me. I recognize the look from a telly programme about American beauty pageants where all these toddlers dressed like hookers paraded around a stage pouting and flirting in some paedo's paradise. Bleuggh! Enda is bestowing upon me the unmistakable smile of a Showbiz Mum.

'Rowena, my little star,' she smarms, her maternal tone suggesting that I sprang from her very own loins. 'And sure won't half the world be there to see your acting debut, your triumphant stage performance, your starring role? I bet it took Dame Judi years to get where you are now. I'm so proud to have been the one who discovered you. Come here, give Enda a hug.'

'Acting debut?' I repeat. 'Stage performance? What are you on about?'

'Don't feign ignorance, you know well what I mean. Sister Bonaventure explained it to you this morning. Now give me that hug.' She draws me to her, half-suffocating me.

'Where are they?' I whisper into her bosoms. 'The bishop and that lot? Where's the meeting?'

'In Bonzo's office,' she replies under her breath. 'Now don't you go listening at doors . . .'

Too late. I wriggle free and vamoose up the stairs.

The door to Sister Bonaventure's room is open just a smidgen, but far enough for me to hear snippets of conversation.

'I saw the marks with my own eyes, on the palms of her hands and across her forehead.' This is Bonzo's syrupy voice. 'It was also reported to me that the girl suffered an agonizing pain in her side.' Oh, triffic. That can only have come from Enda, the gobshite.

'Another time she swore her Father's face appeared to her in a cloud.' Sister Monica's chiming in with her two penn'orth now. 'I saw her fall to her knees in prayer. When I reached the poor child, she was speaking in the voices of angels.'

Bonzo tuts. 'Speaking in tongues is not a practice to be encouraged. We are not *charismatics*, Sister.'

Eminem chips in with the story of how the dustbuster brigade witnessed the face of Jesus in the J-cloth, then she goes on about how the Blessed Virgin appeared in a half-eaten dessert. 'That one's just hearsay,' she adds. 'I believe the incident took place before she had arrived here.'

'Her arrival, yes. That in itself was strange,' says Sister Bonaventure. 'If I recall, she said that our Father appeared to her in a vision and it was He who sent her to us.'

My fists clench and unclench in frustration. I want to leap out from my hiding place and burst into the room saying, 'No, you've got it all wrong. It was *my* father – my dad, Lonnie Vincent – in the dream, not *our* Father, the God bod, Jesus's dad. The time I saw God, it was in real life, in the garden.' But I restrain myself as it would look bad if they knew I'd been earwigging outside the door.

'One could see why some would find these events persuasive,' says a man, the bishop, I guess. 'But what I find remarkable, what almost clinches it for me, is the girl's name. Rowena Vincent, yes?'

Unseen outside the door, I nod my head like a lunatic.

'And our saint is Vincenza of Verona,' he continues. 'Vincenza, of course, would be the Roman equivalent of Vincent. And Rowena is almost an anagram of Verona. I say almost, until we consider that in Latin pronunciation, "v" is pronounced as "w".' He pauses for dramatic effect before playing his trump card. 'Ergo, we have a perfect anagram: Rowena, Werona. Taken all in all, the connection is compelling.'

A group sigh issues from the assembled nuns, accompanied by the clink of china teacups on saucers.

Sister Monica says her piece. 'She is a good-hearted girl. I know that she visits some of the residents in our care home; Miss O'Hara for example.'

'Would that be Miss Teazie O'Hara?' asks the bishop.

'One and the same,' Monica assures him.

'It never harms to have influential friends,' the bishop muses.

My stomach muscles tighten. Influential friends. He must be referring to Hefty and the Mob!

'Good-hearted the girl may be, but isn't she somewhat . . . *earthy* in her demeanour? The way she dresses is a little on the flamboyant side.' Bloody Eminem, trust her to stick her oar in. Old prune.

'That can be disguized by the use of a costume,' suggests Bonzo.

'Have you broached the subject with her?' asks the bishop. 'Is she amenable?'

228

Sister Bonaventure hesitates. 'I mooted the idea with her earlier. She didn't object, although I'm not sure if she absorbed it fully. Her mind might have been set on higher things; she often appears distracted, preoccupied. But I'm sure it will not prove to be a problem. She has a . . . how should I describe it? She has a *theatrical* side to her.'

'Excellent,' says the bishop. 'Her portrayal of St Vincenza will be central to the ceremony. The last thing we need is stage fright, so theatricality, in this situation, is a blessing.' The sisters respond with a muted chortle.

My portrayal of St Vincenza? A theatrical side to me? A costume? What are they skanging on about? It sounds like they're planning a friggin' pantomime! My kneebones rattle. Me – an actress, a stage performer. Fuck-a-doodledoo! Memories of my Shakespearean role as Pease-blossom come flooding back. Lumpen, in Pegg-leg's opinion. Lumpen, wooden and stilted. In other words, shit. Ah, so what? I was young, short on life experience back then. Now I know better. I've seen loads of movies and TV dramas, *ER* and stuff, with proper actors. All I need to do is get in touch with my inner saint and *whoomph*! Oscars beckon. Brad Pitt will insist on me in his next film. Gwyneth Paltrow can kiss my black ass. OK, pinkish, then. A star is born.

But then a terrible thought occurs to me, piercing my heart with a shaft of ice. How far . . .? This is almost too grisly to contemplate. How far do they intend to take the re-enactment of the saint's life? How authentic is it to be? What if, in the interests of dramatic realism, they're planning to gouge out my eyes and pelt me with stones? Am I to die in agony, blinded and bludgeoned by a mob of religious cranks?

Please, God, help me out on this one.

'What did you find out?' Enda's quizzing me as soon as I set foot in the Cleanliness department. 'Where's your colour gone? You're as pale as the head on a Guinness.'

The words come spitting out of my mouth like tacks.

'You knew, didn't you? Every one of you, you all knew about this, but no-one bothered to tell me.' My eyes blaze in fury as I accuse my so-called workmates. 'You set me up like a direct debit. They're expecting me to play the part of St Vincenza for the bison teenery. I bet they'll want to dress me up in some drab, shapeless frock as well. They think I'll be up for it because there's a "theatrical" side to me. What's that about? Just because I wear make-up and they never bother with any? Get real, Julia Roberts wouldn't take the job at a day's notice, not even for twenty million dollars and free underarm hair removal. Not if she knew the crowd was planning to stone her and chisel her eyes out.'

They're all sniggering at my outburst, like my being forced to perform in public is some huge joke.

'Stop it. Shut up, you lot. Just shut it! Can't you see I'm demented with worry?'

Demented is the word. I'm in turbulent brainstorm weather, my thoughts in chaos, head spinning into deep space nine. This is scary. It reminds me of my madolescence, a time when I was completely unhinged, so out of control that *anything* could happen. A bad, bad period in my life, that was, when I turned Menkle. I wasn't responsible for my actions, couldn't help thieving or lying or going off my head or cutting myself or being a total bitch or – well, you catch the way the wind's blowing. Life was a white-knuckle ride, a reckless downslide into insanity, a surrendering of identity, a dammitall leap from Beelzebub's toasting fork into the eternal bonfire.

Lately it seems I've been managing to hold it together. Maybe not by everyone's standards, but by mine. It's all relative, see; that relative being Dad. Dad the abandoner, the cop-out, the dropout, the leaver in the lurch, the wriggler-out of responsibility. I've matured, assumed a sense of purpose, believing that by finding Dad the key to my life will click in the lock, release me, free me, equip me to connect with the world.

If only it were that simple.

Since arriving in Ireland I've been intimidated by Hefty O'Hara, who, by the way, is still on my case for sure, forced to take a menial job in a nunvent, and accused of causing miracles. On the upside, there's Texy, my new best friend, and Joe, the fittest, lushest boy, who I think I've fallen in love with. As plus points, neither is totally problem-free. Texy is mad for Matty, the man with the giant organ. He'd only have to snap his fingers and she'd be off, no looking back. And Joe – well, he's a real puzzle. Does he fancy me or is he toying with my affections, stringing me along?

And now, in a move to top the lot, I'm to become the living embodiment of a murdered saint. It makes me feel so weak and stupid, such a vulnerable innocent abroad, like I've just rolled into town on a wagonload of turnips, while in my head I'm frantic, a wriggling mass of worries labelled Anxieties, Regrets and Foreboding.

'We're all on your side, Rowena,' says Joelle, trying to calm the situation. 'There's no lines to learn, you won't have to say a word. It's all, erm, *impoverished* . . . that thing where you make it up as you go along.'

'Improvized,' says Paula, who perhaps isn't as thick as she appears. 'We'll help you get into character.'

'As far as I can make out, you'll just have to sit still and pose in a tableau,' adds Joelle.

'What's a tableau?' I shriek. 'I ain't posing in *any* undies, and that's an end to it.'

'There'll be no stones or chisels, even if I have to frisk the lot of 'em on the way in,' says Enda. 'This isn't one of your English football matches.' She addresses the girls. 'Let's have three cheers for Rowena, our very own starlet. Hip, hip . . .'

'Hooray!'

'Hip, hip . . .'

'Hooray!'

'Hip, hip . . .'

'Hooraaayyy!'

The girls stamp their feet and holler.

'Stop it!' I yell, covering my ears with my hands. I'm close to tears. They mean well, but they're driving me to the edge of panic. 'Stop! Just stop it!'

Enda silences the noise with a wave of her hands, slipping an arm around my shoulder.

Hardly able to form words, I whisper in her ear. 'I gotta go, Enda, try to get my head around this. Can I leave early?' It kills me to plead but if I don't escape this minute my brain will explode. 'Like, now?'

'Away then. We'll just have to manage without you.' Enda looks at the clock, sighing as if she's made some huge concession. The woman's a bigger martyr than St Vincenza. 'It's a big day tomorrow so make sure you aren't late.'

Heavy-hearted, I plod homeward down the hill. What have I done to deserve this? Why me, God? Why me?

34

A Moral Message

Beep-barp. My nerves are in an advanced state of frayment. I skeg round the café looking for Joe, then I spot him leaning over a grey-haired biddy in a buttoned-up raincoat. He's showing her how to use a mouse. Glancing over at me he rolls his eyes to heaven, making me grin, making me glow inside. I exhale, relieved that last night's confusion seems to have evaporated from my mind. The woman beams her gums at Joe, clearly smitten. I laser an evil brain-to-brain warning via her perm: Hands off da man, bitch, or I'll fry yo' addled head.

'Hi, Rowena.' It takes me a moment to recognize the guy who's calling my name, waving to me from behind the counter. After a double take I realize it's Matty. What a transformation. The grim hairdo has disappeared faster than a speeding mullet, replaced by a buzz cut. He looks five years younger, a zillion times more attractive, like someone who actually lives in the twenty-first century.

'Hey,' I say, approaching him with a stupid smile on my face. 'I dig the hair.'

He runs a hand over his stubbly skull. 'Takes some getting used to. It's that Texy Maguire to blame. She frogmarched me into the barber shop; the old boys in there laughed themselves daft, me being ordered about by a woman. I'll never live it down.'

'You'll survive,' I say. 'Where is she?'

'Gone to see her grandda. She should have brought him along here, it's the Silver Surfers Club on a Wednesday afternoon, or hadn't you noticed?'

I glance around. The place is full of penshies, some tappy-lapping

233

on keyboards, others squinting at monitors, their noses almost touching the screens. Joe is still with the raincoated woman, trying to disengage her arthritic claw from the mouse.

'Jesus H.,' I say, under my breath. Matty snorts and slides a mug of coffee towards me. Yuk, it's that filter stuff so I spoon in three sugars to take the edge off the bitterness.

'I just popped out for a quick break,' says Matty. 'We've been at it non-stop at work, hotel guests arriving all morning. The rooms are booked solid with tourists coming for the shindig at the convent.'

'It's a bison teenery,' I inform him. 'And they're not tourists, they're pilgrims. It's a real big deal, Matty, like a carnival, only for Catlicks. And guess who they've chosen to play the part of the saint?' This is me trying out a confident persona.

He does an exaggerated shoulder-shrug. 'Enlighten me.'

I point to my chest. 'Me, of course. Me!'

'You – playing a saint?' He makes his eyes go big and poppy. 'You're shitting me.'

My face falls. 'Don't wind me up, Matty. I'm shit-scared, if you want the truth. It's not proper acting like on the telly. I don't have to say actual words. They just want me to sit there looking . . . *saintly*.'

'That'll be one hell of a stretch,' he says. Then, noticing my crumpled expression, he goes, 'I'm just teasing, Rowena. You'll be brilliant, and a darn sight easier on the eye than Mother Teresa. Good on you. Tell you what, I'll try to nip off work to cheer you on, add my moral support. Yay, you go, girl. Speaking of which, I must get back myself. Will you keep an eye on the counter?'

'Suppose so.' The oldies had better not rush me demanding mugs of Horlicks or I'll lose it completely.

'See yez.' Matty pulls on a baseball cap and punches me on the shoulder in a jokey goodbye. Joe turns his face to mine and treats me to a wicked smile that suggests he's pleased to see me. I widen my eyes and tap my watch, meaning *How much longer*? He shoots me a thumbs-up, then makes an announcement.

'That's it for today, folks. Would you all log out now please?' The penshies heave a collective sigh of disappointment, close down the computers and grab their old-fashioned coats. Now I understand why the Ballyloony shops are full of prehistoric goods. These people are like extras from *Grannies of the Damned*, zomboid coffin-dodgers with stained dentures and incipient cataracts. Joe shepherds them to the door and they form an untidy, shambolic queue, uttering threats to return next week. He smiles indulgently, almost proudly, as the aged toddlers, his ultra-mature students, shuffle out.

'Hey,' I say, stretching on tippy-toe and pecking him on the cheek to prove that kissing is back on the agenda and that I'm not put off by disfigurement. If you want *de troot*, I love his scar, his mismatched eyes, the way his face is differently featured. His look elevates him above the crowd, distinguishes him as special, emphasizes his Otherness. It's kind of sexy too, until I remember how he acquired the silvery-pink mark. How could his own father, the donor of his DNA, slash his son's face, treat Joe so brutally? Blood against blood. It violates the laws of nature, disrupts the cosmic order of things. No, Rowena, don't go there.

'You've got mail.' Joe's voice breaks into my mental confusion. 'A message from Moral Adair. I haven't opened it, thought you might want to read it in private.'

My scalp feels suddenly too small. The skin creeps as if an army of insects is burrowing inside my brain, depositing zillions of larvae, digging into the grey matter, building a microscopic theme park: World of Bugz. Could anything else go wrong today? How many more shocks can I absorb before my system implodes?

'Joe, this is scary. What if it's bad news?'

'What if it's good news?' smiles Joe. 'Either way, at least you'll know, then you can work out your next move.'

Boom-ba-boom-ba-boom. My heart thumps at 200 bpm. 'Will you open the e-mail, Joe? Then you can break it to me gently if it's something terrible.'

He laughs. 'Have you heard the expression "passing the buck"? Sure, Rowena, sure I'll do it,' he says. 'You can wait upstairs if you'd rather not be here.'

'Uh, yeah.'

I feel unreal, like a waxwork model of myself. Taking the keys, I climb the stairs and collapse on Joe's sofa, staring at nothing, imagining the process of opening the electronic envelope that will reveal my destiny. The world seems unreal – *surreal* – distorted by the unexpected things that are going on. I know that into every life a little shit must fly, but I'm feeling bombarded by foul-smelling turds shot from a cannon in king-size splats, all hitting me at once in an evil, stinking volley. Fear of Hefty O'Hara abducting me into sex slavery, the scary, unknown stuff about Dad, the bison teenery – it's too much to handle. I'll have to make a break for it, stow away on a plane to Ibiza, learn DJ-ing skills, work the clubs, hit the big time, retire to Barbados. Yeah, right, like that's gonna happen. Jeez, my options are all down the toilet. I can't even skulk back to Newcastle, where my majorest fuck-ups will haunt me for ever, where my mother is shacked up with a human fat-bellied pig, where I let down my friends. Yeah, I could run, but could I hide? Doubtful, which is why logic dictates that I maison well stay in this backwater where, although I might not deserve them, I have Texy and Joe on my side. And Matty. And Enda and the lasses from the nunvent, all rooting for me. Friends, I believe they're called. Friends, people who stand up for me, who aren't out to get me. Feck it, I'm staying put.

Thwack, thwack, thwack. Ninja appears at my side, his tail beating against the sofa in time with my heart. He sticks his muzzle against my hand, snuffling, seeking attention, angling for a behind-the-ears scratch. I pat the sofa and the dog jumps up, slurps his tongue over my neck and settles himself on his back with a blissful grumble. Cuddling him in with one hand and stroking his belly with the other, I marvel at his newfound confidence, his perfect timing. Just when comfort is most needed, Ninja forsakes his bathly haven and braves the dangers of the living room to offer me solace. An emotion not unlike love washes over me.

At the sound of the door being unlocked, Ninja and I bristle, suddenly alert. Joe enters, the expression on his face revealing nothing.

'Ninja, you intrepid old hound,' he says, unfolding a sheet of paper in his hand. 'Don't worry,' he addresses me. 'It doesn't tell you that much, to be honest. Want to hear it?'

Choked, I nod. Joe clears his throat and reads.

Dear Rowena,

Yes, I knew your father Lonnie Vincent. We became close friends, although my memory of those times is hazy – much of it is best forgotten. Lonnie and I both spent time in the wilderness, struggling with our weaknesses. The last I heard, he was starting to get his life back on track. I'll put out a few feelers, make enquiries, and contact you again if I come up with anything concrete. Your father deserves some good news. Forgive me for not going into detail over the e-mail.

You are in my prayers. God bless.

Moral Adair

I sit in silence, struggling to absorb the contents of Moral's message, to find some thread of meaning between the lines. It maison well be in code for all the information it offers. Joe passes me the printout. I read the words over and over again, as though constant repetition can make sense of them. Ninja whimpers and snuggles his head beneath my armpit.

'What are you thinking?' Joe rests a hand tenderly on my shoulder.

'Nothing,' I reply. 'I'm thinking nothing.'

'Let me put it another way. What are you feeling?'

I want to ask what Joe is feeling, need to know how far I can trust him. But I daren't.

Sighing, I murmur, 'Alone. On the saddish side of numbness. Let down. But mostly alone.'

He sits on the side of the sofa and drapes both arms around me. I feel paralysed, anaesthetized, stunned and left for dead, as if all my senses have flapped their wings and flown away like a flock of startled birds. My eyes are wide and stary, though unseeing. This is how it must feel to float in a sensory deprivation tank, the initially soothing freedom from everyday stimuli gradually leading to a rising panic. Nothingness. I'm engulfed by nothingness. I am less than nothing. I am whatever I was before I was conceived.

A voice echoes in my ears, or throbs inside my head, or vibrates through my chest, or spreads upwards from my toes. *Loser*, it says. *Dad was a loser*. The voice, it turns out, is mine.

'You don't know that.' Joe's voice reaches me from a distance, as though beamed into space and bounced off a satellite. 'Moral didn't say Lonnie was a loser.'

'Moral!' I'm back, spitting venom. 'I'd like to punch the joker who named him Moral. He had nothing positive to say, Joe. He's full of self-pity, a sympathy-seeker. Poor old Moral.' I mimic a pathetic whine. 'He had a tough time but he pulled himself up by his bootstraps; that's the gist of it. And those things he says about Dad – well, putting two and two together . . .'

'And making how many?' interrupts Joe.

'He made Dad sound a right dosser, or a druggy or an alcoholic, just like Moral used to be, except Moral's been miraculously saved by the Lord, while Dad . . . While Dad's still lying unconscious in some gutter, his matted hair in a pool of vomit.'

'You're exaggerating.' Joe kisses my hair. 'Stop tormenting yourself, Rowena.'

'Dad never ever contacted me, not once, not in years. What am I supposed to think? That he had a knock on the head and got amnesia? Brain damage? Cerebral thingy?'

Ninja wriggles free, jumps off the sofa and scampers to the safety of the bathroom, spooked by my display of Dad-rage, my Moral outburst. Joe slides into the space, holding me close until the anger works itself through my system and eventually subsides.

'What next?' says Joe. 'I vote you put it out of your mind, hang on to see if there's another e-mail. Moral might find out something for definite, like what your dad's doing now, where he's living.'

I exhale deeply, emptying my lungs of used air. An idea, or a feeling, or a realization too weird to make any sense yet, is beginning to take shape, to assume some kind of form. I'm almost afraid to allow the thought into my mind in case . . . In case of *what*? Why do I find it heap big scary?

Because it might destroy the balance of my brain, so recently ravelled. It might render me madder than logs. I *so* don't want to be out of control again, immobilized by paranoia, crushed by the weight of depression, crazy with psychosis, frightened of my own shadow.

There's only one thing to do: face my demons instead of burying them, instead of letting them colonize, multiply and devour me. I have to steel myself to take that one giant leap for Rowenakind.

Please, if any Godlike superpower is out there, give me the strength to confront my darkest fears. Let me see Dad for what he is, a man-person in his own right, free to make and resolve his own mistakes.

Let go, Rowena. It's time you let go.

35

The Unforgetting

To my eyes, Lonnie Vincent, as the Pope to Catlicks, was infallible. I worshipped and adored him, would have died for him. Correction: I'd have *killed* for him. Let's not get carried away here. His status as all-conquering hero was a given, a fixed point, a constant in my weird growing-up life. Dad was a shining beacon in a murky and frightening world. A misunderstood genius, a god, a king amongst dads. He was pure Beckham.

These are beliefs so deeply ingrained in my psyche, so welded and fused into my very bones, that to question his flawlessness as a person, to doubt his perfection, seems unthinkable. *Seemed* unthinkable.

But the madness that has stalked me for years, the mind demon that threatened to leap out from every doorway and mug me senseless, has been taken in for questioning. It's helping the thought police with their inquiries. My selective memory is now the prime suspect in this case.

Regina vs Rowena.
In the matter of the Idealization of Lonnie Vincent.

Sunday mornings, regular as senna pods, Dad and I would visit Nana Vincent, my paternal grandmother. She lived in a Victorian red-brick house with ill-fitting, rattly windows. Draughts whistled through the rooms like arctic blizzards, or a tribe of earthbound spirits whose spectral presence caused the temperature to drop by several degrees. The only warmth came from an old-fashioned coal fire, a source of un-central heating so scant and inefficient that you had to sit practically on top of it to feel the benefit. As soon as you moved away, you froze. Nana's legs were maroon and mottled, as though they'd been sculpted from corned beef, from her habit of warming them in front of the blazing fossil fuels.

'Aren't you going to feed the rabbits?' asked Nana. 'Take Gyp with you.' At the sound of his name, Gyp pricked his ears and wagged his stump. He was a small, snappy dog of unpredictable temperament, even though he had 'papers', meaning a proper pedigree. A pure-bred Jane Russell terrier, according to Nana Vincent.

The rabbits belonged to Old Mr Thing Next Door, or Cloth-Ears as Nana sometimes referred to him. She believed he had no sense of hearing, but I suspected he had selective deafness: he heard what he wanted to hear and ignored the rest. Handy, that.

I trotted through the back gate into Mr Thing's garden. Gyp ran along beside me, yapping mentally, aiming nippy bites at my shins, jumping up and baring his teeth at my knees. He wasn't playing either. He'd have loved to trip me up and tear me limb from limb but Nana Vincent threatened to have him destroyed if he used his teeth in anger, so he stopped just this side of actual evisceration. Canny little bastard.

The rabbits lived in a block of low-rise apartments in a complex of hutches handcrafted, ie. cobbled together from orange-boxes, by Old Mr Thing. I assumed they were pets – ah, the innocence of youth – and had no reason to associate them with the fur mittens and mufflers he gave to his grandchildren every Christmas, nor with the dozens of small bones that Gyp used to crunch in front of the fire and sick up in the yard. One day, catching Mr Thing unawares, at work in his kitchen, I realized that they were *battery* rabbits, bred for the pot and for their pelts. Impossible to forget the sound of scrabbling paws as he grabbed a rabbit by the ears and delivered a killer blow – *thunk!* – to the back of its neck; the sickening noise of a freshly deceased animal having the skin wrenched from its body; the sight of Mr Thing rubbing the non-furry side of the flesh with salt, then stretching and pinning the skin on to a wooden board to cure. Kill or cure. This was kill *and* cure, performed by a council-house-dwelling savage who wore tartan slippers and faked his own deaf.

So anyways, I greeted the rabbits, tempting them to the wire with lettuce and oven-toasted bread. They twitched their noses in reply, swivelling their eyes until it seemed as though they were looking over my shoulder, or just to the right of me. Maybe it's bad rabbit-luck to stare directly into someone's eyes. Gyp went snuffling, rootling in the vegetable patch, getting his fix of carrot tops, which affected him like catnip does cats, sending him into orgasmic heaven, rolling on his back, paws in the air, in a wanton 'I'm anybody's, me' posture of submission. He'd been taught not to yap near the rabbits. By 'taught', I mean thwacked with a rolled-up newspaper by Nana Vincent, or booted sharply up the bum by Old Mr Thing. It's a design flaw with rabbits, see: they're easily frightened to death. One unexpected woof from Gyp could give them heart failure, then they'd be no good for meat nor mittens. Sudden death toughens the sinews, turns the most slowly braised flesh to tasteless leather. The shock also makes the fur stand on end which means it's useless for accessories. In my opinion this could be turned to the good; there's bound to be a gap in the market for punk gloves, but no-one's had the vision to exploit it.

After they'd scratched, nibbled and twitched, the rabbits lost interest and turned their backs on me, so I whistled Gyp out of his personal ecstasy and we returned to Nana Vincent's house. Nana and Dad had pulled up chairs to sit hunched over the fire.

'Fed the rabbits,' I announced. 'Never saw Binky, though.' Binky was a pink-eyed angora, always in moult.

'Aye. He'll have gone to the big hutch in the sky,' said Dad. His voice sounded weird, as though he was speaking through thick fog.

Nana dabbed her eyes with a hanky and sniffed. 'Your dad and I are having a chinwag,' she said. 'Be a good girl and go sit in the front room, watch the TV for a bit.'

'Aww, it's always rubbish on a Sunday,' I groaned, but something shut me up before I could launch into full complaining mode. I padded dutifully into the other room and plonked myself on to the sofa, clutching my knees for comfort.

What was going on?

Muting the sound on the telly I crept along the hallway and glued my ear to the door. *You can't just walk out . . . What will people say? . . . How is Jean going to manage for money? . . . You're such a selfish bugger, Lonnie. I'm ashamed to call you my son . . . Think what it would do to Rowena.* These were the things Nana said to Dad.

And this is what Dad said to Nana Vincent. *I can't help it . . . We should never have got wed in the first place . . . I'm not cut out to be a husband . . . It's driving me round the bend . . . They'll be better off without me . . . Rowena's a tough little nut; she'll cope. She'll soon forget about me.*

Hah! Got you on that one, Daddy dearest. You couldn't have been more wrong.

What a let-down. So it was no biggy after all. The antiest anticlimax. Dad hadn't been summoned to audition with a rock band, hadn't eloped with a famous movie star, hadn't even smuggled rare monkeys into the country down his trousers. He was a dropout, a cop-out. Quite simply, he'd had it with being a husband and a father. He decided to leg it, to abandon his family, find a better life. But the best-laid plans have a habit of going pear-shaped and, reading between the lines of Moral's e-mail, that's what happened to Dad's dreams.

Hang on, what were those words that Joe told me about?

It doesn't matter who my father was; it matters who I remember he was.

The father I remember with a child's eye – not the less-than-perfect version of Dad that's unfolding, the one I'm beginning to unforget – that's who he was. The loving, mysterious, complex, clever father is the one I shall choose to remember. Fun but flawed. Dadly but deep.

He is who he is. A man, not a saint. Look at Elvis: he died on the bog from cheeseburger overdose but does his excess mean we should wipe out his success? Course not. OK, Dad might not be the hero I'd have preferred him to be, but doesn't he deserve to choose his own lifestyle, to triumph or fail on his own terms, without being judged by me?

243

36

De Troot about Herald

To divert myself from thoughts of Dad, I fill Joe in on the details of my forthcoming acting debut. The more I think about it, the less of an ordeal it seems. Who knows, being in the limelight could make my complexion look creamy and unblemished. It doesn't matter that I'm not a professional actor or a graduate of the Mahogany School of Dramatic Arts; all I need to do is strike a pose and not fidget about. There might be some talent scouts in the audience on the lookout for the next Jennifer Lopez. Minus the enormous booty, obviously.

'Joe, would you mind if I stay here tonight?' The words dash out of my mouth on their own, from some half-buried portion of my brain. The Tourette's part.

'Hmmm?' We're still locked together on the sofa, sprawled full-length, cuddling like spoons. The hair on the back of my neck is warm from his breath. 'Are you kidding? Of course you can stay.'

'It's just that with this hooley at the nunvent tomorrow I need to get in a good night's sleep, uninterrupted like.'

'Oh . . . OK, then.' His body loosens. I'm sensing disappointment.

A pitter-patter noise sounds from the hallway, the dog's claws on lino. Ninja creeps into the room and slumps with a sigh into a sleeping position on the floor near me.

'It's incredible,' says Joe. 'That beast has had a personality transplant since you came here. You've done wonders for him. And for me,' he adds in a murmur.

'He must like having someone else around,' I point out. 'Perhaps he was pathologically shy and now he's grown more confident because he saw it didn't faze me. I don't put pressure on him, don't

244

ask him to jump through hoops or act like a poncey poodle, just accept him for what he is.'

Joe squeezes my hand against his mouth and kisses it. 'I'd say that sums up the situation.' His voice is deepdown and husky in a way that's criminally sexy.

My stomach emits a hollow growl.

'Chips, your ladyship?'

'You betcha.'

While Joe's in the kitchen rustling up a snack, I call Texy on her mobile to warn her not to worry as I'm staying at Joe's tonight. She doesn't bother to disguise her glee; it means she and Matty can share a guilt-free night of passion. Matty has already told her about my starring role in the nunvent panto and she quizzes me for details.

'Dunno, search me,' I reply honestly. 'It's no big deal, Tex, it isn't a speaking part. God knows why they roped me into it, they maison well use a shop dummy.'

'I'll bring Bobbo to see you,' she says. 'Remember not to catch my eye or you'll bust out in giggles and ruin the performance.' We share a laugh down the phone. Ninja sits up and thumps his tail, keen to join in the fun.

'Gotta go, babes. Hugs 'n' kisses, mwah mwah.'

'Love you lots, Rowena. Nighty-night.'

My face splits in a broad, cheesy grin as Joe returns with microwaved mini-chips and brown sauce. Mmm, comfort food. Despite everything that's going on in my life, I feel cosseted, warm and needed. Needed? It's an odd choice of word to apply to myself. I can't recall the last time I felt *needed*, but hey, I ain't complaining. It's a top vibe; long may it continue.

Joe sorts out some CDs and we play them one after another. I recognize hardly any of the artists but it doesn't overly bother me. Show me a person who knows everything about everything and I'll show you a buttcrack liar. Then we settle down to watch *American Beauty* on DVD. Given a choice, I'd have said no way, but even though I'm seeing it for the first time, I sort of get most of it and laugh at the same bits Joe laughs at, mostly. After that we chat about Kevin Spacey, how ordinary-looking he is but a dead good actor. To my amazement I remember him playing that gimp, Verbal Kint, in *The Usual Suspects*, fooling the cops with his story about a mysterious crime lord called Keyser Soze. I feel quite proud of myself as movie stuff is usually erased from my memory as soon as the end credits roll, if I manage to stay awake that long. Joe says one of the best lines of all time was in that film, where Verbal says that the greatest trick the Devil ever pulled was convincing the world he didn't exist. It rings so true it could almost be out of the Bible.

By midnight I feel totally chilled, relaxed to the point of narcolepsy. Curled up between Joe and Ninja, all my worries have dissolved into nothingness, or retreated so far to the back of my mind it would take a superhuman effort to retrieve them, an effort I can't be arsed to make.

'So much for your early night,' muses Joe. 'Maybe I should take you to bed before you fall asleep on the sofa.'

'Hmmm.' Too mellow even to form words, I feel bone-meltingly, limb-floppingly swoony in Joe's arms, like a Victorian lady with an attack of the vapours.

'Eeny meeny miny mo,' he murmurs, carrying me along the hallway. 'Where will sleepy baby go?' He pauses outside the spare room. 'In here?'

'Uh-huh,' I murmur.

He touches my forehead in a hint of a kiss, elbows the door and lays me down gently on the bed. 'Think you'll sleep all right on your own?'

'Ysh,' I slur.

'Would you like some time to think about that?' He strokes my cheek in a cobweb-soft gesture.

'S'OK, I'm almost asleep.' Duh, how dumb am I? Can't I see a come-on coming on?

Joe's lips brush against mine and he leaves the room.

Somehow I manage to summon the energy to slip out of my top clothes, strip down to bra and pants and slide under the duvet. Joe must think me a disgrace to hygiene. I haven't brushed my teeth or rinsed my bits, but I'm way too knackered. Please God, don't let there be an unexpected fire in the night or the emergency workers will see me in full make-up and moan about what a total slut I am. Ninja flops down on the floor beside me and licks my hand a couple of times in a goodnight gesture. Me, I'm on a one-way ticket to the land of Nod, drift, drifting away, intoxicated by Joe's lingering fruity fragrance.

At some stage during the night, I snap into wakefulness. My brain is on full mental alert, danger signals pinging from synapse to synapse like steelies in a pinball machine. Hefty O'Hara, who has been chasing me in my sleep, recedes into my mind-shadows.

'Dad! Dad!' This is what I hear myself yell out loud. 'Da-a-a-d, help me!'

I'm scared witless, heart pounding, mouth agape and gulping for air. Ninja yelps as though kicked by an unseen boot, scratches at the carpet, desperate to escape from the crazy fright-witch. The door opens. A male figure stands silhouetted against the dim hall light. He approaches, sits on the bed, puts an arm around me and touches my cheek.

'Joe, is that you?'

'Who else would it be?'

I heave a great sigh of relief. 'I was confused, thought it was a stranger.' Dad, perhaps.

'There, baby, you've had a bad dream,' he whispers soothingly. 'Everything's all right; I'm here now.' I cling to him like a wee monkey to its mother, begging him not to leave me. 'Never. I'll always be here for you, Rowena.'

A part of me – I don't have to spell out *which* part – wants to be next to him. Close and warm and safe. Full-length, naked and uninhibited.

Joe picks up on the feeling.

'Why don't you come into my bed,' he says softly. 'Let me cuddle you.'

A tingle takes hold in my fingertips. My toes curl and uncurl.

'Into your b-b-bed . . .?'

'Ssshhh, just for comfort, I mean,' he adds, as though he's read my thoughts. 'In case you have another nightmare.'

'Erm, all right, if you think it'll help,' I concede, in a muddle of deception and dysfunction.

Wrapping his arms around me, he guides me to his room and lifts up the corner of the duvet. I slide into bed. It's cosy and enveloping and smells faintly of his watermelon hair gel. Instinctively I pat the neighbouring pillow, inviting Joe to climb in and join me. There's no going back. Whatever happens, happens.

We resume our spoon positions, the front of his body fitting neatly against the back of mine, his arms around my waist, his warmth encircling me like a human security blanket. And the hard swelling part of him nestling in my bottom region. A peaceful glow of contentment, an unfamiliar feeling of safety from the madness of the world, a tinge of arousal, spreads through me. A powerful sense that this is where I truly belong. A comforting, nurturing feeling, though short-lived.

'Joe,' I whisper, unsure how awake he is. 'Can we talk a while?'

'Mmm, of course we can talk,' he says in a drowsy murmur. 'What's on your mind?'

'I'm having a bit panic, getting real scared about tomorrow.'

'Sssshh.' He buries his nose in my hair. 'About your part in the celebration?'

I nod, trying to figure a way to duck out of the event altogether. Should I feign a migraine or throw myself downstairs and break a leg?

'What if they're planning to kill me, Joe?'

'Kill you?' He rolls me over on my back, looks into my eyes. '*Kill* you? And the Sisters would do that, why?'

'I know it sounds paranoid, Joe, and I've said crazy things to you before, but this is for real. It's important that you believe me on this one. There's too much evidence stacking up, it has to be true. Listen to this.'

It all comes tumbling out, how Vincenza met a grisly end, how people at the nunvent imagine I'm some kind of reincarnation of their saint.

'Reincarnation: that's Buddhists or Hindus, not Catholics,' says Joe.

'Yeah, whatever. But they think I'm connected to Vincenza in some way, which is why they want me to play her part.'

Joe smiles. 'They chose you because you're special and talented. You're the perfect person to carry it off.'

'But another thing, Joe . . .' My legs and toes are rigid. I hope I don't have an epileptic seizure in front of him. 'It's my birthday tomorrow – that's the same day as the saint's death. There are just too many coincidences and misunderstandings. They've got it into their heads that somehow I *am* Vincenza, and when you think how she died –'

He takes a firm grip of my arms. 'You really think they'll gouge out your eyes and stone you to death? On your birthday? Are you telling me you *really* believe that?'

'Maybe. I dunno.' After a long pause, I shake my head. 'No, I guess not.'

'Nothing bad is going to happen to you. Say it, I want to hear you say it.'

'Nothing . . . Nothing bad is . . . Nothing bad is going to happen to me.' There, it's done, even though it came out in a rush because it felt strange and embarrassing.

'Nothing bad is going to happen to you, not while I'm around.' He strokes my eyebrows with his fingertips. I hardly dare breathe. 'And

I'd like to be around for a long, long time, if you'll let me. Trust me, Rowena.'

My heart almost bursts out of my chest. 'Trust me,' he says. It's an unheard-of concept for me. I haven't trusted a soul since – well, you know. Since Dad dropped out of my life; no warning, nothing. Getting to know Joe better, there's been a definite crumbling of my protective shell, the carapace I've grown to keep people away. I'd give anything to feel I could trust Joe, but scepticism is a deeply ingrained habit, and hard to break.

'You're so good for me, Joe.' I run my fingers through his choppy hair. 'So Zen. I truly don't deserve it.'

'Twaddle and tosh,' he smiles. 'Obscure firm of solicitors. Now let's cuddle in and try for some shuteye, unless there's anything else, any other deep, dark fear, that you'd like to get off your chest.'

'Sleep, please,' I say, turning over and assuming the position. But before I can get cosy a fearful thought strikes me, turning the blood in my veins to ice, sending my body as stiff as an ironing board.

'Out with it,' whispers Joe, rolling me towards him again. 'Come on, worryguts, what's eating you?'

'Nothing,' I lie. 'Nothing much.'

'Do I have to tickle it out of you?' He makes a scuttling spider in my armpit with his fingers.

Wriggling, giggling away, I say, 'Stop that. I'm going to tell you, honestly.' I draw a deep breath and begin. 'OK. It's that mobster I told you about. He's showing up for the procession. What if . . .?' I squeeze Joe's hand. 'What if he does something to hurt me? I've seen it in gangster movies where hitmen use street parades and carnivals as cover while they blast their targets to smithereens.'

'Why would he want to hurt you?' says Joe. 'I thought you said he was grooming you for a job in the sex industry. He's not likely to splatter his investment up a wall, is he?' Although I can't see Joe's face, there's a smile in his voice which means he's not taking this entirely seriously. 'What's he called, this wiseguy?'

250

I let air out between my teeth. 'Promise you won't tell.'

'Crossing my heart as we speak.'

'It's . . . It's Hefty O'Hara.'

'Come again?'

'Hefty O'Hara,' I repeat. 'He wasn't christened Hefty; it's just he hates his proper name. Get this – it's Herald! Can you believe that? It's as bad as Marilyn Manson's real name being Brian.'

Joe does a spluttery laugh. 'Let me get this straight. You're saying Herald, aka Hefty, O'Hara is some kind of criminal mastermind. Call this a wild notion, but could that be the same Herald O'Hara who's ploughed thousands into the convent? The guy who paid for the old people's wing to be adapted so that his own relative could live there? *That* Herald O'Hara?'

'No way!' I cry out. 'There must be two of them. This one – the one who's gunning for me – he's a made man, a capo, probably. How could you possibly know anything about him, even if he did cough up a bit money for the nunvent?'

'You're bustin' my balls,' says Joe in a jokey Noo Joizey accent. It ain't funny. I stiffen. Sensing a bad moon rising, Joe massages my shoulders gently, loosening the tensed-up knots, calming me into a near-functional human being. 'Would you recognize Hefty O'Hara from a photograph?' he says.

I nod. The man is my nemesis; the image of his face is engraved on my eyeballs. He could show up any day now and pimp me to strangers.

'Then we can sort this one easily,' says Joe. 'See, I helped the Sisters with their website after their IT fellow left, and I added a page about one of their benefactors. He was called Herald O'Hara; it's a name that sticks in the mind. There was a picture of him with the Reverend Mother and this relative of his – an aunt, I think it was. He shelled out loads of money for disabled access because she was losing her sight. It was a big thing at the time, I remember.'

251

Gulp. I'm stunned, though the story is still too far-fetched to believe.

'You're wrong, Joe. It must be someone else with the same name. I'd stake my life ... erm, no, my leather jacket ... I mean my *reputation* on it.'

'Last of the high rollers, you,' laughs Joe. He nips out of bed, pads across to a wee table and turns on a laptop. The screen flickers and lights up as Joe swivels the mouse across the mat. 'Here, take a look and tell me if this is the hood who's been chasing you.'

Adjusting my bra and knickies, I tiptoe to the computer and squint at the screen until my eyes focus. My heart plummets to my toes when I clock the picture. There, looking for all the world like the executive he claims to be, is Hefty, handing over a giant-sized cheque to a woman built like a trucker wearing a nun's outfit. It's the same picture that Miss Teazie O'Hara had in her room, except that one was framed. Much like me.

BUSINESSMAN MR HERALD O'HARA (PICTURED LEFT) PRESENTS A CHEQUE TO OUR REVEREND MOTHER (RIGHT). MISS TEAZIE O'HARA (SEATED), AUNT OF THE BENEFACTOR, IS A RESIDENT OF ST PHILOMENA'S CARE HOME WHICH NOW BOASTS UP-TO-THE-MINUTE FACILITIES FOR THE VISUALLY IMPAIRED, THANKS TO MR O'HARA'S GENEROSITY.

I let out a low whistle. 'Fuck!'

Joe laughs. 'He'll be your man, I take it? Herald O'Hara, the philanthropist?'

'What, you mean he bags off with loads of women too?' I'm shocked.

'No, I think that's a philanderer,' grins Joe. 'A philanthropist is someone who does good deeds for his fellow men and women.'

'Oh, yeah, I knew that,' I lie, blushing in confusion. Someone ought to ban big words that sound nearly the same.

'Bang goes your conspiracy theory,' says Joe, but it's a major turnabout for me to absorb. So he handed over loads of dosh to the nunvent. He could still be a mobster.

At the speed of light, I rewind the mindtape containing the known data on Hefty. All this time I've been one hundred per cent certain that he was a baddy, but what did I have to go on? Gossip, tittle-tattle, a wink, a nudge, a tap of the nose, all from the same source: Ray, the driver-bearer from the undertaker's in Newcastle where I used to work. Ray, who cheated his friends at cards, thieved the occasional item when collecting stiffs from their homes (helping with the house clearance, he called it), who wound me up something awful with his sexist 'jokes', who cheated on his wife and referred to her as Swampdonkey behind her back, who sold his son's PlayStation for the price of a pint and an Indian takeaway. How very astute, Rowena. Talk about barking up the wrong tree. Let's just call it barking. The *troot* is right here in front of me, plastered on the website of a bona fide religious organisation. How stupid am I?

I spend a while staring at the monitor, trying to gather my thoughts, rejig them into a new order. All the scary gangster-type stuff about Hefty has been turned on its head. This is how it must feel to find out at my age that you were adopted as a baby. It throws everything into chaos, makes you question and rethink everything you once believed, took for granted, accepted as gospel. Makes you rerun the past, looking for clues, discrepancies.

Let's take a leap of imagination here. Assuming Ray had said nothing of Hefty's bad-boy past, would I have any reason to suspect him of Godfatherish tendencies?

Well, no.

Even if Texy hadn't drummed it into me that Hefty was a businessman, might I have thought the same myself?

Probably.

Do I have any concrete evidence that Hefty was planning to turn me into a sex slave?

Er, no.

Conclusion: I've been deluding myself, scaring myself, about something that had no basis in fact. Hefty O'Hara is on the level, a straight-up guy. Jeez. Dumber than a box of hair, that's me.

Time for a climbdown. 'So I got it wrong,' I mumble. 'These are my hands and I'm holding them up to it. OK? I accept that Hefty O'Hara isn't going to pimp me or waste me. Oh god, oh god, I'm truly sorry for being such a paranoid, whining ninny, Joe.'

He gives me a hug. 'Good. That's another worry we can put to bed. Now shall we put ourselves to bed? It'll soon be time to get up again.'

I glance at the digital alarm. 'Bloody hell, Joe, it's three o'clock.'

'It always is,' he says, 'in the long dark night of the soul.'

I gaze at him in awe. He's so clever, carries so much stuff around in his brain. What does he see in me? How could I possibly deserve him? Stuck for words, I stand up and offer my mouth to him. He glues his lips to mine in a deep-soul kiss, tongues, mingling saliva, the lot. Breathless, I grind my body into his, feeling his excitement, wondering if this is going where I think it is.

'Bed,' he whispers, untangling my arms. 'Sleep,' he says. 'That's why you're here, right?' There's a smile, a tease, in his voice. 'Uninterrupted, is what you said.'

If this is an uninterrupted night's sleep, I'm a gibbon. I'm going to be so knackered. Maybe I should do a bit of speed later to help me through the busy hours ahead. Maybe not, or I'll be chattering away like the aforementioned gibbon when I should be coming across all pious, serene and stuff for the ceremony.

Just before daylight begins to seep through the bamboo blinds, we crawl into bed, reconnecting in a spoonlike fashion. I'd love to turn around and snuggle up facing Joe but I'm afraid my body will let me down and start to writhe and squirm against his when maybe he wouldn't want that. He does like me and all, I can tell that for sure, but apart from kisses and hugs, he's made no attempt to move things on to the next stage. Suits me, though, as I'm feeling too emotionally fragile for anything heavy, plus, on the practical side,

I'm not sure how things stand in the mollies department. I'm pure mad into Joe but I don't want to hurtle headlong into a situation that would burn itself out after a few sessions. He means much more to me than that.

Tonight a minor miracle has occurred: I actually find myself trusting someone. It's like I've found a soulmate, if that doesn't sound too New Age hippy-drippy. Even the rhythm of our breathing is synchronized. In an ideal world, or a parallel universe, we'd be in this for the long haul. Listen to me, going all soppy and teenzine lurve-babble. Yikes!

Blissfully contented, I surrender to the slumber god. For what seems to be about thirty seconds. That's when Joe's clock radio starts to beep and play a cheesy pop song. I slam the snooze button. Lordy, my eyes won't open, they're stuck together with lack-of-sleepness – oh, and yesterday's claggy mascara which has probably run halfway down my face.

Creeping out of bed so as not to disturb Joe, I tiptoe to the bathroom, splash cold water on my eyes and check out the look. Alice Cooper blinks back at me from the mirror. Oh, *très* attractive. It takes no time flat to get ready for work. Who cares whether I'm toshed up in decent togs if the nuns are going to dress me in a bell tent? Does it matter if my hair's a mess when they'll probably scrape it back and stick a veil over it? What's the difference if my make-up is less than immaculo when they'll only slap cleansing lard on it to remove the top three layers? I pop into the bedroom to lay a kiss on sleepyhead Joe and treat Ninja to an ear-tickle, whispering, 'Later, dudes,' to both of them.

37
Mary Belker's Magic Cakes

Boy, what wouldn't I give to spend the day in bed with gorgeous, sexy Joe and my step-dog, Ninja? What cuddles, nuzzles, fondles and snuggles we'd have, the three of us tucked up beneath the perfectly tog-rated duvet. A whimper sneaks out of my mouth just thinking about it. Instead – what? My stage jobby for the bison teenery, my portrayal of Vincenza before the faithful, and here's me not feeling even faintly saintly.

Out in the world of the living, the daylight almost blinds me. Jesus, I must look like a demented bag lady but who cares? There'll be no-one around to see me at this unearthly time of morning. Huh, could I *be* more wrong? The town is full of strangers, non-locals, foreigners more than likely, wandering around and gazing in shop windows. They emerge in gaggles from the tea room; the money-grabbing waitress-witch must have opened early to part them from their euros.

'Hey, Rowena, good luck with your big day.' It's Matty the bald, a fresh love bite peeping above his denim collar. Texy, you bad, bad girl.

'Hi, Matty, what are you doing up and about so early?'

He jerks his head towards a group of incomers. 'The hotel's packed out. Just my luck that our lot wanted to break bread early so they can pray the stations. Tourists!'

'Pilgrims,' I correct him. 'What's praying the stations?'

He explains that it's some sort of Catlick thing where they meditate at a number of points along the way of the Cross, depicting Jesus being convicted, sentenced and crucified. 'You must have noticed the stations in the convent chapel,' he says. 'Those statues in little alcoves set along the wall?'

'Oh, those. Yeah, of course,' I lie, not having a clue what he's on about.

'All these visitors in town, you won't be short of an audience when you strut your saintly stuff,' he grins. 'What time does the gig kick off?'

'Pffft, don't ask me, I'm the last person to find out what's happening. Texy might know.' I glance at my Swatch. 'Lordy, must be off, see you later, Matty.'

'Sure I wouldn't miss it for anything,' he laughs, blowing a daft kiss.

The hill to the nunvent looks steeper this morning, practically perpendicular. It must have grown in the night. Even though I should be shagged out from disturbed slumber, my body seems to have gained a second wind and I half-jog up the incline like Sly Stallone racing up those steps in *Rocky*.

What could be causing this surge of dynamism? See me, I'm bursting with happiness and energy, every cell in my body jam-packed full of pure, unadulterous bliss, ready to explode from sheer joy. These are some of the things I am, *x* a zillion recurring to infinity and beyond. And the explanation, almost too shocking to contemplate, is this.

It must be L-O-V-E!

That's it – I've fallen in love with Joe. Rowena loves Joe. Rowena Vincent loves Joseph Kane. It's scary even to think like this in case it's tempting fate, but then I recall Joe saying he wants to be around for a long, long time.

This could be the big It, total devotion, absolute commitment, together until death do us part and earthworms do us make mincemeat of. It's a glorious, chest-swelling, heart-fluttering, brain-flashing feeling, the highest of highs.

Total swoonage.

I am invincible.

I am also late for work. Only a bit, but still.

Jeez, the nunvent has been transformed overnight into a kind of Santa's grotto. Bunting, streamers and fairy lights adorn the walls, a larger-than-life-size model of St Vincenza, looking heap scary, has been hoist aboard a plinth by the chapel door. She's wearing a grey robe with a blue veil and – get this! – a glow-in-the-dark halo. How trailer-trash is that? At the other side of the door is a board with a painting of Vincenza gurning in a retard way, and beneath that the story of her life and martyrdom, which is the word Catlicks use to describe a gruesome premature death.

Must show my face in the Cleanliness department. It's risky me being here, in the public part of the nunvent, but I figure no-one will dare to yell at me today in case I storm out like a pre-Madonna and they'll be left saintless for the big occasion. To be honest, the carnival atmosphere is having a strange effect on me. I'm starting to feel excited, as if it's Christmas Eve, all dry-mouthed and tingly-bellied, which is a good sign.

'Morning,' I sing, an ear-to-ear beam lighting my face.

Enda's wearing the expression of a vinegar-taster after a twelve-hour shift. 'You're late,' she tuts, but she looks relieved to see me.

'I ain't *that* late. Anyway, no show without Punch, eh?'

Skivvies hop around me like fleas round a cat. 'You'll have to try on your costume, Rowena, in case it needs any alterations,' says Grainne the seamstress, producing a dove-grey thing and holding it up against me. 'Go behind the press and slip into it.'

'The press are here already?' I'm in panic, hoping there'll be time to paint my face before they take photographs.

Grainne points to where the sheets and towels are stored, then I remember that what Irish people call a 'press' is really a cupboard. You'd think they'd speak proper English when they're addressing –

or undressing – me. I snatch the dreaded garment from her and flounce off to the hidey-hole. Check out this robe, man. It's made in typical Ballyloony style, drab, frumpy and out of the Ark. I'd rather donate a kidney than wear it in public.

'How's it looking?' says Grainne.

'Like the Turin Shroud,' I reply. 'It needs taking in just about everywhere. There's no bust, no waist, no bum. It's completely shapeless.'

'But apart from that?' Grainne says hopefully.

I snort. 'Apart from that, Princess Diana, how did you enjoy Paris?'

'You're sick,' exclaims Grainne, pretending to be shocked. 'Come out here, let's see what we can do.'

Slumping like an overladen donkey, I present myself in front of the skivvies. They're struck dumb with the grossness of the sight before them. Fair play to them, at least they're not fawning and saying how great I look.

'Couldn't I wear a bin liner, make out Vincenza was the first punk rock chick?'

'I wish you'd be more respectful, Rowena; you never know who might be listening,' Enda warns, rolling her eyes upwards to indicate the greybacks' quarters. She shuffles across and grabs my upper arms. 'Pull yourself together, girl,' she says underneath her breath. 'Don't be showing me up, I was the one who put a good word in for you.'

Me-me-me, that's all she cares about. 'It'll show you up if you send me out looking like a sack of taties. The pilgrims are gonna piss themselves laughing, and this is supposed to be a sacred occasion.'

Enda sighs. 'It's a fair point she has, Grainne. A tuck here, a dart there – you could make a better fist of it than this, surely? Stand up straight, Rowena, let her measure you properly.'

Grainne inches towards me, like a nervous hunter stalking a grizzly bear with migraine. I just stop myself from baring my teeth in a snarl to make her jump. Her mouth is full of pins. She slips a tape round my bosoms, tugs the grey fabric and fastens it more tightly, then repeats the action at waist and hips, before pulling the robe over my head.

'Tighter,' I say. 'I want it figure-hugging, like a second skin. Think Anastacia.'

Enda flinches, as if someone's smacked her in the face. 'R.E.S.P.E.C.T.,' she reminds me. 'I'll bet whatsisname, Mr Versace, doesn't get all this grief from his models.'

'You're not wrong there,' I say, not bothering to tell her that he was shot unto death by some weirdo.

'I can't make it any more fitted without putting a zip in.' Grainne looks at me pleadingly. 'And we don't have any zips.'

'Use your noddle,' I tell the seamstress, tapping her forehead with my knuckle. 'There's piles of overalls here. How do they fasten? Velcro,' I announce before she has time to formulate a response. 'V.E.double L . . . whatever. Can't you take some off a uniform?'

'Y-y-yes,' she stutters, almost in tears, though god knows why.

'I'm working with cretins!' I slap my forehead in frustration.

'Calm down, Rowena. What's got into you? You're bristlier than a porcupine.' Enda's showing signs of prickliness this morning too. She leads me aside and stares hard at me. 'Look, I understand that you're nervous . . .'

'No, I ain't, not at all,' I bite back.

'But you must try to calm down, compose yourself, otherwise the girls will be quaking in their trainers and I need them to have their wits about them. We're all on edge today. It's so important that everything runs smoothly.'

Here we go. Change the friggin' record, Enda. Resting my weight on one foot and jutting out a hip in a gesture of defiance, I glare at the ceiling.

'Now go and put your clothes back on, and wear your overall on top. Sit in a corner and read up about St Vincenza, think holy thoughts and try not to get above yourself.'

Behind her back, I flick her the finger. Naturally, I'm not going to waste my time and brainpower on method acting. That's for Methodists, not Catlicks. All I'll have to do for my 'performance' is sit still and look a bit on the simple side. How hard can it be? Truth is, my nerve ends are raw from lack of sleep, from feeling excited every time I think about lovely Joe, and from the not-knowingness of how the performance will go, the not-sureness about Dad. On the plus side, my worries about Hefty have melted like an ice lolly on a hot day. And yet I can't keep still. My fingers keep drumming, my knees feel twitchy, I want to wave my arms in the air, dance off my nervous energy. I'm on nature's uppers, ripped to the tits on whizz-like endorphins, adrenaline zooming through my system at a zillion knots.

Something's going on, some secret conversation they're not letting me in on. The girls are whispering and twittering, shooting sidelong glances at me, buzzing and bumbling like the drones they are. Who gives a toss? Maybe they're jealous because I've been chosen to take centre stage in the proceedings. The excitement is getting to me more and more. My feet won't keep still; they're tap, tap, tapping in a crazy, fast tempo rhythm. Then I notice that my fingers are doing the same on the table top, like I'm playing speed garage on a keyboard. My eyeballs feel weird, as though they're swivelling and spinning around in my head. They can't be, of course. It's a case of first-night nerves, that's all. I'll control myself when the time comes.

The coven disperses. The skivvies resume their cleaning and polishing with, it seems to me, exaggerated arm movements, embellished flicks and flourishes of feather dusters, as if they're pantomiming, not actually doing it. After a while Mary Belker pootles towards me with a tray bearing two scrumptious-smelling cakes.

'I'll bet you're starving, Rowena. You haven't had a single biscuit this morning.' She waves the baking tray under my nose, making me slaver. 'These are fresh from the oven, lovely and warm.'

Salivating, I say, 'What are they?' As if I care. I'm so ravenous I'd eat a plate of doggy-doo.

'Muffins,' she says. 'Or scones, sort of. They're luscious, whatever you want to call them. Try a little bite of one.'

I break a cake in half and tuck in. Oh, yummy, it's totally delish. The muffin is muffed out in a matter of seconds. My hand hovers above the other half. 'Can I . . .?'

Mary nods. I guzzle it down my neck. Even after one cake my belly feels stuffed beyond comprehension. Mary smiles and widens her eyes, inviting me to polish off the lone scone.

'I couldn't,' I protest. 'I'll explode.'

'Save it for later then,' she says.

I hesitate for a nanosecond before whipping it off the tray and standing it on a saucer. I'll give that cake two minutes to live, tops. Mary scoots off and waves the empty tray at the others to show what a guzzle-guts I've been. Do I care? Do I buggery.

It's impossible to keep still. Maybe I've caught St Vitus's Dance. Somehow I have to get rid of this energy. Part of me wants to rip off my overall and the rest of my kit and run naked in the fresh air. Two laps of the nunvent should do it, but I'd probably get pneumonia, or arrested. I feel crazy, constricted, as though I'm having the life squeezed out of me by a corset several sizes too small. A PVC one that cinches my waist to the size of a wrist. One that laces so tightly it takes my breath away. One that squashes my internal organs, causes liver failure. I need to break out of the invisible cage before it crushes my ribs, stops my heart, mangles me to death.

'Going to the bogatory,' I say, to no-one in particular, flouncing out of Cleanliness, flying on fairy feet down the below-stairs corridor until I reach the laundry. I peek through the glass in the door. No sign of life. Maybe the scrubbers have been assigned to other duties for the saint's day.

Once inside I check to make sure no-one's around, even glancing in the giant wicker hampers. Alone with my twitching body, I undo the Velcro strips on my overall, rip it off and toss it in the air. It lands in an empty sink. What wouldn't I give for a pair of sharp scissors right now? I feel like running amok, doing damage, slashing, cutting, ripping, slicing. This is how hyper I am. Wild. Reckless. Burning up inside.

It's strip or die. Tearing off my clothes in a frenzy, I lose myself in the music that only I can hear, surrender myself to its voodoo, the insane rhythm of drums throbbing inside my head. I race around the room, picking up wooden tongs, banging and clattering them on every surface, seduced by the crazy beat. I'm flying, floating, at one with the cosmos, thrilled by the energy, the intensity of the experience. Falling to my knees on the quarry tiles, loving the chill of them next to my fiery skin, I clasp my hands and start to sing. The sound that emerges is foreign, other-wordly, incomprehensible. Wonderfully primitive.

'Blanket, over there.' The words twang against the membrane of my consciousness. 'Quick now, get her covered up.' A length of woolly material is thrown over my naked body and swaddled around me. Hands pull me to a standing position. My legs tremble, feet ache with heaviness, arms feel useless. My lips won't keep still, moving in silent mumbles.

I feel reborn.

'I believe it's called ecstasy.'

These are the first words I hear. They appear to be coming from Paula, though I wouldn't swear to it. Somehow I'm back in Cleanliness, lying flat on a bench in the staff cloakroom, wrapped in the blanket, staring at the plastic shade dangling from the ceiling.

Ecstasy? I want to protest that Es are for clubbing, but my mouth is dry and my lips stick together.

'Religious ecstasy,' repeats Paula. She says she never expected to see it personally but she's read about it in books. 'They go into a kind of trance, jig about, don't know what they're up to. Religious rapture. I imagine it's like a kind of fit.'

Someone else speaks. 'Would it be anything to do with the—'

'No,' Mary Belker cuts in firmly. 'I didn't put much in the cake mix. Lightly laced, that's all it was. Just enough to calm her down. Not a word to Enda, right?'

Perhaps these words were genuine, spoken by real people. Perhaps not. They're dead funny, though. They make me laugh.

Why is my forehead tingling? I'm a curly-wurly in the curve of a rainbow. Liquid colours flow through me, melt into a glittering iceberg, re-emerge as a bright, tinkling waterfall. Exotic birds with tails made of harp feathers . . .

Butterflies flutter by. Flamingoes go flaming.

Warble of a natterjack toad. War belove a natter-toed jack.

In the name of the godfather, sun and holy goat. The Dad, the Lad and the Spook.

Bless me, Father, for I am stoned.

'There, a perfect fit. Sure you look like the real thing, Rowena.'

'Thank you, Grainne,' I say humbly. Hey, get the new, docile me, a wee bit giggly but meek enough to inherit the earth.

'And I've taken in the waist so there's no need to wear that Hell's Angels monstrosity.' She means my favourite belt with the steel buckle, a grinning skull with red stones for eyes, that doubles as a concealed weapon in a gang fight.

'You won't be wanting the leather basque either,' says Paula. 'Could I try it on?' I nod blithely. I bet it'll look shit on her.

'Nor the motorcycle boots,' chips in Mary Belker, the purveyor of cakes. I may be temporarily soft in the head, but I draw the line at surrendering my favourite biker footwear.

'The boots stay.' Mary backs off. 'You can borrow them some-time,' I offer.

My hair, lightly backcombed, looks less like a bird's nest than usual, though you'd hardly describe it as sleek. Grainne approaches with the veil, a midnight blue number that reaches to my waist, and attaches it to my bonce using a battery of hairpins.

'Let me see,' fusses Enda, elbowing her way through the girls. 'Ooohh, you look lovely, Rowena. Lovely and holy. Sure it's nothing short of a miracle.' She dabs at her eyes with a hanky as if incapable of absorbing my mutation from sullen Goth to pious virgin. It's a huge suspension of disbelief, I'll admit.

The crowd of girls parts like the Red Sea, heralding the arrival of Sister Monica who's come to inspect me. She looks me up and down, pats my head to check that the veil is firmly fixed in place, and stands back, a satisfied expression on her crinkly old face. She glances at my feet, catching sight of the toes of my biker boots, but decides to overlook this lapse in authenticity, realizing I'd probably get frostbite in sandals.

'I'm amazed,' she declares. 'Amazed. The transformation is quite extraordinary. Now are you sure of what you have to do, Rowena?'

An inane smile spreads across my face. I nod.

'Good. Then I won't interrupt the proceedings a moment longer. Be ready to leave in fifteen minutes, and don't be nervous, there's nothing at all to worry about.'

'It'll be cool, man, Sister. Catch you later then. Mind yourself.' She swishes out. 'Anyone got a fag?' Grainne produces a crumpled pack from her bag and lights one up for me. Enda doesn't say a word, even though the nunvent is a strictly no-smoking establishment. Instead, she nudges Paula in a pre-arranged signal, and out comes a bottle and six tiny glasses on a tray.

'I think we all deserve a little treat,' she says. 'A toast, then. To Rowena, our own St Vincenza.'

The girls raise their glasses, murmur my name and take a wee sip.

Naturally, I knock my drink back in one; well, there's not even half a gobful in the glass. 'Could I have another?' I say, even though it tastes sweet and non-alcoholic. 'I don't suppose you've got anything better stashed away, Aftershock or Baileys?' Paula has a choking fit and dribbles drink through her nose.

Enda bobs over to the table. 'Rowena, I really don't think you ought to drink any more of that grape juice in case it goes straight to your bladder.' Too late. Glug-glug straight from the bottle. I'd love to secrete what's left in my rucksack in case I die of thirst or feel a chill coming on, but Enda whips it away smartish.

'It's for the nerves,' I tell her. Right on cue, I feel gripped by anxiety.

'The Lord's looking after you,' Enda assures me. 'Sure He never gives you more than you can bear.'

If only I had her faith.

38

St Rowena and the Nunettes

I'm tripping, innit. High as an angel's wing-tips. I believe that the things on that tray were hash cakes. This would make Mary Belker my dealer. The nunvent must be as full of gear as a women's prison. How cool is that?

My head feels too floaty to make sense of today's events. First I was twitchy and agitated; now I'm drifting on fluffy clouds, giggling. This is how it must feel to be manic-depressive. I suspect they gave me the spiked cookies to calm me down before the performance. Druns in the nuggery. BVM and LSD. The Blessed Virgin Marijuana. Ooohh, all this thinking, it's making my brain hurt.

There's a bit flurry at the door. Three nuns enter, youngish ones I haven't seen before, and tell me in impenetrable Irish accents that they've come to escort me. They must be new, trainees or something, as they're a bit on the daft side, unless they've been sampling Mary Belker's hash cookies too. Do your laughing while you can, girls, before they knock it out of you. I take the lead; they bustle and fuss around me. It's hardly Madonna and her entourage, or even Atomic Kitten, but it feels like a brush with rock 'n' roll that I hadn't dreamt of before yesterday. St Rowena and the Nunettes. Up the stairs we go and out the staff entrance at the side of the building. Really I should insist on a dramatic exit through the front door but perhaps they want to keep the identity of their 'saint' a secret until the big moment.

It's dusk, and the place is lit up like Blackpool Illuminations with fairy lights and paper lanterns. Small groups of people wander out of the grotto, their loose change rusting at the bottom of St

Vincenza's Pool, a man-made water feature as seen in garden centres. A few hardy pilgrims are on their knees at various stages along the path, others are on their way to pray at the miniature statues which I now know to be the Stations of the Cross. I'd be cross too if I had to keep genuflecting in this weather. There's a chill in the air at this midway point between March coming in like a lion and going out like a lamb.

'Are we nearly there?' Jeez, I sound like a whiny kid on a day trip. The tallest nunette mutters something, but I can't make out a word of it. You'd think they'd supply these country lasses with a translator for occasions when they have to mix with normal people. At a fork in the path I bear left in the direction of the retreat centre, but the spotty nunette takes my elbow and steers me towards the chapel. 'Where are you taking me?' I ask. She titters nervously behind her hand, but says nothing that makes a jot of sense. The cold air is making me shiver, making me consider sending one of the escorts back to get my leather jacket. I pull the veil more tightly around my shoulders, taking care not to dislodge the hairpins.

'Rowena Vincent! That *is* you, isn't it, Rowena?' The broad figure of Hefty O'Hara steps in front of me on the path, blocking my progress. The nunettes brake to a halt, uncertain how to deal with an unscheduled pit stop; they didn't cover such contingencies in rehearsal. Hefty's eyes smile into mine. 'It *is* so. I hardly recognized you in that get-up. Rowena, how're ya?'

Good job my reactions are lightning fast. My first instinct is to flee screaming from a known hardman, but then a brainflash reminds me that Hefty is Mr Big in religious circles so I switch to genuinely pleasant mode.

'I'm good, Hefty. Better than good.' See for yourself, I'm thinking. A fucking *saint*, ain't I?

He gives me the once-over, twice over; then, nodding at my outfit, 'Does this mean you're taking the veil yourself, Rowena?'

'Eh?' Behind me, the nunettes suppress sniggers. I feel a bit giggly myself. 'Oh, no, I amn't, it's just a theatrical costume. I'm playing the part of St Vincenza for the bison teenery thing. One night only, so don't miss it.'

'Wouldn't dream of it. I'm just off to fetch Aunt Teazie now. You've been very kind to her, Rowena, and she's taken a shine to you. Likes your spirit, she says. I hope she doesn't mean you've been leading her astray with the old Black Bush.' He taps his pocket and laughs, before leaning into me and muttering, 'I'll find a way of thanking you for what you've done.'

'It doesn't matter, it was nee bovva, honest.' A sudden icy breeze catches me unawares and I begin to shiver like a half-set jelly.

'Take my coat,' offers Hefty. Before I can protest he's draped it over my shoulders. 'There's nothing in the pockets except my little flask and you're welcome to what's inside it.'

'But –'

'I'm warm enough with all this Irish blood running through me. See you later, Rowena. Break a leg.' He lopes down the path in the direction of the Home for Old Dubs.

The coat is enormous and warms me up immediately. Knowing Hefty and his hi-tech modifications, he's probably had central heating installed in it. Jeez, I hope I don't sweat buckets on to my costume, or collapse from overheating of the organs, or spontaneously combust. Coroner's verdict: Death by cashmere.

They're trying to hurry me along, the nunettes, in their own non-verbal, sign language way, but it's a struggle as I'm sweltering in the Heftywear coat. You'd think one of them would offer to carry it for me. I wonder if I have the power to boss them around or if they'd snitch me up to the Human Resources nun. Eventually, just as I'm on the point of collapse, we reach the chapel. Shitloads of people are milling around, queuing at the entrance, like groupies at a stage door. The nunettes huddle round me, minder-stylee, and bundle me through a door round the side, a florist's or stained-glass-window cleaner's entrance or something.

On the far side of the door is a damp-smelling room. In the dim electric light I see Sister Monica sitting on a bench and next to her, Sister Cuthbert, the kitchen nun, chomping on an apple. They seem relieved to see me.

'You're not before time, Rowena,' says Cuthbert, chucking the apple core into a waste basket. 'Let's take a look at you.'

Heaving the coat off my shoulders, I reveal myself as St Vincenza's alter ego, her prettier, luckier, more stoned sister.

'Is there a mirror in here?' I ask. Sister Monica and Cuthbert exchange glances, but neither bothers to reply. Triffic. I'm appearing before a first-night audience and no-one's thought to provide a mirror for me to check my look before I go on. Nuns are so unshowbiz. I rub my teeth with a finger to remove any lipstick bleed and flatten my fringe with spit. I'll have to do.

'You look fine so,' says Cuthbert, smoothing the crinkles in my costume. 'Isn't that right, Sister?'

Monica smiles and nods.

'Now we need you to climb aboard and try this for size, Rowena.' Monica points towards a wooden cratelike construction, painted an insipid blue. It reminds me of a hutch for a giant, colour-blind rabbit.

'What, in there?' I say, incredulously. No-one told me I had to sit in a box.

'It'll look impressive from a distance,' Monica assures me. Yeah, like from the moon, maybe.

You'd have thought they could have tarted it up a bit, made it more along the lines of, say, Cinderella's golden coach. This resembles a sedan chair knocked up out of timber offcuts, MDF and a glue gun by someone with severe learning difficulties. Giggling, I clamber in through the hole – you couldn't call it a door – and try to park my butt on a narrow plank that serves as a seat. In my unco-ordinated state, I miss the plank and bump my bum on the floor. Sister Monica helps me on to the seat. Talk about tacky: this heap of junk wouldn't make it into a DFS sale. It's the Third World of joinery, the wheelie bin of theatre props, the Jimmy Krankie of transport. I peer through a ragged cut-out which I assume is some kind of a comedy window.

'We'll need something to raise you up a little,' says Cuthbert, 'so that everyone will have a good view.'

My personal view, and this comes gratis, is that we should scrap the whole stupid nonsense and go down the pub, but I keep it to myself.

Naturally, no-one's thought to bring a cushion, so I point wordlessly to Hefty's expensive overcoat. I can't trust myself to speak in my doped-up state. Folding the coat and bunching it beneath my backside, I find the whiskey flask and take a surreptitious sip. Jeez, it's strong stuff, nearly rips my throat out. Immediately my face starts to glow like a traffic light on red.

The nuns fuss, fiddle-faddle and fanny about, straightening my veil, smoothing the robe, whispering stage directions. What's supposed to happen is this. I'll be trotted out in this cobbled-together contraption, supported by four nuns in the manner of pall-bearers. We'll enter the chapel through the concealed door in this larder of a room, straight to the altar where I'll be parked, i.e. dumped. All this time the curtains will be closed, so yours truly won't be visible to the audience, er, congregation. Curtains? They must mean the remnants of red fabric attached by plastic wire to the inside of the so-called windows. My job is to sit there sweating while some churchy bigwig bangs on about God-knows-what for ten minutes or so.

After the religious mumbo-jumbo is done, I'll be raised aloft once more and the nuns will cart me ceremoniously down the aisle. This is known as processing. They'll hoist me and my wooden womb on to a specially built plinth at the entrance to the chapel, next to the one with the saint's statue. Then – get this! – I slide open the curtains and reveal myself, the living embodiment of St Vincenza, for pilgrims to pay their devotions. And offload their loot into the collection bag, although the nuns don't mention that bit. I'm supposed to sit there like a monkey in a friggin' cage while dozens of people file past, staring and pointing and sniggering. This is ritual humiliation. Torture. Human rights abuse.

I take another secret nip of whiskey. It doesn't taste so bad after all.

Cuthbert strains her ears to listen at the door. After a few moments she gives a thumbs-up sign.

'Here's our cue. Ready?' Sister Monica touches my cheek with the back of her hand. Lesbo.

Eager to get the show over, I reply, 'Ready aye ready.' That's one of Nana Vincent's sayings that she got off a Camp Coffee label aeons ago. I hope she isn't watching this farce from heaven with Sadie, her bingo partner, or they'll be incontinent with laughter.

My lifting crew, the holy roadies, comprises the nunettes and Sister Cuthbert. Triffic. Three lasses ranging in size from midget to Amazon, and a nun with one finger missing. Hardly the Rolls-Royce of native bearers. Oh well, here goes nothing.

Shouldering the rickety carriage, they convey me, wibble-wobbling dangerously, through the concealed door into the body of the chapel, plod gracelessly for several steps and set me down with a bump, nearly fracturing my coccyx. I manage to stop myself yelling, 'Fuck, that hurt!'

I can hear a bloke droning on in the background in that weird chanty sing-song voice that church people have. It might be the bishop, or – I realize with a heart murmur – it could even be the Pope! Hell, how would I know? All this Catlick stuff is Greek to me. I have to stuff the veil in my mouth to stop myself laughing out loud. That would go against me in religious circles, send me zooming down the God-charts. After about half an hour, or maybe only five minutes, it's hard to tell, a woman with a deepdown rattly voice takes over. She sounds like a fag fiend with a forty-a-day habit, or someone with a voicebox plugging a hole in her throat, but probably isn't, because smoking baccy is a sin that'll have you on the hi-speed train to Hades.

Jeez, I'm bored-bored-bored to buggeration, but still on the verge of a giggly fit. It's not like they're paying me for this, not even Equity basic, so the least they could do is keep it short. This veil is making my head perspire. If sweat trickles down and smudges my mascara I'll go completely postal and people will think they've hired Gene Simmons from Kiss to portray the saint. I flap the top of the robe to make air, but it just emphasizes the clamminess on my neck. Now there's a tickle in my throat that's making me want to cough. Dare I poke my head out and ask for some water? I wish Fag-ash Lil would hurry it up with the speechifying. My head feels light and full of helium, like a birthday balloon. Dear God, don't let me die in this sweatbox, or when they open it up they'll find a tiny pink blob on the plank. Me, melted in the heat, rendered unto wax. They could always stick a bit of string in the top and use me as a candle. A fitting memorial to all my unstinting work for the Church, I don't think. I swallow hard, fighting the hacking cough that threatens to escape my lungs with the force of a trumpeting elephant. Drink. I need something to sip. Looks like it'll have to be the whiskey then. Glug, glug, glug.

Hang on, something's occurring. The ole jalopy is on the move. I'm bumped and battered as the nunly quartet hump me to shoulder height. Giddy up, we're off! Heading towards fresh air. I hope they don't move too quickly or I might get the bends. Huh, fat chance with this mismatched foursome. I'll be lucky to make it down the aisle. Plus there's an air bubble in my guts, forcing me to clench my sphincter.

The curtains have to be opened sometime around now. I take a peek through a gap in the fabric. Bloody hell! This place is massive, huger than an IKEA warehouse, and even though the lights are down, it's wall-to-wall pilgrims, all holding candles, like matrons at a Barry Manilow concert. All eyes are on my fairy-tale coach.

Fuck! This is scary.

Sippety-sip.

Gluggety-glug.

Lo! the flask hath no more whiskey. I've guzzleth it all. 'Twill verily be a miracle if I speweth not my guts, especially as I'm doped to the tits.

Thud! I'm on terra firma, dumped unceremoniously outside the chapel entrance. Then there's more shaking and bumping while they struggle to raise me on to the plinth. It's a wonder my entrails don't curdle into cottage cheese. Right, now it's my turn to unveil myself, aka St Vincenza, from the inside. I tug and tug but I can't get the frigging curtains open.

'Psst!' Pulling the material open an inch or two, I hiss at one of the farmgirl nuns. 'Oi, Von Trapp, give us a hand, will you?'

The gangly nunette peers through the hole, catches a whiff of my whiskey breath, and steps back sharply. Sister Cuthbert's head appears, followed by her few-fingered hand, and together we yank the curtain rags apart. She sniffs my mouth and regards me with a mega-cross frown.

'Say nowt, Cuthbert,' I smile sweetly, 'and I'll give you a wee snifter.' She tuts and turns her back, frigid old trout.

Concentrate. Breathe deeply. Remember, Rowena *is* St Vincenza.

It's impossible. The look I'm aiming for is saintly, but it comes out as faintly. Faintly pissed, fairly giggly, and frankly incapable. But hey, this is showbiz. It's people like me who keep the Betty Ford Clinic in business. Rehab, Detox and Botox. Another firm of solicitors, rather less obscure.

Gathering my wits, I arrange my face in a benign expression, folding my hands across my lap. I feel like a prossie in an Amsterdam shop window rather than a saint. Pilgrims circle my crate, a sea of human candle holders waxing ecstatic. Wax, Wane and Sputter; don't even go there. Sheesh, I wonder if they'll ask for autographs. How would I sign? St Rowena of Vincent? St Madonna of Child? St Julie of Andrews? Fuck, who knows? I'll tell them I forgot my lucky pen, or I don't put out on a first date, that'll shut 'em up. Cameras whirr. Flashes flash. Tempers fray. Stardom sucks.

'Rowena!' A familiar voice, but whose? 'Rowena, are you all right? You look ill.'

Texy's face drifts into vision in a grid of multicoloured frames, like an Andy Warhol print. 'Well shpotted, man,' I slur, beaming.

'She's pissed!' hisses Matty the shaven, bristling with stubble trouble.

'And stoned, is my guess. Help me get her out of this . . . this *thing*,' says Texy. 'I've got a bottle of water in my bag. We'll walk her up and down, try to sober her up. Keep her in between us, we don't want everyone gawping.'

They manhandle me out of the DIY disaster, the pumpkin that forgot to turn into a coach. The dumpy nunette stares at me, her jaw on the floor.

'Get your holy ass in there,' I say, bundling her inside the box. 'And don't dare move or you'll turn into a block of salt.' She sits upright, motionless, her chins wobbling with fright. The air bubble descends from my stomach and a juicy trump rattles out of my bottom, making me snigger.

Hanging on to Texy's arm and farting with every step, I stumble through the paparazzi of pilgrims, all rubbernecking, clicking and jostling. Matty manoeuvres me through the crowd then half-marches, half-drags me up and down the path at the side of the chapel. Swigging the fizzy mineral water brings on a few burps and dry heaves. I lean against the wall until my head begins to clear and the world fits its jigsaw together until it almost makes sense. Strong hands grip my shoulders and haul me upright. My eyes stop whizzing around long enough for me to recognize Enda. Enda, my boss. The expression on her face registers concern, rather than disgust. Apologize. Lie through your scummy teeth, Rowena.

'I'm so sorry, Enda,' I simper. 'I felt ill, that's why I fucked up

275

bigtime with the curtains. It must have been a bilious attack, or something I ate. I came over really strange, dead nauseous, like. My head was spinning so fast I didn't know where I was for a while.'

She squeezes me, just gently enough so I don't vomit. My stomach still feels jiggly, as if earthworms have set up a breeding colony in there.

'God forgive those girls,' says Enda, 'for what they did to you. They were only trying to help, to calm your nerves, but my brave child, they've ruined your big day. You've shown such courage and fortitude, Rowena. You're truly remarkable.' Her eyes glisten with tears. What oh what is the old bat going on about? I thought she'd come to smack me up for letting the side down.

Then it dawns on me. The hash cakes! She thinks I'm sick because I ate the doped muffins. Thank you, God! Thank you for choking Catlicks with guilt about everything. It's on the tip of my tongue to confess to Enda about how I was sick because I polished off Hefty's single-malt whiskey, but why should I? Here comes a ready-made excuse. My workmates believe that they're to blame for my cack-handed performance. Everything happens for a reason, and if the girls from Cleanliness want to take the rap for my debilitating illness, who am I to deny them?

'I think I'm on the mend now, Enda,' I say. 'It seems to have worked its way through my system. But would you do me one favour?'

'Anything. Anything at all, Rowena, just ask,' she gushes. 'I feel terrible about how they've made you suffer.'

I throw a pathetic gaze heavenwards. 'It's something we martyrs have to go through. At least I still have the sight in my eyes, unlike our own dear saint.' Get a grip, Rowena. Don't milk it dry. Pulling myself together, I say, 'What I'd like you to do, Enda, is explain to the Sisters that it was something I ate that gave me a funny turn and ruined my performance. You don't have to tell them what food it was. I couldn't be certain myself, although I reckon Mary Belker's cakes hadn't been in the oven long enough; they were tasty, but still soggy in the middle. But that's between you and me. No need to upset Mary by mentioning her food was dodgy.'

Enda shrinks with relief, like a deflating soufflé. She's been let off the hook, thanks to my magnitude.

'I'll be glad to speak to the Sisters at the earliest opportunity, Rowena.' She rubs my upper arms. 'You're a truly good person; your honesty shines from every pore.'

Yeah, right, if you say so, only it's more likely sweat. 'I won't keep you, Enda. Maybe you ought to track down some of the Sisters now. I'd hate to think of them worrying unnecessarily.'

Planting a dry kiss on my cheek, the penitent toddles off, guilty but fulfilled. If she only knew how much of her self-sacrifice was involved in the cause of saving my skin. Still, she never will, so who cares? Me, I prefer to call it divine intervention.

Texy gives me a quick visual check-up. 'It isn't fair, you look fantastic. No-one would believe that you were suffering alcohol poisoning a few minutes ago. How do you manage it?'

'It was nothing to do with booze,' I protest. 'Never touched a drop.' Then, winking, I say, 'Perhaps I made a pact with the Devil.'

'It wouldn't surprise me,' she says. 'Was that woman giving you a lecture?'

'Enda? No way. She wouldn't dare, because it was some food from her kitchen that made me sick.' Nothing at all to do with getting shit-faced on whiskey.

How can I look my friend in the eye and tell her a dog-faced lie? Aw, it was so Texy wouldn't feel bad about being an accessory to my under-age drinking.

It's just a *white* lie. That's OK with you, God, innit?

39

The Key to it all

Rowena has left the stadium. The saintly gig is over. Dumpy Nunette, my stunt double, is doing a grand job of crowd-pleasing, posing like a good 'un despite her too many chins and unphotogenic smile. I wonder what the critics will make of my performance? Who else would have given such a convincing portrayal of St Vincenza to the extent of being stoned and blinded, just like our own dear martyr? Stoned on hash cakes and blind drunk on Black Bush. All grassed out and whiskied up. It's called suffering for one's art.

Deflated. That's how I feel. Deflated and lifeless, like a gang-banged blow-up doll. After all the preparations, the excitement, the build-up, the whole event turned out to be nothing but a damp squid. Here I am, alone in a crowd of strangers, feeling shaky and light-headed, trying to hold it together.

The throng of visitors outside the chapel doors parts like the Red Sea. Something is happening. A pure, sweet sound wafts towards me, gradually increasing in volume. My nostrils twitch at the scent of incense. I turn to see the Sisters approaching two by two in their starched white habits, each holding a candle in her hand, gliding down the aisle as though floating on an invisible cushion of air. A young nun sings the solo part of the *Ave*, then the other Sisters join in, their quavery voices accompanying her in heart-breakingly beautiful harmony. Tears prickle behind my eyes. I am over-whelmed by some unnamed emotion. It feels like a near-life experience.

Flattening myself against the wall, I watch the nuns' procession, track them with my eyes as they descend the stone steps and disappear into the dusk followed by the crowds of pilgrims. Who knows how long I stand here, motionless, reluctant to move? Afraid to budge an inch, fearful of breaking the strange spell.

I am all that I have. Am I? It doesn't have to be true. Perhaps I'm not alone. Maybe there *is* a God. Zillions of people from all over the world can't be wrong, can they? I wish I had true faith in something or someone – someone to help share the burden, to help me carry the heavy weight that's dragging me down. And then I *am* down, physically speaking, slumped on the cold stone floor, kneeling in front of a wrought-iron gate at the back of the chapel, a small, zoo-like enclosure with a statue of a woman as an exhibit. I think it might be the Blessed Virgin, but I can't be certain as there isn't a name-tag.

He never gives you more than you can bear. The gospel according to Enda.

A hand on my shoulder startles me. I turn sharply. It's not the hand of God; it's Matty, looking fit with his baldy bonce.

'Here y'are. I've been looking everywhere for you. Come on, things to do, places to be, people to see.'

'What? Where? Who?' I struggle to my feet.

'Ask no questions,' he says, tapping the side of his nose.

Matty takes my arm and whisks me through the groups of pilgrims, past the wheelchairs and kneelers, the snappers and filmers, the disabled, the devout and those who turned out because there was nowt on telly.

'Where are we going? Where's Texy? Where are you taking me?' I say, sounding like a neurotic. 'Matty, what's going on?'

'Don't ask,' he grins, even though that's what I'm doing. 'It's a secret.'

I tug his sleeve. 'Tell me, Matty. I don't like secrets, they make me nervous.'

'No need for nerves.' He steers me past a fat, camera-toting tourist. 'OK, it's not a secret, more a surprise. A *nice* surprise,' he adds, cutting me off in mid-protest.

'But . . .' I begin.

'Mind who you're butting,' he goes, laughing.

We turn on to the path that leads to the main gate. Matty's dragging me along at such a lick that I can hardly get my breath, let alone complain about being abducted, so fast that the sign for the Sisters of Blessed Relief flies past in a blur.

'Fucksake, Matty, tell me what's going on,' I plead.

'Home,' he barks. 'I'm taking you home.' I decide not to point out that technically I'm homeless, assuming that he means we're heading for The Flues. He's propelling me so fast down the hill that my feet are falling over themselves. It's canny dangerous in this useless sack of a theatrical costume. The hairpins in the headdress have come adrift, making the veil blow over my eyes and rendering me intermittently blind. I feel like Muslim Barbie.

'Slow down, Matty, I can hardly see. Please,' I beg him.

He pulls to a halt and takes me in his arms. His touch is surprisingly gentle for one so uncouth.

'Sorry, girl, I'm just rushing cos I'm mad for a drink.' He squeezes me and plants a light kiss on my cheek through the headdress. 'Bet you wouldn't say no to one either. Hey, here's the woman.'

It's Texy, striding across the square to meet us. Boy, am I relieved. I'm pure spooked by the mysterious goings-on and these shenanigans are beyond a joke. My body begins to tremble.

'Rowena, it's all right, I'm here now.' Texy reaches for me and I grab her in a hug. 'There's nothing to worry about, honest. Here, I brought these for you to wear.' She stuffs a bundle into my arms. I can tell by the creaky noise that my leather jacket is in there. Bless the girl! 'I thought you'd be ready to change into something less saintly. You can nip into the ladies' bog and then we'll go into the bar and treat you to a wee drink.'

'Cheers, Texy man, you make me feel human again.'

In no time we're outside The Flues. Texy steers me inside and straight into the loo. I rip off the drab grey gown and veil and slip into my spangly crop top, a glittery thong and black hipster kecks with studs down the sides. I feel like a friggin' Christmas tree. Quel relief, she's even remembered to bring my make-up bag and tailcomb so I tart up my face and backcomb my hair into a moulting dog's bed affair, screwing it up into my fave hairslide which looks like silver barbed wire. It's a big effort just for a drink but what the heck, it's good to be wild once in a while.

Texy leads me out of the boggo into the bar, like I'm some kind of star turn, a strippogram or karaoke queen. Sheesh, it's jammers inside the pub, totally heaving with bodies in various stages of boozy decay.

'Hoorayyy! Hoorayyy! Hoorayyy!' For the second time today, I'm three-cheered.

'F-f-f-f-f ...' I somehow manage to stop myself uttering a profanity.

My jaw drops and my knees are close to collapse as I try to make sense of the sight before me. A crowd of people roars and applauds. Draped above the bar is a banner bearing the legend *Happy 17th Birthday, Rowena!* What the f —?

'H-h-how did you find out?' I gasp to Texy.

'Came across the date in your passport, you dope. You should have said. Happy birthday, sweetheart.' She kisses me on the cheek, adding, 'One more year and you'll be able to drink legally.'

Texy accompanies me as I make my way with faltering steps down the length of the bar. My legs are wobbly and I can feel a stupid Teletubby grin begin as I spot familiar faces. The skivvies from Cleanliness are here, all done up like dogs' dinners. Paula's dressed in my leather basque, the one she bullied me into lending her, although she's spoiled the raunchy effect by wearing it over a pink blouse. Still, she made the effort. Grainne the seamstress is poured into a slinky black number that would look more at home on a pole dancer. She's showing off a great pair of tits, helped by cinching herself in at the waist with my leather biker belt, complete with its buckle of grinning metal skull and glowing red eyes. Who could have guessed such a body would blossom from beneath her nylon overall? Joelle's here too, and Mary Belker, and the knicker-stitchers, the girls who sew undies, all giggling, just this side of paralytic.

'You buggers,' I hiss in a good-natured rebuke. It's hard to believe that they knew about this and never let on. 'Who organized the party, Tex? It was you, wasn't it, you sly vixen?'

She throws up her arms. 'It so wasn't. You'll never guess who it was, either.'

'Enda?' I suggest, on the principle that she's the only person with time on her hands.

'It was someone far more important than that,' teases Texy.

'The Pope? The bishop? Reverend Mother?'

Texy almost chokes on her beer. 'Not quite that high up the Church ladder.'

'Jeez, I could be here all night trying to guess. Tell me, Texy, go on.'

She glances around, her gaze coming to rest on a trestle table set up near a stage affair. Oh, brilliant, there's tucker on. Pork pies, things on sticks, scrummy sausage thingies, plus boring sarnies and salad stuff. The last birthday party I remember, we had jellies and custard and a cake decorated with Smarties. This is a proper grown-up, sophisticated do. I'm more than touched; I'm over-whelmed, dizzy with happiness.

'Who? Spit it out, Tex. Whose idea was the party?'

Drawing me a little to one side, she says, 'Over there. Promise me you won't swear when I tell you.' I cross hands over my bosoms. 'It was Miss Teazie and Mr O'Hara.'

I gulp in astonishment. 'Hefty? Hefty and his aunt? You've got to be kidding me.'

'Nope,' Texy insists. 'The provisional wing of the Rowena Vincent Fan Club, so help me. Miss Teazie organized everything and Mr O'Hara paid for it.'

'But how did they know it was my birthday? I'd forgotten about it myself.'

Texy explains that she told Bobbo because he wanted to thank me in some way for buying his new clothes. Bobbo happened to mention it to Miss O'Hara and it snowballed from there. It turns out that the two of them get along just dandy. Texy says that Bobbo and Miss Teazie have become PFs, meaning Particular Friends, a type of relationship frowned on by the greybacks.

'The Sisters aren't allowed to have PFs because it takes their minds off God and it might lead to, you know,' says Texy.

'What?'

'A pash.' She spells it out in a whisper. 'S.E.X.'

'Yikes! Like geriatric pants stuff, you mean?'

She nods.

'The nuns shouldn't object. They're not called the Blue Spark Sisters for nothing,' chips in Matty, munching on a chicken drumstick.

Texy frowns and shushes him. 'Not now, Matty.'

But this is something that's been puzzling me, so I urge him to tell me, even though Texy says she'll have no part of it because it's disgusting and disrespectful. I push Matty into a booth where he relates the tale, using a quiet, deepdown voice. He begins by pointing out that it's a folklore thing, or an urban myth, but still I insist on hearing about it.

Texy was right. It *is* downright disgusting.

Matty goes off on a long riff about female masturbation, describing a few techniques in general use. Some I know about, others are new and, frankly, unlikely unless the woman happens to be an Olympic gymnast, or at least double-jointed. I listen without interrupting, nodding occasionally to remind him that I'm seventeen and a woman of the world.

'Now for the science bit,' he goes. This is where he loses me. He explains about friction, static electricity and suchlike but the whole deal is taking far too long and I want to go enjoy my own party.

'Cut to the chase,' I say.

The bottom line is . . . remember this is just a story, right? The bottom line, according to Matty, is that if you walk past a convent at night, you can see blue sparks zinging at the windows, some gobbledygook about an electric reaction from the nuns pleasuring themselves.

'Hence the nickname, Blue Spark Sisters,' he says triumphantly, like he's cracked some new theory of physics.

'Thanks for enlightening me on that one, Einstein,' I say, although the tone of sarcasm is wasted on him. Why am I not surprised that it's turned out to be something filthy?

I force my way through the tables to Texy. She's smoking a surreptitious ciggy and grinds it into an ashtray, frowning.

'Sorry about Matty,' she says. 'He found the story on the Internet.'

The Internet! Joe! Where oh where is my lovely Joe? I look round wildly, searching for his face among the sea of partygoers. My heart plummets as I realize that he's nowhere to be seen. But there's hope, as people are still arriving. Enda, for one, dressed in some kind of turquoise Babygro – a catsuit, I believe they used to be called. This is what passes for *haute couture* in Ballyloony. She bulldozes her way to me, plants a wet smacker on my cheek and presents me with a birthday gift. Holding it near a light, I rip off the tacky wrapping paper to reveal a packet of tights. Barely Black, 15 denier. Why is there never a garbage bin when you need one?

'They're l-l-lovely, Enda,' I gush, substituting the word 'lovely' for 'loathsome' at the last second. 'Have you had some supper from the buffet, Enda?'

'Not I,' she says, as if she finds the very thought offensive. 'I daren't eat at this time in the evening. I've got the appetite of a bird, see.'

Yeah, right. A gannet.

'But thanks for asking,' she continues. 'You're a little princess.'

And you're a queen, I'm thinking. Not unlike Elton John, dragged up in that hideous outfit. Then, remembering my lacklustre theatrical performance earlier, I ask her if she managed to square things with the Sisters on my behalf.

'See for yourself,' she replies, pointing a puddingy finger in the direction of the buffet. I can hardly believe my eyes. Looky who's here? Sister Monica, Cuthbert, the Nunettes, plus a few others I'd seen bustling around the nunvent. All tucking into sausages on sticks! The Catlicks have turned out in force for my surprise birthday party!

'I wish I could stay longer, Rowena,' says Enda, 'but I have to get home to see to my Douglas.'

Eeww! Too much information. The last thing I need to hear about is Enda's spousal arousal techniques.

'Douglas is such a darling,' she adds. 'He's an iguana, see. I'm training him to cling to my shoulder on a dog lead so we can go out together.'

This is surreal. 'Don't worry, Enda. I understand,' I murmur, in a mock-serious tone, contorting my face into an expression of gutted-with-disappointment-but-I-daresay-I'll-get-over-it. She pecks me on the cheek with her chapped, dry lips – her *lizardlike* lips – then straightens her catsuit and bustles off to exercise her pet reptile. Bizarreness abounds.

A tug on the sleeve makes me turn round sharply.

'Would you look at me, Rowena. I'm all done up in me dance-hall best.' Bobbo's beaming face and glistening gums send my spirits rocketing skywards. He's wearing the new outfit I boosted for him. A canary-yellow anorak, blood-red nylon pants, and the Monsta Rasta hat. This is its first public outing, as I'd urged him to keep it a secret from Texy until the bison teenery in case she forbade him to wear it. I wonder if Miss Teazie helped him to get dressed.

'Cru-shal, mon. Respeck!' I holler in a mock-Jamaican or Bermondsey accent. 'Increase da peace, Bobbo.' It's pure brilliant to see him looking so wild in his trendy togs.

Texy is incoherent with laughter. 'What have you done, Rowena? He's turned into the granddaddy of hip-hop.'

Bobbo launches into a jig, arms glued to his sides like in Riverdance, knees creaking, dreadlocks flying, dancing to the music of fiddles and flutes inside his head. He holds out a hand towards Texy. Without a moment's hesitation, she takes her place opposite her grandfather and joins him. It ought to be mortally embarrassing, but it isn't. For one thing, they can dance, although Texy's limbs are way more supple than the old man's. But more than that, the sight of a couple from different generations ripping it up twangs the heartstrings, brings a lump to the throat.

After the initial surprise, the other partygoers enter into the spirit, so to speak. Hands clap, keeping strict tempo. Some of the skivvies start to dance, their boldness triggered by the sight of the young girl and the old man glorying in life itself, not to mention the booze. Sister Cuthbert waves her sausage like a conductor's baton. Enda gyrates, her flesh wobbling, threatening to burst through the Babygro, then salsas out of the door to attend to Douglas duty.

A howl of feedback echoes and whistles through the room. Someone taps a microphone. All eyes turn to the stage where Hefty O'Hara, accompanied by his aunt who's been hoist to public view aboard a bar stool, addresses the audience. Jesus, I haven't got around yet to grovelling my appreciation to them for throwing the party.

Hefty begins by thanking everyone for coming, banging on about how we've had such a busy but rewarding day celebrating the bicentenary of our beloved Saint Vincenza. He pauses while the audience applauds. Matty sticks his fingers to his mouth and does an ear-splitting whistle until Texy digs him in the ribs and shoots him a warning look.

Now comes a bit of speechifying about yours truly. Grinning people turn to look at me. I feel embarrassed by the attention, but also anxious about what Hefty is planning to say. A blush spreads across my cheeks as he relates how we ran into one another at the airport and I told him of my quest to find a long-lost family member, even though it meant searching for him in Ireland where I'd never previously set foot. Oh, God, this is mortifying. He burbles about the kindness I showed to him and his aunt. There's a cheer as Miss Teazie O'Hara gets her own name check. She waves regally. The O'Haras really are some major-type deal around here. Just imagine – I used to believe that Hefty was king of the gangsters!

I can't listen. My face is burning up with self-consciousness. There's a ringing in my ears. I think I'm going to faint.

The rest of what he says flies over my head. It's only when the tone of his voice changes and I realize my ordeal is about to end, that I click back to the here and now.

'On behalf of your friends and colleagues – your new *family*, Rowena – I'd like you to accept a gift, with our warmest thanks and our best possible wishes for the future. And here, to present it, is someone else whose life, I'm told, has been positively transformed by knowing you.'

Oh, fuck. What now?

Pushed forward by Texy, steered through the party guests by Matty, I walk stiffly, like an arthritic dummy, towards the stage where Hefty and Miss O'Hara await. People clap loudly. Flustered by the unwanted attention I keep my eyes fixed to the ground, seeing only an assortment of shoes, boots, trainers, feet, paws . . .

Paws?

I raise my eyes, convinced it's all been a crazy dream and I'll wake up to find myself microwaving milk in Enda's kitchenette, my head slumped in a plate of Hobnobs.

But the reality is even stranger. In front of me, wearing a blue bow ribbon, hair brushed to a point like a punky Beckham clone, wagging his tail fit to bust, is Ninja! Ninja the Ginger Cringer, all timidity vanished, stands dignified and proud as if he's just won

Cruft's Best in Show. Around his neck, where a St Bernard mountain dog keeps a brandy barrel, is a soft leather pouch.

'Ninja, you clever boy,' I say, bending to scratch his ear. His tail thumps. A long pink tongue baptizes my ear with spittle. Has someone slipped the mutt a handful of anti-shyness pills?

'Open the purse, Rowena,' urges Hefty. 'There's a gift inside for you.'

I drop to my knees on the stage and untie the blue bow around Ninja's collar region, then fumble with the cord tying the pouch. It isn't easy. The dog's never had so much excitement in one dose. I hope he doesn't wet himself. Stretching across him, I can feel my buttocks making a bid for freedom from the lowslung trousers, exposing my bumcrack to the partygoers. Still, at least Texy's supplied a glittery thong; it's not like I'm wearing my usual frayed and faded knickies in a fetching shade of thousand-wash grey, or I'd die of shame.

'Hold still, Ninja,' I insist in my best dog-whisperer voice, managing at last to untie the pouch strings. I fish out a wrap of tissue paper with something small and rattly inside. I stand, hitching up my kecks, and unfold it to reveal – what?

A necklace. Oh, big deal. It takes a megahuman effort to stop my face from falling to the floor in disappointment.

A *necklace*? I hate necklaces. They're so girly, so not me.

Oh, hang on, there's something attached to the beads. It's a cross. A silver cross with a little man on it. Triffic.

Dangling it aloft, I force out the most insincere smile in history, not counting Mr Tony Blair's, obviously.

A cheer goes up. Voices ring out, demanding *Speech*! *Speech*! Fuckety-fuckety-foo!

From behind, Hefty grabs me in a reverse bear hug and propels me towards the microphone. Who says this man doesn't know about strong-arm tactics? Suddenly I'm desperate to visit the loo.

Speech! they continue to yell. What am I supposed to say? Thanks for the necklace, only I never wear them? Maybe I could donate it as a raffle prize or something.

'Go on, you'll be fine so.' Texy appears at my side and I almost collapse with relief. 'Just thank them, say you're honoured to be presented with the rosary beads.'

'The what?' I say, flustered beyond comprehension.

'There, in your hand, the rosary beads.' She points at the necklace and the cross with the figure of a little man on it. 'Made by the finest craftsmen in Verona. Miss Teazie commissioned them especially for the occasion.'

'Oh, right,' I murmur. I'm hopeless, clueless about this Catlick business, apart from the guilt. I can do guilt big-style. Years of practice, see, and it's paying off right now, in spades. Drenched in guilt I am, plastered in it, overflowing with it, oozing it sweatlike from every pore. The biggest fraud in Christendom, me. An unholy impostor. How could I have faked my way in amongst all these good, kind, God-fearing people, fooled them into accepting – possibly even *liking* – me?

'Just a few words. Keep it short and simple.' It's Joe, bootylicious Joe, whispering advice into my ear, squeezing my hand for comfort. 'Then we'll go home together.'

Joe's deadly smile turns my legs to useless, wobbly things. *Then we'll go home together*, he said. *We* and *home* and *together*. Intimate words that make me feel included, secure, wanted.

It feels almost like an Oscar acceptance speech, only not written down, no umpteen rehearsals in front of a mirror. Even so, I probably make a better fist of it than Halle Berry did and she's supposed to be a professional actor! No, I don't remember the actual words but I don't think I left anyone out and it seemed to go down a storm. They gave me a standing ovation, in fact, even though everyone was standing to begin with. Things I do remember: Miss Teazie's cloudy, unseeing eyes filling up with tears. Bobbo, togged in his hop-hop outfit, draping a canary-coloured arm on her shoulders, dangling his false dreadlocks in her face. Blindness has its consolations. Gangly Nunette taking a sly sip of Joelle's lager. Hefty's cheeks glistening, their ruddiness matching his eyeballs. He looks bushed. Black Bushed. Texy, cheering and applauding like – well, like the clappers. Matty whistling in noisy encouragement. Ninja grinning doggily, his tail in permanent wag mode.

And Joe, darling Joe, gazing at me with something like pride misting his eyes, or maybe just cigarette smoke.

A sudden thought flashes through my brain. Wouldn't Dad be proud if he could see me now? Then a realization, tinged with guilt, that I haven't thought about him in ages.

'You're a star,' Joe whispers, brushing his lips against my cheek. 'A shining, shining star. And that's de troot.'

Something goes off inside me. I squeeze his fingers, murmuring, 'Let's slip away.'

On the way across the square to Joe's place, Ninja hugs the walls, skulking.

'What's with the dog?' I ask. 'I was so proud of him in The Flues but now he's doing that low-self-esteem thing again.'

'He's scared of the dark,' says Joe. 'Me and Matty have been training him in the pub for days and sure, didn't he put on a good show for everyone, but he hates being out in the town at night. Soon be home, lad,' he assures Ninja. 'Calm yourself down, you've another performance to get through.'

'What? What performance?' I say.

'You'll see,' replies Joe, taking hold of my hand like a proper boyfriend would. Ninja twitches his tail half-heartedly then pauses for a micro-widdle in a shop doorway.

Back at the flat above the Mouse Drop-in, I drape myself on the sofa while Joe makes tea in the kitchen. My fingers stumble with the remote and eventually find the button that works the CD player.

There's a disc already in, the last one Joe played. It's P!nk, *Missundazstood*, a favourite of mine, as it goes, although I skip the first track because I'm in no mood to get the party started. Quiet, pensive, almost serious, that's how I'm feeling, Lord knows why. Still, it's been a long day, lots of stuff happening; I'm bound to need a while to rest in peace. Digging inside my bag, I pull out the rosary beads and twiddle them between my fingers. They feel warm and almost alive, like wee ladybirds threaded on a string. Comforting. I wish I knew the words, the ones that Catlicks say when they're counting them. Maybe they're secret, a personal mantra like when people meditate, and the magic won't work if you let slip the word to anyone else. I study the figure, the one of a little man on a cross. Jesus! It's Jesus! Of course, it's so obvious. How could I not have known? Duh.

And then – *zap!* 'Family Portrait' comes on, P!nk's number about an unhappy mum and dad splitting up, as sung by their daughter who wants them to stay together even though they're dead mean to each other. I feel as though I've been shot in the head by a stun gun. Families, huh! Who needs 'em?

'Tea up,' announces Joe, setting a couple of mugs on the table. He clocks my expression, links it with the song, offers to change the CD. What a sensitive soul this boy is. I hold up my hand, indicating no. Time I got my head out of the sand, faced up to de troot. My family, with Lonnie Vincent as the dad, makes the Osbournes seem positively functional. 'You OK, Rowena?' Joe asks, his tone of voice light.

'Sure. Too cool for school, that's me,' I reply.

He passes me a mug. My hands are shaking. I blow on the hot tea and take a slurp. It burns my tongue.

Joe whistles. 'Here, boy,' he says. Ninja trots in, confident again, looking full of buggerment. 'Sit,' orders Joe, and the dog squats down beside me, his body quivering. 'Ninja's brought you a gift.'

'Another one?' I dangle the rosary beads in front of Joe's face.

'You might not want it,' he says, his voice hesitant.

'One way to find out.' I drag Ninja by his collar towards me and firk about inside the leather pouch, teasing out a small item enveloped in gold gift wrap and tied in blue ribbon, just like the bow around Ninja's neck. 'Joe, what is it?'

'Open it and see. There's no obligation for you to keep it if you'd rather not.'

'Ssshhh,' I whisper, unfolding the paper wrapped around the tiny item. Squeezing my eyes shut to prolong the surprise, I hold the contents in my left hand and feel the gift with the fingers of my right. There's a short metal chain attached to two articles, one at each end. One end holds a tiny, hard object, almost but not quite round. At the other is a flat, metallic thingy. The shape feels vaguely familiar but I can't quite put a name to it. It's no good, I'll have to open my eyes.

It's a key. A key attached by a chain to a key ring with a wee mouse on the other end – a computer-type mouse, not a rodent. I twirl the items around between my fingers, not knowing what to say.

'A key,' I mutter at last.

'No flies on you,' says Joe.

'Is it real? Or is it just ornamental – like, a fake accessory?' It wouldn't surprise me if keys are the hippest fashion in this cornball town. 'Or is it,' I continue, 'from Verona?'

Joe tickles Ninja behind the ears. He looks at the floor in something approaching embarrassment. 'None of the above,' he says. 'It's a key for this flat. *Your* key. Just treat this place like a . . . Like your home.'

'Home?' I say, as though it's the first time I've heard of such a thing. '*Home*? You're saying this place could be my home?'

'It's sounding that way. No pressure, no strings or anything. Come and go as you please.'

'Oh.' My heart plummets to my boots. 'Let me get this straight, Joe. So you're not exactly inviting me to move in?' I daren't look at him.

'Well,' he says, staring at the floor. 'You'll be leaving The Flues soon –'

'Tomorrow,' I remind him.

'Tomorrow, right,' he says. 'And your plans after that are?'

I shrug. 'Hadn't given it much thought. I suppose I'd have gone back to Dublin with Texy, although we haven't discussed it.' It dawns on me that I couldn't afford to stay at the Cadogan Hotel anyway. If Hefty hadn't picked up the tab I wouldn't have been able to stay there in the first place. What would I do in Dublin anyway? Texy is the only person I know there and she lives in a single room that goes with her job. So, technically, I suppose I'm homeless. On the plus side, this also means that I'm free. Free to do anything and go anywhere. Free to stay in Ballyloony, where I have a job and friends, people who appear to like me.

And Joe. Darling, bumtastic, choppy-haired, poetic, sensitive, odd-eyed, silver-scarred Joe.

'So are we saying that's a yes or a no? To me moving in, like? We could do it on a trial period if you'd rather, Joe; see how things work out.'

He sighs, but in relief rather than exasperation.

'Come here,' he says, his voice husky. 'Of course I want you to move in. I couldn't imagine anything more wonderful.' He slides towards me. His peculiar, lovable eyes burn into mine. Eventually, he whispers, 'Would you let me undress you? Very, very slowly?'

My heart thuds in a crazy, offbeat rhythm. I'm palpitating. Salivating. Jesus, don't let me die of bliss, not now. Joe draws me to him. His mouth meets mine in a slow-burning, deep-probing kiss that sends showers of sparks cascading through my body, makes my brain tingle. Warm, moist and melty in his arms, I feel myself surrendering, flowering, welcoming his love.

Much later, returning from the bathroom, head whizzing from the latest thrilling developments, body exhausted after a glorious, almost-all-the-way lovemaking session with my man Joe, yet too wide awake to settle, I turn on his laptop computer. After a game or two of blackjack, still I'm not the slightest bit tired, so I log on to the Internet and check out a few websites on celebrity secrets, conspiracy theories, fetish outfits, photos of mingers, stuff like that. *Yawwwn*. It's working. I'm boring myself to sleep here.

Just before logging out, I enter the Shotmail site to check my e-mails, not that I'm expecting to see any. But lo, there are several types of spam littering my inbox. ADD 3 CMS TO YOUR PENIS SIZE. *Delete*. SEE TEEN SLUTS DOWN ON THE FARM. *Delete*. BUY YOURSELF A PHD. LOWEST PRICES FOR VIAGRA ON THE WEB. *Delete, Delete*.

And then, and then . . .

From:	**Moral Adair**
Date:	**19 March 2003**
To:	**Rowena Vincent**
Subject:	**HALLELUJAH! BRILLIANT NEWS! I'VE FOUND LONNIE!**

My stomach does a double-decker flip-over. Palpitations race and thump in my chest. Cold sweat breaks out on my forehead. My internal organs start to judder. This is me, Rowena M. Vincent, on the cusp of life and death.

Moral Adair has found Dad!

The cursor hovers above the OPEN button. My hands shake with nervous palsy.

Dad!

The information I've been searching for so desperately is one click away. Once I open the e-mail and read the contents, my life will change irrevocably.

A snippet of Hefty O'Hara's speech floats back to me. 'Your friends and colleagues – your new *family*.' This is the way he described the people I've met in Ballyloony, the people who have